**FOR CHAR...
ELECTRIF...**

COUNTERSTRIKE

"COUNTERSTRIKE is a wonderful what-if . . . fast, expert, and goes straight for the nerve points. A truly compulsive read!"

Anthony Olcott,
author of *Murder at the Red October*

SILENT HUNTER

"An exciting, suspenseful story of modern submarine warfare!"

—Edward P. Stafford,
author of *The Big E*
and *Little Ship, Big War*

CHOKE POINT

"Realistic, hard-hitting, fast-paced action! Holds you firmly in its grip until the final page."

—J. C. Pollock,
author of *Mission: M.I.A.*

FIRST SALVO

"Taylor writes with a thorough knowledge of sea power!"
—*Seattle Times*

**NOW, HE PRESENTS HIS NEWEST,
MOST EXPLOSIVE NOVEL
OF HIGH-SEAS INTRIGUE . . .**

WAR SHIP

Also by Charles D. Taylor

WAR SHIP

Charles D. Taylor

JOVE BOOKS, NEW YORK

WAR SHIP

A Jove Book / published by arrangement with
the author

PRINTING HISTORY
Jove edition / March 1989

ISBN: 0-515-09952-X

Jove Books are published by the Berkley Publishing Group,
200 Madison Avenue, New York, New York 10016.
The name "JOVE" and the "J" logo
are trademarks belonging to Jove Publications, Inc.

PRINTED IN THE UNITED STATES OF AMERICA

10 9 8 7 6 5 4 3 2 1

For my wife, Georgie, with love—
for sustaining me, us, our family,
while I pursue my muse

ACKNOWLEDGMENTS

What are "Special Operations"?— ". . . un-
orthodox, comparatively low-cost, poten-
tially high-payoff, often covert or clandestine methods that national, subnational,
and theater leaders employ independently
in *peacetime* or to support nuclear/biologi-
cal/chemical and/or conventional warfare
across the conflict spectrum."

> —John M. Collins, Senior Specialist
> in National Defense, Library of Congress
> *U.S. and Soviet Special Operations*
> House Armed Services Committee
> U.S. House of Representatives

I remain indebted to those SEALs, past and present,
whom I singled out in *Counterstrike*. They were willing to
introduce me to their clandestine world of special operations
and I continue to appreciate both their candor and their
desire for anonymity. Lt. Greg Jaquith (USN) was my
escort when I spent a few days with the SEALs in
Coronado, and he has become a valued friend. I owe special
thanks to "Jake" for the time he took to read the sections on
SEAL evolutions for technical accuracy. Any mistakes
remain my own—they are the result of a writer's imagination and profound respect for our SEALs who know

nothing is impossible—". . . anything, anytime, any-place, anyhow."

Captain Dave Schaible, USN (ret.) was the foremost SEAL, and I consider him a mentor, not only for his past technical comments but for his desire that the job be done right—which is the way the SEALs have always done it. From his first enlistment in 1944 to his retirement in 1981, Captain Schaible had five major commands and received twenty-six decorations. He passed away on 9 August 1988 after his toughest battle. Those who knew Dave remember him with awe.

I've known Ted Magnuson since 15 May 1961; that was the cold spring day that we and maybe a hundred others learned that we would share Kilo Company barracks in Newport, hoping that some day we would be officers sailing those ships we saw across the harbor at the destroyer piers. Though we sailed far different oceans, somehow we kept in touch because we both loved writing. Now, in our middle years, we send our manuscripts back and forth across the US for each other to review. I owe Ted a debt of gratitude for the work he did on this book and the changes he suggested to improve it.

Dan Mundy continues to provide suggestions that improve my early drafts. And I am indeed fortunate that I never lost contact with Bill and Anne McDonald; our captain and his lady have returned to our reunions to lead us as our tales of the North Atlantic evolve into legends on those icy February nights around the fireplace. Bill has also become a good friend and I would be remiss if I didn't thank him for his more-than-generous efforts to assist me. Joel Culver of the Bath Iron Works was kind enough to crawl with me for hours through a multitude of spaces aboard Aegis cruisers under construction so that I might appreciate the scope of these futuristic men of war; it was also Joel who suggested that a BIW ship, *Gettysburg,* be the center-piece of *War Ship*. And Bob Donovan deserves a bottomless 'hattan for answering my innumerable questions. The quote at the end of the prologue originally appeared in an article in the April 1988 issue of *Armed Forces Journal International* by Florida congressman Charles E. Bennett. Responsible for *War Ship*'s genesis are Dominick Abel and Natalee Rosenstein.

The situations and characters in this book come entirely from my own imagination, but they could not have appeared without the help of everyone mentioned above and those I may have overlooked. Thanks—all!

"By heaven, man, we are turned round and round in this world, like yonder windless, and Fate is the handspike."

—*Herman Melville*

"I'll be judge, I'll be jury," said the cunning old Fury; "I'll try the whole cause, and condemn you to death."

—*Lewis Carroll*

PROLOGUE

pi-ra-cy [Medieval Latin, *piratia;* Greek, *pei-rateia,* from *peirates,* a pirate]
 1. the act, practice, or crime of robbing ships on the high seas; the taking of property from others by open violence and without authority on the sea.

The high resolution camera could not record the brilliant colors as the sun steamed out of the South China Sea, nor could it relay the arrival of a radiant dawn on the Vietnamese coast. It was also incapable of picking up the cacophony of sound as the sun's rays pierced an awakening jungle growing almost to the sea's edge. In actuality, the sun had been reflecting off its polished shell constantly because this particular camera was orbiting two hundred twenty-five miles above its target. An inanimate object, NAVSAT 27 raced unobtrusively in space, seemingly motionless, sightless, harmless—for the moment. Yet thousands of miles away in Pasadena's JPL, where that same sun was now setting, the men who had been waiting for that Asian sunrise paced nervously, murmuring to themselves until the signal could be sent that would activate that shutter.

Heat was settling over the docks of Cam Ranh Bay even before the bustle of already perspiring workers flowed through the gates of the busy port. It was a muggy warmth, the kind that brought beads of sweat to the brow even before the first crate was lifted. Shimmering waves of heat rose from the pavement distorting the busy scene as hordes of men and women scattered about the huge complex to commence their day's work.

As they scurried from one task to the next with the day growing brighter, each cast an eye at the silhouette of a majestic warship at the head of pier number two. Not only had it arrived mysteriously in the dead of night, unannounced, and unexpected by most everyone there, but it was distinctly foreign—totally different from the Soviet ships normally berthed there. Heavily armed Soviet troops stood guard on the pier, spaced every few feet between its high bow and broad stern. Others, Vietnamese sailors, patrolled the decks, their rifles unslung as if the lowly dock workers would dare to challenge their authority.

Not a soul in Cam Ranh Bay, not even the Russian cadre who now controlled the port, was aware that a signal had finally been flashed from Pasadena to an antenna which then relayed the impulse to that invisible object two hundred and twenty-five miles above them. Not only did they remain ignorant of the maneuvers that activated the camera, they never would have believed that each move they made could be seen thousands of miles away. It would have been impossible to explain to the lowly dock workers, though not the Soviet naval officers, that their faces could be distinguished clearly by people so far away. They would all, however, have acknowledged that the men controlling such an amazing camera had to be motivated by that strange ship.

The men in Pasadena cared nothing for the people milling about the huge port. Their interest was singular—they wanted only to confirm what they found impossible to believe. And in moments, the satellite camera brought the object of their curiosity into perspective. There was no doubting the sharp sweep of the bow, the square stern—and most important—the imposing forward deck house that rose box-like to the telltale fixed-array radar in the superstructure. Intelligence reports received hours earlier had been correct—*USS Gettysburg*, the most sophisticated war ship in the American fleet with her Aegis combat system, was no longer off the Vietnamese coast conducting surveillance of the Russian naval and air expansion. Instead, she was snug alongside a pier in Cam Ranh Bay.

An even more confusing factor was an element introduced by nature, one that man remained incapable of controlling—solar flares! Days before, astronomers had noted unusual sunspot activity in the sun's chromosphere. An unusual number of grouped sunspots were the precursor to the eruption of a rash of solar flares of an intensity never before recorded by observers. These flares radiated violently over the entire magnetic spectrum, from X-rays to radio waves, hurling untold streams of electrons and protons toward earth at the speed of light.

Geomagnetic storms in earth's upper atmosphere had been predicted as a result. The simplest and best understood effect of this phenomenon was the disruption of long-range radio communications, much like the effect of a bolt of lightning on the family radio. However, scientists had predicted the possibility of major communications blackouts since nothing of this magnitude had ever been experienced by today's modern communications equipment. In actuality, global communications were reasonably clear during some periods. At other times, the result of these magnetic storms hurled millions of miles through space by eruptions on the sun was no less than chaos.

No sooner had each man in Pasadena confirmed in his own mind that the worst had indeed taken place than the ultimate insult unfurled before their eyes: a Vietnamese flag was run up her mast. The piracy was complete. The pride of the US Navy had never been more tainted. Not since the *Pueblo* was captured by the North Koreans had there been a darker day—nor had the US ever faced a more serious intelligence coup by a prospective enemy.

The Chief of Naval Operations removed his glasses and rubbed his eyes in frustration. That sentence he'd once underlined with a red marker flashed repeatedly on his eyeballs. It was from an article that so impressed him he'd cut it from a magazine. His wife framed it for his office wall. The still red-lined words were direct—*"If our enemies somehow obtained the Aegis secrets, it would devastate our ability to defend our carrier battle groups at sea."* And those words were doubly frightening now compared with when he first read them!

CHAPTER 1

A breeze—a blessed breeze, Andrew Norman assured himself—had come up about an hour before and now there were whitecaps chasing across the surface from east to west. The South China Sea had been calm and hot that morning and into the afternoon, so damn hot that the cloying stink of red lead and gray paint had risen to Norman's nose like swamp gas. The aroma swirled about his head before blending with a clammy, mildew smell that plagued his uniforms and crept into every compartment on the ship. His stomach churned. It was much worse now than when they'd left San Diego, and it was mostly from sheer nerves.

Norman was a Lieutenant, junior grade (Ltjg) aboard the Aegis cruiser *Gettysburg* and right about now he longed for the sensibility of those navies that prescribed shorts in tropical climates—anything but the heavier khaki uniforms his captain insisted upon at sea. White shorts, like the British wore, seemed more logical in this oppressive heat.

In reality, Lt. Andrew Norman wouldn't have been comfortable in any uniform that day. He was a young man too acutely aware he was once again about to commit the despicable crime of turning against his country. While the timing and method were not his, the act itself was inescapable. The orders, delivered in no uncertain terms by his contact in San Diego two months previous, had been borne with a fateful certainty. He would compromise the most advanced naval warfare system in America, and the means to do so had been prepared just as if the Soviet agent had received his instructions within the vast corridors of the Pentagon. *This is what you will do, Norman, and this is exactly how you will do it.* It was uncanny—and it was terrifying—even after the months (no, years) that he'd been forced to await the inevitable.

And he'd learned there were two others! Yes, there were actually two others the bastards controlled. Of course, they were enlisted. The Russians would never trust some junior officer without the technical background to actually understand the schematics of something like Aegis. Oh, they were making sure: Those bastards never overlooked a thing. Check. Double check. Don't leave anything to chance. When they really needed something as badly as they needed the key to this Aegis system, they'd destroy anything—anyone for that matter—even Andrew Norman. He was simply another step on the ladder, and he hadn't the faintest idea where the top was.

The breeze was cooling. It came almost directly off the starboard beam since *Gettysburg* was barely making headway through the gentle swells at about three knots. The armpits of his shirt were a dark, wet color when he raised his arms to let the moving air flow across his body. Norman was sitting, or perhaps leaning was more correct, against the capstan on the stern, directly across from the Harpoon missile cannisters. He had been there for the last half hour after being relieved from his bridge watch. He had done nothing more in the intervening time than just stare out to the east as the ship eased northward more than fifty miles off the Vietnamese coastline. Cam Ranh Bay lay well over the horizon to port.

His thoughts were anything but complex. He was entirely occupied with his chances for completing the mission. Was it possible, even with the aid of the two others, to access the last of the schematics, photograph them, and slip the tube of film over the stern without being detected? Was that why he was back here now? Was he mentally *casing the joint*? No, definitely not. In the past few weeks, he'd often found himself leaning against this exact same capstan without ever knowing whether or not he would complete the job. The final act would involve dropping the film off the back of the ship no more than a few feet from where he now stared at the sea. How often had he dreamed that he had completed it?

He headed aft purely out of habit. It was quiet back there, a pleasant place on a war ship to contemplate one's destiny—if there was such a thing as a future in Andrew Norman's stars. There were times he would bring a book and read for a while rather than sit around the wardroom table and drink coffee with the others. Was he a loner out of choice—or guilt?

He stared at his watch for perhaps the twentieth time since he'd come off watch. The time had advanced three minutes; the date was irrefutably the same, and it would be until he slipped that waterproof tube over the side in the darkness.

The final message had come in the night. It was very simple. Somehow "they" even had access to those unimportant Red Cross messages to servicemen, even slipping one into the system when they wanted—*Congratulations Uncle, nephew Andrew born*. It explained in a preplanned way exactly when the trailing submarine expected to pick up the watertight tube they'd given him.

It's all so easy, the contact had explained back in San Diego. *The odds are that no one will ever know. You'll be out of the service six months later. We'll never bother you again. This is the one and only time you'll ever be used. . . .*

Andrew Norman glanced out at the whitecaps and saw imaginary periscopes staring back at him, a reminder that one more set of schematics had to be shot before he could complete this ordeal.

He looked again at his watch. Another minute had passed. The two electronics technicians were scheduled to meet him in the ET workshop in a short time. How the hell did the Russians ever get a hold of people like that? Did they do it in the same way? No, not like they got him. These weren't contrary college students willing to accept money and a little excitement to get even with the establishment. There must be a reward later—cash when they're discharged, or maybe it's being socked away in a Swiss bank account like his contact claimed was still being done for him. That was something else he worried about. *Were they really?*

No matter. He'd gone this far. If he didn't carry it through, Norman knew what would happen to him. It had been explained before, with vivid examples of what they did to others who had a change of heart. And his contact didn't pull any punches when he warned Norman against turning himself in to the authorities. They'd infiltrated everything. Didn't that message about his nonexistent sister clarify that?

He peered once more at the imaginary periscopes and saw foamy rooster tails rising off them between the whitecaps. Then he headed forward to the electronics workshop on the third level.

Captain Barney Gold, commanding officer of *Gettysburg*, studied the message on his desk. It seemed innocuous enough. "Sorry, Ted. I can't figure what's so mysterious about this. They named this nephew Andrew after his uncle. That's normal." He shrugged and handed the sheet of paper back to his operations officer. "I saw it, too. I initialed it."

"But that's just it, Captain. I checked his records in the ship's office. Norman doesn't have any brothers or sisters as far as I can tell. No family listed at all, or he hasn't mentioned one since he's been aboard. For that matter, I'm still trying to figure how he got orders to this ship after two years on shore. He'll be out of the navy before he learns anything."

"You don't like him, do you?" Gold smiled gently down a long aquiline nose. He liked Ted Shore because the man had a reason for everything.

Shore had never cared for Andrew Norman, not since the day he reported aboard. The youngster was a tough fit in any department on *Gettysburg*, especially after two years ashore behind a desk. His experience was operations oriented and he was assigned to Shore's department by the executive officer for lack of a better place. "I don't like him because he could care less about the navy. I don't know why he ever signed up and he's been vague about it since the day he reported aboard." Shore pursed his lips thoughtfully. "I've bounced him around each division to see what he takes to and, frankly, he's never seemed to care about anything . . . except fooling around in CIC."

"I ran into a lot like him in my time." The captain's fine black hair was thinning and he ran a hand through it unconsciously. "They're trainable."

"That's when there was a draft, Captain. Shouldn't you expect a little more now?" Shore shook his head in frustration, unaware once again that he was twisting the heavy class ring on his finger. He'd never known another life but the navy since he was seventeen and he found it difficult to understand what motivated outsiders. "Captain, why would a guy like him have such a high security clearance? Hell, there was nothing he did ashore that required more than an idiot IQ. He doesn't need to know anything about this ship or the Aegis system if he's getting out in six months. And the way he hangs around the ETs and the men handling Aegis . . . no, I just don't like it. Maybe I'm paranoid, but there's something wrong with that guy." Shore was short and dark and intense and he searched for a reason for everything.

One of the many reasons Barney Gold commanded a ship

like *Gettysburg* was his understanding of junior officers. He listened to them when they had a hunch. Ted Shore wasn't just good—he was one of the best, headed for an early command. So if he had taken the trouble to learn so much about Norman, it was worth checking further. "OK, Ted, tell me—how do you want to handle it?"

"I want to do this myself, Captain. If I'm wrong, the responsibility is mine alone. I'm going to go directly to him and ask about this message. I can explain that his personnel records don't seem to be complete and with a clearance like his I'm required to . . ."

"Do whatever seems best to you, Ted. You've always handled these things well in the past." Barney Gold stood up politely to show that he had work to do. In his mid-forties, he was still trim and carried his authority with a grace that enhanced his command. "I'm sure you'll keep me informed . . . and let the XO know about our conversation if you would. I want to make sure he's included on everything here. I don't think he's any more excited about Norman than you are. And by the way," he added over his shoulder, "those sunspots or flares or whatever they're called are raising havoc with fleet communications. I'd like you to have young Gibney prepare a report on their effects on *Gettysburg* by morning."

Barney Gold sat down in his desk chair in his cabin and pushed a stack of paper out of the way. Even with the air conditioning, the air was sticky and he had no appetite for busy work. It was time to undertake something he honestly looked forward to—writing his wife back home in San Diego. Rebecca Gold was the unofficial mother of *Gettysburg* and it was time to bring her up to date on her family.

Every other day, Gold made a habit of writing his wife about what was happening aboard the ship. In turn, Becca Gold would compile his information into the *Gettysburg Gazette*, which was published at least once every two weeks, or whenever she had enough information. She had a small copier Barney had purchased when he assumed command of the ship, and Becca ran off enough copies of the *Gazette* to send to the families of each man aboard the ship. It was their way—not just Barney's, but theirs together—of saying that every individual aboard *Gettysburg* was important and that his welfare was a constant concern.

The *Gazette* carried news of professional schools attended, promotions, new babies, and the commanding officer's insightful stories of how each man contributed to the success of *Gettysburg*. Barney Gold felt that pride in their ship and support from home were the basis for any crew making a naval vessel a superior fighting ship. Those who sailed *Gettysburg* had become the proudest men in the fleet, and their families reinforced that pride ashore.

Becca was also a woman with a fulltime job. Not only did she manage the *Gettysburg Gazette*, she worried over new babies, aging parents, and holiday parties when the ship was at sea.

Barney Gold missed Becca terribly from the moment that *Gettysburg* singled up her lines each time to get underway. He wouldn't have been the same man, certainly not the one so revered by his crew, if Becca had not been an integral part of him.

"Come on, Hansen, I'm nervous enough without you screwing around. Is that the right schematic or isn't it?" Andrew Norman was sweating. The air conditioning in the forward electronics workshop was supposedly well controlled but beads of perspiration were evident on his forehead. The room was tiny, no more than six feet wide and fifteen feet deep, and it was crammed with storage space for parts and schematic designs. Since it was an outside space with a hot tropical sun beating down on the overhead, it was also warm and stuffy. Norman's face appeared as soft as his belly, which bulged around his beltline. His round mouth worked nervously as he waited and his eyes moved steadily, unable to concentrate.

"I'm not enjoying this any more than you, Mr. Norman.

But if we don't get this right, someone's going to make us do it over again. Or if they decide to get someone else to do it, we're in deep, deep shit wherever we show our faces. Got that, sir?" There was an emphasis on the last word that left no doubt the sailor cared nothing for Norman or the navy. He was different than the other technicians in the division. Hansen knew his stuff within reason but there was something else about him, almost as if he didn't belong in the navy. Did he feel there was no way out? That he'd take his chances doing this final job correctly rather than face the consequences? Or was he too cocky?

"I don't like this shit either," Norman responded defensively, "but for chrissake will you get your ass in gear." It was false bravado, words he knew he could never back up. He glanced at his watch again—less than two minutes since the last check. "Do you realize what would happen if someone walked in here now?"

"Not much more than if we didn't get the job done right," the second sailor mumbled sarcastically. There was no more respect from him than the other.

Hansen disagreed. "We're going to get this done. I don't want to hear anymore of this bullshit from either of you." Hansen had been warned about the other two, especially the officer, before *Gettysburg* got underway. But Lt. Norman was necessary because there were just some things an officer could get away with that an enlisted man couldn't. There was extra money for Hansen if he made sure they didn't screw up. "Then I hope I never lay eyes on either of you again." After a pause, he added under his breath so that neither of them could hear, *"I'll kill anyone who gets in my way now."* And he knew he would.

Norman remembered the day his contact explained exactly how it would happen: ". . . And on or about that day, the battle group commander will receive a message ordering him to detach *Gettysburg* to close the coast near Cam Ranh Bay. She'll remain well out in neutral waters, but the purpose will be to monitor a slight increase in airborne surveillance activity. The navy always wants to check Aegis's ability to track real live bogies. It should keep your captain on the bridge, and hopefully some others out of your hair." The voice repeating the words now in his subconscious seemed no more disconnected than it had when he first heard it. And the confidence . . . so much confidence that the US Navy would act exactly as the Soviets expected. "There may be some reported sub activity. Don't worry about that. It will be your pick-up boat. This tube is watertight and will sink just three feet below the surface. Don't worry about them being unable to find it. Believe me, this little devil will lead that sub by the nose."

That was exactly the way it had all happened. *Gettysburg* had been sent off for a day of independent ops. The message about his fictional sister's giving birth had come at the appropriate time. And here they were, three men who knew nothing about each other until the two enlisted men reported aboard just before they deployed from San Diego. Norman had been there a few months longer. It was a bit harder to stick an officer aboard a ship just like that.

Another minute had passed when Norman glanced at his watch. "Something wrong with the camera?"

"Mr. Norman, why don't you step outside for a cigarette or something. But leave us the hell alone." Hansen's voice remained quiet yet there was a latent combination of impatience and danger. No respect.

"Hansen, you're setting yourself up for . . ." Norman halted in mid-sentence, wheeling about as the handle on the door rattled. He looked back at the two others, the whites of his eyes wide with fear.

The knob rattled again. Then there was a sharp knock. "Lt. Norman, are you in there?" A pause, then, "Is there anyone in there?"

Andrew Norman's jaw dropped when he heard his name. The other two stared back at him in surprise, yet Hansen never moved from the table, but peered instead over his shoulder without moving. The door was locked. The only other keys belonged to the division officer and the Ops Officer.

The sound of a key slipping into the lock on the opposite side turned three sets of eyes toward the knob. A slight click of the tumblers coincided with the door opening inward.

None of them uttered a sound as LCDR Shore stepped into the tiny room. His eyes fell on Andrew Norman. "Why didn't you answer when I called your name, Norman?" The expression in his eyes reflected a combination of pity and disgust.

His question was met with silence. Norman stared at him, unable to drop his eyes, unable to speak. The door swung shut behind him as the ship rolled gently to starboard.

"How about you—Hansen . . . Filipo . . . ?" Shore asked, looking at the other two out of the corner of his eye. "Why didn't you say anything when I knocked?" Then his eyes picked out the schematic diagrams. He stepped over to the table and glanced at the key in the lower right hand corner of the top one. "There's nothing wrong with the system." He turned back to the other officer. "How about it, Norman? Can you tell me what's going on?"

Norman was searching for the words he wanted to say when he saw Hansen reach inside his shirt. A .45 automatic appeared in his hand, the black metal glistening brightly in the light.

There was never a word from Hansen, not a sound, nor was there a change in his expression. His movement was so fast there was no time for any of them to react, to speak out, before he pulled the trigger.

The explosion in the tiny compartment was deafening. Shore's face remained expressionless as his body careened backward into a metal locker. He clawed frantically at his neck as blood arched from a dark hole. Then his eyes widened with shock. A second shot, seemingly louder than the first, slammed into his chest, spinning him halfway around before he fell facedown on the deck.

CHAPTER 2

Andrew Norman's horror-stricken eyes locked on Shore's crumpled body. One arm was twisted grotesquely underneath him. Blood flowed readily from the bullet holes creating two distinct pools on the rubber deck matting. Hansen still held the gun pointed at the operations officer as if daring him to move. Norman's feet seemed locked in place. He wanted to run but a sixth sense seemed to tell him that would be crazy. There was no place he could run to. And there was that gun. . . .

Hansen looked from the body to Norman. "Roll him over. Make sure he's dead." It was an order that couldn't be refused, even from an enlisted man to an officer.

Norman moved the few steps woodenly, averting his eyes from the corpse as long as possible. Bending from the waist, he placed one hand on Shore's shoulder and attempted to move the body. It was dead weight—*yet he didn't want to come in contact with the blood*. His stomach was churning now, much worse than it had been earlier back on the fantail. He squatted and grabbed the free arm, wrenching fretfully at the body as if he feared it might suddenly rear up and strike back. When Shore was finally on his back, sightless grey eyes seemingly fixed on the three men left no doubt he was dead.

15

There were fan rooms on either side of the workshop, intake trunks forward, uptakes aft, and they were constantly noisy. There was another fan room and an Aegis equipment room across the passageway which then led forward to a radar room. It was quite possible the shots in the closed compartment might not have been heard, but that was a toss-up as far as Hansen was concerned.

"What now?" Filipo asked softly, his eyes on Hansen rather than the officer. If he was afraid, it wasn't evident. He seemed to have little concern for Shore's corpse.

"Big change in plans," Hansen replied slowly. He regarded the gun in his hand with a curious smile as if he was pleased at how well it had worked. "Well, Mr. Norman," he began caustically, "you're the officer. Did they prepare you for something like this?"

Andrew Norman, his eyes still wide with shock, blinked rapidly a few times as his gaze traveled from Shore's body to the gun before settling on Hansen. "Why . . ." he began, his head shaking slowly from side to side, ". . . why did you . . ." but the words he was searching for became lodged somewhere in his throat.

"You saw what was happening. He had us figured—or had you figured—the minute he saw that schematic on the table. I've been taught over the years to react instantly and you'd be surprised how often it's saved my life. You know, Mr. Norman," he wagged the gun in the officer's face, "you know what they'd do to us for spying."

Hansen bent down and unlocked a small cabinet snuggled back in the shadows to one side of the table Filipo had been working at. He extracted three more automatics and a number of clips of ammunition. He slipped one of the guns into the front of his dungarees. The other two were proffered to Filipo. "Take these. They're loaded and don't be afraid to use them." He stuck a number of the clips in his pockets, handing the rest to Filipo. "I don't trust you with a gun, Mr. Norman. You might shoot one of us."

"But now . . ." Norman gestured at Shore's corpse. He

couldn't believe these words from Hansen . . . so . . . callous! There was never supposed to have been any violence. . . .

"Now nothing. It's done. Once again I'm alive. I don't know about you two but I'm going wherever this film was going." Hansen eyed the officer. "That's one thing I wasn't sure about. They never seem to tell any of us about an entire project. How were you going to get rid of it once we were done?"

Norman displayed the tube. "With this . . . it's waterproof . . . over the side. Submarine's supposed to pick it up." *But who was they?* What the hell was Hansen talking about?

"I see." He raised his eyebrows thoughtfully. "Things like that always seem to be reserved for the officers. When is this submarine supposed to appear?"

"Pretty quick after it goes over the side . . . I guess."

"I'm going with it," Hansen concluded. "Better to take my chances that way than . . ."

Filipo interrupted. "You know, we're not going to have any chances to do anything if someone heard those shots. We've got to come up with something fast." He looked briefly at Norman before judging that there were no decisions coming from him, then turned back to Hansen.

"There's only one person this ship can't do without," Hansen murmured as he slipped the gun back inside his shirt. "Call the captain, Mr. Norman. We'll use him. Get his ass down here fast."

The young officer wrinkled his forehead curiously. "I don't know what to say." He was as intimidated by Barney Gold as he had been by Shore, even though *Gettysburg*'s commanding officer had attempted a few times to draw him out.

"I don't give a shit how you say it. Tell him anything. Christ, tell him that Mr. Shore hurt himself. Then you can say Mr. Shore asked you to get Captain Gold so he could tell him something very important. You don't know what it is but Shore seemed to feel it was very important." Hansen pointed irritably at the phone on the bulkhead. "Just do it before I have to use this on you." He patted the gun under his shirt menacingly.

Norman reached tentatively for the phone, his eyes riveted on Hansen's shirt front. Realizing the choice wasn't his to make, he turned away slowly, punched the buttons for the bridge, and waited. When a voice answered on the other end, he responded, "May I speak to the captain, please. This is Mr. Norman."

Hansen studied Norman attentively; Filipo watched Hansen as if the man were putting words in the officer's mouth like a ventriloquist. Hansen displayed some nervousness, but of the three of them he seemed most confident of his next step.

"Captain. This is Mr. Norman." The words came in a flurry. "Commander Shore asked me to call you because he . . . he tripped stepping into the ET shop . . . hurt his ankle, I guess. The corpsman's already on his way. Mr. Shore apologized for asking, but would you mind coming down to talk with him before he goes below to sick bay? He says it's very important, sir." A pause followed. Norman would never know he'd hit upon Shore's earlier conversation with the captain. Then a relieved look spread across his face. "Thank you, sir. He'll appreciate it. Right. It's the forward shop, just across from the 49 radar room." He looked at Hansen after replacing the phone. "He's coming right away. What now?"

"He's our ticket. That's all I know—a ticket to get our asses off this ship somehow." It was the first time there had been the slightest hint of desperation in Hansen's voice. Then he added haltingly, "I don't know . . . what I'll do . . . somehow Captain Gold . . . alive or dead . . . is going to save our asses . . ."

"But . . ." Norman began.

"Just make sure he gets his ass in here," Hansen interrupted nastily. "That's all you got to do. You're the officer. Then," he shrugged uncertainly, looking from Filipo to Norman, "I'll take care of everything. The captain's a god on this ship. Everybody loves him. They're not going to do anything crazy, not if it means their beloved captain may suffer for it. No one's going to touch us once we have him—not with a gun to his head." Then he said as an afterthought, "Not if we hurt him a little bit."

Filipo nodded as Hansen spoke but he seemed more interested in the gun in his hand. He swung it about the tiny compartment, aiming it at various objects, his lips silently muttering *bang* as he destroyed each item in his line of sight.

"You like that gun?" Hansen grinned.

Filipo nodded appreciatively, smiling strangely as it centered briefly on Norman's belly before moving on. "Yeah," he whispered.

"Use it if you have to."

They waited, uneasy with themselves, eyes avoiding each other and the corpse on the deck. Norman knew he was close to tears. Everything had been working so well up to this point. No one had any idea what the three of them were up to. And this was the last effort. After today—*after today*, he sighed inwardly—why they would have been off scot-free! Nothing more to fear . . . fear . . . he'd lived with it so long. . . .

There was a sharp knock at the door. Before the sound had died, Captain Gold pushed it open and stepped into the electronics workshop. His eyes took in the three men quickly, the guns pointed at his midsection, before catching sight of the body on the deck.

"I'll use it if I have to," Hansen murmured huskily.

There was time for Gold's brow to furrow slightly before nodding to himself. "So Ted was right . . ." Barney Gold murmured, his eyes settling on Norman. But there was no change of expression, nothing that would show them he was afraid, perhaps even concerned. He had learned long ago to stop and think a situation out—put the threat to himself aside first. He was inescapably responsible for everyone and everything aboard *Gettysburg*. A dead captain accomplished nothing. He realized instantly he must play for time.

"Pardon me, Captain?" Norman had expected any reaction other than such a passive expression.

"Lock the door," Hansen said quietly to Norman.

There was a quizzical expression on the lieutenant's face as he pushed the door shut. What did Gold mean by that remark?

Hansen knew instinctively. Barney Gold was the most dangerous man aboard the ship. He had to be under their control constantly, physically and mentally. The first part was easier than the second. They would probably have to control him with pain. And to allow him to exert his influence on the crew would be pure suicide.

"He had you figured out, Mr. Norman," Gold answered. "I don't know if he knew anything about these two, but he had his suspicions about you. Is that why you killed him?" The captain's face remained devoid of expression. There was no indication that he was at all concerned with the guns pointing at his midsection. He was the commanding officer of *Gettysburg* and perpetual self-confidence was one of the unwritten requirements inherent in a captain's absolute authority.

"I didn't kill him!" Norman reacted as if he'd been shot himself.

Gold looked at the other two. "Sure you did. I don't care who's holding the gun." He looked over at the table with the schematic layout and the small camera. "Is it the Aegis you're after?"

There was no response.

"So that's it. Aegis," he said softly, folding his arms. Then he looked at each of them separately and stroked his chin. "Three Americans turning against their country." His voice was low and well modulated. Although he was facing a gun, there was even a threat implied in his words.

"No time to play games with us, Captain." Hansen

waved the gun menacingly as if to signify his importance. Gold's calm assurance was disheartening. "We had to use this once, so you better believe we'll do it again. We got to get our asses off this ship now and we need your help." His voice was controlled but it was unable to disguise an inner urgency.

"You can leave any time you want," Gold smiled. "I'll have the ship stopped. You can have a boat, food, water, medical supplies—whatever you want. I can't argue with that," he said gesturing toward the gun. "I don't want to take a chance on your using it on anyone else in my crew." He'd consider just about anything if he could get them off his ship without anyone else getting hurt. Then, if he couldn't destroy them—and that film!—there was a carrier within range that could. But get them off *Gettysburg* before these madmen hurt anyone else!

"Not unless I have to, Captain." Hansen moved over beside him. "From now on, I guarantee I won't leave your side because I don't think there's a soul on this ship who wants to do anything to hurt their captain. They like you too much," he added with a grin. "But if someone does make a move, well you're the first one dead." He sighted down the short barrel between Gold's eyes. "Between the time someone attempts to screw with us and the time they get to me—*bang*," he shouted with all his might, "*you're dead!* Then we start on the others. So your getting blasted won't save anyone else. And we got explosives set down below. We'll blow your ship apart." It sounded like a reasonable threat as it came to him. He pointed at the other sailor. "Filipo's going to have fun with that if you push him."

Filipo grinned at the mention of his name and caressed the gun to emphasize Hansen's point.

Andrew Norman's entire body jerked involuntarily. He knew Hansen meant what he said. But could he really have planted explosives? The promise was in the man's eyes. And he also knew it was probably the only possible way out at this stage. *Oh God,* he said silently to himself closing his eyes, *Oh God, how did I ever get myself into this?* There had been only minutes left until it all would have been over. He could have dropped that tube over the stern and they would have been done with it all. *That's all we'll ever ask of you,* his contact had said.

"How much more to do?" Hansen snapped at Filipo. "Some son of a bitch is going to want the captain any minute."

"Just two more shots. We were almost done when Mr. Shore came in. Just this section," he said, indicating the lower right quadrant of the schematic.

"Then get it over with . . . now . . . before someone comes looking for him." While Filipo returned to his camera, Hansen turned back to Barney Gold. "Now, Captain, you realize the kind of situation we're all in . . . dangerous . . . that sort of thing. So desperate men have to do desperate things. To convince everyone else that I really mean business, I'm going to be behind you all the time and this .45 is going to be in the back of your head. You may not feel it there every minute, but that's where I intend to shoot you if I have to, just one bullet so that I have enough left for anyone else who wants to do something stupid. From right now, don't make any fast moves . . . nothing that would scare me into pulling the trigger. 'Cause I promise—and believe me, I really mean it—that once I put a bullet in your head, I'll be shooting others before you hit the deck. And these other two—or at least Filipo—will also. And we have more clips." He took two out to show Gold. "It'll be a slaughter and you'll be responsible. I'll be able to take some more with me—and that's exactly what you want to avoid." He drew a deep breath and bit his lower lip as if he was trying to conjure up an even better reason. "Remember," he added, "if you're dead, the chances of our getting Aegis off this ship improve with each corpse."

The expression on Gold's face, visible only for an instant, convinced Hansen that he'd touched a critical nerve. He knew men like Gold weren't afraid to die.

Norman was amazed at how comfortable Hansen seemed with Gold, more so because he wouldn't have had the slightest idea what to do when the captain came into the shop. Regardless of what he had now become, he remained in awe of ships' captains—and he'd been afraid of Gold. Whoever Hansen was, he was no average sailor. There was something about the way he operated . . . *the man was too cold.*

Hansen eased behind Barney Gold. "Now I'm going to be behind you at all times, Captain. Just so you know, we're going to be like Siamese twins. My hand's going to be in the back of your belt almost all of the time . . . like this. . . ." He slipped his left hand around the belt and worked his thumb through a belt loop on the captain's pants. "So you'll know I'm always there. I could keep this stuck in the back of your head," he repeated, and he jammed the barrel into Gold's neck for an instant, "but that would be as uncomfortable for me as it would be for you, and neither one of us wants to upset the other."

"How long do you think you can get away with this before we wear you down?" Gold's face remained as calm as the moment he stepped through the door. His objective was to avoid forcing Hansen to pull the trigger. With each moment he bought, Gold felt there was that much more time to find a solution.

"I promise you I've been in worse situations before and lasted for days. But this time, if I can make Mr. Norman here function like an officer, I doubt we'll have to worry about taking that long." He balled the hand on the captain's belt into a fist and dug his knuckles into the man's back. "This is just so you'll know the signal if I think anything's going to happen that I don't like or if I think one of your people is screwing with Filipo or Mr. Norman. I will count to three . . . out loud . . . then, *bang*," he bellowed in Gold's ear, "your brains will scatter."

"Done," Filipo called out. "Let me rewind this film for Mr. Norman and we'll be all set."

"May I ask a question?" Gold said.

"Go."

"Are you really in our navy?"

"For now I am."

"But you're really in someone else's military aren't you?"

"That's possible." All of Hansen's answers had been emotionless.

"You're too comfortable, still calling him Mr. Norman, even though you obviously have as low a regard for him as I do."

"He's still valuable to me because he's considered an officer by this crew and will be able to get certain things done for me more efficiently than I could." Hansen looked over at Filipo, who had handed the tiny roll of film to Norman. "That it?"

"Done."

"Okay, Captain, we're close enough to being ready. Place your hands behind your back."

"What?" Gold had turned slightly as he began to speak when the barrel of Hansen's gun caught him behind the right ear. He stumbled, attempted to catch his balance, then fell forward on his hands and knees as Hansen swung again. Blood ran from a gash under his hair, running across his chin as he struggled to lift his head.

"Stay on your knees," Hansen snapped. "Mr. Norman, I want you to take that wire on the shelf and bind the captain's hands behind his back. Make it tight as you can. I don't particularly care if it hurts him."

Once Gold's hands were secured behind his back, Norman helped him to his feet. Gold swayed, then stumbled against the bulkhead for support. Blood flowing freely stained his shirt a deep crimson.

"How are you going to handle that container . . . that tube, Mr. Norman?" Hansen asked.

"I hadn't thought about it." He was growing increasingly

agitated, continually wiping the sweat from his face. "Put it in my pocket, I guess."

"Put it inside your shirt," Hansen directed. Norman, he could see, would be a liability until they could somehow get out of this mess. "Then take another notch in your belt. Some quick-fingered clown might try to lift it out of your pocket . . . and then I'd be forced to start killing people—our friend here first. Now, both of you," his eyes included Filipo and Norman, "I want you always right by me until I say otherwise. If anyone separated one of us from the other two, that could be the end for all of us. When we're moving anywhere, Mr. Norman keeps his hand in my belt, Filipo in his. We're headed for the pilot house now. Once we're there, we all stay in sight for our own good. All right?"

Hansen explained exactly how they would cover the distance from the electronics shop on the third level above the main deck to the pilot house on the fifth level. The ladders concerned him the most, and he finally decided that Norman and Filipo would lead the way when they were climbing.

They moved forward in the passageway, turning up the ladder by the radar room. Gold stumbled groggily as Hansen half lifted him by the belt. There were two sailors on the fourth level. Both of them shrank back against the bulkhead as their bloodied captain, his eyes dazed, passed with a .45 pressed against the back of his head.

"Stop!" Hansen snapped. For a moment, the six of them remained locked in place. Then Hansen turned to the sailors. "Lie down . . . facing aft . . . on your stomachs." Gold and Norman remained facing forward as the sailors dropped to the deck. But Filipo turned just as Hansen smashed the butt of the gun onto the head of one of the prone sailors. There was a groan as his body went rigid, then relaxed. The second man turned his head and attempted to rise just as Hansen swung at him. There was a sickening sound of bone breaking combined with a low moan. "I don't need anyone warning the bridge," he muttered, then growled to the others, "Okay, keep moving."

The next encounter occurred on the fifth level outside the pilot house just as they appeared at the top of the ladder. The executive officer (XO) had just stepped out of the pilot house and was heading for the ladder.

"Step aside, Commander," Hansen called out to him. And to Gold in a lower voice, "Just keep moving ahead, Captain. I don't intend to stop for anybody."

The XO's glance shifted from face to face. Then he bent down and leaned the clipboard he'd been carrying against the bulkhead. "Captain, what can I—"

"Get out of the way," Hansen snarled.

The XO planted his feet, his arms hanging loosely at his sides. "Just say the word, Captain." His small, dark eyes darted from Barney Gold to Hansen, then back again to Gold.

"Now you're going to feel my fist tighten and see how much I mean business," Hansen said calmly to Gold. "One . . . two . . ."

"Step aside, Glen . . . right now." There was a note of urgency in his voice, though he remained outwardly calm. And when the XO moved back against the bulkhead, he added, "Please stay out of our way," he ordered, struggling to keep his tone even, "until I have more time to think things out."

"Filipo, he's yours," Hansen said as they inched passed the XO. "Mr. Marston, I want you to come back in the pilot house, but stay at least ten feet away from us at all times or you'll see your captain's brains spread all over the pilot house. And Filipo will probably do the same for you. Is that absolutely clear?"

"Captain?" the XO queried.

"Your gun," Hansen growled at Filipo. "I'll count to three and then you shoot him."

Again, a strange look, almost of pleasure, spread over

Filipo's face as the barrel of his gun settled on the XO's chest.

"Do what he says, Glen. Ted Shore's dead. Let's try not to get anyone else hurt. If you want to be a dead hero right now, before we have a chance, you're letting the rest of the men down." He continued to nod confidently to Marston, holding the man's eyes as he spoke.

As Barney Gold stepped over the coaming into the pilot house, one of the men on watch called out instinctively, "Captain's on the br—" but his voice died out as he saw Hansen with a .45 automatic pressed snugly against Gold's head followed by their executive officer in the same situation.

Dead silence magnified the shock as Hansen and their captain, blood still streaming from his head, moved through the interior of the pilot house toward the starboard side where the captain normally sat in his chair. Every eye in the watch section followed them as Hansen turned with the captain and backed against the front corner of the pilot house. He kept his back to the windows so that he could see everything that was going on inside. There was no way anyone could scale the sheer front of the superstructure to surprise him from behind. Norman remained close to Hansen, anxiety etched on his face. Filipo and the executive officer watched from the opposite side.

"Tell everyone to stand easy, Captain, but nobody leaves and nobody communicates with anyone beyond the pilot house without your permission," Hansen said in a low voice. "I guess it would mean a lot more to them if you explain how concerned you are for their lives."

Gold's eyes were still clouded but his expression remained firm as he spoke in a dull monotone. "For the present, I want each of you to continue with your jobs. Do not move from your present position without permission. Do not attempt to contact anyone in any other part of the ship. These men are desperate, they've already killed, and they're willing to kill again. There's no reason to push them yet." He turned his head slightly. "Is that satisfactory?"

Hansen's voice remained calm. "You're using your head, Captain. Let's hope everyone else is as smart as you. Now, it's not going to take more than half a minute for the word to get out on this ship that something's happening on the bridge. I want Mr. Marston to make an announcement over the PA that you are conducting security drills on the bridge and no one is to call or even appear up here until the word is passed that the drill is complete. That might just keep your roving sentry from getting his ass killed, too."

Gold felt the muzzle of the gun pressed tightly below his right ear. If anything, he promised himself, it would help him think more clearly. "Go ahead, Glen. Pass the word. We need time."

"Great, Captain," Hansen murmured in his ear. "Maybe we'll all be alive tomorrow." He waited until the XO finished his announcement, then he brutally slammed the gun against the side of Gold's head. As he fell to the deck with a thud, the executive officer leaped toward Hansen with a cry of rage. But Filipo had been watching him, anticipating something like that. As Marston lunged, the sailor's foot snaked out, tripping the XO. Before his body touched the deck, Filipo's knees slammed into his back followed by his gun slashing across the back of Marston's skull.

Hansen pointed at two of the sailors staring open-mouthed at him. "Pick the captain up. When he comes around, I want him sitting in that chair." He indicated the captain's chair on the starboard side of the pilot house. "And I want his hands behind the back of the chair so he can't move."

Not a word was spoken as Barney Gold was lifted clumsily toward the chair. The two sailors made an effort to be as gentle as possible with their captain. It was awkward, with his wrists still secure behind his back, and they were fearful of injuring him.

"Don't worry about hurting him. If you aren't done by the time I count to ten, you're dead men and two more will finish the job."

Barney Gold was set roughly into the chair. Then Hansen indicated the same should be done with Marston, whose hands were secured with cord from the chart table.

"Now, Mr. Norman," Hansen said, "tell me how we get in touch with that submarine."

"I . . . I don't understand what you mean?" Norman wiped the sweat from his face with a dirty handkerchief. His uniform blouse was dark and wrinkled with perspiration.

"Don't act so dumb," Hansen sneered. "The submarine—the one that's going to pick up that little tube of yours. How do we contact them—tell them they're going to have three extra passengers?"

"I haven't the vaguest idea." A stricken expression spread over Norman's face. What would Hansen do when he found out he couldn't escape? "There's no way we can contact them. This was all a preconceived plan. It was set up months ago. I don't even know how they did it. I just knew approximately when it was supposed to show up, and a message last night confirmed it."

Hansen's look of disbelief frightened him.

"I swear—that's the way it happened," Norman insisted. "I didn't know any more about how it was set up than you knew about how I was supposed to pass it on . . . honestly." His voice dropped to a whisper with the final word, his eyes riveted on the gun in Hansen's hand.

Barney Gold's eyes had opened and he was slowly moving his head from side to side. Now he raised it until his head rested on the back of the chair where he could roll it from side to side. He could feel Hansen's gun barrel grinding into his neck as his eyes came back in focus. "Easy, Hansen," Gold mumbled. "I heard what he said and I bet he's right. I'm sure none of you really knew what the other was supposed to do. That's the way they set these things up in case one of you gets caught. And someone like

Norman isn't exactly capable of being a superspy. You know that as well as I do."

"So much for that," Hansen snarled. Then he called across the pilot house to the quartermaster. "Hey, Cross, tell me where we are right now."

Cross looked to Gold for approval, which came as a painful nod of the head, before he leaned over the chart table. After a moment's hesitation, he said, "About latitude . . . north thirteen . . ."

"Dammit, I want our real location. I'm no navigator. Where the hell's the nearest island?"

Cross was visibly shaken. He picked up a set of dividers, then dropped them on the deck. When he bent to retrieve them, his head slammed on the corner of the chart table. His eyes darted to Hansen's gun before he looked back to the chart. "We're off Vietnam. Cam Ranh Bay is about sixty miles away, almost due west."

"Mr. Norman," Hansen barked with a touch of cockiness. "Take a look at that chart. See if he's right." The beginning of a smile appeared at the corners of his mouth.

The captain's head had slumped forward again, his chin resting on his chest. Occasional soft moans escaped his lips. Each time his eyes opened, they fell on a different man.

Norman edged over to the chart table, careful to avoid each of the watch standers in his path. His hands shook as he picked up the dividers and measured the distance on the chart. He searched helplessly for the distance scale until the quartermaster tapped it with his index finger. "Looks pretty good to me," he called over his shoulder.

"How long would it take us to get there?"

Norman's eyes settled on the quartermaster's with a look of horror. The man's pencil scratched some figures on the chart. "Two or three hours, depending how fast we were moving."

"Mr. Norman," Hansen said, "turn us toward Cam Ranh Bay."

"What are you going to . . ." Norman began.

"I don't know yet," Hansen snapped. "Just do what I say."

"Captain," the Officer of the Deck (OOD), Lt. Wilson, interrupted, "I think . . ." He'd remained quiet after a whispered warning from the executive officer. He failed to comprehend the strategy of appeasing Hansen until an opening appeared and he had no intention of following Hansen's orders.

"Shut up," Hansen said angrily. "He'll handle this." He looked over to Norman. "Go ahead, turn us in that direction."

Norman moved hesitantly toward the ship control console. The helmsman had a stricken look on his face. Lt. Wilson also moved toward the console. "Don't do anything for them," he said to the sailor, placing himself in Norman's path.

Norman looked hesitantly at Hansen.

"Get out of his way," Hansen said cooly.

The OOD glared at him, then stood his ground, staring straight ahead out the window as if his efforts would symbolically solve the problem.

Filipo raised his gun level with the OOD's chest. There was the hint of a grin at the corners of his mouth again.

Norman stopped a few feet behind him, unsure of his next move. He glanced uncertainly at Hansen.

Gold's head came up as he felt Hansen's gun grind into the back of his neck. His eyes studied Filipo.

"One . . . two . . ." Hansen began in a high, tense voice.

"Wilson, get out of his way," Barney Gold ordered.

The OOD looked hesitantly at his captain and took a deep breath. "Captain, I . . ." His mouth was set as he started to speak.

"Three . . . shoot him," Hansen screamed.

The .45 in Filipo's hand bucked once with a sharp explosion that rebounded off the bulkhead.

CHAPTER 3

The OOD staggered backwards, hands clasped to his chest, blood pouring between his fingers. His eyes opened wide in surprise before he crumpled helplessly to the deck at Norman's feet, where he lay groaning softly.

Gold had jerked instinctively as the .45 went off, straining to move against the wire biting deeply into his wrists. The muzzle of Hansen's gun drove mercilessly into the base of his skull. "That's enough, Captain. Don't do anything foolish . . . don't any of you do anything you'll die for," he snarled. His voice rose to a howl as his eyes took in the others in the pilot house. "Don't move a muscle . . . or the next bullet's for your captain and there's still enough to turn this pilot house into a bloody mess."

"There was no call for that," Gold said, his voice noticeably weak. "I was ordering him to . . ."

"He set an example for all the others. Now they understand perfectly that we mean business. Go on, Norman, step over your friend there and turn us toward the land. Don't be afraid," he snickered, "I won't waste a bullet on you."

Not a soul in the pilot house moved. All eyes were fixed on some point beyond the bow as if hoping this was a very bad dream. But it was impossible to avoid noticing Lt.

Wilson's writhing body. Nor could they keep from looking out of the corners of their eyes at Barney Gold and Hansen. Blood still flowed freely from the captain's head while the executive officer slumped forward in his chair, lips moving without sound. Committing suicide by forcing someone else to pull the trigger was a senseless act. They were trapped— trapped by the desire to lash out, yet aware their captain would die before they would. Somehow, Barney Gold would get them out of this if they just gave him time. That's what his eyes seemed to say as they continued to pass from one man to the next. They also glanced questioningly at the unconscious form of their executive officer. Glen Marston had shown no hesitation at dying but these people had chosen not to kill him. *No one moved*.

"Hansen," Gold asked, "will you allow someone to take care of Mr. Wilson . . . please?" It sounded more an order than a plea, but the captain's voice was low enough to be convincing.

"Tell someone to drag him out on the port wing," Hansen decided after a moment's hesitation. "But then they come right back in here. You can call down to sick bay for a corpsman, but that's all. One corpsman, one medical bag. Say that it's part of the security drill. Filipo will inspect the bag before anyone touches him."

As if to reinforce his own importance, Filipo added to no one in particular with a grimace he'd seen in the movies, "Make me nervous just once and this gun goes off again. Understood?"

Gold nodded to the messenger. "Ask the port lookout to help you move Mr. Wilson. Bailey, you call sick bay and explain exactly what Hansen said."

Gettysburg was heeling very slightly when Hansen realized how slowly they were turning. "Mr. Norman, what's our speed?"

"About three knots."

"Christ, it will take us all night. How fast do we have to go to get near the coast in two or three hours?"

"Twenty knots might be good."

"Then increase your speed to whatever we need," he snarled. "Christ, Norman, are your brains up your ass? Do you think we want to crawl all the way?"

Barney Gold closed his eyes. He needed time to clear his head, to think. One sentence kept racing through his head—*save as many lives as you can without giving them Aegis*—until it became a blur. The pain came in surges that brought him close to unconsciousness, yet each time that single sentence returned to hound him until his eyes reopened.

"We're going to have to worry about another problem in awhile, Hansen," Gold murmured. "You can be damn sure that Vietnamese radar is going to notice our change in plans, especially when they track an American cruiser heading right for Cam Ranh Bay at twenty knots. They're more likely to shoot and ask questions later, you know. There's no love lost between us. Maybe you'd like that boat I promised you," he added.

"You're right again, Captain, but not about the boat. Sometimes I'm only good for one idea at a time. Coming in unannounced could make things messy for all of us." He paused for a moment to collect his thoughts. "Mr. Norman, we must know what frequencies the Russians use around here. They've pretty much taken over the port and I bet they have their own primary circuits."

Again that slightly frightened expression spread over Norman's face. "I'm afraid I don't know much about that. . . ."

"How about you, Captain?" Hansen interrupted irritably. "You know everything that goes on aboard this ship."

"We tape a couple of their frequencies. But all we do is listen," Gold answered.

"How about a primary circuit the Russians use most of the time?" Hansen asked.

"You'd have to ask the comm officer. I'm not sure about that," Gold responded. "And communications are very unreliable worldwide right now. Sunspots. Can't do anything about them."

"Captain Gold," Hansen said, pulling the gun barrel away, "Mr. Norman will get the communications officer on the phone for you. You will then ask him which frequency is used most by the Russians. Have that circuit patched into the radio directly above us. I want to be able to send and receive. I'll do the worrying about sunspots when I have to."

In less than a minute, the speaker above Hansen's head crackled into life. A voice came over the intercom from radio central, "You've got that circuit now, Captain. But I don't know what good it's going to do. We've never heard anything but Russian coming over it."

Random transmissions in words none of them understood could be heard in the background. "Remember, Captain, you might not feel my hand all the time but this gun will go off in an instant . . . faster than you can possibly move." When there was a break, Hansen picked up the mike with his free hand and keyed it twice. Then, to everyone's amazement, except perhaps for Barney Gold, he began speaking into the mike in a language they assumed to be Russian. The only recognizable word was *Gettysburg*, which was repeated a few times before he halted to listen.

An eerie silence settled over the pilot house, punctuated by Lt. Wilson's ghastly moans from the port wing.

Andrew Norman stared at Hansen in disbelief. *That had to be Russian,* he assumed, *but why? What was this all about?* He'd understood in San Diego two months ago that there would be technicians on *Gettysburg* who would help him, but everything that had happened in the past hour was so . . . so . . . *bizarre*—that was the word. Like a bad dream. And now this Hansen was speaking Russian as if he was a native!

Barney Gold noted the expression on the young officer's face. "They really fooled you, didn't they?" he said softly. "You should have known there are always spies to spy on the spies." He smiled bitterly at Norman as he felt a warning pressure increasing at the base of his neck. He nodded silently to himself in acknowledgement of Norman's surprise and Hansen's message.

There had been dead silence on the radio. No Soviet station responded to Hansen's call, nor were there any communications among themselves. The circuit seemed lifeless. Irritated, Hansen transmitted his message once again, expanding on whatever had been said previously.

Another thirty seconds passed before a hesitant reply came over the speaker above Gold's head. The voice on the other end completed the message with a single word clearly recognized by every man in the pilot house—*Gettysburg*.

"Captain," Hansen said triumphantly, "I have Soviet Headquarters in Cam Ranh Bay here. However, there seems to be a slight misunderstanding about our mission and what has taken place here. They intend to use an English-speaking officer on the staff who they insist must speak with *Gettysburg*'s captain. They don't seem to be able to accept the fact that we're heading directly for their port to drop off the three of us."

A heavily accented voice came over the speaker. "It is imperative that I speak to the commanding officer of *Gettysburg*. You are in the process of violating territorial waters."

Hansen's gun returned to press against Gold's skull. He handed the microphone over the captain's shoulder. "This is your big chance, Captain. You can talk or you can watch more of your men die before you get a bullet. You know what has to be said. Think about it. Make damn sure of what you say."

Gold accepted the mike and took a deep breath. "This is Captain Gold of the *USS Gettysburg*."

There was a pause, then, "Yes. We have that name for the commanding officer of *Gettysburg*. Is there a way we can establish that you really are Gold?" Another pause with the transmitter still keyed on the other end, then, "This is necessary since we have no record of the person on your ship who contacted this command."

Gold considered his options through the pain that ebbed to a dull throb then surged through his head with a vengeance. *How does one establish his existence to a voice?* His forehead furrowed in frustration. *Why should he?* "Listen, this makes no sense," he snapped. "I have dead and wounded aboard my ship, and I have the individual who called you on this circuit pressing a .45 automatic to the back of my head. My ship is on a course for Cam Ranh Bay and will arrive in Vietnamese waters in less than two hours. If the Vietnamese were to attack *Gettysburg* now, I would be unable to shoot back which would make my superiors most unhappy. Do you understand? Over."

The transmitter on the other end was keyed twice before the voice continued hesitantly, "You are speaking with Soviet Naval Headquarters, Cam Ranh Bay. We are required at this time by international courtesy to ask if you require assistance."

"No, dammit! I am not sinking," Gold snapped. "My ship is currently under the control of a Soviet agent. That is an act of piracy under any international law you care to subscribe to. He and his men want to leave this ship. I insist you take them. Over." He closed his eyes to the pain reverberating through his head.

A second voice, one with less accent, responded quickly. "This command has no knowledge of any Soviet citizen involved with your ship, Captain. We must warn you that you are inviting a forceful response if you persist on your course."

"I have no choice. I have a gun at my head. I request that you provide assistance by accepting the three individuals who insist that you take responsibility for them. Then I will reverse course for international waters." And he would also destroy them and their film regardless of the consequences. "Over."

Before Cam Ranh Bay could answer, Hansen grabbed the

microphone. His voice rose in anger at one point before he ended his tirade.

There was no response.

"What was that all about?" Gold asked.

"I told them what they would have to do to find out about our mission if they had no previous knowledge." He snickered. "Someone there is going to get a hell of a blast when they find out who really controls this mission."

The tension in *Gettysburg*'s pilot house grew thicker with each passing moment. Glen Marston was returning to consciousness. His eyes would open, drift vaguely from man to man, then his head would again fall on his chest as if he was unable to keep awake. *Gettysburg*'s fate—the fate of each man—was controlled by a gun pressed against Barney Gold's skull. Forces beyond their control held their future in the balance. In a short time, their ship would be violating the territorial waters of Vietnam. Unless the situation changed rapidly, unless there was the remotest chance of something less futile than suicide, they were unable to defend themselves. That was the root cause of the tension—they couldn't fight back!

Bang. A single shot echoed through the pilot house with tremendous force.

A sailor, the petty officer of the watch, reeled back against the rear bulkhead by the exit door, blood spreading between fingers that clutched at the agony in his belly.

The door, which had been pulled open by the petty officer, revealed the image of another sailor freeze-framed in the act of reaching for the handle. Filipo's gun crashed twice and the corpsman who had been called to the bridge tumbled backwards into the passageway.

"Don't anyone move! Don't anyone touch either one of them!" Filipo waved the automatic wildly about the pilot house, his eyes alternating between the two men he'd just shot and those who stared back at him in horror.

"What was that all about?" Hansen asked, his voice soft and tentative for the first time.

"I thought Nichols was trying to escape when the door started to open," Filipo responded. "And when the corpsman was standing there, I saw his bag and it just scared the hell out of me." He glanced over to Hansen with eyes that mirrored both fear and hate. Then he reached into a pocket. "I gotta change guns here before I run out of ammo. . . ."

"Don't bother," Hansen interrupted. "Just put in a new clip. You want to have two of them fully loaded all the time. Never can tell when one of these other clowns are going to try something dumb." He punctuated his last sentence with a false laugh. "Well, you showed them. They can see what'll happen," he added for the benefit of his horrified audience.

"Hansen," Captain Gold said softly, "in the name of God, let someone look to these men . . . try to help the ones who are still alive. You can't just let them lie there suffering." He strained to turn his head to look at Hansen and was cuffed in the side of the head for his effort.

"You saw what happened then. Filipo was right. He thought someone might give us some trouble. If we let someone come up here, we're probably just asking for it. No, Captain, you're all just going to have to live with things this way for a while until we're off this ship."

"Hansen?" It was Lt. Norman. "Maybe I could do something for the wounded . . . I mean, you can't just leave . . ."

"Mr. Norman." Hansen's voice sliced through the tension like a knife. "What is our position now?"

Norman pursed his lips and glanced over at the quartermaster who, in turn, looked to Gold for approval.

"Go ahead, Cross. Do whatever he needs. I'd like to know myself."

The quartermaster looked at the chronometer above the table before making a couple of marks on his chart. "A little less than forty miles to land. Close to an hour and a half before we're in trouble from everybody's point of view," he said ruefully. "But your note on the side of the chart, Captain, says Vietnamese ideas on territorial waters already have us in hot water."

As if to emphasize his remark, a jet fighter plane screamed down the port side of the ship with a rumble that shook the windows in the pilot house.

"Where the hell was our radar on that . . ." Gold began. But he cut himself off. The answer was too obvious.

"Our friend here didn't want any communications from any other part of the ship, Captain," the XO mumbled with disdain. "CIC probably had it when it took off from shore."

A second jet passed down the starboard side at bridge level.

"MiG-29, Captain. They're already getting touchy."

"You realize, Hansen, that your Soviet friends may not be able to save your ass before we're all in trouble here." It was the first time Gold's voice had been raised since they appeared on the bridge. Imbedded deeply in his subconscious was the concept that the Russians did not have a habit of warning anyone for long. *Would it be the same as other confrontations? A couple of warning passes, more out of curiosity on their part, before they fired?*

Hansen's reaction was instantaneous. "Nothing changes, Captain. I'm going to wait for their headquarters to call them off."

"I'd like to send the XO down to CIC to see if they're sending out any surface craft yet," Gold countered. "That should be the next step if those MiGs don't fire first."

"The only way anyone leaves here is dead," Hansen growled.

Barney Gold acquiesced for the time being because he could sense a growing nervousness in Hansen. It varied from the pressure at the base of his neck to the odd look in Filipo's eyes to the mood shifts in Hansen's voice. Never push a desperate man, he thought, not if you can get him off the ship. And that's what he wanted to do—get Hansen off before he killed anyone else. To a point, Barney Gold would cooperate to mollify them because he was responsible for each life aboard *Gettysburg*. There was no sense in pushing a lunatic. There was more to being a captain than that. But he would go along for the ride only to the point that the Aegis films might have a chance to leave the ship.

A MiG-29 roared down the port side from the opposite direction, turning sharply across the bow.

"You know," Gold murmured almost to himself, "they might just ruin everything after all your work."

Hansen picked up the mike and spoke rapidly into it, his voice rising slightly. It was difficult to tell if he was also directing his hostility toward the shore but it seemed obvious the MiGs were having their effect on him.

The men on watch in the pilot house continued their effort to effect a calm presence. They glanced at each other from time to time, if for no reason other than reassurance, but they avoided looking toward Hansen while the radio speaker remained silent. No reason to upset him—it was always possible he would direct renewed frustration toward one of them, and he was totally unconcerned about using that gun. *Spetznaz or KGB*, Gold said to himself. *That's what they must be—killing comes so easy.*

Hansen called Cam Ranh Bay a second time. The growing anger in his voice was evident no matter the language.

Once again he was rewarded with an awkward silence broken only by the third jet reappearing directly in front of *Gettysburg* on a course that appeared to bring it right into the pilot house. It seemed to be skimming the whitecaps in an insane game of "chicken" as it grew rapidly larger, boring in on each of them like a bullet. Even Hansen's concentration was momentarily broken as he stared in horror at the approaching MiG. Just before it seemed ready to fly into the pilot house, it rose over their heads as if lifted by an invisible force, a blessed gossamer thread.

The MiG's approach so riveted their attention that it created the illusion of many minutes passing after Hansen's last call, but it was probably no more than thirty seconds before a voice came back over the speaker. The message was short and it was in English. It was not directed to Hansen. "Captain Gold, this command is unable to immediately verify any claims by the individual aboard your ship. The Soviet Union also cannot take any responsibility for possible danger to your crew or your ship at this time. Invading territorial waters is a provocative act. It is recommended you reverse your course immediately."

Hansen roared his response, his anger overflowing as he shifted from Russian to English. "Contact Vladivostok Fleet Headquarters directly. Admiral Markov will confirm the existence of this unit. Please confirm."

Barney Gold's hunch had been correct.

There was no response to Hansen's request. The same voice finally returned in English, "The Soviet Union disclaims any knowledge of non-Americans aboard *Gettysburg*. I am required to inform you that a statement will be issued shortly from Moscow to Washington absolving the Soviet Union of responsibility in this matter."

"Captain," a voice called out, "we have small craft on radar approaching at high speed. They just popped out from the surface return around Cam Ranh Bay."

"See," Hansen crowed triumphantly, "they claim a lack of knowledge yet they're already sending someone out for us." He chuckled good-naturedly, his rages already forgotten. "Captain, I do want to have their commander come to the bridge with his orders before we release you or the ship." He'd already forgotten the jets circling *Gettysburg*.

"No," Gold announced. He did not shout the word, yet it seemed to echo through the pilot house. Glen Marston's eyes fell on Hansen. Would he pull the trigger?

The ominous silence in the pilot house was broken by Hansen. "Figure your options have run out, Captain? No, Filipo, not yet," he cautioned as he saw the man's finger tightening on the trigger. "Captain Gold is more useful to us alive for now. He's our hostage," he announced proudly.

Filipo grinned his comprehension.

The executive officer, Glen Marston, was the first to recognize the flag on the lead boat. "Captain, those aren't Soviet craft approaching. I can make out a Vietnamese flag on the lead boat."

"How about if I take a look through my binoculars?" Gold inquired evenly. "I'm still responsible for this ship. The Vietnamese aren't as friendly as your people seem to be."

"The XO's doing just fine, Captain. There's nothing you can see with binoculars that he can't see with his own eyes. Let's you and me stay right where we are." But the tone of his voice indicated a renewed concern. Barney Gold noted that the Vietnamese flag punctuated the pressure of the muzzle of Hansen's gun.

"You'd be crazy to take chances with these people, too, Hansen." Barney Gold hadn't banked on a third party interferring. Like everyone else, he assumed, or hoped, the Vietnamese danced to Moscow's tune. "I've got to try to establish some sort of contact before something stupid happens. One of the signalmen could try to raise them with a light." The pressure of the gun barrel in his neck eased momentarily before it was jammed hard into his neck at the base of his skull. Gold gasped with the shock. Then his chin gradually slumped down to his chest and his pain-clouded eyes shut.

Hansen said nothing.

The four boats, each armed with surface-to-surface missiles closed *Gettysburg* at high speed. At a range of five miles, they separated, two making a wide circle to port, the others to starboard. They proceeded to stations astern a couple of thousand yards off either quarter. There were no indications one way or the other of their intentions.

There was no change for perhaps fifteen minutes until the speaker above Gold's head crackled with a new voice. In surprisingly clear English, a slightly accented voice said, "*Gettysburg*, you are entering Vietnamese territorial waters, over." Gold's head rose at the sound, his eyes fixed curiously on the speaker.

"Go ahead," Hansen said reaching the mike over the captain's shoulder, "you seem to be handling yourself well so far with these foreigners. They probably have a Russian officer aboard running the show. Tell him you have three passengers for Cam Ranh Bay." He depressed the transmit button.

"This is Captain Gold, Commanding Officer of *USS Gettysburg*." His voice was slightly weaker, the words coming a bit slower, but there was no doubt he understood the situation. "I do not have complete control of my ship at this time. This ship is proceeding under the temporary command of possible Russian nationals who have asked to be put ashore at Cam Ranh Bay. My weapons are not manned, repeat, not manned. . . ." *Time*, that same voice repeated in his brain, *all you need is time*. Would they be fool enough to take Hansen?

"Go ahead," Hansen interrupted. "Tell them we just want to get off if there are Soviet personnel aboard their boats."

"Are there Soviet officials aboard your vessels?" Gold inquired. "Over."

"Negative. These are units of the Vietnamese Navy, entirely separate of any Russian command. My initial orders are to determine your intentions. Over."

"My intentions are controlled by a gun in the back of my head."

Hansen dug the gun barrel painfully into the back of Gold's neck. "Did the Russians send you out to pick us up?" he shouted into the mike.

"We have been monitoring this circuit," came the response. "We are aware of the situation aboard *Gettysburg*." It was as if Hansen had gone unnoticed. "My lead boat, the one on your starboard quarter, will approach for boarding. We do not intend violence. However, our missiles are targeted for your ship if any trouble occurs. You may assume Soviet command in port remains on this circuit and any threatening action on your part will likely invite a reaction from the aircraft currently circling off your starboard bow."

The faceless voice remained calm and polite. Yet it was explaining—no, demanding, Barney Gold realized—that he allow a foreign national to board *Gettysburg* under threat of violence. It was against everything he'd ever been taught. This particular situation was not one covered in any navy manual that had ever been written. This was a new option—could the situation become worse than it already was?

The mike was left dangling over his shoulder by Hansen, who said nothing. His free hand simply returned to Gold's shoulder. Fingers ground fiercely into his flesh as the gun barrel pressed its message home. This time there was also a decided tremor broadcast through those fingers.

Never fool with a desperate man, Barney, the captain said to himself. He was responding to that same tiny inner voice, the one he had struggled to contain until the right moment presented itself, the one that urged him to order retaliation now no matter how long his odds were. Everyone on the bridge would probably die, but there were more than three hundred others who might . . . *No, don't even think of it, not yet, because the men around you don't deserve to die. Give them a chance to live long enough to be able to fight back. That's what Becca would tell you if she was here now.*

Barney Gold could feel the gun quivering in the back of his neck. Was he exercising proper judgment? That inner voice wasn't about to give up. Would other COs approach the problem in this manner? He wouldn't be surrendering in the face of the enemy—no, that wasn't it. He would be trying to use all his powers to save the men who depended on him . . . and *Gettysburg* . . . and Aegis. It was certainly worth the gamble to get rid of these three! He had to try. His men deserved his best effort.

But his answer was, "No." His tone was quiet and firm.

He was incapable of appeasing them further in the hopes of an opening.

Hansen's response was no different than before—an easing of pressure followed by the sharp crunch of the gun's muzzle into Gold's neck. The captain's chin fell to his chest.

"Mr. Norman, you will use the ship's PA to call away a party to receive that boat on the starboard side," Hansen ordered as he responded affirmatively to the Vietnamese request.

Norman had been a silent, frightened observer since Hansen established contact with Cam Ranh Bay. Filipo was content to lounge against the forward bulkhead, his pleasure with the power of a gun evident as he continued to sweep it from man to man. If trouble started, he would enjoy shooting again. But Andrew Norman had been glued to a spot between the ship's control console and the OOD's station since they'd altered course. He'd managed to avoid the blood now drying on the deck, but he was unable to make himself invisible. Each time he attempted to settle into the background, Hansen had warned him back to where he now stood—helpless, yet in a position to assist Hansen if the need arose. What it really involved, he realized, was his remaining in the line of fire, and that was how Hansen planned to control him. So far, it was working. He moved slowly to the PA and called away a party to assist the approaching patrol boat.

Then, Norman, following Hansen's orders, used the PA to explain to the crew what had become obvious in the last twenty minutes—the security drill had been interrupted. Since *Gettysburg* was so close to Vietnamese territorial waters, the captain had graciously acceded to that country's wishes to allow some personnel aboard from the approaching patrol boat. Captain Gold intended to release some dissident crew members responsible for the unfortunate acts on the bridge. All crew members were asked in a spirit of international cooperation to comply with the captain's orders.

Hansen had proved correct. The crew accepted an officer's explanation.

Norman gave the order to stop engines, as he was told, when the Vietnamese boat came alongside. As soon as the quarterdeck reported that a single Vietnamese officer and three armed men were aboard, Hansen ordered them back to speed. He intended to get as close to Cam Ranh Bay as possible while it was still light.

The silhouette of a small, uniformed Vietnamese followed by his three men appeared in the door to the starboard wing soon after the Vietnamese boat accelerated and swung out to starboard. He wore white shorts and a white shirt with gold insignia on the shoulders. A hat with gold braid on the bill seemed to engulf his head making him appear even smaller than he really was. A holstered gun on a belt around his tiny waist appeared too large for him. His eyes moved about the pilot house before settling on Barney Gold, who still appeared unconscious.

Then they fell on Hansen. "So you are the one who has caused so much concern to my compatriots ashore." Taking in the sailor's uniform, he concluded with amusement, "You don't look like a pirate." He stepped into the pilot house, his gaze taking in each individual before returning to Hansen. "If you desire your freedom in Cam Ranh Bay as you have claimed on the radio, you will continue to hold that gun to Captain Gold's head. Agreed?" He turned slightly and nodded to his three men. Their AK-74 automatic rifles dropped in unison from their shoulders to cover the inside of the pilot house.

Hansen looked from the little man to Andrew Norman then back to the Vietnamese again. "Who are you? Do you represent the Russians?" His voice was higher, more strained than before. The cockiness was entirely missing. This was a factor he was entirely unprepared to handle.

"Captain Trang, Vietnamese Navy." Again he inclined

his body forward slightly. "The Vietnamese and the Soviet Union are allies but no, I do not represent anyone but my own country. This is entirely my own decision, or I should say that of my government, to be here at this moment. However, we have heard every word transmitted."

"Why did you come out, Captain Trang?"

"Because it seems the commander in charge in Cam Ranh Bay honestly does not know who you really are. The Soviet Union is an immense country and I have learned over the years that one government unit there often doesn't know what the other is doing. Our intelligence chief assumes that the Soviet objective is your Aegis system, which certainly makes sense from their perspective, but apparently the method of obtaining that information has run into some serious problems. I think they have been frightened. My government has concluded that some of the responsibility for your predicament can be shifted to our shoulders until our Soviet allies sort out their problems." Trang studied Gold for a moment. "Captains are dangerous." He glanced across at Marston. "Who is that?"

"Executive officer," Norman mumbled.

"They're dangerous also." He looked now at Hansen before pointing to Norman. "That officer, is he with you?"

"So far," Hansen replied warily. He had no idea what to expect now.

Trang snapped orders at his men, two of whom shouldered their weapons and roughly lifted Gold's limp body from the chair. "You," he then indicated to Norman, "will show them to the captain's cabin. They will restrain him there. The same will also be done with the executive officer. One of them will remain there as a guard and he will execute them if anyone other than myself attempts to enter the room."

The men in the pilot house watched helplessly as Trang's orders were carried out. The Vietnamese officer remained quiet until a frightened Norman had returned. His eyes next returned to Hansen, whose confusion indicated that he probably understood he was no longer in control of *Gettysburg*. "Do you have any other compatriots in this adventure?"

"Just him." He jerked his head toward Filipo. "He likes to use that gun. And the officer, that scared one there."

"It would appear," Trang commented, "that you have control of the situation here. I think I shall use him again," he said, pointing at Norman.

"You can do anything you want with him. He's useless," Hansen laughed.

"You will show my men where your ship's small arms locker is," Trang said to Norman. Then he spoke to the two remaining men in his own language. "They have orders to shoot anyone who gets in their way. And they also have orders to shoot you if they don't like the way you're responding. Understood?"

Norman's lower lip quivered as he nodded silently.

Trang dismissed them with a wave of his hand and turned toward the quartermaster. "You will be kind enough to use the ship's public address system to assemble all officers forward on the main deck."

The quartermaster's eyes grew larger as he comprehended the situation he was in.

"Do it," Trang ordered sharply.

Still there was hesitation, a man caught between fear and the desire to retaliate.

Trang nodded at Filipo.

The two shots that followed simultaneously hurled the quartermaster's body across his chart table.

"You," Trang said, pointing to the helmsman. "You do it. Let go of the wheel for a moment. Nothing will happen."

Trang moved to the front of the pilot house and peered down on the main deck where a number of officers were milling about near the gun mount peering up toward the bridge. He turned to Hansen and extended his hand for the mike, speaking quickly into it in Vietnamese. Then he said, "My boats will be alongside immediately. I think a combination of automatic weapons and the announcement that they, along with their captain and executive officer and anyone else who shows his face, will be shot should keep them under control." He moved to the windows at the front of the pilot house.

"If you served here in the final war, perhaps you will find Vietnam more attractive now." He turned with a slight smile to survey the people in the pilot house. "See for yourself." He extended his hand toward the bow where a thin, green strip of land on the horizon appeared magnified by a setting sun. "I hope your visit will be a pleasant one and that you and your ship will be able to depart after a short stay."

It was dark when *Gettysburg*, escorted by a small fleet of Vietnamese military craft, docked in Cam Ranh Bay. Captain Trang ordered the crew restricted to their compartments. Only critical personnel were allowed the run of the ship to keep her systems functioning properly under the eye of well armed guards. The officers were sent ashore. Trang had no intention of allowing anyone to assume leadership aboard.

However, *Gettysburg*'s Chief Master at Arms, Ben Gannett, insisted vehemently that Captain Gold, still too weak to walk on his own, be carried on a stretcher.

Gold protested vaguely. He was resting on the deck, his back propped against the bulkhead where he had been left by Trang's men.

"Please, sir." Gannett was holding the simple canvas stretcher under his arm. He dropped to one knee before Gold. "Please, Captain. We'd all feel bad if you didn't let us make sure you went ashore comfortably."

There was a message in the chief's eyes. "Okay." Gold nodded weakly.

As Gannett crouched beside the captain and opened the stretcher, he whispered, "We just had a short meeting in chief's quarters, sir, to set up a resistance. They can't run this ship without us. We'll make it tough for them."

Gold winced with pain as Gannett gently helped him onto

the stretcher. "That's what I needed to know, Chief." As he was carried across the quarterdeck, Barney Gold's voice was clear as it carried to those few crewmen still on deck, "Chief Gannett has assumed command."

CHAPTER 4

The Naval Special Warfare (NSW) Command is as incon-
spicuous as the people who work within it. It is housed in a
low, neat wooden building on the Naval Amphibious Base
in Coronado, California. To the casual observer, the building and its surroundings might appear to have been left over
from a World War Two movie set, so much so that vintage
stars, acting out their roles from a bygone era, would seem
to be in their element.

There are certain exceptions, however, to those bonds
with the past—a chain link fence surrounding the grounds
and topped with barbed wire, security devices implanted
throughout the well kept grounds that are capable of
detecting an earthworm, invisible light beams capable of
being broken by a hummingbird, and smartly uniformed
guards ready to kill instantly without a sound. Only those
specifically invited venture into the NSW Command.

Two hours after actually viewing *Gettysburg* alongside a
pier in Cam Ranh Bay, a small group of naval officers
surrounded Rear Admiral Roland Lyford, commander of
NSW, in his spacious office on the first floor of the neat,
white building in Coronado. With the exception of Lyford,
they were outraged; he had seen or heard or taken part in a
sufficient number of outrages that he wasn't visibly excited,

or likely to become so in the foreseeable future. A few others who appeared only mildly concerned were Navy SEALs, like Lyford. Many of them had what they considered the distinct honor of participating in those outrageous affairs with their admiral. They had become a close-knit group.

The admiral's appearance was anything but that of a professional warrior. His medium height was comfortably balanced on a bulky frame that managed to wrinkle his uniforms within hours. His face was pleasant and he smiled often through a perpetual five o'clock shadow. The single feature that caught people by surprise was a blind eye, one that was slightly off angle from the other, and there were few who were privileged to know which was actually the good eye. Lyford enjoyed watching how often it kept people on edge. If there was a hint of his background, it was his habit of continuing to smile when he was angry.

The admiral made an effort to place the situation in perspective. "Now, gentlemen, you've got to stop thinking that this is the first act of piracy since the Barbary Coast days. It occurs all over the world, sometimes on a daily basis. It happens mostly to helpless people you never heard of in places you've never been and for reasons you would consider utterly ridiculous. It usually involves junks, sampans, dhows, coastal freighters, sometimes even a yacht. The reason you're not aware is because witnesses are usually lacking—dead men tell no tales, nor do they report acts of piracy." Lyford's little speech was given calmly, in the soft voice of an English professor lecturing students who really didn't want to hear what he had to say. But it also had the proper effect: He had their attention.

"This is still different. . . ."

"It's only different to us because some nasty little sons of bitches have been lucky enough to pull off a coup. When they got out of bed this morning, not a one of them had decided they were going to steal an Aegis cruiser. They fell through the outhouse floor and came up with the proverbial ham sandwich—they got *Gettysburg*. If you'll remember, that was a Vietnamese flag that got run up her mast this morning, not Russian."

"But the Vietnamese haven't got the vaguest idea what to do with the Aegis system," a captain said.

"No," another answered, "but just like I've been saying all along, the Russians sure as hell do."

"You bet your ass they do," Lyford agreed. His black, curly hair was thinning but a stranger never would have believed he was approaching fifty. SEALs got older, they lost their hair, they developed wrinkles on their foreheads and worry lines around their eyes like everyone else—but their bodies never gave in to age. They ate properly, dieted whenever a bit of flab appeared around the midsection, often ran ten miles at lunchtime to avoid the temptation of calories, swam for distance a few times a week, and none of them drank like their predecessors. They cared much more about their peers' opinions than what an *outsider* thought. While SEALs came in all sizes, to a man they were in superb physical condition and they looked superb in uniform, contrary to the way Lyford did this day. But when he spoke, even though his voice was soft, he was a commanding presence.

"We're not here to figure why or how or even who. I've got a directive from the White House and it says to keep Aegis from falling into Soviet hands at any cost, and that's exactly what they mean. That's what we're going to arrange before we leave this room." Lyford sat ramrod straight in his chair behind the large desk and managed to look totally at ease as he spoke.

A very junior admiral with gold wings above his left hand pocket said with a half smile, not quite sure himself that he was serious, "We could nuke it. I guarantee that would solve the whole problem . . . Aegis, Cam Ranh Bay, Russians, pirates, the whole lot with one aircraft."

"That is our final option, if we can't get her back," said *Pacfleet*'s Chief of Staff. "It's already been approved by

Washington. We simply say that there were nuclear weapons on board and they messed with them when they shouldn't. BOOM!"

"We'll get her back," Lyford stated quietly. Then he nodded at an officer across the room who had been lounging calmly in a comfortable chair while the others expressed their righteous indignation. "Captain Auger there, from Naval Intelligence, has a knack for turning possibilities into decisions." He indicated a short, neat, trim officer—the opposite of himself—with alert blue eyes gazing beyond a de Gaulle–style nose.

Although Auger's quiet exterior might have given the impression that he was a man of the cloth, he was a superb intelligence specialist. The limited number of ribbons on his chest told the story. There were very few of them because he had spent most of his time in Washington with only brief forays to other intelligence stations around the world. The navy preferred to keep specialists like Auger out of the limelight.

"We have to assume, gentlemen," he began in a husky voice, "that the individual or individuals placed on board *Gettysburg* by the Russians likely completed their part of the job before the Vietnamese took over. That's because the ship was already on a course for Cam Ranh Bay before the locals were alerted. Completion means that there are likely films of Aegis schematics already in someone's hands. I'm not sure how we get those back."

"I take it that's a foregone conclusion?" a voice inquired.

"Not absolute, but highly probable," Auger responded. There was no inflection in his voice. He lived in a world of black and white. "The Soviets are nervous as hell, though. The fact that they are disclaiming any knowledge of the affair means that it was really an undercover job, even within their hierarchy. There are often any number of these little forays underway that are a secret to everyone else. We don't know who was behind it, and the fact that their top dogs in Cam Ranh Bay couldn't find out who was directing

it means whatever film is available is probably still there—
at least for the time being. That's supposition," he concluded with no expression. "The people who want it are
going to be on the pipe to the Kremlin super fast screaming
for their property. How long that takes is anyone's guess.
As far as time is concerned, we've already run out. It's all
borrowed from this moment on."

Pacfleet's Chief of Staff snorted, "With *Teddy Roosevelt*
charging around the vicinity, I think that would make them
pay attention. If they aren't scared to death with her just off
their coast, then they're a lot dumber than I figured." He
was one of those people who particularly frightened Lyford
because he had no respect for whoever the enemy might be.

"They're not scared at all," Auger answered drily. "They
survived the best we had to offer them twenty years ago.
Your birdfarms are a pain in the ass to them, but they're not
afraid. They have half a dozen missiles for every aircraft on
that ship. But," and it was the first time he'd shown any
emotion, "*they know we're pissed*. That means nothing
happens ashore until they receive a directive from Moscow.
And that means someone has to justify enraging us as much
as Washington has already indicated. Remember, the Russians didn't swipe *Gettysburg*. The Vietnamese did it.
They're just sort of presenting her to their buddies as a gift,
and the Soviets aren't so sure they want to even acknowledge it."

Auger's eyes swung about the room as if to ensure that
everyone was listening. "I've explained to Admiral Lyford
that we appear to have a bit of time—as much as forty-eight
hours if we're lucky—because Washington is pulling out
every stop to make Moscow realize we are royally pissed."
He seemed to enjoy employing his mild curses. "We *will*
turn Cam Ranh Bay into glass if we're forced to, and State
is trying to get that idea across. But first we think the
admiral's men ought to have a shot at getting her back. We
have to show our allies that we made a maximum effort
before a decision like that. I can run statistics through the

computer until I'm blue in the face to determine what their odds are, but there are certain elements in SEAL operations that can't be included in any analysis. If we have nothing in forty-eight hours, then—*boom*!"

"Do you have anyone you can get in there that quickly?" the Chief of Staff asked curiously.

"He and a few of his men were ferried out to *Roosevelt* even before we had satellite confirmation. They should be transferring to a submarine shortly." Lyford glanced at his watch as he spoke. "Unfortunately, we didn't have any boats out there equipped for SEALs, but Chance and his boys can handle themselves anywhere. . . ."

"Who was that again?" one of the surface admirals asked. "I didn't get the name." He'd gotten the name the first time. There had been no doubt in his mind who should do it. He just needed reassurance.

"Chance. David Chance."

"Wasn't he the one in El Salvador who . . ."

"That's the one. He was in Japan for a little R&R, then this popped up. I'll be honest. It's almost like it was planned from the start. He has contacts up the shoot over there. About twenty years ago, he did three tours, every place from the Parrot's Beak to the Rung Sat Special Zone to some of those nasty little ops in the Ca Mau. He worked with the Provincial Reconnaissance Units twice." Lyford remembered how much he, himself, had enjoyed operating with David Chance and the PRUs during the Phoenix Program. He thought of mentioning their relationship but, considering some of the new young faces who had never been involved in something like this before, thought better of it. There was no reason to mention Phoenix—it was too difficult to explain to the uninitiated. "Chance liked working with the Vietnamese and he made a lot of friends over there, enough so that he's been back a couple of times since then."

"How can you be sure these friends of his are still

friendly toward us, Admiral? There's been a lot of changes since we pulled out, and now the Russians . . ."

"Men were willing to die to work with Chance," Lyford responded softly. "Too many of them did. The survivors owe him more than you can imagine, and there are still good people there who never will forget. That's why he was willing to go back. They even got word out to us once that we might be able to find some of our POWs, even arranged to provide some guides each time. But there was no joy."

"Admiral, how can we be sure this Chance will hook up with one of his old buddies so soon? If my history serves me right, the SEALs spent most of their time way down south, at least that's the way the books have been written. If we've got forty-eight hours, hell, he could spend weeks before he found . . ."

"Your history is about as accurate as the SEALs want it to be. They were everywhere—north, south . . . Saigon . . . Hanoi . . . try Laos or Cambodia." His normally soft voice took on a distinctly sharp tone. "Our base of operations has always been anywhere in the world and almost nobody ever knows SEALs were there afterwards. But rather than bullshit you, I'll say outright that Chance already knows who he intends to get to. North of the airfield at Cam Ranh, the peninsula narrows down to no more than two or three thousand yards. The harbor's also easy to get across and there's a town called Suoi Hoa on the other side that's sort of a bedroom for the port at Cam Ranh. Comparing it to San Diego Harbor and Coronado will give you an idea. His man was moved there by the government some years ago. There's a story there but I've never been let in on it. He trained as a SEAL and operated with Chance until they were just like brothers. Chance was the one who got him a new identity when his family died. That's as much as I know."

The Chief of Staff glanced over with raised eyebrows. "But you trust this local?"

"I trust David Chance." Admiral Lyford picked up a folder on his desk to show that he had nothing more to say. "That's all. Here are the instructions Chance gave me. I've made copies for each person with a need to know."

The young aviator-admiral looked at the notes quizzically. "You say you've talked with this Chance?"

"Scrambler—just before he flew out to *Roosevelt*. It was secure, believe me." He was still smiling. "It didn't last long with those sunspots—but long enough that he knows how Washington feels."

"It's not that, sir," the aviator answered. "I was . . . I was just interested in a commander telling you what he wanted. I'm not questioning this guy, Chance, of course. You must admit it's rather unique. . . ."

Admiral Lyford grinned. "I've taken a lot of orders from Chance in my career. I've always been glad I did."

CHAPTER 5

David Chance was as ready to lock out as he was ever going to be; it couldn't come soon enough. Submarines—he hated them! A man couldn't control his own destiny in one of those elongated coffins. It was a united effort in those things—one for all, all for one, everybody survived or everybody died—and it was not the method he would choose for his own demise. When his turn came, it would be man-to-man—*and let the better man win*!

The men on this submarine were no different than on any of the others. They were in awe of the SEALs, or maybe they just thanked their lucky stars they could stay with the boat rather than go ashore. If a submariner was in the position he was now, it would be for only one reason—his boat was beyond hope. The only purpose for a sailor to ever think of locking out would be that one final attempt to survive a dead submarine.

Chance smiled inwardly. Wouldn't it be convenient if every man could eventually choose his own poison? But life wasn't like that. Some men went down to the sea in ships while others, like David Chance, crept out of the sea like the first creature that stole clandestinely ashore.

It would have been so much simpler if there had been one of those new SEAL-equipped submarines available. They could have locked out together with all their gear and allowed the submarine to escape quickly back to its own element. It was unfortunate that so many of man's creations were designed for only one purpose.

The boat's captain had been pleasant to them considering how little time—just hours—he'd had to prepare. It was tough to yank a submarine away from its designated mission and send it close to hostile shores, but this captain was as cooperative as could be. Perhaps it was also that he was thanking the powers-that-be that someone else was going ashore at Cam Ranh Bay. The men had been actually apologetic when he'd shaken their hands in the control room. Maybe he'd seen one too many movies where the CO wished his passengers well before their departure because he knew he'd never see them again—at least not alive. Or perhaps he was one of those super-organized types who needed to know everything about an operation before it started. In this case, an American destroyer's sonar had brought him to the surface and there'd hardly been any information to provide. Between the sunspots ruining communications and the time element, there was none.

Locking out of an unconverted submarine was the method they had learned before a few of the retired missile submarines were modified for SEALs. It was slower, more dangerous, but the same purpose was served in the end.

A SEAL officer Chance knew only by name had been sent out to act as liaison in the control room. Someone, probably Rolly Lyford if Chance had only one guess, had pulled Hank Taron out of a covert mission with a team of Korean SEALs and flown him out to the carrier in time to be the trunk operator. Taron, one of the early SEALs, had probably escaped from as many submarines as bars in his career; but he was an automatic choice for a mission like this one. Hank handled the valves and vents to control rates of flood and air pressure. If someone couldn't clear their ears, their safety—more often their lives—was in Hank Taron's hands, the best hands in the world! And anything could happen with the submarine itself—a change in speed or depth variation since they had to keep way on to hold trim—so that the liaison officer in control was as vital as the trunk operator. But the escape trunk was still better than their final option, locking out of a torpedo tube with no light, valves, or communication.

They would lock out in pairs—*the buddy system*—flood the lock, empty the lock, next pair, flood the lock, empty the lock, good-bye submarine! On your own! But it was also better than jumping out of a plane, high altitude or low. Chance hated *halo* jumping. It wasn't the danger involved before the mission began, so much as the possibility of radar picking up their aircraft, which could ruin your whole day. All things considered, he still preferred swimming ashore.

There was the signal! Chance rechecked his equipment. Weapons sealed tightly, breathing apparatus set, he pulled the mask over his face. Taron worked the valves equalizing inside air pressure with outside sea water pressure. They listened to the procedures called out by Taron and repeated back by the liaison officer in control. The water bubbled around their ankles and began to rise. Pressure increased. Chance saw the smile broaden on Gates's face and he knew it reflected his own. Then Chance smiled inwardly. He was returning to *his* element. It was time. He nodded at Gates. *They were a team again!* Merry and York would feel the same way. Somehow, when the water caressed your body and that brief shudder of power clutched the heart, a SEAL was whole once again.

Lock out!

Merry and York worked their way forward against the motion of the submarine on the line strung by Chance. The first two had already opened the compartment on the submarine's deck which housed the Swimmer Propulsion Units (SPU) but they were forced to wait for the others. There had been no place along the hull to secure their equipment so all four were needed for the last phase; submarines were designed to slice silently through the water like a snake rather than provide conveniences for uninvited SEALs. They all held on awkwardly to the watertight bags while preparing the SPUs.

The captain had taken a final look through the night periscope and reported all clear before the last two had locked out. Merry passed on the message by hand signals to Chance when they made their rendezvous at twenty feet. Time was precious but that clearance and a final compass check were standard before moving out. The submarine wouldn't turn away and head back out to deep water until they were well clear.

The SPUs transformed them into human submarines, propelling them silently through the black water toward a hostile shore. It was quite possible to become disoriented in this inky environment and even Chance, a veteran of more night approaches than most men could imagine, checked his course periodically. He planned to come ashore well north of the Cam Ranh Bay airfield, beyond the end of the paved road that tailed off into beach scrub.

The first indication they were closing the beach was the current effect from the slight undertow. Chance slowly began to rise to the surface. The others followed, staying slightly lower and spreading out parallel to the beach. If by some freak possibility an individual ashore was shining a spotlight in their direction, only one might possibly be seen. It was literally impossible to see a man in the water at that range in the dead of night but SEALs survived by betting on the impossible.

Chance's head broke the surface first. His movement was slow. There was barely a ripple. He could just as easily be a chunk of driftwood floating in the dark water. Even at that range, the horizon was barely discernible. The merger of black sky and sea was broken only by wave foam that was no clearer than the clusters of stars that pierced the humid night air. He heard the soft rumble of waves breaking before he could see the milky white outline. There were no lights, no sign of any human presence out there, but he waited.

That was another method of survival. Never proceed on
your first impression. Give the other guy a chance to make
the first move—it was preferable that he became the dead
one.

Nothing. No movement. Not a fisherman, not even the
nocturnal bark of a stray dog to give them away. While his
eyes adjusted to staring into the distance, a barely perceived
look of misty light appeared to his left—the airfield at Cam
Ranh Bay. If there was electricity in Suoi Hoa, there was no
evidence it was in use at this hour.

Everything would be quiet there now. Nguyen van Dinh
would make sure of that. There was a generator in Suoi
Hoa—that was how Chance had been able to make contact
earlier from *Roosevelt*. Dinh guarded that circuit religiously
one hour every other evening, taking messages for the tiny
underground that struggled to flourish in Vietnam, and
hoping that some day the Americans might come back.
Hatred inspired him, hatred of the communists, even more
hatred for the Russians who had slaughtered Dinh's family
and now lorded over the huge port of Cam Ranh Bay.

Chance was anxious to see Dinh again. If there was an
even better name for the concept of loyalty, it was *Nguyen
van Dinh*. When the government told Dinh that he would
have to move north to the Cam Ranh Bay facility from his
village outside Ho Chi Minh City, which he continued to
call Saigon, Dinh was crushed. That is, he was crushed
until Chance returned that first time. As they struggled
through the jungle trails searching for that mysterious POW
camp, he explained how critical Dinh's presence might be
some day in Cam Ranh Bay since the Russians were turning
the facility into their first warm water port in the Pacific.
And the truth of those words had now been substantiated.

Satisfied now that there was no threat, Chance gave the
signal and the four men began the last leg of their swim
toward the shoreline. The beach was flat and they struggled
the last fifty yards through a crisscross undertow that would
have given them away if there had been anyone watching.

Wind-whipped sand had created small dunes crested with thin grass and scrub bushes. Chance picked out the largest and marked off thirty paces parallel to but well up from the waterline. That was where they buried their SPUs and breathing gear in a waterproof plastic cover. Gates and Merry wrestled a beached log over the cache, then swept away all traces of their presence.

They crossed the narrow spit and slipped into the warm water of the upper bay pulling the watertight bags of weapons and explosives behind them. It was a casual swim since they had actually moved into the water ten minutes ahead of schedule. But if Dinh was his old self, the signal would come at the precise moment they'd agreed upon. Chance had no desire to surprise any villagers who would more than likely turn them in the next morning.

They floated, they swam in circles, they studied individual sectors of the dark land ahead of them until York saw the red lamp—two long, one short, two long. It was a little to the south of where Chance had anticipated.

They waited five minutes. Then the next signal came— two short, one long, two short. After the first signal, Dinh had sent two others around to check their surroundings. It was a lesson that Chance had taught him long ago and was one of the reasons he was there this evening. If there was a war and real bullets were in vogue, one never responded to the first signal. Someone just as smart might be waiting. Take the time for that secondary search. Any cautious SEAL would explain that at least half of security was common sense. That's why the casualty rate for the experienced men was so low. Dinh had learned that lesson working with David Chance twenty years before, and he had found it saved his life more than once. The two survivors had made one hell of a team!

Nguyen van Dinh, blending in with the background in black pajamas, met them at the water's edge, a muting finger against his lips. He made a single movement with his hand and the four men followed him through a wooded area to a small clearing. Dinh again indicated they should remain silent as he disappeared into the darkness.

He returned in two minutes and whispered his first words in clear English, "There's no one nearby to bother us now. You may remove the rest of your equipment and stow it here with your weapons." Dinh bent down to lift what appeared in the shadows to be a patch of buffalo grass. There was a neat storage space underneath that would have accommodated enough for ten of them. "Don't worry about dampness. It's lined," he whispered. Then he added expressly for Chance, "We will greet each other properly as soon as we arrive at my secure hut."

Dinh waited patiently for them before leading off on a trail so black it seemed to fold in on top of them. For fifteen minutes they followed each other through the darkness, more by sense than sight, before they entered another clearing with a low structure set off to one side. Dinh maintained another hut in the village of Suoi Hoa, the one that was his permanent home. Only a few trusted friends were aware of this one.

Dinh lit a lantern as soon as York pulled a cloth cover tightly around the entrance. Then he extended his hand to Chance. "So . . . David . . . I am pleased to see you again." A white, even smile set off by a gold front tooth seemed to cover his entire face. His black eyes literally danced with happiness. Dinh was small like most Vietnamese, no more than five foot three, and there wasn't an extra ounce of fat on his body. But he was muscular, so much so that he could become embarrassed when he appeared without a shirt around many of his contemporaries who appeared undernourished in comparison. Thick black hair hung just above his eyebrows and his face was smooth enough and unwrinkled that his age would be impossible to guess.

"So . . . Dinh . . . my friend . . ." Chance squeezed the other's hand then stepped forward and bear hugged him, lifting him off the ground. He swung Dinh around in a complete circle as if they were engaged in an impromptu dance. He set the smaller man down and holding him at arm's length said, "So, Dinh, what makes you think you can greet a brother with a simple handshake? It's been three years and you act like you were meeting a village chief."

The little man stepped forward, his face suddenly serious. "Thank you for saying that, David." Then he put his arms around Chance's shoulders, barely able to lock his own hands around the much bigger man, and squeezed. "Thank you . . . my brother." Gates and Merry and York each saw the tears in Dinh's eyes reflected in the lantern's flame. But they were a display of comradeship. Nguyen van Dinh and David Chance had fought together. Those tears signified love and respect.

David Chance was average in height, no more than five foot nine inches, but his weight was well over two hundred pounds and age and gravity had turned his waist from a trim thirty to a mature thirty-four. He had a football player's neck, which flared even wider as it joined his broad shoulders. His barrel chest appeared overinflated. He had short, thick legs, the kind that others called tree trunks, and he could use them as lethal weapons. In his early forties, Chance was partially balding now, but his remaining black hair helped to emphasize the heavy eyebrows over wide set hazel eyes. He had very white teeth and smiled often, even when he wasn't happy because he'd once been told he was mysterious when he did that.

They were an odd couple—the small, wiry Vietnamese and the dark, stocky American—but they had learned to depend on each other. They'd fought a war together and were as close as brothers could become. Dinh claimed to anyone who would listen that Chance understood Vietnam's war better than the people themselves. But most important of all, they understood each other.

"Well, David, now I really have a chance to help you,"

Dinh sighed and then smiled, his gold tooth winking in the lantern light like a firefly. "Finally."

"You've helped me before, Dinh, more than you can imagine. It was only three years ago when you helped me search for that camp."

"But we never found anything then, none of your comrades. Now, there really is something I can offer you. I can help return your ship. I saw her today and she really is beautiful . . . so big . . ." He extended his arms to show his fascination with *Gettysburg*.

"Yes, she's a beautiful ship, Dinh. But that's not what they really want. No one can see what they're really after. Only the scientists understand that. There's a powerful system of radars and computers inside that ship named Aegis. *Gettysburg* can keep track of all the targets approaching an entire battle group—submarines, surface ships, airplanes, even the missiles they fire. She can either attack them herself or assign other ships to do the job and she'll keep track of each target until it's been destroyed. What that really means is that we can launch our attack aircraft before anyone can get through to stop them. The Russians have to know how Aegis works in order to defend against it."

Dinh understood. "I think I see—a secret weapon."

"That's as good a way to look at it as any. For them, understanding Aegis means everything in their strategic plans. If they compromise that system, we lose much of our ability to defend our carriers against attack. I think they've got a lot of the technical data they intended to get, but they didn't want the ship and they don't quite know what to do now that the Vietnamese have delivered the ship. The Russians don't like to get caught like this. Washington has threatened everything you can imagine to make them think twice. We're lucky if we have thirty hours left, Dinh."

"I don't think we could even get close to your ship in that time." The little man appeared thoughtful for a moment before commenting, "Vietnamese sailors are still aboard the ship. They stole it—they still consider it theirs. And it doesn't appear the Russians want to take charge of it. But the ship is surrounded by their marines, David. It would be a slaughter to try to capture her now."

"Then we won't try that. We'll do it their way. We'll surround them." He winked at Dinh as if they had a private joke no one would ever know. "Remember how we did it in the Parrot's Beak? How we grabbed back all the prisoners at Song Be? We went right into the lion's den. . . ."

Earlier that same day, the Kremlin was not a pleasant place to be invited. It was exactly as David Chance had anticipated—Russia did not appreciate being caught with her pants around her ankles. It was embarrassing. It attracted attention. It made every individual from the General Secretary on down appear foolish. In a word, whatever the end purpose had been, the means were *stupid*. Someone was going to pay.

The Soviet leader had been awakened from a sound sleep to learn of the event. His initial reaction—that the situation was so bizarre, that such stupidity was impossible—was quickly refuted by a general in Cam Ranh Bay who was so enraged that he literally screamed over the phone at the most powerful individual in the Soviet Union.

The situation was critical enough to call an emergency meeting of the Defense Council, the highest decision-making body for all aspects of national security. Chaired by the General Secretary, the Council included the Minister of Defense, the Chief of the General Staff, the chairman of the KGB, the chairman of the Council of Ministers, the chairman of GOSPLAN, and other critical party figures. There was no doubt in the Soviet leader's mind that *Gettysburg* could present a challenge to the survival of the state if the situation deteriorated further. He would require the advice of these men. The balance of his military leaders were not included because he was sure one of them had authorized this travesty.

The General Secretary began with the head of the KGB. "Are you prepared to state unequivocally that your organization had nothing to do with this?" That had been KGB's first reaction when the Minister of Defense had called him.

The KGB leader set his jaw. "I have yet to talk with anyone in my organization who is aware of anything involving this ship *Gettysburg*." He stared down at his hands for he knew firm denial would mean his life if some fool underling had authorized it. "I can't say that there may not be someone involved in it. . . ."

"If you were sitting in the White House," the General Secretary asked, turning to the Minister of Defense, "what would your options be at this stage?"

"I would demand the immediate release of the ship."

"I've already talked with their Secretary of State. He demanded."

". . . and then, knowing that such things do take time, I would give us a time limit . . ."

"Less than forty-eight hours now."

". . . and if the ship were not at sea at the end of that time . . ." he spread his hands helplessly, ". . . I guess I'd do something pretty drastic."

The General Secretary nodded. "I would have insisted on twenty-four hours myself. What would you consider drastic?" he persisted. "How bad? Would you start a war over it?"

The minister avoided the question. "Frankly, I don't think they'd lose any other country's support whatever they did. The fault—the initial fault anyway—appears to lie with us, without a doubt."

"Do we possess the key data to this Aegis system now that the ship is being offered to us?"

The Defense Minister spread his hands in frustration. "I don't know." He glanced over to the KGB man. "You know more about that than I do."

KGB was equally upset. "This General Brusilov, the one who commands at Cam Ranh, he's not sure. He's so angry he's almost impossible to speak to rationally. He says there are three American sailors, an officer and two technicians, who claim they have everything needed. The officer is an American who speaks no Russian and is terrified. He doesn't understand anything about this Aegis. One of the technicians, the one who says he has everything we could ever dream about, claims he is Soviet military. He also says he's assigned to the KGB and was planted in the United States for this mission. The officer says he heard the word Spetznaz, but they insist they know nothing about him. Nor do I know anything about him yet," he added quickly. "Brusilov claims he's the one who contributed to this mess but remains so arrogant he thinks he deserves a medal. Brusilov would like to send him to the firing squad. The third says nothing. He's also a killer . . . brutal . . . apparently enjoys it . . . even scares the other two. None of them trusts the other. It's going to take some time to see what is real and what is imaginary."

"The Americans have no intention of giving you the luxury of time, and I don't blame them." The General Secretary was barely controlling his anger. His gaze took in each man at the table as he spoke without expression in his voice. "Before this day ends, I want to know what we actually have on Aegis, what we must do with that ship, and recommendations for salvaging some respect after this is over." His last words were for the Minister of Defense. "I don't think you have any other choice than to set Condition One. We must be prepared to defend ourselves. The President is the type of man who would follow through on his words without another warning." He stroked his chin thoughtfully. "It's going to be most difficult—just about impossible—to attract sympathy to ourselves."

CHAPTER 6

For a moment both men, David Chance and Nguyen van Dinh, were incapable of preventing their minds from drifting back *twenty years earlier*. . . .

The Parrot's Beak was a savage little piece of Cambodia jutting rudely into the upper delta country of Vietnam to the west of Saigon. The Beak was a platform for the Viet Cong and the North Vietnamese Army (NVA) to launch their attacks on Saigon and the rich countryside surrounding the capital. It was a supply center funneling arms, food, fuel, and medical supplies to an army that appeared only when it wished to be seen, and fought only on its own terms. And most of all, it was a sanctuary that denied the Americans an opportunity to pursue the enemy back into their lair. Official Washington—the President, the Secretary of Defense, but definitely not the military—had created the sanctuary to counter criticism. As a result, Americans died every day because of this arrogant political stance.

The Parrot's Beak was where the VC spirited their most important prisoners for interrogation. That was why David Chance was ordered to select six others at the Nha Be base for insertion thirty miles from the prison camp. He chose two American and four Vietnamese SEALs, a choice combination of highly trained special forces. The Vietnamese operated under the Provincial Reconnaissance Units (PRU). Their missions often involved removing communist officials in the same manner as the VC emasculated the village leadership. It was all coordinated under a program called "Phoenix."

They'd heloed in the last fifty miles along the treetops. The other Hueys, the ones used to decoy the VC, were a little more obvious. Since most operations in Vietnam could not remain secure for more than a limited amount of time, even SEAL ops, they took every precaution. There were six other Hueys that darted into open spaces in the jungle near the Parrot's Beak as if they were on a mission. They were preceded by strike aircraft dumping five-hundred-pound-bombs and napalm to sanitize each area, and accompanied by others who flew shotgun at the insertion point as if US strategy depended on their attack. It was an impressive display.

But no one accompanied the single Huey that skittered over the treetops and dropped David Chance and six others in a tiny clearing that had been guaranteed clean by a SEAL recon team. The bird never touched the ground. Seven men, without a word spoken between them, leaped out with all the supplies they would need for three days and disappeared instantly into the jungle cover. The helo lifted back over the trees twenty seconds later.

They squatted in the dense undergrowth, invisible, silent, listening for the slightest indication that they might not be alone, that a stray patrol might have heard the sounds of their insertion. Only dead men underestimated the VC. Chance had moved instantly to a point twenty yards beyond. Two of the Vietnamese, the point man who would be in front of Chance and the radioman behind him, had immediately gone to either side of him without an order being given. It had all become automatic. They kept each other alive.

These men were unlike any others who operated in the dense jungle. They wore camouflaged uniforms with floppy jungle hats shading their painted faces. They thrived here. Chance and one of the Vietnamese carried M-16s with 203 grenade launchers attached under the barrels. The point man and rear security were armed with shotguns. Two of the Vietnamese carried Stoners, a light rapid-fire machine gun for close-in combat. The automatic weapons specialist, Bobby Campbell, hefted a powerful M-60 as if it was a toy. Ammunition belts crisscrossed their chests. Grenades dangled from their belts along with razor-sharp Gerber combat knives and garroting wire. Claymores took much of the space in their packs. Food was secondary baggage on such operations. They could forage when they had to. Water was more critical in the jungle heat. Their most valuable weapons, and their quietest—their hands—required no extra space. They were lethal.

There were no helmets, no flak jackets. Those were heavy and bulky. They inhibited movement. A SEAL's most reliable defense was his training. He moved stealthily, silently, patiently, able to crouch in one position, barely breathing, unmoving, waiting for danger to pass by. They rarely showed themselves. Firefights brought injuries, even death, both unacceptable. SEALs were survivors trained to eliminate their enemy by surprise, by cunning, by invisibility. Their missions were always successful because each man was a professional who stuck by the next. Their movement around an objective was orchestrated to take advantage of each individual's talents.

SEALs were feared by their enemy.

They remained in position for an hour, immovable, inanimate objects. Nothing changed. There was no indication of enemy activity. The jungle noises, the monkeys, the birds, insects, all continued uninterrupted after their arrival. At the end of that hour, Chance made a single hand signal and they moved out.

The point man, Nuan, was an experienced tracker with a keen sense of danger. He chose each step carefully, watching for the slightest trace of previous activity in their path.

He was responsible for avoiding booby traps—any possible change in the vegetation to cover a mine, a trip wire for claymores, a hole in the ground filled with bamboo stakes dipped in human excrement, a noose ready to sweep the unwary into knife-sharp stakes. The ways of dying were endless. The SEALs had seen them all. Like the animals in the jungle, they had learned how to survive under adversity. The point man's short-barreled shotgun was ready for first contact.

Chance, as patrol leader, was the second in line followed by Tranh, the radioman. Bob Campbell secured the middle with his fire power. Behind him came Vuong, the corpsman, Dinh acting as assistant leader, and Graham Nelson covering rear security. They had rehearsed their assignments and hand signals in the brief time they'd had before boarding the Huey—their familiarity with each other from other missions made up for the lack of preparation. They knew automatically what each of them would do when crossing roads or streams, circling up, setting ambush, even resting for the night. Knowing each other's walk, movement, habits, the special characteristics of the one ahead and behind would save their lives. If they were forced to reverse direction, the responsibilities would reverse accordingly but not their original order—Nelson at rear security would become point, Dinh the patrol leader. It was second nature.

Chance expected to cover the distance to the camp at Song Be by noon of the following day. That would give them enough hours of daylight to reconnoiter enemy defenses. The following day, they would hit the camp. Their extraction point was much closer. It would have been foolish to return to the original drop zone or even travel so far when they were already exhausted—someone could just as easily have picked up their trail and would be waiting. Only the careless were ambushed. Even more obvious was that no human being, not even a SEAL, could backtrack that same thirty miles with a pack of escaped prisoners and not expect that every able-bodied VC, including old men and small children, wouldn't be after them.

The jungle was alive as they moved. It also changed each hour. Early mornings in the dry season were cool and damp. And no man could stay asleep with the raucous sounds of the natural inhabitants awakening. The dew disappeared wherever the sun's rays struck, and the heat grew heavy in staggering increments. Jungle smells altered with the daily drying of the vegetation. Birds, bugs, animals, slithering creatures—all of them played, hunted, killed, ate, slept at different times. The noises they made varied with their activities. Everything about the jungle was alive, and a man became an integral part of it in order to survive until the next day's sunrise.

When the sun ducked below the horizon, the jungle suddenly became dark for the early evening light was unable to penetrate the dense overhead cover. Familiar sounds would fade to be replaced by those of the night creatures.

Chance gave the signal to circle up and settled down with his radioman. Nuan, on point, moved to twelve o'clock, rear security to six, while the other three settled in their positions. It was a time to rest, eat just a little, drink some water, but most of all to give each man time to familiarize himself with the darkness and the new sounds. Campbell and three of the Viet SEALs moved out to guard points. Chance and Dinh and Graham Nelson stretched out side by side against a large tree. They said nothing until Nuan came back in thirty minutes later to report the area secure.

Dinh was the first to speak in the hushed whisper Chance had taught him that included as many hand signals as words. He had been fighting for so long that there was little that bothered him, but this time Chance could detect a rare note of concern. "The Russians who were reported to be in Song Be—what do you think brings them there? They usually aren't involved this close to our land."

"Intelligence. Someone obviously thinks they have some

very valuable prisoners." Chance paused for a moment, considering how he should explain himself. "Perhaps they are important," he concluded. "Maybe that's why we're supposed to kill them if we can't get them out. That usually means something. . . ."

"I wasn't aware . . ." Dinh began. The prisoners weren't Americans. They were his people. It was even possible they were friends . . . perhaps family.

"Don't bother yourself about it. I was told to keep my mouth shut until we were in the jungle."

Chance got up and moved a few paces away. After relieving himself and covering the fresh hole he'd dug for the purpose, he stretched out a few paces away from Dinh and closed his eyes. There had been too many words already, enough for three days. "Get some sleep if you can. We'll start out again after our watch." That would be before the sun rose. Chance knew he wouldn't sleep. He never did this early into an operation. There was too much to think about. But he didn't want to lie to Dinh. Better not to say anything.

The prison camp was twenty miles beyond the Cambodian border. Two months before, the site had been pure jungle. Intelligence couldn't say for sure what had inspired this particular camp but the presence of Russian military personnel partially explained the reason—interrogation. The Soviets were willing to make two major contributions to their communist allies. Their military supplies had helped to modernize the rebel armies, but it was their ability to meld superb intelligence gathering with guerrilla tactics that really appealed to the VC leadership. They explained that it was sometimes better to bring in senior officers and political leaders for interrogation than to slaughter them.

There were other camps designed primarily for Soviet interrogation purposes, but the new one in the Parrot's Beak seemed destined to house the cream of South Vietnamese leadership—if it was allowed to exist. Air attacks had been considered but the Cambodians would have screamed bloody murder to the UN, and the left wing in the States would have taken up the cry. MACV in Saigon had decided the only sure method of taking out the camp was SEALs. The operation would be delicate and the planning occupied much of a series of senior staff meetings until the VC forced the issue—they kidnapped a number of district leaders and three senior military planners right from the ARVN general staff. That was when Chance's name came up.

There was no time for the careful planning that might increase their odds. Chance and his men were on their way before the prisoners even arrived at Song Be. And his orders were to either get those prisoners out or dispose of them. *Time*—it meant so much when there wasn't any to be had. Chance's preference in any operation of this nature was to develop a preliminary plan based on intelligence, then confirm his intuition once he could scout his target. This time it would all have to be done when they arrived.

Chance had picked Graham Nelson and Bobby Campbell (they had been his life insurance so often), then decided the four Vietnamese would be preferable to any more Americans. He told Dinh to pick his own people. They turned out to be exactly the ones he would have chosen, Nuan, Vuong, and Tranh. He'd worked with all of them before. They were as good as any SEALs he could have selected himself.

Song Be had been carved out of the jungle like an angry sore, a place designed eventually to be deserted. There was no sense of permanency.

Chance lay at the edge of the jungle studying the camp's layout. There were no roads leading to it, no rivers nearby, nothing more than a stream off to one side. His nose told him it had already become a sewer. It was obvious that supplies came by helicopter, at least for the Russians in the camp. There was no way they could subsist on the meager diet of their allies. And, Chance decided, these intelligence specialists probably weren't trained to disappear into the jungle like the Vietnamese if they were attacked.

Chance had assigned each of his men a different position around the camp. With no concrete plans, it was vital to understand from seven different perspectives how Song Be operated and they had less than twenty-four hours to do so. Where were the prisoners kept? How were they fed, exercised, and interrogated? What times did the guard change? How many protected the camp? Were there different shifts for prisoner guards and camp security? Did they have men on the perimeter only or did they also send squads into the surrounding jungle? Most important was an accurate head count. When seven people planned to move against an armed camp, every detail became magnified. One error and there would be seven more prisoners, or more likely a single mistake in knowing their enemy would produce seven corpses.

Everything they saw indicated that Song Be was temporary. Building construction was flimsy. It appeared that the Vietnamese ate and slept on platforms protected only by thatched roofs. The Russians preferred the security of walls, even if they were made of plywood. Their roofs were shiny tin which, Chance decided, was a poor tradeoff—status for life in an oven. The prisoners were kept on one side of the camp in a long, low building with no windows. They were herded singly or in twos to a nearby structure, another of those with a tin roof, where they must have been interrogated by the Soviets. Vietnamese acted as guards though none of them ever entered that particular building. The Russians were cautious like that—they'd never trusted any of their allies.

On the other hand, there were no guard houses. The NVA would never have been that casual, but the Russians must have assumed it would be almost impossible to approach Song Be, situated as it was in the midst of the Cambodian jungle—and they obviously had no intention of remaining longer than need be. After studying how the guards moved from the jungle's edge back to the buildings with no concern for the ground they covered, it became obvious no protective minefields had been established on the perimeter. Only a single five-man patrol had gone into the jungle each four-hour period and that was insignificant since they covered only a circular path around the camp. Such confidence minimized their security.

The SEALs remained just out of sight through two complete watches. If nothing else, the Russians had imposed a sense of order on the camp regardless of their disdain for danger in this remote jungle. Chance had observed how quickly and efficiently this systematic approach had been established in the past. It would be foolish to rely on absolutes after only eight hours but the Soviet passion for order meant there was much he could count on.

It was two hours after midnight and in a secure area when they gathered around Chance again. "What we can't be absolutely sure of is when their patrols come back. The second one yesterday came in sooner than I expected. I don't know whether they figure they're too isolated to be worried or just plain dumb. Either way, they went out and came back through the same point. The one for this watch is already in." Once again, much of what he explained was in hand signals; his words covered only speculation. "Nuan, take off now and set up some *welcome-home* claymores after the next patrol moves out. Make sure that every man goes down." Chance winked at the Vietnamese. "If we get off schedule, circle back to this position the moment any fireworks start. And if we don't have any trouble, be back here at zero six hundred." He waved Nuan off before glancing around the circle. His next hand signals conveyed the words he'd used before boarding the Huey. "Remember, this is our base. We move out toward the landing zone from here whether or not everyone's back." That was understood, an accepted practice—a man who failed to show was most likely a dead man anyway.

They were squatting on their heels Vietnamese style in a

small clearing half a mile from the edge of the Song Be camp. Chance was the only one to speak. Each man had explained to the others in succinct detail exactly what he'd observed the previous day. It was normal procedure in every operation David Chance commanded—observe, withdraw to a secure area, report, then don't say another word. His method involved mutual trust and an understanding by each member of the team of every other's job. No man had a chance to doze off until he had a complete understanding of every other's responsibilities.

They'd studied aerial photos before taking off and Chance confirmed now in hand signals what he'd said then: "When they catch on to what's happening, we want them to chase us back here, and we want them to follow our tracks. Before we go in, we set claymores no more than ten yards back from the edge of the clearing. I don't want the undergrowth absorbing all the blast. Then a second batch another hundred yards along. Dinh, you're in charge of LZ security. Helos will be in the zone at exactly zero seventhirty. Move out double quick ahead of us. If there're bad guys in the area, Tranh will take radio control of the gunships. We'll stay out of the way until we get the word from you. Tranh and Nelson will herd the prisoners we take out. Campbell and I and Vuong will drop back to take out any stragglers."

No raid had ever gone exactly the way it was planned and Song Be was no different. Although the sky was just lightening above the jungle, six prisoners were taken into the interrogation hut just before Chance gave the signal to move out. That meant they had two buildings to sort through. Their orders were to bring back or kill every one of the prisoners. Now their chances of detection had just doubled. Their greatest advantage beyond sloppy security was that the camp was just coming to life.

Dinh and Tranh removed the guards at either end of the building housing the prisoners. Their work was silent, efficient and bloodless. They dragged the bodies behind the building, switched into the guards' uniforms, and resumed the posts outside either door. There was little chance of being noticed through the early morning haze rising off the damp ground.

Campbell slipped inside. Six prisoners were capable of traveling. Tranh and Vuong, who were covering the exit facing away from the center of the camp, coordinated their escape one at a time into the bush where Nuan had already returned. When the last man had gone, Campbell removed a needle and syringe from his pack. The four remaining prisoners had been horribly tortured. It would have been cruel if any of them had ever regained consciousness.

Tranh and Vuong took over as guards at the front entrance while Dinh proceeded to the interrogation building. The Vietnamese guard at the single entrance was sloppy. He paid no attention to Dinh's approach, seemingly unaware of the other until he was called over to the corner of the structure. He, too, disappeared into the jungle just as the guards at the other building.

Chance and Nelson darted unseen from the edge of the jungle through the door. It was a calculated move—there hadn't been enough time to establish absolutes. Surprise was their only advantage. They dropped automatically into a crouch in firing position on either side of the entrance.

They were greeted with shocked silence by three Russians—two officers and a sergeant—and two VC guards who had leaned their rifles against the far wall. Once again there was too much comfort in the remoteness of Song Be, and too little attention to security. The guards were obviously there to handle the prisoners, five of whom were seated on wooden stools, their arms lashed behind them. Two of them were unrecognizable, their faces swollen and bleeding. The other three stared back at the Americans through puffy, half closed eyes. A sixth man lay on the floor, blood streaming from his mouth.

Neither the Russians nor the guards moved, their eyes seemingly hypnotized by the automatic weapons swinging back and forth across their chests. The shock of the moment magnified the silence until Campbell called out softly, "Dinh, send Tranh in here."

One of the Soviet officers, a stocky blond man, blinked and shifted his feet slightly. He wore a major's insignia and appeared to be the most senior of the Soviets they had seen in the camp.

Chance leveled his M-16 on the man's chest. "Don't move a muscle," he growled in Russian.

The major's eyes narrowed in astonishment and his mouth opened as if he intended to say something.

"Silence," Chance snapped, waving the M-16 for emphasis.

Tranh slipped silently into the room. Chance nodded toward the five men on the stools. "Make sure they can travel—our speed. Otherwise . . ." There was no need to add the obvious.

One by one, Tranh released each of the men, speaking gently with them in his own language and nodding to Chance each time he was sure. He sent them to the door one by one where Dinh pointed out where they should slip into the jungle to join the others waiting with Nuan. It took Tranh only a second with the remaining one before he shook his head and reached into his pocket.

As the needle slipped into the limp arm, Dinh appeared inside the doorway. "Quickly," he hissed, "coming this way . . . Russians and VC." It was enough to create a distraction, one that wasn't lost among the five men who had seen their destinies in the gun muzzles. If there'd been no chance before, perhaps there was one now. One of the VC, a man who was taller than average, surprised everyone when he hissed a single word of recognition, "Dinh!"

Dinh's mouth dropped open in surprise. "Po!" Gunfire cracked outside. Dinh turned and bolted out the door, his M-16 firing as he lunged to one side.

The moment of shocked recognition, the firing outside—each accentuated the desperate situation for the five men.

The other VC guard took a step toward Tranh, who was still kneeling over the remaining prisoner. The junior Russian officer reached for the Tokarev on his hip. The stifling air inside the little building was shattered as Nelson blasted them both with his shotgun. The Russian sergeant took one step to the side before he, too, was flung backward by the impact of Chance's firing.

"Now," Dinh shouted back inside. "Too many . . ." were his last clear words as the sound of shooting increased, punctuated by the murderous automatic fire of Campbell's M-60 just outside the entrance.

"Outside . . . now," Chance bellowed. He leaped through the doorway, his M-16 blazing as he balanced on his knees. Tranh followed.

Campbell turned his head back into the doorway toward the remaining VC, the one called Po, and the Soviet major just as they dove behind a desk on the far side of the room. Campbell fired a burst that sent splinters flying. He might have gotten a hit . . . he fired once more . . . more splinters from the disintegrating furniture . . . but he was sure there wasn't a kill because the M-60 would have tossed the corpses about the room. He vaulted back through the doorway into the firefight.

Although all firefights seemed to last forever to the participants, this one was short. Song Be had been unprepared for any kind of raid. When Tranh, Vuong, and Campbell opened up with their murderous automatic weapons, Soviet troops and VC alike scattered for cover. They were down and confused just long enough for the SEALs to resume their plan. They weren't there for a firefight. Their objective was to bring back the prisoners. One at a time, covering each other, they escaped into the jungle exactly at the spot Chance had designated, allowing themselves to be followed closely, until the claymores were triggered. That allowed precious minutes more. Blasts from the opposite side of the camp, the claymores set by Nuan, neutralized the incoming patrol.

Everything else had worked after that. Dinh had gone ahead to the extraction point but there had been no need for the covering gunships. The LZ was clean. Campbell and Chance set one more covering ambush with their last claymores. When those were tripped, they crouched near the edge of the LZ and waited for stragglers. But the jungle remained silent after that. The Hueys lifted them out without incident. Two hours later, Chance was making his report and Dinh and the other three Vietnamese were heading back to their villages.

It had been a successful operation . . . except for that VC who had recognized Dinh. What was his name? *Po*. That was it, Po. That was the only aspect that bothered Chance when he had a moment to sit back and reflect before he made his report. The VC took their revenge whenever and wherever. And Campbell had been honest—he'd tried to take them out but there wasn't enough time and he was sure Po and that Russian major were still alive. . . .

And now, twenty years later, Chance could still remember Po's name—and the name of the Russian commander at Song Be who had ordered the ensuing massacre—*Brusilov*! Major Georgi Brusilov.

Chance would always retain a vivid picture of the agony the following morning when Dinh had appeared at the front of his tent. He was covered with blood and he was carrying his only remaining possession, a framed photograph of his wife, Mai, a fine, quiet woman Chance had grown to respect. Beside Dinh, naked, raw with blisters from the flames she'd barely escaped, was his daughter Phuong, the only other survivor from their tiny village of Can Fat— which no longer existed.

Squatting in flickering lantern light in a hut near the village of Suoi Hoa twenty years later, Chance closed his eyes to shut out that same horror as Dinh repeated, "That's correct, David. The commander of the base at Cam Ranh Bay is General Georgi Brusilov . . . the same one . . . he arrived late last year." Dinh bit off his words with a sob.

CHAPTER 7

Dinh meant as much to David Chance as a brother could mean to any man. Back in that long ago when the SEALs challenged for every square foot of the Delta, in an operation in the Ca Mau, Chance heard the footsteps of death racing toward him on the bare feet of a VC. It was the only moment in his short life when he had been unable to defend himself. This particular mission had become a game of hide and seek where the objective was to hold down the enemy until a flanking position could be established. Chance sensed rather than heard the soft patter of feet on the jungle floor an instant before the telltale sound of a grenade launcher, followed seconds later by a rustling in the leaves above him. A grenade fell through the green overhead canopy to his right. He hurled himself in the opposite direction as the weapon burst a few feet from where he'd been crouching. The concussion from the blast and the hard ground left him groggy. His Stoner had landed three feet beyond.

As Chance struggled to regain his senses, the bush parted in front of him. A small man in black pajamas appeared, cradling a Soviet AK-47. For a split second, he stared down at Chance, his face devoid of expression. The Stoner seemed so close yet the distance widened as his mind attempted to will his stunned body to reach out for it. The AK-47 swung around in his direction. It was as fast as the VC could move but to Chance death seemed to be approaching in slow motion.

In retrospect, he had really not heard another set of footsteps, yet a patter of bare feet now seemed to echo through his head. While the SEALs had seen death around them in a variety of forms, they had yet to hear footsteps. But it was an expression each of them often recounted when they returned to base after a firefight. If there really had been a sound for Chance, it was the final beats of his heart.

Then the explosion of gunfire Chance dreaded erupted around him. But it was the VC who died, lifted off his feet by a long burst from behind Chance. His heart was still pounding, reverberating through his body. He was alive! And Dinh was kneeling down beside him, a worried look turning to relief as Chance rolled over. It was the closest he'd ever come to death. But instead of reliving the memory of that AK-47 swinging toward him, he had always carried the expression on Dinh's face from that incident in the Ca Mau.

Affection for one another is different with men, but if one man could love another, David Chance felt love for Nguyen van Dinh from that moment on. And it wasn't completely the fact that Dinh had saved his life as much as the agony he'd seen in the man's face, the fear that his friend had been close to death, so close they had both sensed the footsteps.

Now, as Dinh wept quietly in the hut at Suoi Hoa twenty years later, Chance reached out his hand. He was sure he was seeing the same picture in his own mind that was haunting Dinh. Mai had been a beautiful young lady then, and she would have been now as a mature woman. Tentatively, he placed his hand on Dinh's shoulder and squeezed. Then he leaned forward and put both arms around his friend and hugged him. The massacre at Can Fat . . . Georgi Brusilov here . . . now . . .

They relived Dinh's horror together, silently, each remembering in their own way that morning after Song Be until Dinh's shoulders ceased their shaking. Chance released him and sat back cautiously, concern evident on his face until Dinh drew in one deep breath after another to regain his composure.

The others, Gates and Merry and York, waited quietly, unembarrassed. They were familiar with such stories. Those outside the SEAL community rarely learned of the exploits of this small band of professionals because they were satisfied to keep such feats among themselves. But these incidents survived the years and were passed on as new men joined the teams. The other three also knew that Chance and Dinh had made a solemn promise to each other—someday the Soviet major who ordered the massacre of Dinh's village would die.

"David, it seems as if we are once again back with Phoenix. You and I . . . even this Brusilov . . ." Dinh paused for a moment, nodding to the other three men as if to involve them in his innermost thoughts. "It hasn't changed much in our country, really, just the time."

Twenty years before, missions like Song Be involving the Vietnamese Provincial Reconnaissance Units (PRU) and the SEALs under the code name of "Phoenix" created a furor among the non-military types. The name had been dropped. Now, as the three younger men watched, they understood they were being invited to relive the past.

"They understand, Dinh. They know of Song Be . . . and about Can Fat. They knew before they volunteered to join us."

Dinh nodded in their direction again, as if he were now welcoming them to share the secret of his past. His personal loss had been commonplace in those days. Slaughter of civilians occurred almost every day throughout his country. Little notice had been taken of his own tragedy at the time. What he did not understand was that SEALs remembered such experiences when they happened to one of their own, and Nguyen van Dinh had become *one of their own* forever—the moment he saved Chance's life. Gates and Merry and York had already assimilated that experience as an integral element in the SEAL mystique.

"How well do you know the docks where they're keeping our ship, Dinh?"

"As well as you know the back of your hand. I work there, David. I learned everything there was to know about Cam Ranh Bay before they ever dreamed about bringing an American ship in there. I know the docks, the shore facilities, the airbase, the command center. I also know everything possible about General Brusilov. I know because . . . because Phuong works for him." The last words came in a rush as if he would explode if they didn't escape immediately.

"Phuong . . ." Chance murmured, remembering the naked, burned little girl at Dinh's side so many years before. She'd been terrified, unable to speak, whimpering as she clung to her father. He remembered her once later, a gawky teenager who treated him like a god. "She's a young lady now. She must be about . . ."

"She's twenty-four years old," Dinh interrupted. "Not only is she highly intelligent, she has become a very attractive young woman."

"How much have you told her about Brusilov?"

"It would have been a mistake to say anything, David. She wouldn't have been able to stay there if she'd known." He cocked his head to one side and it might have appeared to a stranger that he was smiling when he added, "Would you have been able to greet a man with a smile each morning if you knew that he had been personally responsible for the murder of your mother . . . your brothers and sisters . . . grandparents . . . aunts and uncles . . ." he paused and blinked his eyes each time, ". . . that he burned your village . . . all because . . ." Dinh seemed to run out of energy and concluded, instead, "No, David, I couldn't tell her that because I needed to know everything about that man so that he couldn't escape me. I wanted the time to plan his death so I would enjoy it fully and he would suffer the pain of understanding as much about the pain of death. This has been all I've lived for, David. After so many years of believing I would never have the opportunity, a little more time, a year or so, meant nothing to me."

Chance knew without taking his eyes from Dinh that the other three were looking in his direction. Emotions had no place in a military operation. They blurred that fine line that allowed men to function beyond their normal abilities—*and that's what got men killed needlessly*! There were no more than thirty hours to gain *Gettysburg*'s release and now there were three men hanging on his response.

"I understand, Dinh, and I want to help you. But I also intend to get that ship back. If we do, then I will be beside you to make sure Brusilov doesn't get away. And if we fail, you have nothing to worry about because Brusilov and Cam Ranh Bay and you and me will all disappear in one great blast." It wasn't what he'd been planning on saying in front of the others, but they'd understood implicitly when they volunteered to join him. "You're like me, Dinh. You'd much rather enjoy the pleasure of knowing he's dead—but we have to be successful, and we have to stay alive to do that."

"I understand. Revenge is only sweet if one can enjoy it." He inclined his head in the direction of the other three. "I have worked in the past with SEALs. I know what you expect. You have my promise that I will do nothing to endanger you. If you see me wavering at any time, treat me like one of your own." Then he turned back to Chance. "I think it's important now for us to plan how we're going to release this ship of your's. There are a number of people loyal to me who will help . . . and you must meet Phuong." The gold tooth gleamed once again in the flickering light. "She is so excited you have come."

An observer from the outside would never have had the slightest idea that anything out of the ordinary was occurring inside Naval Special Warfare Headquarters. That was simply the nature of Admiral Lyford's leadership— "The extraordinary is our business," he was fond of saying. Even inside the NSW building, there was a semblance of order, a business-as-usual attitude. Lyford had succeeded in shooing out many of the staff types from the other commands who were not nearly as valuable to him as they thought. Captain Auger from Naval Intelligence had been specifically requested to remain. In fact, Lyford had arranged for a cot for the captain. They had worked together often in the past and had grown to enjoy each other's company. Lyford knew that behind that quiet ministerial mien was a mind able to fathom each move the Russians might make.

The unique requirements of special warfare demanded unusual individuals, especially in their leaders. Admiral Lyford possessed the ability to view a situation from his enemy's vantage point, a talent which he'd passed on to many of the most talented members of the six SEAL teams. He claimed this was often as valuable as their training.

Lyford would have done exactly what the Soviet leader did—establish Condition One. The situation from the Kremlin's viewpoint had to be bleak. They obviously had yet to determine how someone's attempt to compromise the Aegis system had evolved into high seas piracy of an American war ship. It was only logical to anticipate the US would go to almost any length to get that ship back and to prevent Aegis falling into Soviet hands. This was one time bluff wasn't going to work. The goddamned ship was sitting alongside a pier in Cam Ranh Bay for the world to see. Condition One was an obvious indication Moscow would protect herself from attack. But, would she go to war if Cam Ranh Bay simply disappeared? He wasn't sure.

"What do you think, Jules?" Lyford asked the intelligence officer. "Is it worthwhile going to the wall over something like this?"

Captain Auger rubbed his chin thoughtfully as if the beard he once had was still there. "It depends who fesses up. If it's a KGB higher-up with a reason that appeals to the Defense Council, maybe yes. Any other, not a chance."

"What would you do with all those self-important fleet types who want to get a piece of the action?" He was smiling as if involved in a huge practical joke rather than worrying about a number of admirals who suddenly wanted to become special warfare experts.

"I'd call their immediate superiors and tell them you want their asses out of here double fast because the President agrees this is your baby and your's alone."

"And if they question that?"

Auger grinned. "Then you have no choice but to get the President on the pipe and tell him frankly that these guys are anxious to test their new toys and he could have a war on his hands. That's the type of thing he understands."

Lyford looked grim. "Easy for you to say. When was the last time you called the President and got him to answer?"

"Condition One in the Soviet Union changes all that. Why do you think the President hasn't retaliated and set the same thing himself?"

"Because he knows, just like you and I know, that they're waiting for us to make a move. It was purely defensive on their part. The President isn't going to order a ground attack, no massive carrier launch, not even a B-1 out of Okinawa, or anything of a magnitude that's going to be challenging all out war. It'll be a Tomahawk, I think, probably from a sub—just one—just enough to obliterate the place. Then he'd wait to see their next move. I said I'd let him know what's happening with Chance as soon as we heard ourselves, that is if communications improve soon. He agrees that the best thing that can happen is to see *Gettysburg* steaming out of Cam Ranh Bay on its own." Lyford glanced at his watch. "When the hell is Chance going to call?"

Auger rubbed his chin again. "It's not like he can pick up a phone and call. Someone's got to get to that radio, which is set up in a village outside the base, and then establish contact with Japan, if there's any chance of any radio working when we want it to, and then . . ." He waved a hand around in circles to show how complex the process was no matter how urgent the situation might be.

An aide knocked and entered the room to explain how many people were upset that Admiral Lyford had managed to avoid them for the past half hour. They were anxious to prepare themselves for a showdown with a Soviet Union that hoped for anything but that.

Barney Gold could see his ship from the window in Brusilov's large office. The building faced to the west and was situated about a hundred yards back from the water between the seven piers that jutted into Cam Ranh Bay. *Gettysburg* was alongside the second pier from the north, her high bow pointing toward the land. The Vietnamese flag flew at her mast, rather than her stern as was normal in port. It was an insult that would not go away no matter how many times Gold squeezed his eyes tightly shut. At that moment, the sun on the pilot house windows reflected back in his face, creating a pattern on the far wall of the room.

Gold's features revealed the abuse received from Hansen the previous day. Thick, white clots of bandage covered shaved sections of his head where he'd been struck repeatedly by Hansen's gun. Blue-black bruises ran from his right ear under his eye to his nose, and his upper lip puffed out where he'd landed on the pilot house deck after the last assault. The physical pain was there—his head throbbed— but it couldn't match the pain in his heart as he stared out at *Gettysburg*.

"She seems to be calling you, Captain, looking for you right in this office. Sort of eerie, wouldn't you say?" Brusilov's English was grammatically perfect though his pronunciation was clipped. Like Gold, he had been awake much of the night trying to come up with a solution to this problem. *Gettysburg* had been dropped in his lap as a gift, an unwelcome one at that.

Captain Trang's enthusiasm for *Gettysburg* had not been transferred to Brusilov. The last thing he could have wanted or imagined was an American ship, especially an Aegis cruiser, brought to him as a gift. Neither he nor Trang had been aware initially of Andrew Norman's mission. As worthy as the objective appeared, the presence of the ship did not balance the intelligence to be derived as far as Brusilov was concerned. Trang thought it a wonderful coup, a slap in the face for an America he'd been taught to hate over the years. Brusilov wanted that ship out of Cam Ranh Bay as quickly as possible. It presented a danger he was totally unable to convey to Trang. He knew the United States would not allow *Gettysburg* to remain at that pier for long.

On the other hand, wouldn't it be a feather in his cap if he could deliver the key to Aegis to Moscow? His intelligence people were once again interrogating the three men who claimed to be Soviet agents. So far, the results were no different than they had been the first time. If this was a KGB operation, it was definitely second rate.

Barney Gold squinted his eyes against the reflection from the distant pilot house windows. Yes, *Gettysburg* seemed to be calling him but he was damned if he'd admit it to this cocky Russian asshole smiling benignly at him from behind that ostentatious desk. "I repeat again, I would like a detailed report on the status of my crew."

"Your officers have been escorted ashore and will remain here until we can reach some sort of a decision. Your crew has been allowed to remain aboard under guard of Vietnamese troops, of course." Brusilov shook his large head in mock wonder and raised his eyebrows. "It appears their Captain Trang wants to make a gift of your ship to me but he won't trust my people to guard it. I promise you there has been no damage. Your men are operating the ship exactly as if you were aboard. I have made port facilities available to them so there is no discomfort." The Russian general was making every effort to be as pleasant as possible. It was not his normal way, but Brusilov really had no interest in encouraging additional problems with this American. He also had no intention of being condescending. Perhaps, he'd decided, a show of neutrality would be the best approach.

"But we are all prisoners. I insist . . ." Gold began abrasively.

"Be quiet for a moment, Captain Gold," Brusilov growled. He was a man of little patience no matter how much he attempted to exhibit a pleasant outward appearance. "You are in no position to insist on anything. Your ship is alongside a pier in an unfriendly country and it is guarded by men who are most fanatical about keeping it right there, regardless of what I say. Anything that happens to your benefit will occur because of me." He leaned forward and once again raised a set of very bushy eyebrows. "Understood?" Brusilov was of average height, but his shoulders were broad over a thick body. He was built like a wrestler and wide-set eyes over high cheekbones added to a slightly menacing appearance. His voice remained gruff even when he made an effort at pleasantries.

"Then I'm your prisoner!" Gold snapped.

"We're not at war, Captain. Don't try to make my life any more difficult. Since you weren't invited here, let's call it protective custody, unless someone can offer a better explanation. You and your men will be treated as much like guests as possible."

"Then we can come and go as we please . . ." Gold persisted.

"There is a term I was taught by a man who spent many years in the United States. It covers you thoroughly, Captain Gold—*pain in the ass*! If you want to persist in being one, I can make your life unpleasant enough." He folded his hands and placed them on the desk, leaning slightly forward.

"Since my ship possesses a system that your country has attempted to steal, and your agents shot a number of my men in the process, I have no choice but to assume you are involved. And since we were delivered to you, it appears that you are responsible. All I require, General, is that you return me and my officers to our ship and allow us to leave. Until you do so, I have no choice but to consider myself a prisoner." Barney Gold saw no other course of action. There was no way of knowing what was taking place between Washington and Moscow, nor could he imagine what attempt might be made to free *Gettysburg*. Aegis was his responsibility and he was the sole individual who could arrange her freedom. But he was being forced to reach for straws.

Even when he smiled, General Brusilov's appearance remained mostly unchanged. Now, his eyes brightened slightly and his cheeks dimpled around the corners of his mouth. His lips remained straight. "You may consider whatever you want then. Since you have no intention of cooperating with me to reach a meeting of the minds, I have no choice but to place you under protective custody. I can't have you running around creating problems for me today."

They were interrupted by a knock on the door. Before Brusilov could answer, a delicately attractive Vietnamese woman took three steps into the room. Her hands remained at her sides. "Good morning, General." Taller than most Vietnamese women, she was appealingly slender in a beautiful *ao dai*. Shiny black hair hung almost to her waist. Her soft, round face was one of the loveliest Barney Gold had ever seen, yet there was no expression, neither smile nor frown. It was empty . . . empty was the only word that came to him as he stared at her. She had yet to look at him.

"Good morning." Brusilov barely took notice of her. "Tea, if you please . . ." Then he halted in midsentence. "Captain Gold, I'll make one more effort. Would you join me in a cup of tea? I've taught Miss Phuong to make a good pot of Russian tea."

It was at that moment that the girl's eyes settled on Gold. There was something in that woman's expression, Gold thought, almost as if she recognized him. "Yes," he answered. Her face remained empty, but had she nodded slightly when she saw him? "Yes, I'd like that."

"Phuong, my guest will join me in a cup of tea."

"At once, General," she said without expression. This time her eyes held Gold's long enough for a hint of recognition to pass between them. It was not a glance that anyone else, not even Brusilov, would have noticed. Yet it lasted long enough for a message to be conveyed to Barney Gold. When he inclined his head just the slightest bit to acknowledge that he'd sensed an effort on her part, her lips turned up slightly at the corners.

"If you will be patient, Captain, I have a few items on my desk that require my attention. Then perhaps we can attempt to understand each other over some tea. The Vietnamese make some sweet rolls that I've grown to enjoy. I'm sure Phuong will bring some of those, too." Brusilov leaned over his desk without waiting for a response.

When Phuong returned, she carried a tray which she set down on a table to the right of the window. Gold saw her twice make a point of glancing out at *Gettysburg* then briefly looking back to him. She poured the tea into large glasses set in pewter holders in the Russian manner. Brusilov was served first, a small bowl of sugar and a plate of tiny rolls placed at his right hand. Then she moved a small table over beside Gold's chair and placed a plate of rolls on top of it, followed by a glass of tea.

She picked up a creamer and sugar bowl and stepped in front of Gold. "Cream and sugar, sir?" She held them in front of her at arm's length.

"No. Thank you, no," Gold responded as he looked down at her hands. He'd been correct. He'd sensed she wanted to express something to him before she left the room the first time. A slip of paper peaked from underneath the sugar bowl with a single word scrawled on it.

SEALs!

Phuong closed her eyes tightly, so that she wouldn't

have the slightest chance of Brusilov noting any change of expression. Thank God it had worked! When she opened her eyes, she acknowledged Gold's raised eyebrows with the slightest of nods. Then she returned the cream and sugar to the tray and Gold saw her bunch the piece of paper into a tight ball and place it in her mouth when her back was turned to the general. Without another word, she was gone from the room before Brusilov looked up from his desk.

"Now, Captain Gold, let's see if we can't come to a truce with each other, since the only way you'll be able to leave will be through diplomatic channels."

CHAPTER 8

The United States had managed to foot the bill for one of the finest new support bases in Southeast Asia. And once the Americans departed, Cam Ranh Bay grew rapidly. The Russians, who recognized the ultimate potential of the area, then expanded this American gift into one of the largest forward deployment installations outside the Soviet Union. Eventually, it included a naval base, an expanded air base capable of servicing strategic bombers, a logistics center, and a headquarters for communications and intelligence activities.

It was the warm water port that the Russians had never before possessed. With their major naval bases icebound part of the year and open to the high seas only via straits controlled by other nations, Cam Ranh Bay was the ultimate gift from America. To achieve total control of the installation, Moscow poured billions of rubles into Hanoi. They gave until the Vietnamese couldn't say no. And once Cam Ranh Bay grew to the point that it became absolutely critical to Soviet strategy, the Russians excluded their hosts.

It wasn't so much a matter of throwing the Vietnamese off their own soil. There just was no purpose in their disputing the awesome military power the Soviets brought with them. Long-range Bear and Badger strategic bombers challenged American might in the South Pacific. New control in the South China Sea brought the Soviets a vital link between their eastern ports and the Indian Ocean, not to mention a new challenge to the American base at Subic Bay *if* the Philippine government allowed them to keep it. The Vietnamese skies were protected by MiG fighters. Cruisers, destroyers and frigates that had no compunction about steaming brazenly alongside their American counterparts called Cam Ranh Bay their home. Both cruise missile attack submarines and their smaller diesel powered sisters that protected the coastal waters joined the growing fleet. The Russian naval and air forces stayed because there was finally a warm water facility that provided rest and recreation, repair services, and supplies, all at their largest military installation outside the Soviet Union.

And in return, the Vietnamese catered to the Russians and remained out of their way—that is, until Captain Trang delivered his present to General Brusilov. And that was a gift Andrew Norman could have done without. He had become increasingly concerned with his fate from the time he learned that Hansen and Filipo were involved in the same mission aboard *Gettysburg*. Their responsibilities demanded a capability he couldn't have fulfilled, but the more people who became involved the greater the chance of detection as far as he was concerned. How the hell had he ever gotten himself into this mess?

First it was Lt. Shore blundering into the ET workshop, followed by Hansen taking control even though he was a goddamned enlisted man! . . . *or was he*? No, he wasn't! He didn't know what Hansen's background was but it sure as hell wasn't American. Norman knew he should have just stopped it all right then, rather than letting Hansen talk him into calling Captain Gold. From that point on, it was all a crazy dream—like shooting the OOD right there in the pilot house, and beating Captain Gold and Mr. Marston and all the others who'd been hurt, turning the ship toward Cam Ranh Bay, Hansen talking over the radio as if he was a

Russian . . . he must be . . . Oh, God, that had been as much of a shock as the killings.

Then, Captain Trang had interfered. *That* was the kiss of death!

"Lt. Norman, we have yet to find anyone who knows you." His interrogator was a Soviet captain who seemed bored with his job. He had been chosen for his ability with the English language and was disappointed that his first assignment was so dull. This American was scared to death. If his story wasn't so absurd, he might almost be believed. "Moscow is in direct communication with us and they continue to disclaim any knowledge of your fantastic story. I'm almost beginning to feel sorry for you. Can't you give me some names . . . some places?"

Norman looked up with tears forming in the corners of his eyes. Was this man asking him another of those inane questions? Did he expect an answer to what he'd just said, or was that a simple statement? Nothing seemed to make sense as this bewildering questioning wore on. He knew he could never go back to his own country. Yet these Russians, who should have accepted him as some kind of a hero, were treating him like a common criminal.

The Russian looked down at Norman and, seeing a large tear run down his cheek, shook his head in disgust and walked back to his desk. He shuffled through some papers as if the answer he was searching for might somehow be hidden there. *It was embarrassing to question a grown man who cried! How could a piece of shit like this*, the officer wondered, *possibly be working for us? What had the KGB come to if they ran agents like this in America?* He hurled the papers angrily into the corner. *We're all doomed!*

Andrew Norman's head hung on his chest in despair until he heard the Russian's fist slam the desk, followed by a howl of anger. He looked up just as the man lunged at him, a broad fist slamming into his face just below the cheek bone. Norman, who had been sitting in a simple wooden chair, went over backwards hitting his head hard on the floor. Brightly colored images flashed through his head, followed by a dull pain that seemed to spread to every cell in his skull. He was confused. What had he done to deserve that? Nothing had been said. The room swam before him like a reflection in an oily pond.

"You disgusting piece of shit, tell me how I can find out who you really are?" The voice was brutal.

Is he talking to me? Norman wondered as the far wall shimmered from a blue haze into a red blur. It seemed that just a moment ago this man had been trying to reason with him.

The toe of a boot slammed into Norman's ribs. "Why would you turn against a man like your Captain Gold?" The Russians had been impressed by Barney Gold's absolute disdain for their courtesies. He was as Russian as they were. But this simpering lieutenant! "Why do you allow those enlisted men to push you around?"

Another kick. How in the world could he *stop* them from pushing him around? Filipo really didn't do anything rude—he just acted like I wasn't there. It was Hansen. He had no regard for officers. He acted like I couldn't handle the situation . . . just took over right after Lt. Shore came barging into the workshop . . .

"Get on your feet."

The tone of the voice was a threat of even worse things to come if he failed to obey. It was enough to force Norman to roll over on his stomach and slowly rise to his knees. He looked over his shoulder and saw the Russian captain staring down at him, an unfathomable expression on his face. There was no telling what he might do next. Very slowly, hesitantly, tipping the chair upright and holding onto it for support, he rose shakily to his feet. The dizziness that overtook him threatened his stability. "I've got to sit down," he said, surprised at how distant his own voice was to him.

"Sit," the Russian growled with disgust. Then, "The

other two men, the enlisteds, the ones you claim you were working with, how long did you work together?"

"I never knew them before the *Gettysburg*. I . . . I didn't even know they were going to be there," he stammered.

"Did you expect to do that entire job yourself?"

"I was just told I'd be contacted by someone who would help on the technical details. I was on board ship for a few months before Hansen. Talk to them. They'll tell you."

"I've already talked with them. Now I'm asking you the questions and I don't believe that you're as dumb as you want me to believe. This one called Hansen has already given us another name and claims that he's one of us. Who is he?"

Norman shrugged. His vision had cleared considerably now. He kept opening and shutting his mouth because his jaw hurt, and his entire head now throbbed. "Maybe he's right. I don't know. He was speaking your language when he used the ship's radio. Listen," he continued pleadingly, "I didn't care who he was. I was involved because I didn't have a choice. Now I'll never be able to go home again. Please," he whimpered, "don't you understand?"

No, the captain didn't understand. Nor did he care. And he had no idea what he was going to report to General Brusilov. This worthless officer he was ready to give up on obviously didn't have the backbone to lie. His story seemed to coincide with the enlisted men. Pain brought nothing additional from any of them. The one called Filipo just stared back in anger while the blood ran down his face. And that Hansen, he refused to speak English. He'd lashed out in anger with his own fists, as if he expected them to draw back out of respect. He had to be restrained to complete his interrogation and promised retaliation when his superiors were informed of his treatment.

Whoever had engineered this compromise of the American Aegis system had designed a superb—but not quite foolproof—plan. It should have worked . . . it might have even, if they'd had a better understanding of the personalities they'd chosen to join *Gettysburg*. People make all the difference. As it was now, General Brusilov wasn't sure if he was in the position to deliver Aegis to Moscow or if he was the victim of a failed plot that could destroy his career. He possessed a watertight container with film in it, which these people claimed was enough to compromise the Aegis system. But he had yet to find a soul in Moscow who would claim responsibility for that film. As a matter of fact, what might have been a simple and efficient act of espionage had ended in an act of piracy that had brought distress to his doorstep. One thing he was certain about—if the Americans had attempted to steal something as vital as Aegis from the Russians, he knew how Moscow would have reacted.

There was one person who insisted that the intelligence coup of the century had been accomplished. He was known to everyone concerned as Hansen, an electronics technician from *Gettysburg*, although he now insisted his real name was Golikhov and that he had been trained by the KGB at a secret center in East Germany. No one had yet come forth to substantiate this.

As a result, the cause of the *Gettysburg* affair remained in doubt. Hansen's closest accomplice, Filipo, said nothing; he claimed he was an American who had been blackmailed into the situation. His interrogators concluded early on that he was probably a lunatic, after analyzing his delight in shooting people, and they were just as happy that he claimed to be an American. Lt. Andrew Norman had already been judged useless by Soviet interrogators. One by one, they reported exactly the same conclusion to Brusilov—that he was a *useless piece of shit* and the KGB couldn't possibly have hired him in their wildest dreams. The General had no one in Cam Ranh Bay who could tell him whether or not the films were of value. He had even toyed with the idea of destroying them, sending *Gettysburg* on her way, and hoping that Moscow wouldn't demand his neck. On the other hand, if there was an individual yet to come forward in the Kremlin, and he possessed unlimited power . . .

Washington had even less idea of whether Aegis was in danger. The navy had explained in no uncertain terms that this could be at least as bad for surface warfare as the Walker case had been for submarines. It was preferable to slough off the idea of compromise. So the decision was made almost immediately to emphasize the piracy aspect rather than the security problem. That would unite the free world, and even much of the third-world community which was the primary victim of twentieth-century piracy.

That left Moscow in a corner with literally only Vietnam to sympathize with her. Those few in the Soviet scientific community who might have been able to comment one way or the other on the worth of the films refused to get involved since the power structure that controlled them still denied responsibility. Besides, these were obviously amateurs and amateurs usually failed to deliver. But one thing the leaders in the Kremlin understood was that there was not enough time to get that film back to Moscow and into the hands of people they trusted for some sort of intelligence evaluation of its worth before the Americans retaliated. To get involved in a missile exchange over useless film would have been absurd.

Was it worth prolonging the threat?

David Chance strolled boldly down a Cam Ranh Bay street leading toward the pier. He wore the uniform of a Navy Captain 3rd Rank in the Soviet navy. The night before in Suoi Hoa, Dinh had shown him a hut full of uniforms that his small group had been amassing over the years. It was wiser, Dinh had insisted, to wear a navy uniform—so many Soviet ships stopped in Cam Ranh Bay that no one could possibly keep track of so many naval officers, especially one waiting by the piers. Gates, Merry, and York were off in different directions in other uniforms. By nightfall, their combined knowledge of the base would create a perfect map for any situation.

They'd entered the base hidden in the back of a truck. Security, as Dinh had reassured them, was minimal because the gate guards were familiar with all of the Vietnamese who came each day to work on the base. Dinh was often given the privilege of driving a Russian truck so that he could return in the mornings with fresh local fruit and vegetables for the officers messes. He never failed to provide the guards with something also—and they never failed to wave him directly through.

Phuong had joined them briefly before dawn. With a squeal of delight, she'd flown into the arms of a thoroughly surprised David Chance. She had never forgotten the American who had helped to nurse her back to health when she was a little girl, always bringing such wonderful surprises when she was in the hospital after her return from the burn center in Manila. And after he'd gone back to his own country, somehow he managed to get things to her father for her. A few years before, when Chance had returned briefly, he had brought her a beautiful dress from Hong Kong, the first really fashionable one she'd ever had—"You're growing too fast for me, Phuong," he'd said, "so I thought you needed something more grown up."

It was Phuong who explained how the base was laid out. She drew the floor plan of each building for Chance and then he and the other three did the same thing until they had memorized the location of each of the vital elements of Cam Ranh Bay's nervous system—communications, radar, intelligence, and operations. None of them would enter any building until necessary, but today they would learn how the rest of the base related to Brusilov's command center. Chance had decided they would have to sever Cam Ranh Bay's contact with the outside world if *Gettysburg* were ever to get underway. With long-range communications as unreliable as they were, he also knew Rollie Lyford back in

Coronado would just have to—*keep the faith, baby*. He always had.

Cam Ranh Bay had been well layed out by the Americans. The Russians had improved on that ingenuity. Seven piers, more than when the US ran the base, jutted out into the water to the west. The major street ran north and south with wide feeders leading out to the piers and smaller ones connecting them, including one along the waterfront. Smaller streets allowing access to the various support activities and warehouses ran parallel and were connected to the main one, which continued three miles north to the huge airbase.

Chance paused to look across at *Gettysburg*. The Russians maintained security around the ship. Soviet marines stood guard at the head of the pier while others patrolled along its length. The entire complex swarmed with Vietnamese yard workers. Vietnamese sailors with automatic rifles provided security aboard the ship. The wooden gangway leading from the pier to the quarterdeck acted almost as a boundary between the two nations. But there was no mistaking the Vietnamese flag on the mast. That was more than a token. That was a symbol General Brusilov continued to allow for the people who daily came to work on the base and then returned to their villages at night. The huge American ship was theirs—for the time being.

"Do you have dreams of sailing aboard her, Captain?" The gruff voice shocked Chance. He whirled about as if he'd been threatened, which surprised the man who had come up behind him.

"Why . . . good morning, General." He came to attention instantly, his right hand snapping up in a sharp salute. Chance remained rigid until the other returned his salute. "You . . . you surprised me, sir," he began, searching for the words to mask an expression that must have mirrored shock. The man staring back at him was Brusilov. There was no mistaking it. A bit older certainly, but he remained much the same as he'd been twenty years before. The stars on his broad shoulders and five rows of medals created an aura of authority, but the face—the face had changed little outside of some natural aging lines. The body was as blocky as ever, still not fat. But it was the eyes, Chance realized, that brought back that day so long ago. They were dark and set wide under the heavy eyebrows that monopolized his face.

"I didn't mean to scare you, Captain. Were you expecting someone else?"

"Not at all, General." His eyes went back to *Gettysburg*. Was it possible Brusilov might recognize him as well after all these years? "I was simply trying to develop a more exact image of this American ship in my mind." He was searching desperately for an appropriate response. "I've never seen one this close before. She doesn't seem to display her power like our own."

"They're not intended to be seen like this," Brusilov answered. "If the Americans had their way, you'd never see them. The only warning that they were in the same ocean would be the electronic pulses from their radar or the sound of one of their missiles just before it hit your ship. I assume you are from one of the ships tied up at five or six?" He pointed in the direction of the other piers.

"Yes, General." Chance stared hard at the Soviet war ships to his left. What the hell were the names he'd been told to memorize while they were en route? He gestured toward the new, smooth lined destroyer closest to the head of pier five, "The *Admiral Kulakov*, sir. Not quite as big as the American but more appealing lines, I'd say." That was the correct ship, wasn't it? It was one of those big ones bristling with all types of sophisticated weapons.

Either he was right or the general didn't know a hell of a lot about the navy. "Every sailor should feel that way about his ship. But the American one is a beauty, too." His voice seemed to drop with the last few words. Then he added, "She also makes an appealing target today . . . or tomorrow. . . ." His voice dropped off with that last word.

"Pardon me, General?" What did he mean by that? He glanced curiously at Brusilov.

"If I were an American, I'd destroy this base and everyone here if I didn't have it back in twenty-four hours. That's what Moscow thinks right now, too—that's why we're in Condition One. It looks like the Americans don't have the guts to do that. At least I hope not. . . ." His eyes fell back on Chance and he studied his face as if he would have known this naval officer.

Chance looked away. Those eyes were no easier to meet than during their last brief encounter, and perhaps the years had made Brusilov even more menacing than before. *If I could recognize him instantly, why shouldn't he have the same ability?* "I've noticed some of her enlisted men on the decks, sir, but none of the officers. Are they still aboard?" The question was meant to be as casual as possible. It was something he needed to confirm but he hadn't anticipated this opportunity. Take your chances while you can. He didn't look at the general when he asked it.

"Why do you ask?" It was a simple question but there was nothing simple in the way it had been asked.

"I'm in charge of security on my own ship, General. I guess I'm more curious than anything else."

"They're ashore. Since you asked, you should always know, Captain, that you should immediately separate the leaders from their men." He seemed to be enjoying his little lesson for this naval officer as he concluded, "And the captain should always be separated from his officers for the same reason."

Chance knew better than to pursue the conversation further. He'd learned enough. They were separated from Gold. One of them had to find where *Gettysburg*'s officers were located before the end of the day. It seemed obvious that Barney Gold would be kept somewhere around the main building.

He half turned, still looking toward the piers, and said, "General, I appreciate your willingness to talk with me for a few moments. I must get back to my ship." Chance came to attention and held his salute until Brusilov returned it. "Good day, sir."

The general's hand touched his sleeves as he was about to leave. "I didn't get the name . . ."

"*Kulakov*, sir . . . *Admiral Kulakov* . . ."

"No, no, not your ship. What is *your* name? I always like to remember the names of the men I meet here, in case I run into their commanding officers."

For a moment, no name would come to Chance. The only one that kept thundering through his head was . . . Brusilov . . . and he'd almost uttered that name in his anxiety to clear his mind. He remembered the man he'd once met at the Russian Aide Society and the pleasant conversation they'd had. "Captain Third Class Nikitin, sir."

"And what is your billet?"

"Weapons, General."

"Good, very good, Nikitin. You seem to be an ambitious sort of person. I'll remember to tell your captain about our conversation when he pays a call on me tonight."

"Thank you, General." Chance strode off toward the piers without looking back. If the commanding officer of the *Kulakov* really was going to meet with Brusilov that evening . . .

CHAPTER 9

Nguyen van Dinh was the first to learn where *Gettysburg*'s officers had been taken for safekeeping. Building 408 was well back from the docks. It was one of the oldest structures on the base, probably dating back to the earliest days of the Seabees in Cam Ranh Bay. One story and sheet metal, he knew it must have been brutally hot every day. The sign on the outside wall indicated its main use was spare parts storage for diesel engines—that meant primarily submarines were serviced from the building.

He was certain there had to be more than diesel engine parts in there for who in the world would have placed two black-bereted Soviet marines by the entrance to guard chunks of metal for aging submarines? Building 408 obviously contained much more valuable property, and the only addition to the base in the last day was an American ship.

Dinh had worked at Cam Ranh Bay for almost five years, long enough to earn a position of trust among Vietnamese and Russians alike. He'd seen three base commanders come through before Brusilov arrived. The run of the base was his and no one would ever question where he went or what his latest assignment might be.

After spending half an hour noting the few who passed through the doors of 408—primarily intelligence specialists from the headquarters—he sauntered back to the central supply depot. There he leafed through the catalogs to the diesel engine section and wrote down half a dozen part numbers on a requisition form. Then he selected one of the open electric carts used for transport and headed back to 408. Time was much too short to rely on guess work. He must make sure.

The Soviet marines had been assigned to guard 408 on a moment's notice. This wasn't in their normal line of duty and they had no idea of what was real or fraudulent. Dinh proffered the correct papers and was allowed access to the building. A low rumbling sound punctuated the wheeze of air-conditioning equipment that had been repaired too often with makeshift parts. The air was stuffy. An aroma of metal and grease mixed with the odor of unwashed humans.

There were three men lazing about the long counter at the front of the building which was separated from the ware-house section by a wire mesh fence. Behind that, rows of shelves containing a variety of diesel engine parts ran all the way to the end of the building. The smell of human sweat assaulting Dinh's nose was created by more than three men, and two Vietnamese marines relaxing near a door that led to an adjacent storeroom to one side seemed to confirm that. Voices drifted over the half wall that separated the two sections of the warehouse. As he discussed the time of day with the clerks, Dinh struggled to catch bits of conversation from the area beyond. Yes, there were occasional words in English that he could pick up. He must be correct!

Then he heard the words that left no doubt in his mind. "You don't have the vaguest idea what to do with us. Why don't you just take all your questions and stuff them up your ass. . . ." He missed the final words because they were drowned out by laughter. Obviously, cooperation was nonexistent.

There was no doubt where *Gettysburg*'s wardroom had set up shop.

• • •

Jimmy Gates had impersonated a Russian officer once before. That situation had been different, a little more secure. That particular Soviet Embassy, comfortable in a satellite country, simply hadn't been ready for such an outrageous mission. Gates had entered the embassy alone and departed less than twenty minutes later with a native of that same country who could have compromised a vital American intelligence plant. Once again, Gates wasn't comfortable but he had no doubt about pulling this one off, too.

He'd sauntered down to the pier from the far side of *Gettysburg* and his reasoning had been justified. There were few guards paying any attention to the outboard side. The only thing to look at was the detritus floating in the harbor. Virtually everything they would have to worry about would be on the pier side. Most of the Vietnamese sailors posted aboard ship were armed with rifles which remained slung from their shoulders, more show than anything else. He wouldn't worry himself too much about them.

The Russian marines were another matter. Gates moved along the head of the pier studying the various types of weapons—and they were a reason for concern. There were too many automatics, the kind used for close-in operations, and the marines wore flak-type vests. It didn't make sense! They couldn't possibly expect an invasion of any kind.

But it came to him as he turned up the pier toward the check point, and it made sense. The Vietnamese! That's who the Russians were really worried about. They probably figured the Americans could be kept at arm's length diplomatically until someone came up with a solution to *Gettysburg*, but they were scared the Vietnamese would do something crazy. After all, that's who had swiped the ship in the first place. Their flag was at the top of the mast. The ship was their booty; things seemed no different now than two hundred years earlier, when pirates roamed the seas. And the Russians must have figured that they'd be held personally responsible for anything that happened to the ship while it was in their hands.

Gates wore a Soviet officer's cap above a starched but obviously well-worn jumpsuit with a captain lieutenant's insignia on the collar. He was blond and blue-eyed and picked up languages as if he was a native. His Vietnamese became fluent from five tours during the war. An official looking clipboard was tucked under his arm. Jimmy Gates truly enjoyed these charades.

A marine came to attention as he approached a makeshift gate of rope and sawhorses. Gates returned the salute crisply and removed an ID card from his breast pocket. "Engineering inspection," he said curtly.

The guard glanced briefly at the card before saluting once again. "Yes, sir. If you'll just sign here, we'll give you a badge. You'll have to return it when you sign out after you're finished on the ship." Then, seeing the expression on Gates's face, he added, "General Brusilov's orders, sir. He doesn't trust the Vietnamese at all with this thing. We want to make sure that they don't interfere with any of our people."

"No problem," Gates muttered, and signed the name that appeared on his ID. The signature was barely intelligible. It should take their intelligence people more time than he was worried about to figure out who had passed through the gate in an engineer's jumpsuit.

Cradling the clipboard on his forearm, he strolled slowly down the pier, stopping occasionally to make notes. The lines from *Gettysburg* to the pier belonged to the ship. No substitution by the Russians. They were heavy but standard issue, and there was no wire braided through the nylon if it became necessary to cut them with an axe. He peered over the side into the water. Nothing else appeared in the water—no booby traps. Moving toward the stern, he saw that the screws appeared completely clear. There were no lines from the pier disappearing into the water, nothing he could see as he peered below the surface that might incapacitate the ship's movement.

Satisfied, he moved back to the gangway and climbed up to the main deck where he waited austerely until the quarterdeck sentry came over to him and saluted reluctantly. The other Vietnamese wandering on the periphery eyed him suspiciously, peering at the badge clipped to his jumpsuit then at the clipboard. He asked the sentry for directions to main control.

"I'm sorry, sir. I haven't been beyond this point right here. I'm just in charge of the duty section on guard." He indicated the Vietnamese who were watching them without apparently following what was being said. "I don't think any of them have been below either. The Americans have been very belligerent whenever they've made an attempt."

"How about one of the ship's crew?"

"They're restricted to their quarters mostly, sir. There's a lieutenant of ours on board acting as interpreter. He's waiting in their wardroom wondering what to do, and he's very nervous. I can call him on this phone." The sentry obviously wasn't anxious to cooperate with a Soviet officer unless he had to.

"Please do," Gates smiled. He crossed his arms indicating that he intended to remain there until he was satisfied. "I have a lot to do today. No telling when we might release the ship."

A moment later a young Vietnamese naval lieutenant appeared on the quarterdeck blinking at the bright sun. He was indeed nervous and he stuttered slightly after saluting when he recognized Gates's more senior insignia. He was no more excited than the sentry to see this Soviet officer.

"I'm here to inspect the engineering spaces," Gates explained. "Much of it is computerized and, of course, of interest to us. My English is almost non-existent. Would you please call for one of their engineering chief petty officers to assist me?"

"Yes, s-s-sir," the younger man stammered. "But I'm not

supposed to leave their wardroom . . . just in case other officers like yourself come aboard for something. I can't interpret for you and still follow my orders."

"No need. I just need one of them to show me the way. I can understand most everything I see in an engineering space after a while. Be good and quick about it now, and get one of them up here for me." Gates turned away and stared up at the impressive superstructure.

The lieutenant stuttered an awkwardly worded request in broken English, half order and half plea, over the ship's PA system. It took more than five minutes before a chief in worn khakies sauntered up to the quarterdeck. There were no salutes. His arms folded as he stared at the young lieutenant with obvious distaste.

"This officer requests . . ." The translator searched for the proper words. "Y-you escort him to the m-main engineering . . ."

"I don't escort any Russian anywhere," the chief interrupted.

Gates looked the Vietnamese translator in the eye disdainfully and said, "Would you explain that Commander Hanafee, his engineering officer, gave me permission."

As the lieutenant translated, the chief studied Gates closely as if he might be transporting some rare disease. He knew there were few reasons for the chief engineer to allow anyone into main control. Yet there was a bemused expression on this Russian officer's face, one of long suffering patience, as he stared back. "How do I know he's talked with my chief engineer?"

The translator turned to Gates to inquire. "They have all been making everything difficult, sir," he added as an excuse.

Without saying a word to the chief, Gates handed him the clipboard. "The ship's engineer wrote down something that he said would allow me to go below with one of his men," he reassured the translator.

The chief noted some of the phrases carelessly scrawled

on the paper. They were barely legible but he could make out enough to spark his curiosity—*screws clear* . . . *Viets no hazard* . . . *no booby traps* . . . He handed it back and turned to the interpreter saying contemptuously, "I'll take him down. But just this once. Understand? No more." Then he jerked his head in the direction of the midships passageway as an indication to follow and moved toward the far side of the ship, turning down an interior passageway without a word. It was worth a gamble.

Gates followed the chief for a short distance until he turned left and disappeared down a ladder. They emerged in a bright room unlike any engineering space he had ever seen. There was a perfectly scrubbed, gray rubber mat covering the deck plates, and a complete absence of oil or grease stains. Shiny electronic display panels covered the forward bulkhead. Digital indicators were evident alongside buttons and levers that obviously controlled the engineering spaces below where they now stood. A large easy chair before what must have been the master control panel appeared to be the chief engineer's or watch officer's station, while equally comfortable chairs were set before other panels throughout the large space.

The chief sat down at a desk and stared back at Gates uncertainly. A plastic strip across one corner of the desk had *Ferro, MMCM* punched onto it. Gates glanced around. There were two sailors looking busy who stole quick looks at him from the moment he arrived at the front of the ladder, but they seemed to be the only others in the space.

"Ferro?" Gates asked, pointing first at the name tape, then at the chief.

The man knit his brows, then nodded. "You read English," he growled. "Do you speak it, too?"

Gates looked quickly at the two sailors, then turned toward what appeared to be the main control panel. He began to jot notes on his clipboard, his fingers running quickly over each indicator.

"Now wait a minute . . ." Chief Ferro was on his feet

instantly and beside Gates, snatching the board from his hands. He read the barely legible words that had just been written—*are there any other men in this space*? He looked at Gates in astonishment, his eyes wide, before he shook his head.

Gates retrieved the clipboard. *Send those two away from us*, he wrote.

"Smitty . . . Harvey . . . get another fuel reading for me. I need something just in case we have to shift to ship's power again." The expression on his face was neutral, as much for the two sailors, Gates assumed, as it was concerning his presence.

As soon as the other two were beyond hearing, Ferro said in a low voice, "Mister, I'm not sure what . . ." but he stopped and his eyes widened as he saw five letters appear on the paper— *SEALs*. He stared at the man next to him and saw two, very clear blue eyes holding his own. The man nodded his head once to confirm what Ferro had just read.

Gates crossed out the word quickly. "Don't say another fucking word, Chief," he whispered, his tone a direct order. Each word was enunciated so clearly there could be no doubt that the speaker was making a point. "Just follow me around."

More pencil markings filled the sheet, many of them numbers along with some jottings that appeared to be in the Cyrillic alphabet. As Chief Ferro followed closely, the man beside him said little:

"I have to make notes in Russian in case I'm stopped."

"Careful—there could be Russian plants aboard."

"After I've spent enough time here, I need to see your Chief Master at Arms."

Each minute that passed, as Gates wandered from one control board to the next, increased Chief Ferro's anxiety. His men returned with a fuel report that was no different than the one completed earlier that day. "Why are you wasting your time with that creep, Master Chief?" one of them said, giving Gates the finger when he turned toward the voice. His only reaction was a smile as he recognized the gesture.

Finally, Ferro saw the words briefly scrawled on the board—*CMAA— Where?—must be secure.* While the pencil quickly blackened out the question, Ferro was on the phone to chief's quarters. Gates heard the brief conversation. "That's right, Ben, this guy has Mr. Hanafee's okay and seems pretty definite about seeing the control console in the pilot house as far as I can figure, but I want you up there with me . . . and just you. I don't want to have a party up there."

It was hot as hell in the pilot house. A tropical sun beat down on the metal roof raising the temperature inside to a hundred and ten degrees. There was no breeze. Chief Master at Arms Gannett, *Gettysburg*'s chief of police, was unhappy about being called from the air-conditioned chief's quarters and his face showed it. He eyed Ferro curiously. "This better be good, Mark." Ben Gannett had never wasted his time suffering fools.

Gates scrawled a quick note on his clipboard—*more secure outside.*

"Signal bridge," Chief Ferro murmured softly, gesturing with one hand toward the starboard door. They went out on the starboard wing and moved along the outer bulkhead of the pilot house past the signal shelter. There was no one in sight.

Gannett leaned against the back of the shelter, his sharp brown eyes switching from Gates to Ferro. Perspiration dripped down the back of his neck and he took off his hat to wipe his bald head with a handkerchief. "So what's the big secret? If this guy's trying to slip some broads aboard I'll start with two." There was no humor in his voice.

"Not at all, Chief," Gates responded. "On the contrary, you're going to help me get this ship out of here in less than twenty-four hours."

Gannett's eyes narrowed. He was known at times for a short temper. "I don't know who you are." He could think of nothing else to say. This Russian officer was speaking English with a Boston accent.

"*SEALs*. My name's Gates. There are four of us on this base right now. We came into Suoi Hoa last night off a sub." Gates shook his head and continued talking as Gannett reached out in an attempt to shake his hand. "Don't give any indication that you're friendly toward me. Someone ashore, even in those buildings farther back, might see us. Right now, the others are locating your captain and the officers. We figure they have to be separated. While we're breaking them out tonight, you're going to take over this ship and hold it until we get them back here. That means you've got to get into the small arms locker and distribute weapons to this crew."

"They never took my keys," Gannett answered. "I've got them rat-holed now. It doesn't look like they realize what we have aboard. You can see for yourself. They've got a lot of sentries spread around and they're trying to limit our movement around the ship. But we can pull it off." He grinned wickedly at Ferro. "The Russians seem to be more worried about the Viets, and those guys don't like anybody."

"I'm worried about one thing though, Chief. What do you think about the Soviets having another plant on this ship? You know, maybe someone who hasn't tipped his hand yet."

"There was one officer and two ETs." Gannett shrugged. "I can't think of anyone else." He could become upset when someone proposed an idea that wasn't his own, especially one the ship's police chief should have considered. Ferro enjoyed teasing him, explaining that a martini drinker like him among a bunch of beer lovers was subject to those strange blanks.

"How about the officers? Any new ones report recently?"

"No," Gannett responded thoughtfully. "Mr. Norman was the last and he was the bad guy—a real asshole." He always said what he thought and considered the consequences later.

"They're all ashore so we'll worry about them ourselves. Forget them."

"It's tougher to figure with the enlisted . . . so many come and go on a ship this size."

"How about chief's quarters. Anyone new down there?"

"Not in the last ten or twelve months. Mark here was the last one I remember coming aboard . . ."

"Almost a year now," Ferro said. "I was transferred from *Antietam* at Captain Gold's request. We'd been together before."

"Okay," Gates decided, "it looks like we'll use you people to sanitize. What you want to do this afternoon is have each chief go over every man in his division. Sort out the ones who've been on board less than a year. I don't know how you're going to review each one of them, but you're going to have to be a bunch of pricks. Anyone you can't be absolutely sure of is going to have to be handled differently. Maybe one of your leading petty officers can keep an eye on them . . . or whatever you decide. If you have any real problems, you may have to lock them up out of the way until it's over."

"We could end up with some really pissed off guys," Ferro said with an amused grin.

"Better than someone blowing the whistle on you," Gates answered. "You can do it however you want, but I'm depending on you," he said, looking directly at Gannett, "to make sure this ship is ready to get underway when the shooting starts. If we can forget the ship until the last minute, the odds increase a hell of a lot."

"You got it." Gannett had never worked with the SEALs before, but he'd heard the stories. They never screwed up, always got their part of the job done. He'd be damned if *Gettysburg* would create a problem. "Captain Gold spoke to me just before they took him away. He said the ship was mine until he got back—said to start a resistance. Shit, we're more than half there."

Gettysburg would be humming when he gave her back to Gold!

General Brusilov had finally found someone who knew something about the Aegis project, and a lot more than he had admitted up to that point. An intelligence officer in Vladivostok had given the general the name of a KGB officer in Moscow. Brusilov kept a clerk on the phone continuously until the man finally came on the other end of the line.

"You realize, General," a high, thin, featureless voice stated, "that our objective was to effect a compromise of the system without anyone being the wiser—not you, not anyone in the navy if we could help it. This is scientific intelligence, not military, and we really wanted to avoid your people. The more military aware of such a program, the more chances of someone slipping. There are too many in this clandestine world of ours who would sell that sort of information to the Americans, and then they might have had a chance to build some sort of defense for their Aegis." He concluded this last sentence with arrogance and a finality which seemed to indicate there was no further purpose in their conversation.

Brusilov experienced a moment of sheer anger, the kind that leaves a man shaking, more in fear of what he might have done or said in the next moment if control wasn't regained. He wasn't as concerned for his own position after hearing garbage like that. "You mean to say that no one outside of your little organization was kept informed because the KGB felt there might be someone in the navy who would . . ." He couldn't finish the sentence. It had no ending because this person on the other end made no sense at all to him.

"The best mission is one that is known only to those involved," answered the faceless voice.

Brusilov considered replacing the phone in the cradle. Was he losing his mind? Had the Moscow power structure already talked to this man and dismissed him as a certified lunatic? The world really was coming apart by the seams, at least the one he was involved with. Who the hell was running the KGB these days? For that matter, who was answering the phone in the Kremlin? Had this individual escaped their notice? Not so many years ago they never had to worry about such . . . such . . . what was the word? The Americans had one for it that covered their own CIA's misdeeds. It would come to him.

"Do you realize," Brusilov inquired carefully, "what this secrecy of yours has done to us? This isn't just another one of your silly little international incidents that will be forgotten in a couple of weeks. This is piracy." He stopped for just a moment to consider what he was saying before he decided he really didn't care. He'd take his chances. "Do you know what that word means? Do you understand what that entails in the twentieth century? I wouldn't blame the Americans if they simply annihilated this entire complex." He paused again to seek the proper words. This genius he was talking to in Moscow might just possibly have a powerful boss who had condoned this travesty. "I don't even know if we have the proper data on the Aegis system now that your people are in our hands."

"Ah, good then." Nothing Brusilov had said had apparently sunk in. "I'd heard that only three of them had been rescued from the Americans. You have the other man, too?"

"Who's that?" the general snapped.

"Oh, I couldn't tell you that yet, not if he's free."

One of them had yet to step forward! What manner of men were coordinating this operation? What was there to be gained at this stage by keeping a plant aboard *Gettysburg*? Such a person was more a hazard if he, Brusilov, had no idea who he was. He could cause more damage . . .

General Brusilov slammed the phone down.

CHAPTER 10

Dinh pulled the truck to the edge of the road and turned off the engine. He wasn't quite sure why he'd parked. Although these moments were relatively rare now, he wasn't really surprised it was happening. It was almost an instinctive act, as if something greater than his own soul was now controlling his destiny. He looked out across the water toward Cam Phuc, no more than a mile or so distant. There was no wind and heat rose from the nearby sand in shimmering ripples that turned the land on the far side of Cam Ranh Bay into a green wave. The surface of the bay was so calm that the sun's reflection oscillated with hypnotic surges. If he had been standing, Dinh might have fallen.

After leaving Building 408 where *Gettysburg*'s officers were interned, he'd met York near the supply depot and explained where the American officers were being detained. Then he'd driven north toward the airfield. *There was so much to think about.* After so many years of plotting revenge against a man he'd been sure he'd never see again, Georgi Brusilov had appeared in Cam Ranh Bay as if by miracle. Perhaps he could have, should have, killed him right away—simply shot him dead in his office, or even in the street as he went off to one of those fancy dinners at the officers' club. But Dinh had planned instead, planned exactly how he could exact his revenge while Brusilov suffered for as long as possible. *The man had to know why!*

But *Gettysburg* had changed much of that. He knew he must work closely now with David Chance if they were to be successful, yet Brusilov was almost in his hands! His mind was torn in two directions—but he knew he must help David first. Every time he willed himself to concentrate on what could be their last mission together, that vision returned and he was once again back in his village . . . so long ago.

He pushed open the door of the truck and stumbled out across the beach. Hot sand filtered through his sandals forcing him to move more quickly until he reached the water's edge. Its coolness eased the searing heat on his feet but the visions grew stronger. The tide was out and the waves of heat from the sand combined with the fetid aroma of the bay mud to assault his lungs. It seemed he would suffocate. The land across the bay at Cam Phuc seemed to tilt, first down so that he seemed forced to run, then back up until he was climbing . . . then sliding . . . then climbing . . .

Dinh sank to his knees in the water. The vision was real! He could smell the smoke now, even before he could see it, and he was running toward the village he'd always lived in—Can Fat. The jungle undergrowth tore at his clothes, whipping at his face until blood began to run freely, but he never noticed it. His village, his home, his family were burning up.

Dinh broke into the clearing, gasping for breath, and faced a hell he only could have imagined until that moment. The chatter of gunfire that had come vaguely to his ears as he ran was now all about him and people—old men, women, children—people he knew, relatives, friends, were running, screaming, tumbling from the impact of bullets. There were Russians there in their neat tan uniforms, but for the most part they weren't shooting; they were watching, directing, sometimes even pointing out human targets. It was the VC, his own people who were methodically destroying Can Fat and its innocent victims.

His own hut was at the far end, beyond a cluster of palms, and Dinh ran as fast as he could. He was unaware of the men who fired in his direction, unable to hear the bullets that slapped into the dirt around his feet or screamed past his face. The only thoughts that registered at all were the fears for his family whose faces appeared before him in an album of flash sequences—his wife, Mai, the boys, Nuan and Tri, his daughter, Phuong.

He was oblivious to the smoke swirling through the village as flames leaped from one hut to the next. Sparks from collapsing grass roofs snapped at his flesh. The screams of those who were dying mingled with the chatter of automatic weapons, but Dinh experienced none of it. It would come to him so many times in the future when his subconscious wouldn't allow him to forget the horror, but now he was blind to everything but his own family.

There was his hut . . . flames licking out at him from what had been the doorway, the thatch roof totally involved in flame. He stopped ten feet away, feeling the intense heat for the first time—because of a body curled grotesquely at his feet. His oldest son, Nuan, the one who had promised he would become a soldier when he was fourteen, had been shredded by automatic weapon fire and lay in a pool of still-flowing blood. Beyond, barely out of reach of the flames, was Tri, his ten-year-old body so torn that he might have been a discarded doll.

Dinh raced around behind the hut, hoping against hopeless odds that he would find Mai and Phuong hiding until all the horror disappeared. But there was nothing. No one. No hope. Then, just as he was about to give up, he heard a muffled wail from inside the burning hut. But . . . *nothing could survive in that*! It was impossible.

One of the outer walls fell away as he circled. These were

nothing really, just a simple frame with mud walls, a roof covered with woven leaves for a little privacy, a pounded dirt floor. They burned quickly. Leaping through the hot coals into what had been their single main room, Dinh stumbled over something solid. Thick smoke limited his vision and choked him. He dropped to his knees and reached out frantically. His hands came in contact with flesh, and, as he bent down, he peered directly into Mai's wide-open eyes staring up at him. She was dead, mercifully, and he hoped it had been quick. Her body was completely charred. Only her face, which had always been the most beautiful sight in the world to Dinh, remained untouched.

The agony of loss that surged into his throat was interrupted by the same sound that had drawn him into the hut. A wail, more animal than human, rose from a smoldering pile in the far corner near the family altar. A small metal foot locker, a gift from Chance, lay on top of the heap and he heaved that away. Underneath were the heavy blankets that Chance had also given him only a few weeks before. They were soaking wet and steamy hot from the flames, and there were blackened sections where burning fronds from the roof had fallen. Another wail of fear and pain emerged from underneath as he tore them away and found Phuong huddled in a ball, her eyes closed tight. There was no movement when he bent down, only the subhuman sound that emerged from her mouth with each strangled breath. She was close to suffocating. Mai must have wrapped her in the wet blankets, then the chest had fallen on top—or had it been placed there for added protection?

His memories of the next moments were so distinct that it seemed as if time had stopped, yet it was only seconds. He lifted Phuong up, squeezing her to his chest and murmuring in her ear. She was bleeding from numerous cuts, and he could faintly see sections of her body that had been seared by the flames, but she was alive. Dinh closed his eyes momentarily and pictured the scene—before the hut had been entirely involved in flame, Mai must have wrapped her in the wet blankets, hoping that she might survive by some miracle.

As Dinh squeezed the tiny body tightly, he became aware of the smell of his own hair. It was burning. He could feel blisters rising on his skin wherever the flesh was exposed. Breathing was almost impossible.

Reality returned with the pain. The last section of the roof collapsed nearby. Enveloping Phuong in his arms, he charged through the smoke back into the terror of the village, where flames and gunfire seemed to have engulfed the entire world.

His neighbor, an old man named Thuc who had helped him to build the hut, tottered toward them, the clothes burned completely off his body. At about the same moment Thuc raised his hand toward Dinh, an explosion of automatic rifle fire hurled his skinny little body backwards into the dust. Dinh whirled in the direction of the gunfire to see the tall VC, the one called Po who had recognized him earlier at Song Be, with his AK-47 swinging in their direction.

Dinh stared back transfixed, unsure of his next move, until the tiny body snuggling against his chest moved. There were only seconds and they would be her last . . . that thought catapulted Dinh back into the present—*survival*! He could accept his own death, but Phuong's life suddenly became paramount. The .45 he carried during the operation at Song Be still hung from his hip and now, as he let his daughter's body fall at his feet, his right hand snaked down to the holster.

Po's gun barked as Dinh hurled himself sideways, rolling in the dust until he was far enough from Phuong. Then, bringing his own semi-automatic up, he fired—once, twice, three times—the .45 jumped in his hand. Three times he watched Po's body shudder as the slugs hit him. He staggered backwards from the impact of the first two before the third spun him around, the AK-47 flung outward and landing at Dinh's feet.

There were more shots in his direction. Puffs of dirt flew up around him, too many dangerously close to Phuong, who stared back at him unmoving, her black eyes reflecting the horror around her.

Dinh looked to his right. No more than thirty yards away was the Soviet officer who had been in charge at Song Be. The man was pointing at him excitedly as two of the VC fired wildly in his direction. There was no chance to fire back, no reason to do anything but escape before Phuong was hit.

He scooped up Phuong and sprinted with her under one arm, darting in first one direction, then another, until they were in the relative safety of the nearby undergrowth. Bullets splattered through the leaves, thudding into trees, but Dinh remained low and raced further into the thickening vegetation where it would be next to impossible to follow.

Dinh had no idea how long he ran, but it was far enough away that they could no longer hear the shots and the screams of their fellow villagers or smell the smoke as Can Fat disappeared from the face of the earth.

Dinh choked back the salt water spilling down his throat. It burned his nose. Some had gotten all the way to his stomach and the gulp of fresh air he took before coughing it up immediately tasted of bile.

He was on his hands and knees in the water. The sun continued to beat down mercilessly on his shoulders and the intense heat combined with the thick, still atmosphere brought on a spasm of choking. He reared up, sucking in more air, and stumbled to his feet.

His clothes were dripping wet and clung to his body. There still was no breeze to refresh him. That might come later in the day. He turned in a slow circle to get his bearings. There was Cam Phuc shimmering across the water. And as he turned toward shore, shielding his eyes from the reflection off the hot sand, that was his truck parked at the side of the road.

It was that same recurring vision, he knew, of Can Fat—and little Phuong—that had left him paralyzed and on his hands and knees in the water. She had been all that was left to him. The family altar had been destroyed. The others were all gone . . . both boys . . . there were no more heirs. *His family had disappeared!* There were times he had been sure that picture was gone forever. Then it would return when he least expected it. Today was one of those days, and it had been brought on by thoughts of his Phuong having to serve . . . serve *that man*, and of the ensuing hours—when he would finally be able to gain his vengeance on Georgi Brusilov.

Phuong slipped her arm through Chance's, explaining with a confident smile that there were a number of Soviet officers who had Vietnamese girls, and it would look even more natural for the two of them to be seen that way. Secretly, she was thrilled to be so close to him. Ever since she could remember, she had been in love with this American.

But her memories were unlike most women her age. The days before Can Fat were lost to her, a convenient blank in her existence. The only life she remembered began after that, and all her memories of Chance were happy ones. When she was still little, she thought of him as an uncle, a handsome one that her friends envied her for. As she grew into her teens and became a young woman, she was positive she loved him. There would never be another man like him in the world.

She had dreamed over those years of being able to stroll down a street with her arm through his, and now she actually was—even if it might last only for this day, even if this very brief escape into her dreams was along the main thoroughfare by the docks in Cam Ranh Bay.

For his part, Chance experienced an odd sensation, almost of awe, more for himself than anything else. Without a word passing between them, he understood what was going on in Phuong's mind. This lovely woman, whom he'd always thought of as a daughter, worshipped him. It was in her eyes when she met him in the street. There was no reason for him to chide her for mistaking their real relationship. If it was real love on her side, he was absolutely sure it was puppy love, nothing more. His remaining time in Cam Ranh Bay was short, less than twenty-four hours, and there was no reason to disappoint her. If she wanted to make believe she was in love with a man old enough to be her father, no harm could come from his being kind to her.

David Chance looked down at the slim, soft hand resting on his forearm. He saw grace and beauty in the clear, nut-brown skin that had once been so close to constant pain and ugliness. That mental picture of Dinh and Phuong standing before his tent returned in a brilliant flash. He'd seen many men like Dinh, wounded and bleeding, hair singed, outrage flashing in their eyes. But they were the lucky ones for they were alive.

The children were the real sufferers. They were unable to understand the reason for their pain and misfortune. Phuong had been no more than five years old, tiny, skinny, even smaller in her nakedness and fear. The blood from her many cuts had been smeared until it was impossible to tell how serious those injuries might be. Ugly blisters marred her skin and one foot that might have strayed from under the wet blankets was blackened. She was in shock. There were no tears—nor was there any sign of recognition. She simply stared blankly at him, her body shaking uncontrollably, while Dinh related in a torrent of words what had happened to Can Fat. It took no more than thirty seconds, and in that time Chance had already swept Phuong into his arms and was heading for the dispensary with Dinh moving along beside, tears of rage running down his cheeks. It was only later that Dinh had explained what her name translated to in English—*Phoenix!* Like the bird, she had risen from the ashes. And it was even stranger that her father and Chance were involved in the Phoenix Program where they often left only ashes!

The young doctor knew better than to argue when the two men insisted on joining him during the surgery performed on Phuong. He'd been attached to the SEALs for six months and knew there was nothing to be gained from it. These were unusual people and their minds were normally made up ahead of time, and this Chance was not one to cross.

Her wounds were minor and could be treated there but the doctor was more worried about the burns, especially on her foot. He simply wasn't equipped to handle that sort of injury there. The closest place to treat her was Manila, but he explained how the powers-that-be frowned on civilians in military hospitals. He shrugged. There was nothing he could do about it.

That was when Chance stormed out of the dispensary, bellowing over his shoulder that the doctor better get his ass in gear and prepare the girl for the trip. Six hours later, Phuong was on her way to Manila.

When she returned, with the prewarned doctors assuring Chance that there would be no scarring, there was a new village of Can Fat. With the help of the Seabees, the SEALs had constructed a more secure location near the old one and the few survivors had moved back. David Chance visited her at every opportunity, always bringing some kind of present until he was shipped back to the States. Even then, gifts arrived once a month until the communists took over the country.

He was an uncle she never forgot. When she grew into her teens, she dreamed of the day Chance would return and be so amazed that she had grown into a young lady that he would instantly fall in love with her . . . as she knew she would with him. But there were only two visits after that, both short, both missions where he disappeared with her father—and she knew on both occasions that she was still too young and skinny for any man to notice.

Now, as she ran her fingers through the curly hair on his

tanned arms, she had no doubt he was aware of her as a woman. It made no difference that they were in Cam Ranh Bay, or that he might once again be gone before they could understand each other's feelings. Nor was she concerned that he was wearing a Soviet uniform and depending on her to find the captain of *Gettysburg* so that he might once again disappear from her. Just the fact that he was there was enough for Phuong.

"It seems impossible that you can get into that house, David. General Brusilov has never trusted the Vietnamese. There are always guards all around. And they use dogs." She had just finished explaining that Barney Gold was being kept in Brusilov's personal quarters. "That's the most secure place in Cam Ranh Bay."

"You've been in there before . . . in his home?"

"As a translator. The general speaks our language but there are very few people who visit here from Russia who do. Sometimes I escort them when they're traveling around the base. When he has dinners, I have even acted as a hostess, sitting between one of our people and one of theirs in order that they might carry on a conversation." She giggled. "It's odd because sometimes they think out loud in their own language and have to warn me not to translate. Often they don't like each other. I can tell that right away." She increased the pressure on his arm to slow their pace. She knew it might be forever before they were like this again.

The day was viciously hot, so much so that even Phuong could feel the dampness on the back of her neck. She delighted in the perspiration that rose on Chance's arms and she rubbed gently until the hairs lay flat against his skin. It was something she'd never done before—never realized in her wildest dreams how something so simple could mean so much to her. *This*, she thought, *is what it means to love . . . and it's so easy*.

She looked up to see if he was aware of her thoughts and found him smiling at her. There was nothing in his eyes to indicate his own feelings, but she decided she didn't care. "I will tell you all about the general's quarters and what must be done to release your Captain Gold, if you'll let yourself relax for a few moments." She smiled when he nodded his assent. "There's a beach just a few miles north of here toward the airbase where I often go when I want to get away for a while. Perhaps there will even be a breeze. We can wade in the water—or I will even if you don't—and I can explain where the security is located. I'll even draw pictures in the sand for you," she laughed with delight.

Chance knit his brows slightly. "What ever made you learn all that?"

"My father. He told me that someday we will chase the Russians from our country, and he said I could help by memorizing everything I could about the general's quarters." She squeezed his arm. "I really don't remember what it was like—their not being here, I mean. But it seems to mean so much to him." Then she removed her arm from his and stopped. When he had turned around with an inquiring look on his face, she asked, "Why does he hate General Brusilov so much?"

Chance could see the trust in her eyes and he knew he wouldn't be able to explain part of it without telling her the entire story. "It's up to him to tell you that, Phuong. He has his reasons, and he also has his reasons for waiting until he thinks you should know." He reached for her hand because he knew the gesture would allow him to change the subject. "Come on. Let's go up to your beach and you can show me what a fine little spy you've become."

They arrived at Phuong's beach just as an obviously distraught Dinh was stumbling up from the water toward his truck. The horror that had been Vietnam was once again deeply etched on his face. His daughter would never have to ask that question again. He was willing at that very moment to tell her why he hated Georgi Brusilov more than anything else in the world.

CHAPTER 11

The President's press secretary was fond of reminding others on the staff that "the impossible is impossible to keep quiet." He enjoyed rubbing that fact in people's faces whenever the impossible was somehow leaked to the press. Shortly after the satellite's magic eye revealed *Gettysburg* alongside the pier in Cam Ranh Bay, he made a point of telling anyone who would listen that this was one incident that would be all over the world in no time flat—even though their boss insisted on secrecy.

All that the President needed was a little time to think, a little time to analyze all the advice he knew would be directed at him. As it turned out in an era of instant communications, the press secretary was correct. While it was considered next to impossible to trace the initial leak, the Vietnamese were deemed the most likely source. They were more than proud of their efforts. *Gettysburg* was a major international coup.

The unfortunate result was that the world got to take part in an incident that might have been more quickly solved if the Kremlin and the White House were the only ones involved.

The remainder of the international community saw the incident exactly as both the Americans and the Russians did— *piracy*. Not a soul blamed the American President for the public denunciation he was forced to issue, even though he had hoped for some precious time to marshal US reaction. While most rational people realized it would be weeks or even months before the truth about the incident was revealed, neither did they blame the Kremlin for setting Condition One. That was a logical step in self-defense, especially since the Soviets appeared to be caught with their pants down.

Many in the world were more frightened than they would have been over an orderly and well carried out buildup for war, say a massing of Warsaw Pact troops on the European borders. That would have allowed time for political intervention, negotiation, and a hopeful cooling-off period. The taking of *Gettysburg* was an irrational act that most feared would result in an irrational response. The war alerts in Washington and Moscow meant quite simply that fingers were approaching buttons—panic was starting to overrule reason.

The results were predictable. In addition to the United Nations Security Council, every other governing body of any size offered to mediate, to intervene on behalf of one party or the other, and some less secure nations even announced the taking of sides—just in case. The outcome gave both the White House and the Kremlin some anxious moments since neither could communicate effectively with the other through the overwhelming chaos. In addition, the magnetic storms resulting from the powerful solar flares continued to inhibit effective electronic communications between the seats of government and their military commanders.

The initial discussions in Moscow, centered around KGB assumptions, were to go ahead and analyze the films as quickly as possible. Perhaps whoever had coordinated this debacle had somehow been lucky. Maybe there was enough solid intelligence on Aegis to salvage something out of this mess. They even argued that additional data could be retrieved quickly before *Gettysburg*, which was the equivalent of a gift horse, was released. Their theory was simple and logical—take advantage of a good thing, regardless of how it fell into their laps.

The counterarguments were based solely on the absurdity of the situation. Admit a mistake. Try to salvage some honor before it was too late. It was dangerous but the General Secretary's close relationship with the KGB convinced him that enough trouble had already been caused, that another day or so might not matter. Those international leaders who knew him felt he was pushing his luck, and they said so. His ears were closed to their appeals.

Piracy was a word that flowed over the airwaves from Washington. It had been a long time since the United States felt that the righteousness of their cause was indisputable. Threats should be taken seriously. If *Gettysburg*'s release could be won by the four-man SEAL team that had gone into Vietnam the night before, the Russians would be humiliated for years to come. And, if the President was forced to order retaliation, it would be the most accepted violence since the Cold War began. The American leader knew in his heart he would not allow the Soviets to compromise the Aegis system, one way or the other.

Admiral Lyford replaced the phone in its cradle and looked glumly at his intelligence specialist. It was the first time he had been anything but positive. "Jules, that man is being pushed too hard." He had just finished talking directly with the President.

"And he wants us to solve all his problems." Captain Auger's face cracked slightly with a smile. "I never thought I'd see the day when the President of the United States would find me so important. . . ."

"And so much to blame," Lyford interrupted, "if we don't establish communications damned soon with Chance." He knew that was next to impossible but Jules should know everything that was said.

"Even if communications were perfect, there's only one way we can do that . . . and that's if he tries to contact us. That's a big *if* when you consider that he went in there already running out of time."

Lyford touched his fingertips together unconsciously. He was staring into space. When you sent men—SEALs—into another country on an operation like this one, you didn't ask them to take time out to give you a call. Chance's time was limited, his odds were short, and now the White House wanted to know what he was doing! "Twenty-four hours seems to be it. The man's getting pinged on from every angle, and he's weakening. I think he'll make Cam Ranh Bay disappear by then if he has any inkling that they've compromised Aegis."

"How will he know?"

"I haven't got the vaguest idea. It seems like just hours ago that I felt real good about Chance." When he turned toward his friend this time, neither eye seemed to really be looking at the intelligence specialist.

Auger's Adam's apple bobbed perceptibly. "It was. Don't give up hope. Has he ever disappointed you before?"

Georgi Brusilov squared his broad shoulders and stared into the mirror. The private bathroom just off his office had been a stroke of luck. There simply hadn't been time to change his uniform this day and he couldn't imagine when he might have a moment to slip back to his quarters to do so. The hell with it. His uniform looked decent enough. It was just that he preferred to appear as sharp as the ship captains when they came to visit him each week. This idea had been his own and he wasn't about to alter it just because of *Gettysburg*. Once a week, he held a reception for the commanding officers of those ships in Cam Ranh Bay and he intended to continue that pleasant tradition regardless of the situation—and his pride also had a great deal to do with that decision.

He reflected on the session just an hour ago. Things had

become messy with that Hansen or Golikhov, or whatever the name of that *Gettysburg* sailor really was. The KGB always seemed to produce some interesting agents at the wrong time, and this one had been no exception if he was indeed one of them. Arrogance was a trait that too often displaced good common sense. For a while, this Golikhov possessed an almost proprietary attitude toward the Aegis films, insisting that he was the only one who should handle them. That had been short-lived since the KGB resident in Cam Ranh Bay had no prior knowledge of the project and could learn of no one who did between there and Moscow.

Brusilov decided there was no point in mentioning that he had finally been led to someone in Moscow who was aware of the operation and the fact that there was still another plant aboard *Gettysburg*. This Golikhov had no idea his superiors hadn't trusted him completely, so why tell anyone. Perhaps this other plant might be useful in an emergency. Certainly Golikhov would be of no value until he recovered from his interrogation.

General Brusilov splashed cold water on his face, smoothed his uniform, and decided he was ready. The gold stars on his uniform would more than make up for any wrinkles with these navy officers. Then he passed through the outer office and down the hall to the briefing room that was also used as a reception hall.

He knew when he stepped into the room that it had been a wise decision to insist that the naval officers appear as usual. There was the usual table brimming with the delicacies from home—smoked fish of all kinds, caviar, boiled eggs, meat-stuffed pierogis, and it was all laid out by his chef in an appealing display to emphasize the delightful colors. On either end of the table were a number of liter bottles of various vodkas—lemon, lime, pepper, and pure—set in cakes of ice. It was just like home! Before he arrived, Cam Ranh Bay had been an outpost. Now, after just a few short months of his tenure, it was civilized!

"General Brusilov." His aide's voice had been soft but

the name seemed to echo through the room like a rifle shot. Both of them always enjoyed the reaction. The naval officers, many of whom had been away from their home-ports for months, had been sampling from the table with obvious relish. At the sound of his name, they turned instantly in his direction and snapped to attention, food and drink forgotten. Brusilov smiled inwardly. Yes, that extra gold on his uniform did mean a great deal, certainly enough to draw their attention away from a few wrinkles.

"At ease, gentlemen, at ease," he said, his face remaining set as before, the menacing countenance a trademark. "I don't hold inspections on the navy. This is supposed to be a pleasant evening where we can eat and drink together and help each other." He allowed just a trace of a smile.

There were no balalaika players strumming in a corner, but there was a tape playing similar music from home in the background. Brusilov recognized the commodore of a destroyer squadron, the senior naval officer present, and motioned him over by the vodka. The general poured a glass for each of them, then turned to the assembly and offered a toast to the Soviet Navy and her valiant officers. The commodore had witnessed this general toast before and knew that Brusilov always achieved his desired effect.

The general was built for this kind of drinking. His stocky wrestler's body appeared to thrive on it. But he also knew enough to sample the foods profusely as he made a point of talking directly with each of the captains. A few of them had attended these parties previously and had grown comfortable enough to bask in the glow of one of the more powerful reputations in the military. Although it was difficult for many of them to imagine the stories they'd heard of the man's brutality, a healthy fear, combined with enough vodka, attracted them to Brusilov with a level of respect that bordered on awe.

"I don't believe I've had the pleasure." The general extended a hand to the youthful-looking officer who appeared much too young to be a captain second rank and offered what passed as a smile. "This must be your first time in Cam Ranh Bay."

The other inclined his head slightly, his own smile no more pronounced than Brusilov's. "Captain Pietr Boldin, sir. My ship is the *Vice Admiral Kulakov* and this is our first time in Cam Ranh Bay." His words were clipped and precise, his demeanor much like the man he was speaking to. He looked about the table and gestured, almost in disapproval. "It's been a long time since any of us have seen anything quite like this. My crew would be impressed with such splendor so far from home. I'm sorry they aren't allowed to join us. But I thank you for inviting me." It was exactly the response he'd been trained to offer.

Brusilov had met this type before, promoted above the others in his age group and, as a result, cool and arrogant. They were generally overconfident and had a certain disdain for senior officers, especially those outside the navy. "I would consider it a distinct honor if you would join me in a glass of vodka, Captain." He poured a glass of the pure, clear liquid before Boldin could refuse and handed it to the man. "I met one of your officers earlier today and I wanted to say how impressed I was with him. But first, a toast to the success of *Vice Admiral Kulakov*." He downed his glass in one gulp, his eyes never leaving the other's face, as an indication that he expected the same from Boldin.

The strained smile disappeared from the younger man's face and one eyebrow rose slightly. Boldin had never been a drinker. But it was a matter of respect—and self-respect—to do the same. He closed his eyes and drained the glass, taking a series of deep breaths to force the liquid down his throat.

"Another, Captain?" Brusilov had already refilled his glass, his point made.

"Thank you, General, but no," Boldin answered. Both his voice and the expression on his face had softened. He could not match this army general, nor was there any purpose in trying. It was mutually understood that Brusilov knew Boldin was similar to him but that there would be only one Brusilov on this base. They both smiled at the same time, acknowledging this meeting of the minds between themselves, without anyone else in the room noticing.

Brusilov instantly liked the man. He preferred the cocky ones to the subservient. He even enjoyed those, like Boldin, who chose to test him. "Your weapons officer is the one I met on the pier today. A fine young man."

Boldin looked at the general curiously. "My weapons officer? I wasn't aware that he'd left the ship today. Are you talking about Captain Surkov, sir?"

Brusilov folded his arms thoughtfully trying to remember the name. "A pleasant young fellow, mid-size, built like I am, but very dark eyes . . . piercing eyes. He said his name was . . . Nikitin . . . a captain third rank. He must be one of your senior officers . . ." Brusilov had been looking away as he described Nikitin but he stopped in mid-sentence as he turned back and saw the expression on Boldin's face.

"There is no man by that name on *Kulakov*, General. Nor do any of my officers fit that description." He placed the glass he had been holding on the table. "Are you sure he was from *Kulakov*?"

It was Brusilov's turn to be uneasy. "He also said he was involved in security procedures."

"I'm sorry, sir." There was a curious inflection to his voice as he continued with a rather odd expression on his face, "I have no one by that name. There is obviously some mistake."

The general could drink a great deal and the effect of the vodka had created only a minor sensation in the back of his head. He was surprised now to find himself completely sober as he stared back at Boldin. Who the hell was this Nikitin? Were there more KGB prowling about Cam Ranh Bay already? It certainly couldn't be anyone else. . . .

Very quietly, so that he might not be overheard, Boldin said, "I understand your surprise. There has been a great deal happening here in the past day or so. I promise you there is no Nikitin on my ship and I'm sure, as much as you must be, that this has something to do with that American ship."

"Yes . . . yes, I'm sure it does." After a moment's hesitation, Brusilov added, "You know, if I had any choice in the matter, I would have turned that ship around and sent her right back to sea."

"I agree, General. And I'd like to make a suggestion, if you'll be kind enough to consider it. You're so busy with all the problems this ship has created, let me offer to assist you. I don't like being fooled any more than you do. Let me look into this matter further. No one really knows me around here. If I can help, it will make both of us look good." The smile that creased his face was meant to be conspiratorial. "I think we both understand each other."

It was a suggestion Brusilov might have made in the same position. "I appreciate your offer, but what do you think you might be able to contribute?"

"I was assigned to our embassy in London for eighteen months. I speak English quite well. I also spent a great deal of time in intelligence while I was there. Who knows what I can do? Your time is limited and your problems are going to increase before they let up. Is there any harm in letting me try?"

"None, Captain." Why did he bother to mention that he was fluent in English? "What would you like to do?"

"I'm selfish. I'd like to talk with the captain of that American ship first. I'd like to learn more about her." He decided Brusilov possessed the insight to figure out his motives. There was nothing to be gained by being coy. "I plan to wear gold like yours, General. Being the first Russian naval officer to visit one of those Aegis cruisers would mean a great deal."

"He's tough."

"I would assume he would be. But I think I can handle myself."

Yes, this one could take care of himself. Why not? He just might come up with something we've overlooked. "Fine, Captain. I'll ask my aide to arrange it for you," he concluded curtly. With that, Brusilov excused himself, said his goodbyes to the other naval officers and, after a word with his aide, departed.

Back in his office, he found himself reflecting on a whirlwind of problems. Why, he wondered, did I agree to that? That was when he acknowledged to himself that the situation with *Gettysburg* posed more problems than he could handle. He had no idea who was operating covertly in Cam Ranh Bay, but he knew such things happened. The KGB did things like that. But why now? And wasn't the base secure?

There were any number of spaces on a ship the size of *Gettysburg* where a sailor could disappear for as long as he wanted. Chief petty officers made it a point to know each one of these compartments. It was rare that a chief utilized one of these spaces himself, rarer still when they monopolized them as they had done that day.

Under the direction of Ben Gannett, each of them had been pouring through the service records of every man in their division who had been aboard less than a year. It was boring work, more so because it was almost impossible to stay awake in those spaces, many of which weren't air conditioned. A service record provided the same level of excitement as paint drying. Looking for the unusual in these records was akin to searching for the proverbial needle in a haystack. But two enlisted men and an officer had already been able to fool the entire navy. It made sense there could be more, and Gates had made it clear that one more plant could mean the end of *Gettysburg*, even the loss of every man on the ship. When they reported back to Gannett, every division had at least one man who could be suspect.

"Now that we did this, what the hell are you going to do about it, Ben. I can guarantee you Steinberg isn't going to be happy about spending time in the brig, even for a reason like this. He considers himself very intellectual, very much above the rest of us, and . . ."

"And if there's the slightest reason to wonder about him, it's what we call tough shit." Gannett had a way of making the obvious blunt. "Besides, I'm not sticking them in the brig. You're just going to have to explain to him . . ."

"You explain to him. He doesn't listen like other people do."

Gannett grinned at the chief radarman who ended up with more than his share of eggheads, the bright ones who joined the navy because they had no idea what to do with themselves. They scored so high on their tests that they spent their first year in the service in schools where they were told how bright and wonderful they were. Then chiefs like Hennessey, who'd joined the old navy, won them and sputtered every night in chiefs quarters about the spoiled brats they were sent.

"I'll speak to Steinberg, Mike. But what do you have on him?"

"Only six months aboard, doesn't spend much time ashore with the others, reads a lot of strange stuff on the side, and he likes to take the opposite side whenever his watch section is talking about something. That seems to qualify for strange in the navy."

"I'll tell you, Mike, any other time we did something like this we'd have a discrimination suit on our hands and there'd be all sorts of pointy-nosed lawyers wandering around the ship. But Steinberg is going to disappear for at least twenty-four hours if you say so."

Hennessey snorted. "It'll probably be the best twenty-four hours I've had in the last six months . . . regardless of what happens . . ."

It was the same with the other chiefs. Some had Steinbergs they were worried about. Others had stronger or weaker reasons. But in the end, there were eleven sailors who were quietly spirited away. Seven of them were slow enough to even agree with Chief Gannett that they were about to make a unique contribution to their ship. Steinberg and three others disagreed as had been predicted.

Only one, a radioman, put up a struggle. He was terrified. The convincing occurred on the port side of the main deck, opposite from the pier. There was a scuffle, some shouts, and the man was almost secured when one of the Vietnamese guards appeared. As Gannett said later, they were lucky his rifle was slung at his shoulder. Before he could bring it level, he had been disarmed, knocked unconscious, and followed the unlucky radioman down into the engineering spaces.

The noise brought other guards, their rifles ready. But all they encountered was a bunch of sailors wrestling on the port side of the ship. They shouted some vague threats in Vietnamese and left the Americans to their foolishness.

Chief Gannett had accomplished everything the SEAL, Jimmy Gates, had asked of him before the sun set that day. There was only one problem—the Vietnamese guard now hidden in the engineering spaces. How long would it be before he was missed? What would they do then? It seemed more than likely that he would have to go over the side.

Nguyen van Dinh had not left the base that night with the other Vietnamese workers. Even if he had been ordered to go, it would have been impossible in his state of mind. That afternoon had been a brutal, wrenching experience, his memories of Can Fat boiling to the surface in a vivid machine-gun–like display of scenes he could never wipe from his mind.

Again and again, he saw the bodies of relatives and friends staring sightlessly back at him as the Viet Cong methodically destroyed the village. It was pure retribution. There had been no mercy. Blood and flames seemed to leap at him from every direction as he knelt at the edge of the water of Cam Ranh Bay that afternoon. Only his wife, Mai, appeared to him unscathed, her face as beautiful and peaceful as ever—it was always that way until the end when the dead paraded before him. Many of the victims had been murdered in full view of Dinh and Phuong and their deaths were repeated once again. Always, always their eyes, no matter how dead they were, seemed to focus on him and ask—*why? Why had this massacre been visited upon Can Fat?*

And Po would always appear to him again, the man who shouted his name during the raid on Song Be in the Parrot's Beak, and the only one Dinh was able to kill during that fateful afternoon. The last vision was of Brusilov, shooting at the two of them, Dinh and Phuong, as they escaped from the village, his bullets spattering in the dirt around them, tearing at the undergrowth as they disappeared into the jungle.

Now, there would be no more running. After all these years, his time had come. *Revenge.* He had lived for revenge. No, not completely. That wasn't entirely true. Seeing Phuong grow up had been equally important. But now she was a woman . . . and his mission, with the exception of Brusilov, seemed complete. Brusilov had taken his sons from him, had burned the altar of his ancestors, had taken his honorable family—and for that he would die.

Now Chance had returned. That was so important. The sensations that swept over him from the moment David Chance had appeared on the beach had triggered these emotions. That was why he had once again been tormented by the visions of Can Fat—because Chance would see this through to the end. He would make it happen. Brusilov would not survive the following day. He didn't care about himself, whether he lived or died, but he did care about Phuong—*Phuong whose name meant Phoenix*—and who like the phoenix bird had literally risen from the ashes.

This was *Phoenix* all over again! This time the job would be finished. More than twenty years before, Dinh's own PRU and the SEALs had set the stage to reverse the terrorism, to give back to the VC and to the Russians the same thing that had horrified innocent villagers. But there had always been one difference. During the Phoenix Program, they had gone after the VC officers and cadre who were ordering or perpetrating the murders. *Take out the leaders and they'll think twice*.

And so it was. Song Be . . . retake their prisoners, kill the captors, and they'll leave you alone. They'll understand that if they continue, the Phoenix Program will make their lives miserable. It had worked for a while. But after Song Be . . . less than twenty-four hours. . . .

There had been one hole in the fabric, one glaring hole that Dinh could do nothing about over the years. Brusilov had escaped them!

But in less than twenty-four hours, he would have revenge.

There was so much to think about, and so much sorrow —sorrow for everyone in Can Fat who had believed in him—intruding upon his mind. That was why he had experienced one of those recurring attacks on the beach. But it would be the last one. The emotion had overwhelmed him for the final time . . . or was it the fact that he wanted to make sure he saved Brusilov for himself?

Dinh looked in the rearview mirror in the truck he was sitting in and his gold tooth winked back. Tears ran down his cheeks but he was actually smiling. Everything should be all right now. He was smiling because Brusilov would soon be dead. Then these dreams that came to him, even when he was awake, these horrible fantasies, would be gone.

Phuong's head snapped around as the engine in the old truck coughed into life. Her eyes were still red but she'd stopped crying. The hot sun had quickly dried the tears on her cheeks.

For that moment, the sorrow and anger generated by her father's story of Can Fat was replaced by fear. She found quite suddenly that she really did not know her father well, at least not this secret part that he'd kept within himself for so many years. Would he remain irrational enough from this fit of anger that he might do something foolish, something that could endanger him?

Chance took her shaking hands in his. "Your father can control himself now. He has that one objective in mind. But he won't do anything until *Gettysburg* is released. He promised me."

"And then?" Her dark eyes appeared even more beautiful to him when they were sad.

"And then I'm glad that my name isn't Georgi Brusilov." He gently brushed another tear from the corner of her eye. "I can't tell you exactly what will happen by this time tomorrow. I hope everything will be over by then. But if the general is still alive, he'll wish he wasn't." *And*, Chance thought, *if any of us are alive then the Kremlin will have won*.

"Why didn't my father ever tell me before?" The answer was already so obvious. Her lips twisted into a hurt pout before the words were out. "I would have done whatever he asked," she protested, knowing she was wrong.

Chance smiled. "The perfect daughter? Is that what you want me to think?" He placed a finger to his lips. "No. You know the answer as well as I do. You couldn't have done what you already have if you'd known who Brusilov really was. And you might have tried something silly yourself and ruined it for everybody. Your father was right. Everything you have learned is going to be very important."

Her eyes held his own momentarily. She didn't want to believe him. She didn't want to hear the truth. Then she looked down at their intertwined hands and nodded. Everything seemed so right at this moment.

"He's been very patient over these years," Chance continued. "You don't understand Phoenix and you don't know what people did to each other—family to family, sometimes brother to brother. Your country is one nation now and these things belong to people like your father. He's waited a long time—we both have—and revenge is for those who have suffered with patience. Somehow, you don't remember Can Fat. Do you understand what I mean?"

Again, she nodded, this time without looking up at him.

"Your father knows that the most important thing is to free the ship. He's a military man once again. Today is more important than the past. He won't do anything else until that's done. Then it's his turn."

She looked over her shoulder as the sounds of the truck shifting into gear came to them across the sand. As it moved down the road, they could see Dinh waving a hand to them above the truck's cab.

"See, he's all right now. He just had to get it out of his system. We all have different ways of doing that. His way frightened you."

"Perhaps you know my father better than I do." The pout was there again.

"Only at times like this, Phuong. And these are the only times Dinh and I really have had together. Maybe that's why we became such good friends." He shrugged. "We're so much alike."

When he said that, she looked up and studied his eyes. What she saw, or sensed, shattered the dreams she'd toyed with as they strolled down the street on the base just a few hours before. He was right. That same hardness, almost an opacity, lurked in the back of his eyes. She'd seen it from time to time in her father. It was intentional and there was no room for anyone else.

"You want to know about Brusilov's quarters," she said abruptly, withdrawing her hands from his.

Chance appeared surprised. He reached out, as if she'd just taken something away from him, then pulled back just as quickly. She was right. "The ship's captain is all alone," he said. "Brusilov was smart to separate him from his officers . . ." and then, "I have to."

She drew diagrams of the structure in the sand, showing

the location of each of the security devices. Her memory was exacting, even to the point of being sure where Barney Gold was being held. "You can get through all of these. I'm sure of that. But the dogs . . ." Once again her eyes reflected the same fear that she'd held for Dinh.

He took her hands, brushing away the sand. "Thank you for caring. I'll be able to handle it, if you'll be around to help me afterwards . . ."

She tried to resurrect the pout. Her lips twitched two or three times before the smile appeared, slight at first, then full as tears once again flowed down her cheeks.

CHAPTER 12

Barney Gold had spent much of the day staring out of the single window of the room he occupied in General Brusilov's quarters. An efficient doctor had thoroughly checked him, two nurses had tended to his wounds, and he'd been told that nothing that had happened to him was life-threatening even though he might feel that his head was collapsing inward. He'd refused all but the simplest medications. The window looked across to the piers of Cam Ranh Bay. There was certainly nothing better to do, and he'd convinced himself that whatever he might see could offer a great deal more than any intelligence specialist could figure out with a satellite photo. If he ever got out of here, his impressions would certainly be expected during his debriefing.

He'd even been studying the Soviet naval officer walking briskly toward Brusilov's quarters with interest. This man, just in the assurance of his stride, was the type to attract attention. Although it had been a hot day, with the early evening not much cooler, this one seemed unconcerned with the heat. His uniform looked fresh, he appeared comfortable, and there was a definite purpose in his gait. Some people just appeared to be thinking. Perhaps that was the reason he caught Gold's eye.

When the door to his room opened, Gold expected to see a Soviet marine with his dinner. They had been overzealous in their treatment. Instead, the door was held open by his marine guard for the naval officer Gold had been watching moments before.

"Good evening, Captain Gold. I'm told that you're feeling better and I hope you don't mind a visitor." The accent was distinct and harsh, but the words were spoken with a precision that mirrored the purpose Gold had noted from his window. This tall, slender officer obviously had used English for more than simple conversation. He was conscious of pronouncing each word for the benefit of his listener. "Forced separation can make one very lonely."

Gold nodded. "I doubt I have much choice in the matter." He studied very serious blue eyes set close together in a thin, aquiline face and saw that these, too, radiated a seriousness of purpose. "Is this another interrogation session?"

"On the contrary." This time the words ran together as if they had been rehearsed by someone who didn't really understand them. "I came on my own—with General Brusilov's permission, of course. You don't have to talk with me."

"Who are you?"

"Captain Pietr Boldin, commanding officer of the destroyer *Kulakov*." He walked over to the window and pointed. "That one, the new one at the pier beyond your's. The lines of our ships are quite different, Captain, the purposes much the same."

"What do you want?"

Boldin spread his hands in front of him. "To talk . . . to exchange ideas . . . to learn more about your ship. I promise I'm not here to interrogate. I'll exchange any information I can with you. I don't expect you to provide me with any state secrets. . . ."

"Everyone else here seems to."

"That's only because you're here, Captain. It's convenient. Wouldn't your people do the same if I happened to be in your place?"

"Probably. But I didn't choose to come here."

"I have yet to meet anyone who planned on your unusual visit." Boldin's blue eyes were disconcerting. He was trying to make pleasant conversation, but they still gave the appearance of boring into his listener's. "It is unfortunate . . . but you must make the best of it. I can call for some vodka. Would you care . . ."

"No. I'm satisfied with what I've been given."

"Would you try to escape from us if you had the opportunity, Captain?"

"Certainly. Wouldn't you?" Gold snapped back irritably.

Boldin smiled and nodded in agreement. "Is there someone trying to assist you to escape from here?"

Gold frowned. "Hardly. How could someone do that if we weren't expected to visit?" He was quite certain his own facial expression revealed nothing—*could they have already learned that there were SEALs on the base?* After all, there had been but one brief contact and there'd been moments when he seriously doubted that.

"Just a question." There was no indication whether or not he'd seen anything beyond Gold's response. "I was curious . . . because someone claiming to be an officer from my ship talked with General Brusilov today. He was not my officer."

"So?"

"Curious. That's all." He studied Gold for a moment. "Boredom must be difficult, especially all alone like this."

"There must be a reason you're here."

"There's a reason for everything I do." Boldin's smile was mirthless. "I want very much to see your ship. In return, I am willing to offer you a personal tour of my *Kulakov*."

"Why not just wander over to the pier and go aboard. I would imagine anyone who wants to can do that," he concluded disdainfully.

Boldin's lips turned up at the corners again. "If you watch more closely, I think that you will see very few people allowed aboard your ship. There are Vietnamese sailors acting as guards and they're very difficult to pass. Although their Captain Trang's intent was to turn your ship over to us, it seems she is an unwelcome gift and no political rewards, or whatever these people were hoping for, have been promised yet. That's not what Trang expected. The result is that access is difficult. I'm also told that your people are uncooperative."

"Well trained, I'd say." It was Barney Gold's turn to smile.

"If I found myself in the same position, I'd hope my crew would act in the same manner." Boldin pulled out a chair for himself. "That's why I didn't want to go aboard as an uninvited guest. What do you say?"

"Of course, I'd like to get back on my ship, even under those terms. That would have to be up to your General Brusilov."

"If I get him to agree, do we have a deal?" There was anticipation this time behind the mirthless smile.

Gold nodded. "Being an uninvited guest, and a suspicious American, I would like a tour of your ship first, Captain." He wasn't sure why Boldin was offering him such an opportunity, but anything was better than waiting in this room. There was also a chance to see a new Soviet destroyer firsthand, something no other American had yet done. Once he was aboard *Gettysburg*, regardless of the situation, there might be a chance for something . . . anything . . . "Is that fair enough?"

"Considering what you've been through in the past couple of days, I might agree with you." Boldin studied the bruises across Gold's face and the white patches on his head. This American was tough. "However, the only way you're going to be released from this room is if you go along with General Brusilov's wishes. And that means your ship first, Captain Gold." He rose to his feet. "I can also see that you don't trust me. But, if I can get you out of here for even a couple of hours, will you accept that as the favor of a curious brother naval officer?"

"I'll try." Gold didn't believe for a second what Boldin was saying but there were more chances for something to happen beyond the walls of this room that was his prison.

Phuong drew in a deep breath, held it, and exhaled very slowly. Then she squeezed her eyes tightly shut. Even though there was enough light from the far end of the building where the night guard's desk was located, she had to prove to herself that it could be done in the dark.

With her lower lip clenched firmly between her teeth, eyes closed, she moved down the corridor, her bare feet soundless. Her slippers remained outside by the window she had used to gain access to the building. Phuong had prepared herself for something like this, just as her father had taught her, but she had never imagined what it would be like to actually do it. Now, with each step, she understood exactly how it felt to be taking such a chance. She was terrified, not as much by what she was about to do but by what she now knew about General Brusilov.

It had been hard for her to comprehend the brutality of the man she worked for, harder still to realize that she and her family had once been the enemy. She knew now she was afraid of Brusilov but she also was aware of an unreasonable hatred. If she was caught, was it possible that she might be forced to reveal the presence of Chance and his SEALs? Would they torture her?

Her father had explained how such methods were a way of life with Brusilov. Chance had elaborated on it less than an hour ago, encouraging her to succeed, preparing her for the worst. Then he had kissed her goodbye. Phuong was sure he felt nothing, more a kiss for a sister about to go on a long trip—but for her it was the most romantic experience in her short life. The man she knew she was desperately in love with had taken the time to work with her, to expand on everything Dinh had taught her, to share some of his own knowledge and daring—*and he had sent her off with a kiss*!

She had taken the proper number of steps. Now she turned to the right, extending her arm in case she was about to walk into the wall. One step . . . two . . . three . . . nothing. She peeked. There was no wall, nothing but the next corridor exactly where anticipated. A couple of more steps, just as she had been instructed, then stop . . . listen, with your eyes closed. *Always listen with your eyes closed and you will hear sounds you never imagined*—Chance had said that. She strained her ears. Nothing, not even the rustle of a cockroach.

Phuong opened her eyes. The light from the night guard's desk did not affect this corridor. Turning, she saw that it provided only a faint glow behind her. And her father had been correct—her vision was much improved by keeping her eyes shut. Ahead, she could discern shadows that indicated her position but she also knew she could find her way even if she were blind.

The stairs were ahead. She counted her steps once again, pleased when she executed a right turn and found herself almost at the center of the first stair. Ten steps . . . then four more around the first landing . . . and another ten steps brought her to the second floor. Turn left. Retrace her path on the first floor. . . .

Don't try to be too careful with each step. You make less noise if you walk as you normally would. Chance had been right. Her confidence was growing.

And there it was—her own tiny office, the one next to Brusilov's. The general's was directly over the night guard's position, the front of the building so that he could view the piers. Once again, she took a deep breath as she removed the key from the container in her pocket and inserted it into the lock of Brusilov's outer door. Quietly, softly—Dinh had explained that this was done with the gentleness of brushing something from one's eye, not with the anxiety of punishing a mosquito—the key turned in the

lock. She held it in that position, pushing open the door
before releasing and withdrawing the key. Then she inserted
it in the lock on the opposite side and once again turned it.
Then, so gently that she appeared to be smoothing a curtain,
she pushed the door shut, releasing the lock only when she
was sure it was firmly against the frame.

There. She'd done it! The door was locked to the outside.
Dinh had explained that unless she made a noise during the
night guard's rounds, he would only rattle the door handle
to make sure it was secure. No Russian's office had ever
been disturbed since they'd come to Cam Ranh Bay. There
was no reason to expect it would happen now. She mar-
velled at the advice from her father and Chance. They must
have been wonderful working together, wonderful and
terrifying at the same time . . .

Phuong took the small container from her pocket and
pressed the door key into the soft wax, the same she had
used over a period of time to make an impression of each of
the office keys. Then she removed the key next to it.

Chance had warned her to act exactly as if she belonged
there. If she was too stiff, too cautious in her actions, there
would be a mistake. *You can do it. You come from good
blood—the best!* So she pulled back Brusilov's chair and sat
down, just as he would. When the top center drawer of his
desk was unlocked, all the others were also. She used a tiny,
narrow-beamed flashlight to inspect the contents of each
one. Nothing was moved from side to side. *One at a time or
you'll make a mistake.* Each item was picked up to find
what was beneath, then replaced in exactly the same
location.

She covered each drawer in this manner but there was no
sign of any of the Aegis film from *Gettysburg*. Brusilov
couldn't have sent it off anywhere. That she was sure of.
She'd overheard him on that phone call to Moscow,
repeating that anything could happen to that film en route
and then where would they be? The proper equipment to
develop this type of film wasn't available in Cam Ranh Bay.

An expert would arrive there tomorrow morning with the right materials to inspect it and confirm what this Hansen/ Golikhov person claimed. So it had to be in this office.

The most logical place was the general's file cabinet, one which he alone used. That key had been a difficult one to copy since he kept that locked in his desk drawer. She remembered waiting many days before her opportunity came. Brusilov had left his desk open when he went to use the toilet at the rear of his office. In that time she'd tried to locate the key in his top drawer to make the wax impression, terrified that he would return at any moment. But her fear had gotten the best of her and she fumbled through the drawer unable to locate it, almost fainting with fear when she heard the telltale flush. Afterwards, her father had been most understanding, saying there was no need to take such a chance as long as the one key, the desk key, would allow access to the other.

Once again, she shut her eyes tightly. This time she had no interest in enhancing the sounds around her. She was thinking of Chance, remembering that goodbye kiss. Could he be thinking about it now? Would he realize how important it had been to her? He must understand that he had sent a woman, no longer a girl, no longer the skinny teenager he'd seen the last time, but a sensitive woman off to Brusilov's office on a very important mission. Would he have allowed her to do it if he loved her?

No . . . no that wasn't what she should be thinking. That had nothing to do with anything. Her father had trained her for this and Chance had simply taken the time to offer more help. But did he? . . . No! She opened her eyes. There was so much to do. Forget such thoughts for now.

She took out the file key, leaving the top drawer of the desk open, and went about her search in the same manner. It was a two-drawer cabinet perched on a small table. There seemed no method in Brusilov's record keeping. Nothing appeared in order to her. None of the file folders were named. Instead there were symbols that apparently meant something only to the general. Phuong knew that she was supposed to locate some type of film, but she had no idea if it would simply be placed inside the folder or in an envelope. As a result, she was forced to search each envelope she encountered. It was time-consuming, and her concentration overwhelmed her senses. Also, it was a struggle to push thoughts of Chance from her mind.

Her mind was wandering when she should have had an ear cocked. When the door handle rattled, it was already too late. Instantly, her body grew rigid with fear, a folder in her left hand still held up to her flashlight. The guard was outlined against the glass of the door by the loom of his own light. Once again, he shook the door handle. Then she saw him press his face against the glass. Some silent warning in the back of her mind forced her to extinguish the tiny beam of her own light.

As the sudden blackness enveloped her, Phuong realized the guard would also have noted that. If only . . . but it was too late to correct that. Then she studied her own hand curiously, unaware of how she was willing it to move as it replaced the folder in the drawer. She knew there was a reason for such an automatic reaction. But she could not yet move the rest of her body.

In the enveloping darkness, it seemed as if she were part of a dream, that she was somewhere else, observing the action. Everything experienced in her fear was in slow motion, the guard's movements outside, the sound of his key in the door, the handle turning . . .

Something began to move in her mind, some electrical signal seemed to be jostling brain cells, sending a message that was overpowering her fear. If she was caught . . . if she was caught . . . if she was caught—the message struggled against other impulses that attempted to push that basic fear once again to the forefront. But finally the message became too powerful. *If she was caught, the entire effort would be doomed. Her father, Chance, each of the*

SEALs, and how many others would all die if she failed in her part of the mission.

There was a provision for such a problem. Her father had provided it; Chance had insisted that she prove to him she could use it. Then he made her promise. Yes, there was still a way to avoid compromising the entire plan.

The door swung open slowly. *The guard must be just as scared!* She was granted one more second to return to rational thought. His light flashed to the opposite corner of Brusilov's office. She reached into the front of her blouse, fumbling for the small instrument.

The light swung toward the desk, falling on the opened top drawer. It held there momentarily.

Phuong pulled the weapon out, dropping her flashlight in the process. It clattered on the floor as she struggled to hold the vicious little instrument properly.

The light shifted in her direction. *Was it still all in slow motion or was that just the way it seemed when you expected to die?*

She held it in her right hand and pushed the button. There was no sensation, no sound, no indication that it was operating as she had been instructed.

The beam of the guard's light settled on Phuong, momentarily blinding her. She could see nothing, had no idea what he would do next, aware only that her own breathing had ceased. Then there was a soft grunt, more of surprise than anything else. First the light, then the gun, fell to the floor with a clatter Phuong was positive reverberated through Cam Ranh Bay. She could see no more in the resulting blackness than in the glare of the light. Then there was a crash as the guard pitched forward onto the floor. Surely the sound must have awakened the entire base.

Her father had been absolutely right about how quickly the poison worked. He said it had been effective back in the days of the Phoenix Program, but she never imagined anything could work like that. The little needle gun was effective only at close range. Usually the victim had no idea of his fate because there was no sound. The poison attacked the nervous system so quickly that there was no opportunity to cry out. Chance had explained how he'd watched the Montagnards use that in the mountains at much longer distances. There, the victim never knew there was a soul nearby, never knew the sound and horror of being a target. But they were dead before they hit the ground . . . just like the night guard. The SEALs had been in awe of this silent killer.

Then she was trembling, first the hand holding the weapon, then her whole arm, finally her entire body. She dropped to her knees, holding the needle gun before her as if it were an offering to some vengeful god. This was the first time she had ever done anything like this to another human being. Even now, she had trouble scolding the village children when they disturbed the old ones. She had never known violence and, until that day, had been unaware how much of it had taken place around her. *Can Fat* had been a name totally unknown to her.

The shaking graduated to an odd numbness. Reason began to return as she hugged herself, hands rubbing her body in a desperate attempt to halt the trembling. More messages were racing to her brain, so quickly that it was impossible to put them in order. *She must move!*

The guard's light—that was the first thing. It was still shining. She crawled over on her hands and knees and snapped it off. Then, very tentatively, and only because her father had explained how wise it was to make sure, she reached out for his wrist to check for a pulse. There was no doubt about it, none at all, no sign of life.

She rose slowly to her feet, as if any rapid motion might shatter her trembling body. Shivering? Yes, she felt cold all over. It was a totally foreign experience. She'd known this sensation of cold only when she was sick with a fever. The trembling, the numb feeling, both sensations seemed to have left. She was just cold.

Did she have time to continue to search for the film? Of

course, that was her mission! The needle gun had slipped to the floor when the trembling began and now she replaced it inside her blouse. The tiny flashlight once again was in her hand as she climbed to her feet, pushed the outer door shut, and returned to the files.

But this time she would be alert to anything new that might become a problem. She wasn't about to be surprised this time.

And that's when she heard the ringing. It was a long way off, almost too far to be heard, but her senses had become heightened by such a close call. It was a phone ringing . . . somewhere in the building . . . somewhere . . . why it was the phone at the guard's desk. That's why she heard it. It was right below where she now stood.

If it wasn't answered, why . . . someone would be appearing quickly!

Her hands moved more rapidly through the files. She was halfway through the second drawer when she found a small section of film in an envelope. Even held against her flashlight, it made no sense. But it shouldn't have meant anything to her in the first place—and this was the only film to be found. There was printing on the outside but it was in the Russian alphabet.

What to do? She'd been told to look for rolls of film in a tube of some kind. This was flat. She couldn't turn on a light to study it, and she wouldn't understand it anyway. Any moment someone might come in downstairs to search for the night guard. Maybe Chance—or someone—might be able to read what was on the front of the envelope if she copied it down.

She tore a sheet off the notepad on Brusilov's desk and wrote down the Russian letters as best she could, stuffing the paper in her pocket.

What now? Should I . . .

The phone on Brusilov's desk jangled raucously. Phuong jumped back in surprise. Who would call the general at this hour? It rang three more times. If there was no answer below at the guard's desk, someone might check to see if Brusilov was working late as he did occasionally. With no answer to either one . . .

Don't leave a reason for anyone to think you might have been there. Chance had explained that if something was obviously wrong, then people tended to search more carefully. If everything seemed normal at first glance, they would go on to the next place. Why wasn't he here right now, beside her, holding her . . . anything . . . would he ever know how much she loved him? Would he ever know how much she needed him right now?

She had replaced everything she had looked at. All the drawers were closed and locked again. The only obvious problem lay at her feet as she moved warily from behind the desk—the night guard. There was nowhere to hide him in the office. He was much too heavy to carry for any distance.

Then she remembered the day she had tried to copy the key to the file cabinet, when the sound of the toilet flushing had been a warning. That was the only chance she had now. She pulled open the door. Yes, that could be it. It was tiny, but it was the only place—*and it was her only chance.*

Phuong turned back to the corpse with a churning stomach. She bent over very gradually, her eyes shut against the horror until she was forced to open them to see what she was doing, and grasped the guard's arm. With all her might, she began to drag him toward the bathroom at the back of the office. He was limp, a dead weight. But inch by inch she yanked and dragged until the body was in front of the doorway. She slumped against the wall, exhausted, positive she hadn't an ounce of strength left. But in the background, she heard the telephone ringing persistently underneath at the night guard's desk, and that was all the encouragement she needed.

With one final burst of energy, she pulled the corpse into the bathroom and pushed the door shut. But it wouldn't close. Tears formed at the corners of her eyes. It wasn't going to work. But something told her to turn on her light.

She shuddered as the beam fell on a foot twisted grotesquely through the door jam. Once again, she could feel the trembling resume as she gingerly bent the corpse's leg so she could shut the door. The cold she'd felt moments before became a chill coursing down her spine. She had to get out. If she didn't, she would faint and that would ruin everything for Chance, for her father, for everyone.

As she ran down the corridor, she remembered her last rational steps. Her father had explained in detail what she should do. Chance had been more pleasant, softer perhaps—because he explained why she should cover her tracks, how much it would mean to them all. And she had done exactly as she was told—before the hysteria took over—closing the bathroom door, checking the desk and the file cabinet once again, shining her light on the floor and seeing the guard's gun and flashlight lying there, throwing them in with the corpse, and remembering to lock the door as she left. Then she ran.

She didn't need to see. She had no idea of her location as she passed down the hallway to the stairs, tripping down them two at a time, down the first floor corridor.

There was a ringing sound in her ears that grew louder until it seemed to surround her. It increased in intensity until she was sure she would scream. But she had to keep moving.

Approaching the lighted area near the front of the building, she realized it was the phone at the guard station, insistent, incessant. The sound probed into the depths of her brain. There was intense pain, or was she just imagining all of this. Would it kill her before she escaped through the front door?

She pushed open the door and rushed into the night . . . colliding headlong with another person!

My God . . . my God . . . she said to herself, . . . *I've failed . . . I've . . .* and she felt herself swimming into unconsciousness. The world seemed to swirl faster and faster as she sensed strong arms holding her. She struggled briefly . . . but they were too much for her.

Had she failed? She strained her eyes through the enveloping darkness and the last object she recognized as a dark wave of unconsciousness settled over her body was David Chance's face.

She was unaware of being placed in the front seat of a truck or of the short trip to safety.

CHAPTER 13

Fran York had been named *Sergeant York* by the SEAL instructors the first day he reported for BUD/S training in Coronado. It was a nickname that stuck and he had more than lived up to it on distant shores during a legendary career. Peter Merry, his partner, had never received a nickname but there was no person who met him who could ever forget the man. All SEALs were adept in appearing without warning and dispatching their enemies silently, but York and Merry were superior to most. They considered these abilities an art form and their unique talents were the major reason Chance insisted they accompany him to Cam Ranh Bay.

Like the others, they had come on the base from Suoi Hoa in Soviet naval uniforms but their assignments required enlisted dress. Dinh had not been able to acquire any Russian marine uniforms. Their initial assignment was to analyze the two armories Dinh had designated for them the night before. If there was a command decision made by the Kremlin that could be considered dangerous to Cam Ranh Bay, it was simply that the base was considered so secure by Vietnamese and Russian alike that little attention had been directed toward contingencies. While Chance realized that the first indication of a firefight would bring out the heavy weapons, he also had learned from Dinh that they were normally stored inside the armories. If access to the heavy weapons remained open, there was no possibility that four SEALs and a couple of dozen unarmed naval officers could survive such large caliber fire and still free *Gettysburg.* The obvious answer was to neutralize each armory with explosive charges that could be detonated by an electronic signal when the time was right.

Soviet marines had been assigned to guard both the officers and the armories. Since it was a foregone conclusion that both York and Merry would enhance their chances over the next twenty-four hours with marine uniforms, it was simply a matter of selecting the proper time and place to acquire them.

Marines were apparently the same worldwide. The Russians followed the traditional four-hour watch schedule, splitting the evening dogs for meals. That meant that those who relieved at eight that evening would remain off watch until at least the same time the following morning. That was more than enough time for York and Merry to complete the first part of their job.

Part of their plan was a gamble, but, luckily, the Soviets had transported their traditions to Cam Ranh Bay. It seemed that stopping for a beer after duty was not a lost art with the Russians. The enlisted men's club was just to the south of the piers, not far from one of the armories. The marine barracks were at the northern end of the base and it was a long walk back to their bunks for those who enjoyed too many beers.

York and Merry meandered into the club shortly after the eight marines just off watch had made themselves comfortable at a large table. The SEALs sipped the foul-tasting Russian beer and watched. They would wait until just before the last two marines were ready to leave. Four of them eventually rose in a group and departed. The others looked as if they would stick together. Now it was awkward. What if the other four were to leave together also?

"Drinking games?" York asked with a grin.

"Doesn't look like we have a choice," Merry replied. "But it's going to have to be your ball game." He was a Vietnamese specialist and his command of Russian was weaker. "You do the talking. I'll do the drinking."

"Mind if we join you?" York inquired as they sauntered over. "We'll buy the next round." He knew their regular navy uniforms lowered them in the marines' eyes, but they were still senior to all of the men at the table. "I recognize you from home," York continued, thrusting a large hand toward one of the marines.

His hand was accepted tentatively by the other, who looked at him curiously. "No, you must be mistaken. I don't think I've ever seen you in my life."

York clapped him on the back. "Of course you have. Shuya! You're from Shuya! I've always been good with faces."

The marine withdrew his hand. "I've never heard of Shuya before. Where the hell is that?" A look of irritation spread across his face.

York reached in his pocket and slipped some money into Merry's hand. "A round for everyone here while my friend and I figure out where we've met each other before." They couldn't let this opportunity slip away. He pulled back a chair and sat down by the marine. "Why Shuya is northwest of Moscow. You mean to say you really aren't from there?" He laughed good-naturedly. "You're playing a game with me."

"I come from Orel, the opposite direction," the marine replied. He folded his arms across his chest.

"Then maybe we were at the same station together." York recognized one of the ribbons on the man's chest. "How about Africa? I was on the horn a few years back. . . ." He'd been there in Yemen with a dozen SEALs on a covert operation that set the Russians back six months.

The marine's eyebrows raised and he studied York more closely. "Yemen? Were you there?"

York broke into a huge smile and clapped the man on the back again. "You see, it just took a little time. I was wrong about Shuya . . . but, like I said, I never forget a face."

The two men talked for a few minutes until Merry returned with a tray of beer and passed it around the table. It was unusual for Soviet marines to mix with sailors and York insisted on a toast to old friends, then to the marines who were the best fighters he'd ever seen. He gave the quieter Merry money for another tray of beer.

"How about my friend there, do you recognize him, too?"

The marine squinted at Merry's face. "Was he there at the same time?"

"That's where we became good friends. He doesn't say much but there's no better man in a tough situation. He saved my life once. We're lucky to be stationed together again."

York remained the life of the party. He made sure the marines never had to buy a round and he kept the conversation away from Merry. When one of the marines rose unsteadily to his feet and suggested that they all return to the barracks, York shook his hand and that of the man next to him who also looked like he was finished for the night. "Maybe tomorrow night we'll do this again. I enjoyed talking with you."

And as Merry mumbled the same words, York turned to his new friend, "Hey, have one more with me. This doesn't happen every night. Let them go back and we'll show how friends drink to old times."

It was an offer presented in a manner that couldn't be refused, and the two remaining marines returned to their seats for one more. And before that last beer was finished, Merry somehow had another round on the table.

The marines were more than happy to explain their system of operation to their new friends. They told where the kennels were located, when and how many dogs were used and how they were rotated, how often an officer checked on the guards, what kind of security backups existed, even about the makeshift system for guarding *Gettysburg*'s officers at the warehouse. It was all very efficient, they pointed out, exactly as it should be when Soviet marines were on duty.

When it finally came time, York asked, "Do you have a ride back to your barracks?" aware that the marines walked everywhere on the base per order of their senior officer.

"Never ride anywhere," came the tipsy response. "Marines walk all the time in Cam Ranh Bay . . . to set an example for everyone else."

"Well, you can use one this time. My friend here has the use of a truck over behind the frozen foods warehouse. You come with us and we'll give you a ride close to your barracks. Your officer will never know, and you can catch up on some extra sleep before you go on duty in the morning." He winked at Merry and shooed him toward the bar. "He's going to get some sausages at the counter so we have something to eat on the way back."

It was too good an offer to refuse at that time of night. The idea of avoiding a kilometer and a half walk and eating some good sausage at the same time allowed the two marines to die with pleasant thoughts. They never knew that Merry's truck didn't exist because their necks were neatly broken within seconds after they rounded the corner of the frozen food warehouse and stepped into the shadows. The sausages, never touched, remained for the dogs. It was quick and absolutely silent and in less than ten minutes their corpses were stuffed under a tarpaulin at the far end of the lot. *Gettysburg* would be gone before they were found.

Tom Davis, *Gettysburg*'s communications officer, was the first one to notice the odd, irritating sounds from above. He'd been dozing off on the tiny cot issued to each one of them but the two by six canvas offered little comfort. Snores indicated some were having better luck than he. There were five others involved in a quiet poker game in the far corner. He struggled to shake off the daze that comes between the netherworld of sleep and wakefulness. Often, sounds that would normally go unnoticed are enhanced during this return to consciousness, and that was exactly what was pulling Davis back into the real world.

It was a scratching sound, almost like a mouse, and it came from overhead. The lights on that side of the room had been extinguished so that the roof was a hazy outline above him, but Davis knew no mouse could be that persistent, not in the same location—a smart mouse kept on the move. As he concentrated on the sound, it seemed to become louder, and eventually it centered on an exhaust duct. He seemed to be able to magnify it simply by staring at its source.

The thought of waking the others crossed his mind, but he dismissed that quickly. If it was all in his imagination, he'd look foolish. And it was even possible that he might create enough noise by waking the others that the guards would take a look in at them. He was wide enough awake now to know that no one, Russian or Vietnamese, would be wandering around on the roof at this hour. Whoever it was had to be looking for *Gettysburg*'s officers. *Just keep your mouth shut, Davis, until you're sure of what's happening.*

It was a fascinating, almost hypnotic, experience until he was sure, even in the shadows, that he saw the roof move. Now his eyes were wide open. This was no dream. There had definitely been a persistent sound and, now that he thought about it, it sounded more like someone working with a screwdriver. And it wasn't a dream when the duct—not the roof—actually moved. With a grinding of metal, it twisted to one side, held for a moment, then slid back in place. That was it. That was enough. No telling what was going to happen next, but it was definitely time to do something.

"Hey, Commander, wake up." He shook Glen Marston, the ship's executive officer, who was sleeping quietly next to him. "Tell me I'm not dreaming." He pointed upwards. "Look at that duct, right where my finger's pointing. Just keep your eyes on it."

The duct cooperated, once again sliding to the side. This time, a hand appeared to bend it tightly back, where it remained.

Marston looked over at Davis, then rose on an elbow. "It moved," he commented thickly. "What the . . ." He had only one good eye. The other was swollen shut. His neck and one side of his face were discolored from the beating he'd received from Filipo. His head throbbed when he rose to a sitting position.

Davis jabbed him again, pointing upwards. A face peered through the hole where the duct had been and surveyed the room. The eyes stopped on Davis who was staring back. An arm appeared and its hand pointed down to the floor below where some of the others were sleeping and made a signal indicating that space should be cleared. Then both the arm and face were retracted.

The two officers stared in wonder as if they were privileged to be seeing a magic show put on exclusively for them. Then, silently, they moved from cot to cot, shaking each man awake with a warning whisper to remain quiet. Soon, the face reappeared, saw that the space had been cleared, and pulled back. A pair of mystical black boots appeared in the opening, followed by legs covered by black pants tucked into the boots.

The man who was lowering himself slowly from the roof also wore a black shirt and a black beret. He dropped easily to the floor with a loud thud among the men who stood in a curious circle. The poker players turned from their game to study this individual in the uniform of a Soviet marine.

The value of the shock factor had once again been proved. Not a sound had been made since this stranger landed so gracefully but one finger had already gone to his lips pleading for silence. "Sergeant York here," he hissed, grinning broadly. He'd used his nickname in that manner before and he loved the reaction each time. In bars, it drew laughs. In situations such as this, it guaranteed he was an American before there was any chance of trouble. "You gentlemen would probably like to break out of here soon, compliments of the SEALs, of course."

York had the advantage of surprise. There was barely a murmur as he spoke. The SEALs' reputation was based on credibility. When York finished explaining when they would be leaving, and how they would get back to the ship, they believed him. Then they boosted him back through the hole in the roof and he pulled the duct back into place. There was no reason at this hour to reseal it. There was also no chance that any of *Gettysburg*'s officers would sleep again that night.

Merry and York were demolition experts. They enjoyed explosives like others enjoyed investments or the law. Since they were unsure which building they might have to enter, much of their daylight hours on the base had been spent studying access to critical structures. Blowing up buildings wasn't all that difficult. It was selecting the absolutely critical location to set your charges, then completing the job as quickly as possible and getting out intact that demanded special consideration. The results almost always justified the effort. The two SEALs had already decided where the critical structural locations existed at the two armories. Security had been a greater concern until their drinking partners of a few hours before had solved what they considered their final problem.

A barbed-wire fence, more for show than security, surrounded the largest armory. It might have slowed a mob intent on storming the place but Merry, after satisfying himself that there were no security devices buried beneath the dirt surface, simply crawled under on his belly.

There was a single dog roaming the grounds that night, just as the Soviet marines had claimed. It was a powerful, mean-looking animal but it also suffered from what proved to be a fatal weakness. Once it was engrossed with the sausage Peter Merry had saved from earlier in the evening, he clubbed the dog hard behind the right ear. The animal crumpled without a whimper. The Soviet guards continued to do exactly what he had anticipated, nothing. Manning the front gate appeared to be a self-fulfilling job that evening.

According to their drinking friends, this was the building where the explosives, possibly even the highly sensitive plastic, had been stored in a specially designed rear addition. That was simple confirmation of what they had already expected after sauntering past the building a couple of times earlier that day. York had claimed that additions to armories, particularly when they appeared to be of special construction, usually meant sophisticated explosives.

This was exactly the type of challenge Merry appreciated. He loved explosives, loved that instant of demolition when all his training peaked in a terrific blast. One well-placed charge on either side of that rear extension, plus a smaller one inserted by the air vent, would keep the fire fighters, and a hell of a lot of others he expected, involved for enough time. With luck, he might be able to set the whole damned building off, Merry decided, as he finished placing his explosives.

They'd agreed the second one would be tougher. Merry had spent some time studying the sentries' habits to see if they were any more diligent than the others, and he was glad when York appeared. Until that time, the marines seemed to be far more interested in a discussion they were having. Occasionally, Peter had picked up some of their words drifting across to him and York confirmed what Merry suspected—the marines were involved in an analysis of certain Vietnamese women, and some of the comments involved especially detailed descriptions of their capabilities. Tradition once again—that was certain to keep them busy for a long time.

"Have you seen the dog yet?" York whispered.

"Don't know where the hell he is. The last one was on his

own . . . just wandering and sniffing . . . doing a better job than any of the marines we've seen. If I had to guess, I'd bet there isn't one if we haven't seen it yet."

"Keep your eyes open anyway. I don't think we have anything to worry about with those guys." York put his finger to his lips and listened to more of their discussion before snickering, "They're talking about some young lovelies we really need the time to meet some day." They were both on their bellies now. "Any trouble getting under the fence at the other building?"

"None. Not a thing buried in the dirt. No security to speak of. These guys are feeling awfully damn comfortable. If there wasn't anything at that first one, I can't imagine why this one would be any more secure. But I did save the heaviest charges for this one. I don't think they have anything inside to add to the show." He indicated the canvas sack behind him. "I picked up the second bag on the way over. We ought to have enough to at least bring down that back wall . . . four charges."

"Let's do it. Chance is going to be pissing his pants if we don't get back in time."

That section of the base was deathly quiet. There was no breeze, nothing to mask any sound they might make. After probing cautiously in the ground with his knife, Merry was first under the fence. Then, carefully, he hauled in the sack of charges that York slipped under after him. He crawled over to the safety of the closest wall, stretching his body flat on the ground, until York joined him.

"You know," York whispered, "now that I think about it, this is one of the buildings the Seabees put up before our guys had to beat it out of here. It's one of those with the reinforced structural supports against the walls, the ones that are supposed to stand up against the typhoons. You know what I mean?"

"Yeah. Isn't that the type that's supposed to keep the roof up even if the wall blows in?"

"And if a support beam like that went down . . . then

the whole goddamn roof ought to cave in." York was silent for a second. "What the hell. Let's give it a shot . . . two charges right in the middle where that support should be. This is where they store the heavy, long-range stuff."

"If it comes down, I promise I'll tell everyone it was your idea," Merry snickered. But even as the last muffled sounds were coming out of his mouth, he was sucking in his breath in surprise. One hand moved cautiously along the ground and grasped York's arm tightly.

Neither of them moved for a good twenty seconds. Then York felt the iron hold gradually ease until Merry's hand was off his own. Without having to look, he knew the other was going for his knife. Every movement was in slow motion, calculated not to excite whatever or whoever had caught Merry's attention.

York sensed there was someone or something nearby. Merry was good close in—as good as anyone he'd ever seen—but York sensed it might take two of them to handle this. The only part of his body that moved was his head. As he lifted it and turned with painful slowness, he stared out at a huge dog. It was standing stock-still no more than twenty-five feet away, eyes peering intently in their direction. He'd seen them like that before. The dog would be quivering in anticipation, nose twitching in an attempt to identify this alien intrusion, heart pounding as it prepared to attack.

Perhaps it couldn't smell them, York thought. The air was dead. He had been taught to put himself in the place of the other creature, man or animal, at a time like this. He'd been told to imagine what the animal senses and then he'd know how to cope if it attacked. Dogs' eyes weren't that great, not on a dark night like this, but that beast knew there was something foreign in the shadows of that building, something that hadn't been there previously.

There was no sound. Of course not! That kind of animal would never make a peep unless it was attacking . . . or about to! How many seconds? York caught the faint glint of steel out of the corner of his eye. Merry's knife was ready. But if that animal attacked, surer than hell there'd be all sorts of noise and those guards would instantly forget all about that Vietnamese honey.

The dog was moving! One step forward, nose up searching for something, then another, then rock still sniffing the air. Another step. Head now down close to the ground, then gradually rising higher until it was stretching for any smell that would identify whatever was up against the building. A couple of more steps! Now there was no chance it would turn away.

York knew there had to be a potent aroma about them, especially with that beer earlier. Now he could taste it once again. It had become suddenly overpowering, that sour, flat flavor that assaults the tongue half an hour after the fir.. . beer—especially that Russian piss, he concluded.

The dog took two steps to one side, again lowering its head, craning its neck from one side to the other. No, the eyes weren't so great but the senses were superb! Then a few more steps in the other direction. And it was getting closer, no more than eight or ten feet away at the most. Christ, he thought, it could leap that far. As he imagined the animal flying through the air in his direction, York also tried to concentrate on exactly what he would do, how he would turn his body to defend himself, the quickest movement to get his knife up.

The goddamn animal was airborn! There was no warning, no sound. He'd been absolutely wrong about the growling or snarling. It was just coming at them, looking bigger and bigger, mouth open with white teeth exposed, ready to slash . . . about to screw up the entire. . . .

Merry's knife seemed to rise from nowhere as his body rolled to one side. Instinctively, York was moving in the other direction, away from the dog. The next sound he heard was the impact of the knife as the dog landed full force on top of it, the weight of its body driving Merry back down. Then there was a low howl—just a very short one—as the shock and pain reached the animal's brain. But it was loud enough to be heard.

Merry and the dog became one as they rolled away from him. It was as much the impact of the animal's charge as anything planned by Merry. York reacted, springing on top of both of them. He found the dog's muzzle and wrapped his hands around it in a powerful grip before another sound could escape—and before the beast might lock his jaws on the other man's throat.

York could feel the heat of the animal, the heavy fur, as his right arm slipped down to lock around its throat. Then he was pulling the head back, yanking it away from the man underneath, anticipating that the huge body would writhe under him, attempting to escape . . . to kill . . .

"Hey . . . hey . . . easy man. It's dead." Merry's voice was soft but urgent. "How about getting off me. You're going to break my leg . . . son of a bitch . . ." he hissed as York rolled aside, the dog still in his grip with the creature's blood pumping out on his arm. "No kidding, you can let go. It's really dead . . ."

York released his grip. The dog's head flopped limply to one side. There was no movement. He pushed it off onto the ground. "Christ, that's one hell of an aim you had there."

"Luck. Pure, stupid luck . . . goddamned thing landed right on the knife and just plain impaled itself." A sigh of relief escaped Merry's lips. He reached over and removed the knife. "Now we know where the dog was . . ." He wiped the blade off on his pants before carefully drying the handle.

"And with the yelp that thing let out, you better bet your ass that someone's going to be wondering what the hell's going on. One of those guys out by the gate has to be back here super quick." York paused, recognizing the glow of a flashlight coming toward the near corner. "Stay right where you are. Don't move. If it's just one of them coming around that corner, I'll take him. Two . . . we'll just have to play it by ear . . ." His last words disappeared into the night air as he faded back against the building, crouching down as low as he could to become just one more shadow.

The guard behind the light exhibited too little caution as he meandered around the corner of the building. The loom from the flashlight swung from one side to the other until it caught the outline of two forms on the ground. Merry remained as still as the dog. The guard stopped instantly, dropping into a half crouch. Carelessness became caution. York saw his hand flash down to the gun on his hip.

The light moved in a wider arc, revealing nothing other than the two prone forms, then settled back momentarily on the dog before swinging onto Merry. What the guard saw was a dog with a pool of red blood spreading beside it, and a Soviet marine nearby, apparently hurt, certainly motionless, or perhaps even dead. Advancing slowly on the body, the guard bent down and extended a hand, touching Merry's shoulder tentatively.

From the moment the guard's concentration centered on Merry, York was moving like a cat, quickly and very close to the ground. He brought an open hand up swiftly under the man's chin with such force that his head snapped back at the same moment his body was being driven forward into the ground by York's weight. There was no sound beyond the collision of the two bodies—except for the sharp crack as the guard's neck snapped. Even before the guard's dead body hit the ground under York, Merry was on his feet with his knife ready.

"That's one," York grunted, perched on the limp body like a jockey. "But if he doesn't show up at that gate soon, his buddy's going to get nervous."

"No problem." York couldn't make out Merry's face well in the dark, but he could sense that the other was grinning as he answered. "You speak their language like a native. Go out there and surround that other guy. I'll set the charges. How's that for a deal?"

Merry peered cautiously around the corner of the building

after he was finished. He could tell by the shape of the guard at the gate that it was York. He sauntered up to the opening in the fence. "Where's your friend?"

"Asleep." York pointed to the figure perched on a chair inside the tiny guardhouse. "When they come to relieve him though, he's never going to wake up."

"Chance isn't going to be happy about this. It was all supposed to be done without leaving a trail."

"It almost was. If all we had to worry about was ourselves, we'd have made it. Come on, we'll prop the other guy in here, too."

When the two guards were set in chairs like a couple of drunks, York stepped back to consider their work. "Perfect. Not a mark on them. Maybe a little dirty, though I suppose that can't be helped. If there's no reason for anyone to nose around the building for a while, these guys might give us that last little bit of spare time we need, except one of us is going to have to stop back when the watch section changes to greet the next two sentries. Now, that's just one more problem on our shopping list."

Merry looked perplexed. "What's that?"

"I promised *Gettysburg*'s XO that we'd try to get them some small arms." He was feeling cocky now. "Can you imagine how you'd feel running around an enemy base waiting for people to shoot at you?"

"I'll bet everything we could ever want is laid out in the produce section—just inside." Merry jerked a finger over his shoulder.

Ten minutes later, they had disappeared into the night with their stolen truck loaded with weapons for *Gettysburg*'s officers.

CHAPTER 14

After twenty-six years in the navy, much of it in naval intelligence, Jules Auger found that one side of a telephone conversation was usually more than adequate for his purposes. Perched on the arm of the sofa across from Admiral Lyford, he amused himself by studying mood changes while the head of special warfare chatted with an unknown party on the other end. It had been a direct call, no intermediaries this time. Captain Auger decided the boys in Washington were getting edgy after analyzing the moves of their counterparts in Moscow. There was obviously big game on the other end. That was for sure. Since it was Washington, he guessed it might even be the President's national security adviser. Rolly Lyford rarely called anyone "sir" unless he decided the other man had earned it.

"No, sir, there is no better man than Chance for the job." How many times did he have to explain that? "If he can't do it, then no once can." He smiled to himself as he said that and, as his lips turned up at the corners, his dimples emphasized his five o'clock shadow. He was badly in need of a shave.

"About twenty years now, sir." Lyford's forehead wrinkled while he jogged his memory. "First time was right here in Coronado when he was in training . . . then two years later when I commanded the teams in the Delta . . . and then a couple of other operations . . ." He'd covered enough background for the party on the other end because Auger could see he'd been interrupted.

"Yes, sir, I fully understand your position. In situations like this one, David and I have always just made a habit of trusting each other. Chance said they would be in contact *if* there was time." He placed a great deal of emphasis on the *if*. "If not, then we assume he just didn't have an opportunity. I'm still comfortable with that." Patience was reflected in his eyes as they wandered about the room separately, eventually settling on Auger with a look of resignation.

"My firm recommendation is to stick with the original plan, sir. Absolutely. With this sunspot problem, we might not be able to talk anyway. This may be his toughest assignment but I assure you there have been others that demanded just as much. . . ." Lyford's eyebrows rose as he stared back at Auger, this time indicating there was a lot more he would have liked to say if he hadn't been interrupted again. But, obviously, you also didn't argue with this one.

"I appreciate your honesty, sir, and I agree you have no choice but to go ahead with your original plans if she's still alongside that pier when your time limit expires. But I'd be ashamed of myself," he nodded unconsciously, "if I failed to recommend strongly that we give Chance at least the full amount of time we agreed upon . . ." His eyebrows were raised again but this time he smiled and nodded as the third interruption was to agree with his position.

"Yes, sir, I know you've always been a man of your word. That's consistently made our job a lot easier." He jotted something down on his desk pad as he listened. "Yes, sir. I will. Right away."

Jules Auger wished he'd had a tape recorder. He'd seen people dub in the other end of a conversation before and this one would have been terrific for a takeoff on the guy in Washington. When Lyford placed the phone back on the receiver, Auger said with a knowing grin, "Don't tell me. Let me guess—Harry Allen."

The admiral shook his head. It wasn't the Secretary of the Navy.

"OK. How about the national security adviser . . . what's his name?"

Lyford's head continued in the negative.

"How about Magnuson, his old buddy who's always hanging around whenever things get tough."

"Wrong again." He was enjoying the game.

"I don't do games very well, Rolly." His Adam's apple bobbed as he wet his lips. "I give up. Who?"

"The President."

"Called direct?" It was Auger's turn to raise eyebrows.

"I assume he still knows how to dial a phone." Lyford winked. It wasn't often he had Jules on the defensive. "When I answered, he was on the other end. No one else involved." He held up the desk pad to display the telephone number he'd written down. "See. Direct line. No White House operator, no Harry Allen, no Magnuson, no nobody but number one. Wake him up any time, he said."

Very little managed to impress a jaded old intelligence officer like Jules Auger but he decided right then that he and Lyford had one hell of a job for the next five hours or so—keeping the President from panicking before David Chance could do his job.

The sleepy guard in Building 408 yawned, blinked a couple of times, and knew it was time to start worrying. He wasn't the type to fret unnecessarily and he was still comfortable because his prisoners were behind a reasonably secure metal grillwork. But there was obvious reason for concern—all of the Americans were wide awake and it was still the middle of the night.

Earlier in the evening, everything had seemed normal. Some of them played cards while others talked or slept. But for the past half hour they had been gathered in a circle around one of their group. At first, he was just curious. Now his attitude was changing. There was definitely something afoot. The guard wished he could speak English so he might have some idea of their discussion. It seemed quite animated at times, almost a little scary. The most unusual feature was that none of them were heckling him. When he realized that, then he also experienced a healthy fear.

He decided to wake up the other guard. As far as he was concerned, their agreement concerning sleep was viable only while everything remained calm—and this didn't look right, even if there was no earthly way the Americans could escape. After all, where would they go in Cam Ranh Bay if they did? Certainly not their own ship!

"I'll take my group this way," Glen Marston continued. "Just in case the captain's not there, I should try to be the first on board along with the chief," he added, nodding at Mike Hanafee, the chief engineer. The executive officer pointed out the path he would take back to *Gettysburg* as soon as they were released. Considering they were all avoiding the most commonly used streets, it was the most direct one.

York had left a crude map of the base with the various routes Dinh had laid out for them. Chance, he explained, said it would be crazy for the officers to travel as a group, too easy to be seen, recaptured, or even shot on the spot. There would hopefully be some weapons available, York added. He and Merry just had no idea what they'd be able to provide in such a short time.

"Tommy," the XO said to Tom Davis, "you take this southerly path on my left. It's going to take you closer to the Soviet ships, and probably to sentries, so we'll make sure you have the heaviest artillery. Jim, you and Rick can decide which of you takes the paths on my right. I really don't care." Marston was sending the younger officers with Jim Ellard and Rick Ireland. They'd move faster with the impatience of youth and he was hoping there would be enough confusion brought on by four separate groups that more of them might make it back to *Gettysburg*. Junior officers were slightly more expendable. "If there's any firing down our way, you got to act just like the cavalry."

Jim Ellard was spirited. He enjoyed an opportunity to blow off steam. "I'll take the farthest route. The four of us can keep everyone busy for a while." It was the cockiness of youth.

Marston pointed a finger in Ellard's direction. "Remember, Jim, think first. Don't draw fire for the hell of it. We're separating because this SEAL says that's the way to do it. We've got no idea yet what he's going to be doing and we don't want to screw up his plans. This is a one-shot deal."

Ireland just beamed. He and Ellard had become friends, one of the reasons the XO hoped they'd coordinate if anything went wrong. "I'll put him on a short tether, yank his chain if he screws up." It all sounded like a marvelous adventure.

"Just think . . . think about liberty somewhere if any shooting starts," Marston responded. They had been too young to know the other Vietnam. "You guys have never run into that kind of thing before." The sound of the guard opening the door ended their talk. Marston tore the paper into tiny shreds as the *Gettysburg* officers turned to their nervous guards with broad smiles and made the peace symbol.

There was nothing the guard could say or do.

Jimmy Gates had always been invisible—when he was referred to as *The Shadow*, it was with respect. Chance strained his eyes for even the slightest movement. Nothing. His ears detected only the normal night sounds that he'd been listening to for ten minutes. Very cautiously, so there could be no way a soul would know he was there, Chance cupped his watch and pushed the button. The face lit up for only the instant that it was depressed. Gates was ten minutes late.

Then Chance sensed movement, rather than saw or felt it, at his side. Pure gut reaction caused him to suck in his breath.

"Sorry about that. I had to take the long way . . . and I needed to make sure it was you." Jimmy Gates materialized next to him. "By the way, I'd squat down next time I checked my watch. People don't usually look down for a light like that." He touched Chance's arm. "I don't mean to be critical, but I would have cut your throat if I hadn't figured it was you."

Chance squeezed Gates's hand. "You're right, Jimmy. You scared the shit out of me. I've put in a hell of a lot more hours than this without doing something stupid. Must be age creeping up on me. Keep an eye on me, my friend."

Gates touched Chance's hand again. "Care for one of these?"

"Not yet . . . not if I can avoid it. The old bod doesn't react to those things like it used to." In days gone by, they used pills by the second day, anything to keep alert. Of course, they could last so much longer back then, and still get home safe and sound. But these days Chance found he couldn't handle the crash that came when they wore off. What did they call it—age, wisdom, common sense? It was one of those he knew.

Jimmy Gates was a youngster when he decided to become a SEAL. Blond and blue-eyed, barely shaving, but muscled like a young stallion, he was looking for action. He was the type who eventually might have hired out if he hadn't found the SEALs. Jimmy was a San Diego kid who used to watch from the stern of his father's fishing boat when the SEALs took their trainees to swim in the cold water of the bay. Later on, he perched on the rocks above the Hotel Del and watched them flounder ashore from their rubber boats. Every horror story he heard about SEAL training made it all sound like that much more fun.

The navy recruiter decided the kid might be a little crazy to claim, right from the start, that he was enlisting to become a SEAL. His civilian friends were absolutely sure he'd gone off the deep end. And his instructors, after they did everything they could to understand what motivated him, accepted Jimmy Gates, even encouraged him. It was never necessary for him to assimilate the mystique of the SEALs—he arrived with the raw desire.

In Vietnam, David Chance at first dismissed the new, blond kid as one more recruit who had to be weaned no matter how tough a man was to qualify for that duty. The kids—the cocky ones who thought they'd live forever, regardless—were usually early casualties. After the first mission, one that moved over the border into Cambodia twice in four days, Chance was told that Jimmy Gates was the best point man in the business, at least the best since David Chance. The boy had the instincts of a cat. There was little to teach him that he didn't already sense. He seemed to work as well in the dark as midday. His superb hearing was balanced by his sense of smell.

Jimmy Gates never graduated from high school, yet after three months in country he spoke fluent Vietnamese. When he returned for his final tour with a PRU during Phoenix, he became Vietnamese. He wore black pajamas and tire sandals and he took his meals with the unit he advised, squatting back on his heels by their cookfires eating strange food covered with fish sauce from a bowl just like theirs.

But Jimmy was blond and blue-eyed and his skin burned after too much time in the sun. That became part of the legend that grew in the Delta because "the white haired one who travelled at night" took no prisoners. The intelligence he provided was unquestionable but he was never willing to take the chance of returning with a prisoner because that might endanger his unit. That encouraged the VC to put up "wanted" posters with a picture someone had filched from his service record. They said his head would be adequate to claim the reward and some even said the senior cadre would have been satisfied with a blond scalp.

They never came close.

Jimmy Gates never cared about the reward for his head, but he was upset when his war ended abruptly. The SEALs were sent home. Jimmy began looking at the ads in *Soldier of Fortune*.

David Chance was the one who probably saved Gates from himself. For years after that, he took a personal interest in making sure that the young SEAL was sent off on those special details that often produced results, but never medals—not when they never took place officially. And when life was quiet, he saw to it that Gates was in another country training indigenous special forces.

In return for his interest, Gates was available whenever Chance was given command of a new operation. There were no more than a half dozen SEALs needed for those missions because Chance picked only men like Gates, men who adapted to those situations like a second skin. That was why he'd sent Jimmy aboard *Gettysburg* that afternoon. He had learned to speak Russian as well as any Soviet officer. But his favorite part was always walking into the lion's den—*just to say that he'd been there*.

Now, as Chance thought about the pills Jimmy had just offered him, he wondered for a moment if perhaps his legend might have fallen victim to those little chemical wonders. "Tell me, Jimmy, how many . . ."

"First time this trip, sir. Don't worry, only special occasions . . . weddings . . . christenings . . . some-one else's funeral," he chuckled. "Don't worry about me, sir. Just don't want to make any of those little mistakes. I'm clean."

"If I keep doing those dumb things, I'm going to need a bodyguard. Stick close to me, Jimmy."

"Always have, sir." They were whispering softly but Chance could tell when Gates's tone changed. There was a concern rarely voiced. "I'm ready for whatever you want me to do next, sir. . . ."

"But?" Chance asked.

"But I'm worried about that ship. Those chiefs I talked to are good. Everything's supposed to be set up the way you wanted. But we could screw up awfully big if we showed up just a little bit too early. I'd just like to be sure they're as ready as we're going to be. I want them mounted up and ready before any of us show."

"I don't think anyone's going to fall for the Russian officer routine again, not at three in the morning."

"Oh no, sir. Don't worry about me. I can handle myself. There's any number of ways I can get back on board."

"Go ahead, Jimmy. I won't insult you by asking how. You know where I'm going to be at first light. Either meet us at that little shack Dinh's got fixed up between the warehouses or make sure someone passes on whatever you find. Let me know somehow."

He did not see or hear Gates depart. He simply sensed that the man was gone. It was Chance's turn now to slip away. He must find Barney Gold.

Peter Merry turned to his right. He didn't expect to see York and he knew he couldn't be seen. But he could be heard and he had to say something. "You stink," Merry whispered with disgust.

"You're no charmer yourself." York watched the forms of three Soviet marines amble by in front of them. They were outlined against the glow of lights from the main base a mile distant. "I remember Dinh warning us about something like this, but I never paid much attention."

What Dinh had explained before they ever left Suoi Hoa was that the main base had been built by the Americans and expanded by Russians complete with sanitary facilities. But, not too far from that bastion of western civilization, one could find the old-fashioned drainage ditches alongside the roads. The Vietnamese used these for every conceivable purpose. Both Merry and York were now more than ready to acknowledge that fact, and there was nobody to blame but themselves. Perhaps they'd been just a touch off guard after setting the explosives around the armories. Whatever, they'd failed to hear the approaching marines until there was no choice but to jump into the ditch.

"Every goddamned mutt on the entire base is going to love us," Merry murmured. "We need a bath."

"The beach isn't too far from here. That's our only choice."

"Lost time." Merry was proud of his efficiency. Stupid mistakes bothered him.

"Like I said, no choice." York crept out of the muck and slithered to the edge of the road. He could neither see nor hear anything. "I remember seeing a path back here a bit," he said, standing up.

They had one more target to prepare, the auxiliary generating station. Dinh and his people would handle the main power plant when the appropriate time came. The Russians had allowed the Vietnamese to run it since they took over the base. Dinh knew there would be nothing unusual at first when his people showed up there.

York and Merry placed their weapons and remaining explosives at the juncture of beach and vegetation and, without a word to each other, waded sheepishly into the water fully clothed. It was a unique situation. Dirt had never been a concern to a SEAL on patrol but each piece of clothing now had to be removed and scrubbed. They had already learned how effective dogs could be. So far that night, the four-legged guards had been more of a problem than the two-legged variety.

They crept close enough to the auxiliary station to study their objective. Once again, they saw in the light cast from the guard shack that a dog would again require a new approach.

"Thank God for baths. Suggestion?" Fran York asked.

"There are a lot of dogs I've been very fond of—never met a guard I liked. Why take chances this time with a pissed off dog upsetting that guy in the shack?"

"All right," York agreed. "You get on the other side and get his attention. I'll make sure he doesn't have too much time to get curious."

The guard was tired and had lost his edge. He wandered out of his shack with a flashlight to see what was causing a commotion in the brush, never once looking back. While the dog howled and leaped against the fence in angry warning, York's knife opened the man's throat without a sound.

Merry found a bayonet on the guard's web belt and attached it to the rifle in the guard house. When he opened the gate and stepped beyond the fence the enraged dog charged and impaled itself on the bayonet.

While York settled comfortably into the guard's chair, Merry set charges around the equipment inside the small building and attached a mechanical timer. This target was far enough from the base that they didn't have the luxury of waiting until the time was right. If they were a little off schedule and it blew a little too soon, it would be minor. Dinh claimed it most likely would be no problem. It was an auxiliary station and an explosion could just as easily be considered an accident for the little remaining time the operation would consume.

"There's no point in drawing attention to an empty guard shack," York said. He turned out all the lights. "It's sort of a dead end out here anyway. I'll give odds no one will pay attention before morning."

They disappeared into the night.

The layout of General Brusilov's quarters was exactly as Phuong had outlined it. She had drawn each floor in the sand that afternoon, taking great pains to point out the location of each security device. Perhaps she had taken longer than necessary to explain the building to Chance, but each moment with him meant so much more than the last. She even offered, quite seriously, to take him herself. It was only when he insisted that her own mission in Brusilov's office was just as important that she was convinced.

It was an easy job. Just as she explained, a single orderly was posted in the large front room in case the general or his guests required anything at night. The man was nodding when Chance looked in the window. There were no other guards. Brusilov assumed that no one would dare to enter unless they had a specific, approved purpose. He also had tremendous confidence in the modern security devices sent by Moscow. Chance was familiar with each of them.

Now it seemed that one of the most complex parts of the job—they'd explained that Barney Gold was almost as vital as *Gettysburg* herself—would be one of the easiest. The Russians desperately needed the Aegis data, but the greatest bargaining factor was the commanding officer himself. *Get him back*, Admiral Lyford had said. *And if you run into a dead end, you're authorized to kill him!* How Aegis was used was almost as vital as how Aegis was designed. But Chance wanted Gold to know he had nothing to worry about. He would bring Barney Gold home. He'd never had to kill an American yet.

Chance enjoyed working in the dark. It wasn't the challenge of blindness in a strange place as much as the heightened sensitivity that resulted. It was almost electric. Sound, smell, even touch when he reached out and found an object exactly where he expected it, expanded to unimagined levels. There were no mistakes permitted, no allowable error factor. He'd been at this game much too long. When he was younger, it was self-preservation combined with an element of cockiness. That had matured to pure professionalism because he had nothing more to prove. As each year passed, he would promise himself that if he ever made a mistake, and still managed to survive, he'd resign. There was no such thing as two mistakes in this business.

Moving like a cat, quickly, cautiously, he came to the room Barney Gold occupied. No light escaped from under the door. Using his tiny pencil beam for the first time,

Chance studied the door lock. It was simple enough, not really designed to hold someone who really was capable of escaping, but it did its job. The occupant could not leave the room unless a special key, usable only from the outside, released the lock. It could be smashed in an emergency, but that would activate an alarm. Unsure of what else might set it off, Chance disconnected the adjacent power source.

Then, using the key that Phuong had given him, he silently opened the door and stepped into the darkened room.

But something was wrong!

He paused, not moving, not breathing, searching with his senses for the sleeping prisoner. There was no sound of heavy breathing, no scent of another human being in the room. Chance felt a chill run down his neck as he reached again for the pencil light, knowing he would find nothing.

The tiny beam swept the room reassuring Chance that Gold was not in there—dead. The place was empty. And it must have been the Russians who took him away because there had been no guards in his path. That's why it was all so easy.

The most important man in the entire operation was missing! *He couldn't leave a live Barney Gold behind.*

CHAPTER 15

Georgi Brusilov was a man who survived as much by his instincts as his special talents. Any individual who had ever worked with the man, and even those who knew him only by reputation, would acknowledge that he was uniquely qualified for the most complex assignments. He was more than a survivor in a system that treated its people ruthlessly.

If there was a singular reason for his success, it was simply that there were no enemies to stand in his way. The general was a brutal man. Those who crossed him, even those few who attempted to question his methods, were summarily dispatched. They disappeared. Brusilov eliminated problems. Only a very few of his superiors understood what motivated the man. His father not only had been very close to Joseph Stalin, but had actually survived every purge. As a result, Stalin had served as a role model for the boy. Like his father, Georgi Brusilov knew what it took to survive.

His most powerful instinct, if it could be called that, was premonition. He was a seer. The problems that might arise in the future were anticipated and he confronted them head on. *Never wait for trouble*, he cautioned his favorites. *Grab it by the ass and shake it, stomp it—kill it if it's mortal.* Senior officers understood his methods and silently approved. There were no problems where Brusilov commanded. His peers stood aside for their own safety.

That evening, the general had done some thinking. It was obvious there would be no sleep that night. His senses were on edge, warning him of something, something that continued to elude him, but the message remained unclear. After midnight, he'd gone down to the interrogation unit where that Hansen/Golikhov, the sailor from *Gettysburg* who claimed he had been working under KGB orders, was being held. Even though Brusilov's men had employed a number of different methods to challenge the man's background, the story remained the same.

"I am told by my contact in Moscow that you have done exactly as you were ordered . . . that you have done a good job." Brusilov smiled down at the young man. It was a decidedly different approach.

A look of relief spread over the young man's face. If nothing else, the arrogance had been knocked out of him in the last twenty-four hours. "You've actually found one of the controllers." A smile formed at the corner of his swollen mouth. He'd been under tremendous pressure since delivering the film. "Then he explained that I'm telling the truth." The willingness to talk was written across his face even through the bruises.

"They would like to see the films first." It was an oblique answer, intended to set him up for the next question.

"But I completed everything they . . ."

"You didn't tell us about another agent on board the ship, one whom I assume is still there." Brusilov's voice remained steady and calm, considering the menacing expression on his face. The pressure had returned with a vengeance. "Tell me his name."

Golikhov's mouth dropped. "Another . . . ?" He looked unsteadily at Brusilov. "I wasn't told."

"Just his name. It's critical at this point." The wide-set eyes and heavy eyebrows were unforgiving.

"But I don't . . ."

"How do you expect me to believe everything else you've told us if you don't give me his name? For all I know, this man could be a double agent. Your officer, your Lt. Norman, was a worthless piece of shit. He would sell his mother to get out of here. The other one is stupid. Why should I allow someone who may be a double agent to survive here? Once more—just his name."

Fear drained the younger man's face to an unhealthy chalk white when he recognized Brusilov's expression. He hung his head. "I wasn't aware." Then he forced himself to look up into the general's eyes, a final act of defiance.

Brusilov turned on his heel. "See if he'll be more willing to cooperate on my next visit," he called over his shoulder as he stalked out the door. "Use any methods you find necessary." That usually meant experimentation and, more often than not, the prisoner rarely survived. He couldn't imagine it would be a great loss to anyone.

The American, Lt. Norman, was in an adjacent room. This visit was equally useless. Norman's answers were drivel. Pressure was of no value. The man was terrified. He reeked of his own waste. If he did know anything of value, he was the finest actor Brusilov had seen in years. There were no answers there either. He left the same instructions as he had for Golikhov.

Perhaps, Brusilov pondered, I should talk with their captain again. But he remembered that Captain Boldin from the *Kulakov* had asked permission to have Gold as his guest for a few hours, for intelligence purposes as much as anything. Boldin was driven by ambition and the time of night meant nothing to him. He also harbored a fear that somehow *Gettysburg* would disappear before he had an opportunity to study her close up. So he had told the general he would like to have Gold that night. Brusilov had acceded to the request, assuming that possibly Boldin might come up with something useful. He glanced at his watch. There was no purpose in interrupting them now. Daylight would be coming in a few hours.

He ordered his driver to take him to the docks, then excused the man, sending him back to his barracks to sleep for a couple of hours. Bright lights illuminated the gray ships nestled alongside the piers. *Gettysburg* stood out among the others, her block-like superstructure rearing straight up from the smooth main deck, her weapons invisible beneath her shining gray skin. The Soviet ships were a counterpoint. Low in the water, their deck housing rising like a wedding cake, they bristled with weapons. Vietnamese sailors still paraded about *Gettysburg*'s decks, rifles slung from their shoulders, pistols in web belts around their waists, *as if they actually presented a challenge to the Russians who remained on the pier,* he thought.

There was nothing about the American ship that satisfied this vague sense that had been bothering him. There was supposed to be one more KGB agent aboard this ship who had yet to show his face. Why? Was there something below the surface that continued to evade Brusilov? How could someone in Moscow be sure this man was still aboard? For that matter, how could they be sure he still belonged to them? There was a final consideration that Brusilov had been avoiding—was he somehow in danger because of this unknown individual?

After staring hard at the American ship as if he might make it disappear, the general decided to return to his office. Normally, he preferred to avoid the place this late at night. But his best thinking was done there. Perhaps the solitude of an empty office with no phones ringing would bring him an answer.

Upon entering the building to sign in, he was surprised to find there was no guard at the desk. But at that hour of the night, there was probably only one man on duty. Brusilov placed his signature in the appropriate place in the book and headed down the hall. He would probably encounter the man making his hourly rounds. He remembered being told that the guard toured the building once an hour. Perhaps, he decided as he rounded the corner to his office, *I should* recommend two men for that duty. Then he decided two guards for a darkened building in Cam Ranh Bay just weren't necessary. *Such foolishness!* Excesses like that were reserved for fat generals in Moscow. He chalked that idea up to lack of sleep.

The general unlocked his office and stepped inside, hesitating for a moment almost in mid-stride. *What . . . ? Forget it . . . too nervous in your old age.* But as he was removing the key from the lock, he stopped and half turned to look over his shoulder. *What was it . . . ?* His eyes darted about the room. Nothing seemed out of place.

Pocketing the key, he was walking toward his desk when he realized quite suddenly what had bothered him. A smell—no, no, it wasn't that so much, not a real or powerful smell—but the aroma of the room was different somehow.

Very cautiously, careful not to touch anything, he slowly walked around his office, eyes alert for the slightest oddity. He would have noticed any item missing or even anything moved barely out of place. Brusilov was that particular about his habits, that careful about his personal safety.

Then he checked the locks on his file cabinet and desk. Both secure. But someone had been in that room since he'd left the previous evening. Of that he was sure.

General Brusilov sat at his desk and folded his hands, eyes once again moving slowly about the large office. There was little of value for a common thief, just some souvenirs he'd acquired in his travels, mostly with a personal meaning. He could imagine no reason for anyone to break in unless they were searching for something to do with the American ship. But even the Aegis films had not been left here, although not a soul in Cam Ranh Bay knew that. They'd been on his person, in his uniform, since he'd taken personal custody of them, and he intended to keep that film until the expert from Moscow arrived to analyze it.

But that wouldn't preclude someone from looking . . . would it?

He unlocked his desk, then his file cabinet, searching each one carefully. Nothing was missing, nothing out of order.

His phone rang, its sharpness in the quiet of the night startling him. No one knew he was here.

He lifted the phone gently from its cradle, curious, and even a bit tentative. "Yes, this is General Brusilov."

"My apologies for disturbing you, sir. This is Lt. Belov down at the night guard's desk. I saw your name in the book. Is everything all right, sir?"

"Of course it is," Brusilov answered irritably. "You weren't at your post when I came in the building. Why are you bothering me now?"

"My apologies, General. I wasn't on duty here. The regularly assigned night guard failed to make his standard call to the duty officer's desk during the previous hour and I was sent over here to check on him." There was a short pause and then, "I assume you have seen him, sir."

"Of course not," Brusilov snapped. "I'm not in the habit of searching for sleeping guards." He had no idea why he was being rude to Belov. He didn't even know the man.

"General, you are the only one signed into the building this evening and I apologize for intruding. But I am responsible for locating this guard. It was just that you are the only other . . ."

"Forget it. It's late. I . . ." Brusilov paused and thought back to the moment he entered the office. *That smell. The only people normally in his office were the Vietnamese girl, Miss Phuong, and occasionally his subordinates. And that odor was heavy . . . was it an unwashed smell?* "Lieutenant, kindly wait one moment."

Brusilov lay the phone on his desk and walked over to his closet. He pulled open the door cautiously. Nothing. Then he moved to his private bathroom, snapped on the outside light switch and pushed the door, tentatively, until something seemed to hold it. He looked down. There was a uniformed leg keeping the door from opening further.

Peering around the edge of the door, he saw what his nose had already identified—the night guard, obviously quite dead.

Brusilov tiptoed, as if he might somehow disturb the guard, back to the phone. "Lieutenant," he said in an odd, brittle voice, "I have located your guard's body. Before you come up here, call the duty officer. I want to double the sentries on the American ship and I want an additional squad sent to Building 408. Then, I want the American captain brought directly to me."

There was one final piece in this puzzle that seemed to have no solution. He called Moscow. Perhaps Hansen/Golikhov really didn't know. Those people in Moscow did things that way at times. It was a long wait to locate the KGB manager who was aware of another operative aboard *Gettysburg*, but he was finally connected with the man. There were many interruptions as one superior after another was contacted. It seemed nobody could make a decision. The minutes ticked on interminably until Brusilov was finally given the name he wanted. Then he called the duty officer and requested that a sailor on board the American ship be delivered to his office immediately—the man's name was Donald Kelly. The duty officer was responsible for Kelly's well-being and could remove him from *Gettysburg* any way he saw fit.

Phuong was hysterical when she located Dinh. He was exactly where he promised he would be but that did nothing to calm her. Somehow she was still able to explain through her sobbing how she had been forced to kill the night guard in Brusilov's office. There had been no alternative. And when she explained this, more tears streamed down her face. She'd never considered killing anything in her life, and she recoiled earlier in the evening when Dinh explained how necessary it might be to use the tiny dart gun. There was only one reason: if it would help Chance.

Dinh was normally a calm individual but he understood

how close to the edge he had come that day. Whenever he closed his eyes, a vision of the massacre at Can Fat would return; and each time it would end with a picture of a younger Brusilov, the flames of Can Fat surging about him while he fired repeatedly in their direction as they escaped into the undergrowth. Phuong was his daughter, the only human being remaining to him after Can Fat, and he wanted desperately to take her away from this horror. But there was no time. He hoped they would be alive on the following day so he could console her as he so desperately wanted to, but their time was too precious now. There were perhaps two more hours until sunrise and he had no idea how much the others had accomplished.

He reached out and grasped her shoulders firmly, shaking her until she looked up into his eyes. It pained him to be so rough. "You'll have time for tears later, but there is none now. Listen to me, please. Think about David." It was so cruel to use Chance's name in that matter. "Are the guards on the same system as the other buildings? Do they check in with someone during their watch?"

"Yes." She rubbed her eyes with the back of her hand. "I think so, but I don't know how often." Her father was right. She must think of David.

"Someone will come looking for him when he doesn't call in." Dinh's mind was awhirl. Where were the other SEALs? Each of them had gone on a different assignment. He had no idea where Chance was now, and it was imperative that he should be warned as quickly as possible. What to do?

"Come with me," he said softly, rising and moving off quietly in the darkness. They skirted the lighted areas, choosing the alleys and shadows. Phuong said nothing, barely paying attention to their path as she followed her father. Her mind was awhirl. Visions of David Chance became a counterpoint to the revulsion at what she had been forced to do in Brusilov's office.

Dinh knew exactly where he was heading. It would be the

first place he would see anything out of the ordinary if that guard's body had been found. Their path was circuitous but they moved rapidly until they were in a position to watch the barracks where the marine guards were billeted. He'd been correct in his suspicions. There was already activity before they arrived. The front section of the first floor was ablaze with lights. As they watched, a platoon fell out into formation in front of the building. Two officers barked out a series of orders. As Dinh and Phuong watched, the group broke up into three units, the largest moving at double time toward the piers. Dinh understood that much Russian.

"I think," Dinh murmured softly, "that your guard has been found and that perhaps General Brusilov has ordered additional sentries."

Phuong's hands flew to her face as she sucked in her breath. "Do you think he knows about David?" she gasped, her brown, almond-shaped eyes filling with tears once again.

"I don't think so. There's no way he could learn that yet, not unless one of them had been caught. But the general is a very cautious man." Dinh had momentarily forgotten his inner rage. This was a new challenge, one that Chance and the others must know about as soon as possible.

"What?"

"I want you to go to the shed and wait there." It was a tiny building behind the machine shop, probably built many years before by the Americans and now forgotten by the Russians behind weeds and mounds of junk. Dinh had carefully prepared it over the past few months, anticipating the day when he might use it in some manner to avenge Can Fat. He had brought them there very early that day so they would know of one safe place. They also planned to meet there once more before sunrise. "Whichever one appears first will know what to do." He was still holding her shoulders tightly. "I'll try to find David."

Phuong nodded and squeezed her eyes tightly shut. When she opened them, Dinh was gone.

• • •

The water was warm and comforting, wrapping around Jimmy Gates like a soft, black, silken quilt. He'd waded in a few hundred yards above the first pier and swam well out before turning toward the ships. Once he was off *Gettysburg*'s stern, he would float and study the situation for a while before he moved in.

He preferred warm water. Some of the others claimed that the colder the water, the more alert you remained. Jimmy disagreed. You might be sharper for a short time, but that was because you were so damn cold. After half an hour, he usually found himself slowing down as the cold wormed its way into his core. It was the water he was sure, not his age. He knew that if he admitted it they'd watch him more closely, and if they decided he was getting too old for that sort of thing he'd end the rest of his career ashore. So he kept quiet and thanked whatever lucky star stayed over him whenever they sent him on a warm water operation.

This wasn't his first time in Vietnamese waters although he'd never been in Cam Ranh Bay before. Years before he'd worked out of the Delta. He remembered names like Nha Be, the Rung Sat Special Zone, and the Ca Mau Peninsula. Those were just places, large areas of jungle and paddies and rivers and canals that disappeared into an impenetrable undergrowth. The battles, large and small, often had no names. They were places along a river or a canal where the PBRs nuzzled into a muddy bank and dropped them off—places with no names, places no one wanted to name afterwards. He remembered them mostly by body counts, more clearly if American bodies were involved.

That water had been brown, more fresh than salt. Brackish was the word that covered a variety of sins. Gates always tasted the water before he slipped in. It was a silly habit that had grown into a superstition—if he tasted the water first, he was somehow anointed, somehow mysteriously shielded from harm. Sometimes that Delta water tasted of mud, sometimes salt, and too often of blood. But it had also kept him alive.

Cam Ranh Bay was salty. No doubt about it. There was some fresh water in the background because he could taste mud. And there was also a dollop of oil, the residue from the ships at the piers. He was glad the tide was going out or more than likely sewage from the base would have greeted him also. The water also tasted *wet* and that was proof that he was once again in his element. Jimmy Gates felt safer in water than on land. Perhaps that was why so long ago he'd gotten into the habit of taking a mouthful. They had once been called *frogmen*, so perhaps frogs did the same thing to save them from their predators.

Cold stars and a quarter moon offered little illumination. Dinh had explained that there were no small boat patrols off the piers so Gates would remain invisible out in the bay. He'd blackened his skin and a black bandana was tied around his head over his blond hair. Even close in he had the advantage. The brilliant lighting around the piers outlined everything he needed to see, but it ruined the night vision of those ashore, or on the ships.

He swam comfortably, enjoying the clinging, velvety sensation of water pressing the black pajamas he now wore to his skin. Wet suits were clammy, rubbery, heavy. They'd never appealed to him—he would brag to anyone who would listen that Jimmy Gates wasn't designed to be encased in a black condom, just like a dick. When they were a necessity, he accepted them grudgingly. He would claim they slowed a man down in the water, even when others moved ahead of him. Yet even with his peculiar prejudices and superstitions, Jimmy Gates was superb at his job. He never made a mistake.

Treading water softly a couple of hundred yards beyond the sterns of the nearest ships, he studied the activities of the sentries ashore and on *Gettysburg*. Then he swam closer to get an idea of their routine. The Russians on the pier seemed much more aware of their responsibilities, their weapons properly slung, uniforms orderly. There was little talking or smoking. The Vietnamese, on the other hand, seemed to be more casual aboard the ship. They chattered among themselves, gathering in small groups on the fantail to smoke. Some took time to piss in the water—*his water*!

The Russians were still apparently responsible for what occurred on the pier and for making sure that no one went aboard or came ashore without a reason. It was more difficult to determine just what the Vietnamese were accomplishing, *other than fouling his water*. Gates considered any body of water that he was operating in as *his water*.

As he was about to head toward the pier, he observed a number of Soviet marines round the warehouse at the top of the pier. He waited. They didn't relieve the current sentries as he'd expected. Instead, an officer apparently in charge disbursed them among the current sentries. Another of the newly arrived officers moved from man to man with instructions. Something had obviously gone wrong ashore.

Very steadily, and without a sound or a ripple, Gates approached the pier, swimming the last thirty yards underwater. He surfaced beneath the pier near *Gettysburg*'s stern, exhaling slowly.

He listened carefully. Apparently the arrival of additional Soviet marines had little effect on the Vietnamese other than to alert them that there may be a problem. They were sure the Russians would not come aboard their ship—*their ship*! There was also talk of women and a suggestion about starting a card game. It wasn't that they were unconcerned with the ship—rather, they felt that the guards on the pier protected the ship from aggression and that the crew, so quiet that they surprised their guards, was under control. It was the cards that finally succeeded. Guards still remained at critical positions on the ship. The lone sentry on the stern section lounged on a chock on the pier side, watching the goings-on ashore.

Gates moved out from under the pier to the darkened far side of the ship, swimming halfway forward to assure himself there were no hidden guards. No one stirred. It must have been a high stakes game.

Back off the stern, he located the NIXIE port on the starboard side, an opening in the hull for towing a device to draw torpedos away from the ship. It was well above the waterline but Jimmy Gates managed to launch his body high enough above the surface to get a hand grip in the port. Then, concentrating his strength in a desperate effort, he hauled himself up until he was able to gain a tenuous foothold. The main deck was five feet above his head. This would be the trickiest part, but he'd already anticipated the problem with Chance. If he was lucky, the sentry would remain on the far side watching the activity on the pier.

Gates was not excited about placing his knife between his teeth. Although they did it that way in the movies, it wasn't a wise way to function. Yet he had no option at this stage. Then he removed a thin nylon line from his pocket and flipped the weighted Turk's head just high enough so that it flopped over the top lifeline on the main deck. He jerked the line until the weight slipped back through the outboard side of the other lines. Then he let it drop back down until he could tie the ends together. He yanked hard twice. That also was the way it was done in the movies, but this time it was the common-sense way to operate.

Leaning back for a moment until the nylon held his weight completely, he hauled himself straight up, walking his bare feet up the side of the hull until he could peer over the edge. The sentry remained occupied with the pierside activity. Then Gates pulled himself the rest of the way up like a monkey scurrying up a tree. He grabbed the bottom lifeline, then the next, and the next until he had one foot on the deck. There was no purpose in stopping now. He was committed.

Gates hauled his body upright, vaulting silently over the lines, ready to meet the sentry. He landed on the balls of his feet, his knife ready. The guard hadn't noticed a thing. He might even sneak by without being seen, but Gates never played odds like that.

Above him, smoking quietly on top of the hangar, a

single chief petty officer watched curiously from the moment he'd seen the dark figure grasp the lifeline. What he saw in the following seconds he was sure was the most amazing display he'd ever witnessed. The individual, apparently black from head to foot, inched his way across the deck until he was directly behind the sentry. Perhaps the Vietnamese sensed something. Whatever it was, he turned to look over his shoulder. The black figure moved with incredible speed. One moment the guard was perched on the chock, the next he was being dragged across the deck. There had never been a sound.

Not more than ten seconds had passed before a second Vietnamese called out for the first. *Another non-card player*, Gates growled to himself, *who has just made a fatal mistake*. The second guard wandered casually out onto the stern already beginning a conversation as if *Gettysburg* were a cruise ship. The chief was sure the man never saw the creature in black—the chief wasn't so sure he had even seen what took place—and that he was dead before his body ever hit the deck.

But the chief was quite certain about what was occurring. He headed for chief's quarters to let Ben Gannett know he was about to receive a visitor.

Mark Ferro met Gates in the passageway. He had no doubt who was approaching, but the figure in black pajamas, a black bandana covering his blond hair, and his skin covered with black camouflage paint, bore no resemblance to the neat Soviet officer who had come aboard the previous day in freshly starched coveralls. "SEAL?" was the only word he uttered, partially in surprise, mostly in relief.

Gates's voice was his only means of identification. "Let's sit down with Gannett and the others pronto. Life is changing rapidly out there."

Chief's quarters in an Aegis cruiser bore no resemblance to those on the submarines Jimmy Gates had ridden. It was spacious, almost a home, with sleeping quarters, a lounge, even a galley. None of the CPOs were asleep. They were gathered in the lounge.

"We've got about an hour and a half until dawn," Gates said, sipping the first coffee he'd had since leaving Japan two days before. "Sooner or later, someone is going to recognize there are two less guards topside."

"Three," Gannett interrupted. "We had problems ourselves." He shook his head in wonder. "I can't imagine how sloppy these guys have grown. They were sharp during the day, but they seemed to take us for granted when the crew stayed below after dark. Our mistake is already over the side and your's may be a problem if they're still around."

"I couldn't put them over the side without a splash," Gates said. "I've got them stuffed under a tarp on the stern, but a mess like that's easy to find. If that happens, the shit hits the fan."

Gannett glanced at the chief boatswain. "How about rallying a couple of your boys. Just have them lower the stiffs over the side nice and easy and let the tide take them—and make sure they wash down afterwards."

"Something also happened ashore," Gates said. "I don't know what but it's something that's got the Russians on their tippy toes. They've doubled the sentries on the pier. And they're a little more competent than the clowns aboard this ship. They look to me like they know exactly what they're about. And they're definitely on to something—one too many officers staying out there with them. I'd say the easy part is over."

They were interrupted by the buzzing of the phone. One of the chiefs picked it up, listened for a moment, then responded nastily, "If you want something, asshole, you talk with Chief Gannett." He gestured in Gannett's direction. "Ben, some Russian on the quarterdeck says he has orders to pick up some of the crew. You talk to him."

Gannett identified himself bruskly and listened, his brows gradually knitting into a frown. "I think you've got a couple of incorrect names," he said evenly. "Must be a language problem." He listened for a moment before replying, "I don't think I ever heard of him. You sure you got the right name?" He nodded toward Gates as if to say—*you're right about them being on to something*.

There was a discussion at the other end while Gannett waited.

"No, I don't have any Donald Keeley aboard this ship either. You'd better check those names again." Gannett replaced the phone. "I'm going to get another call in about a minute. The silly shit just couldn't pronounce the name right."

"What is it?" Gates asked.

"Russian officer on the other end," Gannett answered. "Excellent command of English . . . except for names." He grinned at the chief radarman. "I guess your boy, Steinberg, is OK, Hennessey, even if he is a bit strange. I was going to put my money on him until that call."

Gates's face lit up, his white teeth flashing against the black on his face. "Their fourth man?"

"Looks like it," Gannett said. "One of the kids that made the biggest squawk when we rounded them up was a radioman named Donald Kelly. And that's who they want to borrow for a while. This guy had a list of names, trying to throw us off, maybe. But I could tell that's the one they really want."

The phone buzzed once again and Gannett picked it up. After listening patiently, he responded, "I still don't think I understand who you want."

The answer came loud enough for the others in the room to hear it. There was no doubt he wanted Donald Kelly and they could hear him sound out each letter as he spelled it.

"We'll have him there in a few minutes. Takes a while to find someone on a ship this size, you understand." He hung up before there was an answer. "I sure as shit don't want them to start searching the ship for Kelly."

Gates looked at the other faces. "One of you must be a corpsman?" he exclaimed.

"I'm the doc," a large, round-faced man answered. "Hogan . . . Brian Hogan." There was already a grin on his face. He knew exactly what Gates expected.

"What have you got in your grab bag that will put this Kelly out of the picture for four or five hours?"

"I can put him out forever." The corpsman leered maliciously. "It would be a pleasure."

"The prick probably deserves it," Gates said. "But if we delivered a stiff to the Russians, we'd have them swarming all over us. We need something that'll keep him conscious . . . but you can't let him talk."

"Where is the gentleman?" Hogan asked. "I can have him moving under his own power with a little help, but he'll be so incoherent in thirty seconds they won't figure out his problem for hours."

"If you'll remember," Gannett said with a sad expression, "he was being very difficult—wouldn't listen to reason. He must have figured we already had the drop on him." He shrugged. "So we put him forward in the port chain locker. I figured he could make all the racket he wanted up there and no one would pay attention."

Gates nodded at the corpsman. "You'd better get on up there with Gannett and zap him quick. The Russians are definitely into hardball right now. If that officer of theirs has to wait five seconds longer than he wants to on the quarterdeck, he'll figure you're playing games with his boy. And," he added, "have one damned good story ready when he asks what Kelly's problem is."

"I've had a pint of medicinal brandy I've been saving for just the right time. I guess I'm going to have to waste it now. We'll baptize him with it, Ben," Hogan laughed maliciously, and gave Gannett a slap on the rump as they left. "He's going to look very drunk when we deliver him, so we might as well make it realistic."

When Gates was ready to leave David Chance an hour before, Chance had pretty much finalized in his own mind how they would free *Gettysburg*. If things changed or fell apart, they'd just have to ad-lib. But he wanted it made clear that he was leaving it up to Gannett to neutralize *Gettysburg*. Gannett's crew—he laughed every time he claimed he could turn technicians into marines for a day—would be able to protect their ship with the small arms he'd issued and the odds were that the SEALs would appreciate that added firepower, too. And, Gates asserted in chiefs quarters, it was vital that the ship be completely ready to get underway as soon as Captain Gold was aboard.

"How are you going to get Captain Gold off that Russian ship?" Ferro inquired. "That's going to be a pretty trick if they've still got him there."

Gates's mouth dropped open. "What ship? He's supposed to be in Brusilov's quarters. That's where Chance was headed when I left him." He could see the ad-lib was quickly becoming the most critical part of their plan.

"A couple of hours ago he was here with some Russian," Gannett answered. "Christ, the captain looked like hell. He could barely walk. He took me aside when he had a chance and said that for some crazy reason the CO of that Russian ship—*Kulakov*—had gotten permission to spring him for a while, probably digging for something. Captain said it was the only way he could let me know there were SEALs loose on the base and something was bound to happen. He was happy as a clam when I explained that you'd already been aboard and it was probably going to hit the fan in the early AM. He told me that I was as good as CO and to get this ship under way somehow. The captain said not to worry about him. The SEALs might be able to help him but I was to get this ship and Aegis the hell out of here if you guys gave us a shot. He was being taken to that Russian's ship afterwards, I guess."

"Shit!" Gates gripped his bottom lip between his teeth for a moment while he looked thoughtfully down at his folded hands. This was the kind of glitch Chance was worried about. Then he looked up at Gannett. "Got any idea where this ship is that Captain Gold might be on?"

"Next pier over. One of their new ones. *Kulakov*, I think. Does that sound familiar?"

"Don't know the name . . . but I did see a new one over there." Gates rose to his feet. "Time for another swim. Don't worry about your captain. We'll have him here . . . somehow. But you get this ship out of here if you see the slightest opening."

Jimmy Gates was floating very quietly about twenty yards astern of the new Soviet ship when he saw a car pull up alongside the quarterdeck. An officer climbed out, followed by two armed marines. Less than a minute after boarding the ship, Gates saw them depart with Barney Gold, their weapons drawn as if they feared someone might attempt to take him away.

They were making it all so much more difficult.

For the first time since the *Gettysburg* incident had begun, Jules Auger saw the expression on Admiral Lyford's face change to despair for a moment. Whatever had been in that message he'd just received had been unexpected. Auger waited patiently, knowing it wouldn't remain private.

"Here." Lyford finally extended the sheet of paper across the desk.

The initial thought that crossed Auger's mind as he read it was basic—*I thought I'd be able to accept anything.* Through all his years in the navy, the intelligence specialist was sure there was nothing that would shock him. But this did.

The top-secret message was addressed to the commanding officer of the aircraft carrier *Theodore Roosevelt*, the one nearest to Cam Ranh Bay. There were very few individuals vital to the operation who had been included, even for information purposes. *Roosevelt*'s captain was directed to prepare an attack aircraft armed with a nuclear weapon. The target was Cam Ranh Bay. The real shocker was that the plane was to be airborne before the President's deadline. That would have the target within range at the precise moment he'd threatened. Certainly Cam Ranh Bay would know what the aircraft was there for the minute it was picked up on radar. The President was into a heavy bluff or he had no intention of granting additional time.

"I thought he'd give us more time . . . if it looked like we needed it. It could be so close."

"Maybe the message got lost in the magnetic storm . . . maybe *Roosevelt* hasn't. . . ."

"It requires a receipt," Jules answered. "They'll just keep at it until *Roosevelt* acknowledges."

CHAPTER 16

David Chance was the first of the SEALs to appear at the little building Dinh had prepared behind the machine shop. His approach was typically cautious, suspicious by habit. He crept through the rubble and weeds silently, stopping every few steps to listen. Each of his senses was attuned to anything unnatural. But it was only when he was just outside the door that he heard the strange sound. He paused, listening to what sounded almost like a lost, frightened child weeping. There was nothing in this sound that warned him of danger. Rather, it was almost a siren song calling for him, imploring him.

He dropped to his hands and knees, gradually pushing the door in without a sound. Easing down onto his belly and palming his knife, Chance wriggled through the door. Someone, perhaps a child, was on the far side of the shack still unaware of his presence. There was no other sound—just two of them inside. His pencil beam slashed through the darkness.

Phuong was huddled in the far corner, sobbing quietly when the fine line of light pierced the black. She gasped audibly, but did not look up, instead seeming to draw herself into a tighter ball of misery.

Chance knelt beside her, placing a comforting arm on her

slender shoulders. His words were tentative. "Phuong, it's me—David." He stroked her back and shoulders. "Please, talk to me. It's David."

She didn't move but he noticed that her breathing gradually became more steady as he continued to rub her back. The choked sobbing grew quieter until she was able to draw a couple of deep breaths.

"Phuong, will you talk to me—please?" He sat down beside her, his back against the wall. "I know something happened. I need to know what it was." His hand never left her back, stroking up and down, moving across her shoulders, massaging her neck. "It's going to be light soon."

With a suddenness that took him by surprise, she turned and snuggled up next to him with her head on his chest. "Don't let me go, please," she whispered, her voice choked with emotion. "Put your arm around me. Please . . . hold me . . . hold me tight."

He slipped his right arm around her shoulders and squeezed her tightly, trying to absorb the fear that had been in her voice. He stroked her head with his other hand, sweeping her hair back. "Whatever happened, you're safe now." He cut off his next words as a deep sigh escaped, almost as if she were consciously expelling some horror.

"David . . . I killed someone tonight." Her voice trembled. "I really did. I killed someone." The words seemed to rise from her chest in a steady flow. "I didn't have a choice . . . the night guard found me in Brusilov's office . . . and if I didn't do it, everything would have fallen apart . . . and something would have happened to you. . . ." Another gulping sob escaped when she said that, but she caught herself and continued. "And I think someone must have found the body, even though I tried to hide it. My father sent me here because they've called out many more marines. . . ."

He covered her lips with his fingers. "Shh, wait a minute. Catch your breath." He bent his head and brushed her hair with his lips. "You're going to be all right. Just relax for a bit longer and get your thoughts together." He squeezed her closer and rubbed his cheek gently back and forth through her hair. "I'm sorry I put you in such a position. It won't happen again. I promise you that." He rubbed her cheek with his hand and held her quietly.

Phuong broke the silence. "David?"

"I'm still right here."

"Do you love me?"

"Of course I do." He smiled to himself in the darkness. "Ever since the first day I saw you, when you were a little girl. You've always been my favorite little girl."

"No. I didn't mean that. But do you love me?" She lifted her head. "Do you love me . . . as a woman?" Even before her voice had died away, she could feel his muscles tighten. She buried her face in his chest.

Chance was silent for a moment. Then he said, "Why do you ask . . . ?"

She raised her head slightly. "Because it is very important to me. I must know. It will be sunrise soon and then you'll be gone . . . or if you aren't, then you'll be . . ." She couldn't finish the sentence.

It was if she'd opened a door for Chance and nothing he'd expected was on the other side. *She'd just said in so many words she was in love with him.* Of course—that little girl was no longer that pitiful child standing in front of him, naked, burned, and terrified. Nor was she even Dinh's daughter anymore. She had become an individual, entirely separate from past attachments. She was making a life of her own. She'd gone into Brusilov's office by herself—*to help him.* She'd acted on her own accord. And now, she was making it absolutely clear that Nguyen thi Phuong was in love with him.

"Yes, Phuong." There would be no harm in making her happy. In another few hours . . . yes, she was absolutely right. He would either be gone—*Gettysburg* would be gone—or he would be dead. "Yes, I do love you. And it's not because of your father and not because I've known you since you were a little girl. I love a very beautiful woman named Phuong." He kissed the top of her head softly. "I'm sorry that it has to be this way . . . in this place."

She raised her head. "It doesn't matter where we are. Really, it doesn't." The darkness could never mask the smile that was so obviously on her lips. "Because I love you so very much." She straightened up until he knew she was face to face with him. "I never felt beautiful in my life . . . not until you said I was. Please, will you kiss me, David, just as you would kiss a beautiful woman if we were in the right place at the right time?"

Chance placed two fingers under her chin and gently lifted her head until he could feel her lips with his own. He was gentle at first, still unsure of who either of them had become in the darkness. She returned his kiss more strongly than he ever would have imagined. His arms circled around Phuong and he pulled her close. Her body strained against his. David Chance could no longer recall the picture of that little girl. She was gone forever.

He was in love with her.

When they separated at last, Phuong was content to rest with her head on his chest. She held his free hand in her own, sometimes lifting it to her lips. They said nothing for a while. There was no need for words.

Finally. "I'll have to leave soon," Chance said. He was tired. If he allowed himself to relax anymore . . . but no more than ten minutes had actually passed. It was little enough time to realize how much that one kiss had changed their relationship. He squeezed his eyes shut tightly. *Not now. Don't let go now!* "You never said what you found in Brusilov's office . . . the film?" It was cruel to have done that. He was glad Phuong couldn't see his face and understand that all he really wanted to do was take her in his arms.

She bit her lip as he spoke. Then, "Yes, but I don't think it was right." *Why did he do that?* She explained what she'd told her father—about the files with a single section of flat film—and that Dinh had also doubted that was what they were after. "But I did write down what was on the file."

Chance briefly illuminated the scrap of paper with the Cyrillic letters she'd copied. It was too quick for her to see his face. "No, this has nothing to do with the ship. But you did well—very well, Phuong." After a pause, he asked, "Did your father say he would meet me somewhere else?"

"No. He said there was no reason to change anything like that. He would be there when he said he would, and his people would be ready." She explained where Dinh had been since Chance saw him last. Then, after a second's hesitation, she asked in a tentative voice, "David, what was so wrong with the Phoenix Program that my father never talked about it before? Was it really so dangerous to my own people?"

"Why do you ask?" After the massacre at Can Fat, Dinh had made him swear on the graves of his ancestors that nothing would ever be said about Phoenix. His daughter, Phuong—who'd been named after the Phoenix—had risen from the ashes created by his part in the Phoenix Program.

She could feel his muscles tighten. "My father . . . my father says that there were times when you both hated the work you were doing."

"Did Dinh say he regretted what he'd done?"

"No, not at all." He'd only spoken about it one time, and it had been earlier that day. It was so hard to put it into words. Yet it was so important to her—it would explain so much about her father, about a secret he'd held inside for so long . . . even about a mother she couldn't remember. "He just said there were innocent people . . ."

"I know what he said," Chance interrupted. How could he answer her without invading Dinh's privacy? "Your country had been at war for so long and we—my people— were just one more invader . . . no, not invader . . . I guess intruder is a better word." He had begun in a monotone but found himself struggling now to keep his voice soft. "Phoenix was the first to introduce a little frontier justice." As soon as he said that, he knew she couldn't understand what he meant. "We went after the VC cadre and the northerners who were slaughtering your leaders in their own villages. We took the terror to the terrorists, then we added a little extra to discourage them. It worked, too. There were abuses—innocent people were hurt—but for a while it seemed to work. It provided intelligence for our military and it stripped some of the most dangerous leaders from the other side."

"Then why—"

"Why did we leave?" Chance was silent for a moment. He never really understood why they'd pulled out. "We left because it was time to go. And there were a lot of the wrong reasons we left. That's why your father is bitter about it." He didn't want to talk about Can Fat.

"He says nothing against you."

"Dinh knows I didn't give the orders to leave. And I've been back since then. He knew someday I'd come back to help him with Brusilov." There he was—getting dangerously close to Can Fat!

He could feel her body shudder at the mention of that name. "General Brusilov scares me now . . . now that I know. I wish my father had told me about him sooner. I used to ask him about my mother and his answer was always that she died in the war. He never said how—just that it was the war." She was silent for a moment before she asked, "How did he know Brusilov would come here some day? It seems a twist of fate that they ever ended up in the same place after all these years."

Fate! Chance had never placed much faith in that concept until now. He'd always allowed room in his relationship with Dinh for the little man's never-ending plans for revenge, but never had it seemed remotely possible that the opportunity would present itself. He'd stuck with Dinh because the two men had learned to love each other and never had Chance considered breaking the ties. Dinh had saved his life! If he couldn't owe Dinh a life in return, at

least he could offer him hope. Phuong was right. It was a
twist of fate. Dinh deserved it.

"If your father had told you about Brusilov earlier . . ."
He stopped in mid-sentence. There was no point in discuss-
ing it further. "The Phoenix Program isn't over yet,"
Chance concluded, more to himself than her. *Gettysburg*
had ensured that.

Georgi Brusilov extended his arm very slowly, curious to
see if this would confirm his suspicions. His fingers were
balled into a fist which moved in a tight circle before
stopping just short of Donald Kelly's nose. The sailor's blue
eyes flickered, barely registering that an alien object had
come close to making contact with his face. Then Brusilov
drew back the fist quickly and swung, this time stopping
directly in front of the left eye. Kelly did not move. He
blinked, but that was the only indication that he might have
noted a possible bodily assault.

"Drunk, you say?" The general's voice echoed off the
walls of the closed room. "Have you ever seen anyone that
drunk before?" he inquired of the marine officer standing
beside him.

"I don't think so, sir." What else was he supposed to say?
"Though I have seen some of my men pretty close to that."
What else was he supposed to say? The American was so
drunk only the cold water was keeping him awake.

Brusilov's expression was one of sour disapproval. "You
said that your men have been physical with him."

"Yes, General. One of them thought it might bring him
around before you arrived."

"And did he vomit?"

"No, sir. There was very little response."

"And you still think he is drunk?" Brusilov concluded
derisively.

The marine stared back unsure of the answer he was
expected to give.

"If he was really drunk—so drunk that he could barely

respond to the threat of being smashed in the face—the treatment by your men would have made him sick. He should have vomited all over them." The general shook his head. "That's what a normal drunk would do. This man's been drugged. To you, he looks drunk, and he certainly smells that way, and that's exactly what you're expected to think."

The marine colored slightly. He looked at the American sailor, then his eyes returned to Brusilov. "He was like this when they turned him over to me. The one in charge on the ship appeared to be very disgusted with this one. He was the only one in this condition."

"Of course he was. That's exactly what you were expected to think." The general turned away abruptly. "I wonder how they found out," he muttered. "Send the others back to their ship. They're useless. I don't even want to waste food on them," he growled over his shoulder as he stalked out of the room. Perhaps he might learn something more from *Gettysburg*'s captain—but he doubted it.

Barney Gold had slept very little in the past two days and there were puffy circles under his dark eyes to enhance the bruises which were now turning a deep purple. But those same eyes also remained as alert as the first moment Brusilov saw the man. Gold obviously had used the adjacent toilet in Brusilov's office while he waited for the general's return since his thin, black hair was as neatly combed as possible around the bandages. His white uniform blouse was wrinkled but it had been smoothed as much as possible in front, the sides hand-pleated and tucked neatly into the back of slightly soiled white pants. He did not stand up, nor did he remove his feet from the other chair. Captain Gold was the picture of self-confidence as he glared haughtily down his aquiline nose at Brusilov. There was no indication of the obvious discomfort he must have been experiencing.

There is something . . . he knows it . . . no man would make the effort to look like that if he expected to remain a prisoner, Brusilov decided. "Well, Captain Gold, you must be tired after your long day." He glanced at his watch. "And an even longer night. We'll be seeing the sun very shortly."

"I hadn't noticed the time," Gold responded drily. There was no reason to offer this Russian anything, nor was there any purpose in becoming belligerent.

Brusilov smiled briefly without expression. "I'm surprised you didn't wait until tomorrow to take your little tour with Captain Boldin. Now that I think about it, it doesn't make much sense for us to allow a man in your position to be wandering around in the middle of the night." His thick eyebrows rose and his broad forehead wrinkled. "It would be rude of us to deny you some rest." He waited for a response.

"Maybe it's just habit," Gold answered. "Ship captains break their old habits very quickly. It's a twenty-four hour a day job when you're at sea. I suppose Captain Boldin is as used to living that way as I am. He didn't seem very tired either, and he was most anxious to see my ship."

"I'm sure he was," Brusilov remarked thoughtfully. Perhaps Pietr Boldin was afraid *Gettysburg* wouldn't be around for too much longer. "It also seems rather unusual to me now—more so than when Captain Boldin suggested it—that you'd allow a Soviet officer to tour your ship. As a matter of fact, it seems like the last thing you'd agree to." The general leaned forward across his desk. His carefully folded hands indicated an inner calm, but his irritation was evident as soon as the fingers on one hand began to drum on the knuckles of the other.

"As I said, I'm not in the habit of sleeping, not at times like this." Gold shrugged casually. "It was a fair exchange. I'm sure Captain Boldin decided it was worth it to exchange visits at any time, just on the off chance that some special new intelligence might appear that he was unaware of. I don't think I gave anything away. I looked at it the same way he did. At least it seemed like a fair idea until your marines came to drag me off Captain Boldin's ship before I'd been given a complete tour. Any reason for that?"

"There is a reason for everything I do." Brusilov leaned back in his chair and studied Gold's face. He saw a man much more relaxed than he should have been considering his situation. "I'm being left out of something. I can sense it," he said with assurance. "There are even a couple of little clues, nothing concrete but still they're there. Would you care to include me in your little secret?" He extended his hands, palms up, toward the American. "I am aware that something is happening around this base and I have no doubt it is due to your presence. I don't even know how you've become part of it but I have taken certain measures to make sure nothing gets out of hand."

"I'm afraid I can't help you," Barney Gold responded. "I haven't the vaguest idea what you're talking about." He held Brusilov's eyes with a blank, uncomprehending stare.

There was no purpose in spending more time with the American. "I'm sure there's no point in our wasting time in further discussion." The general glanced at the marine officer standing by the door. "Would you escort Captain Gold back to his room at my quarters. I want guards—your very best, marines, no sailors, no Vietnamese—at every door to the building, as many as you think necessary in the reception area, and I want you to personally remain outside his door until you hear from me." Brusilov waved his hand toward the door in a sign of dismissal.

Dinh followed Gold and his escort at a discrete distance until they reached Brusilov's quarters. Even in the dim street light, he could see the black berets on the squad of ten Soviet marines who waited at attention outside the building. He hung back, blending into the night until the light snapped on in Barney Gold's room, thankful that the street remained deserted. When the American appeared in the window, staring down onto the street, Dinh stepped from the shadows for no more than a second, barely long enough to be seen. He cupped his hands in a circle around his face as if he might be peering through a diver's mask, desperately hoping his message might be understood—*they had not forgotten Barney Gold*.

Then Dinh headed off for the tiny shack. The others would be there. Any moment now the first faint glow of dawn would be on the eastern horizon.

At the same time Nguyen van Dinh was scurrying through the shadows of the base at Cam Ranh Bay, a small group of men had assembled at one end of the hangar bay aboard *Theodore Roosevelt*. Heavy tarpaulins suspended from the overhead shielded them as they worked. On the opposite side of the tarp, armed marines were positioned every ten feet. No other individual among the more than six thousand men living aboard would observe what took place.

Those present included the carrier's commanding officer, weapons officer, nuclear weapons coordinator, the pilot selected for the mission, and three chief petty officers specially trained in nuclear weapons. The captain had first called the group together in his cabin shortly after receiving the President's message to detail the stipulations in their orders. These were equally vital to the mission, whether or not it was ever completed. If the mission was aborted for any reason, there would be no record of the flight. The aircraft would continue on to a secret base in Thailand rather than return to the ship to be disarmed. There were no other copies of the President's orders and the captain burned his in an ashtray after each of the participants had read it. It was understood before they ever left the captain's cabin that they would never say a word to another soul about their activities that morning.

The B61 bomb did not really have the appearance of a nuclear device, at least certainly not to civilian eyes. It wasn't as imposing as the two-thousand–pound conventional bombs and certainly bore no resemblance to those bulky versions of thirty years before. It was long and comparatively slender, pointed up front, fins in the back.

The casual observer might have likened it to a torpedo. When it was stored aboard *Theodore Roosevelt*, it was absolutely harmless. Specialists like the three chiefs were needed to prepare the weapon and the officers present were necessary because of the nature of the mission.

When the weapon was ready, they moved it by dolly to a position beneath an A-7 Corsair. There it was lifted into position, the interlock devices fitted, and the release system tested from the cockpit. It had been repainted to look as much as possible like a Sidewinder missile in the darkness. They were as ready as they ever would be.

The next step in the commanding officer's plan now began. Essential members of the crew were awakened for an emergency launch. Vitally needed medical supplies for a Thai village had been requested instantly, and the fastest available source was *Theodore Roosevelt*. A Corsair, they were told, was already loading on the hangar deck and would be ready shortly for launching to ferry the emergency supplies.

The process was a natural one, instinctive after so many thousands of launches. A tractor operator appeared to tow the aircraft to the starboard elevator. Two more men raised the A-7 to the carrier's flight deck where it was towed forward and spotted into the proper position. As *Roosevelt* began its turn into the wind, she was followed by a single destroyer hustling into plane guard station. There had been no purpose in disturbing an entire helicopter crew.

It would all take a little longer than normal but the captain didn't care to arouse the entire forty-man crew normally required for a catapult operation. He assumed the air boss's duties in pri-fly high above the flight deck. The fewer people involved, the fewer curious eyes.

In the darkness, the catapult officer depended on the reports coming through his earphones to report completion of each evolution in other areas of the ship. As he squinted into the darkness, the launch bar was engaged with the catapult, the holdback bar was set to prevent early launch, the jet blast deflectors reared up behind the Corsair, and each of the safety checks were confirmed.

Satisfied on the flight deck, the cat officer waved his green flashlight wand to the pilot. The A-7's engines roared at full power against the deflectors and, as soon as the pilot completed his own control checks, the exterior lights winked on.

The catapult operator gave his ready signal and the cat officer bent down in the traditional method to touch his green wand to the deck before thrusting his entire body forward with his launch signal. The operator's hand slammed down on the launch button. Instantly, the giant steam valve below decks opened to deliver hundreds of pounds of pressure to the catapult piston. The Corsair hurtled down the deck with tremendous force. It dipped slightly at the end of the flight deck before lifting its pilot and precious cargo into the black sky as if it was the most natural thing to do.

The captain's voice came down from pri-fly to each man wearing earphones, and it was passed on to those who weren't. He thanked each man for his professional devotion to duty in seeing that the vital package was now on its way. Then he called his air wing commander and asked that a squadron of Tomcats be ready on deck in one hour. It wasn't in his orders, but a sixth sense told him that anything was possible and *Gettysburg* just might beat the President's deadline. If she did, she could use air cover.

When the sun rose over the South China Sea that morning, a single A-7 Corsair was circling its assigned station at thirty-five-thousand feet awaiting a message from the President of the United States.

CHAPTER 17

Rick Ireland was the only *Gettysburg* officer in Building 408 to truly appreciate the SEALs' efficiency. It was purely by accident. He had no idea what had attracted his attention to the Vietnamese guard. Once again, there was only one of them awake and he seemed to be staring into space through drooping eyes that could close at any moment. The other had propped himself in a chair against the wall and was sleeping soundly. So Ireland glared back with what he was sure was a classic sneer.

The next moment's action was so rapid that he blinked involuntarily to make certain it had actually happened. Perhaps it was all his imagination. In that brief part of a second when his brain recorded the image of that hand snaking around over the guard's mouth until his eyes confirmed the action, he saw the man's head wrenched back. There was fear—raw, basic fear—instantly evident in those eyes as they opened wide, so wide that the whites seemed to fill his face. Sheer terror was replaced by the agony of recognition as his neck snapped. With that sound came brief resolution as the guard relaxed and accepted the inevitable death that was already clouding his eyes.

It was over so quickly that Ireland had not been able to convey what he had just witnessed to any of the others. It had only been a matter of seconds. Not a sound had been made. There was never any indication that the second guard was aware of what had taken place. As Rick was in the process of calling out to the executive officer, the intruder had whirled on his toes in anticipation. But he was not needed. A second man was already in the process of dispatching the guard in a slightly different but equally effective manner. This time there was no need for absolute silence. The chair he'd been perched on clattered to the floor as he was hauled out of it with a single sweep of a powerful arm. He was already dead before his body touched the floor. Once again, there had been no chance to sound any type of warning.

What the officers of *Gettysburg* now saw were two husky men clad in Soviet marine uniforms. One ripped a key ring off the belt loop of one of the dead guards and unlocked the door. As he stepped inside, a half-smile spreading on his face, Glen Marston recognized the SEAL who had dropped through the roof just hours earlier.

"Can I be absolutely sure you're anxious to get going?" Fran York enjoyed understating the obvious. The smile broadened as if he had just invited them on a picnic. He included the entire group with a sweep of his hand as he looked toward the executive officer. "They already divided into groups?"

"I don't think anyone's slept a wink since you were here," Marston answered. "I think the only problem we could possibly run into is that some of my younger ones have some idea about getting even." He was sure of the reaction; he just wanted it to come from another source.

Merry stepped inside, his eyes settling on the junior officers already grouped together. "I'm afraid there's no time for excitement." He was the opposite of York. "Look at yourselves." He gestured at their white uniforms. "Perfect targets. How many Russians do you expect to see running around this base at sunrise dressed in whites and carrying guns? The first cowboy who pulls a trigger without good reason is probably going to be responsible for getting a couple of you guys killed. You might as well get the romance out of your systems before you go out the door," he growled, "or end up like those two." He jerked his head back toward the guards' corpses. "Pretty naval officers bleed the same way. Dead is dead."

He was met with absolute silence.

"I'll break out the gear out there," he said to York as he headed for the door. "It'll be ready before these guys come tumbling out the door."

"We've got a small truck outside," York announced. "We couldn't get a hell of a lot of firepower for you because I guess their small arms are mostly in the barracks. But there are enough pistols and AK-74s to go around." He stepped over by the door and peered outside, acknowledging a sign from Merry with a wave of his hand. "Looks clear for now." He turned back to Marston. "OK, the three other group leaders first—you and your boys stick with me until they're gone."

Davis, Ireland and Ellard moved up beside York. "Now I want each of you out there one by one, but only when I tell you to. Someone could come along at any minute and be very unhappy about this. Peter will provide each of you with a weapon and some ammunition and tell you where to go to wait for the rest of your team. We'll try to make it as even as possible. Once you've got your team together, you're on your own. You know the route you need to take. Stay in the shadows as much as possible. The sun's ready to come up soon so you're going to be moving in the light before you get back to the ship." He shook an index finger at them as if he were talking to a group of schoolchildren. "Like Peter said, don't pull a trigger unless it's absolutely necessary because that will be the end of our little surprise and each of you will know exactly what target practice means." He looked down at his watch. "Now, do we all have close to the same time?"

SEALs were trained to function together like timepieces.

They knew each other's strengths and limitations and used them well. Their operations functioned with precision, even in the chaos of a firefight. It was awkward to be working with naval officers whose lives were built around missiles and computers.

York turned around to the others. "About fifteen minutes from now, you're going to hear some very loud explosions. Those should take out all the heavy artillery they might have had time to drag out otherwise. And there's not going to be any power on the base or to any of the Soviet ships. All phone lines will also be cut. So there's probably going to be some very angry people shooting at the ship and anybody they can see. Don't you start shooting unless you absolutely have to. And for God's sake, don't shoot at any Vietnamese civilians. There's going to be a bunch of them on your side and they're putting their lives on the line for something that I can't understand myself. If you've got a question, this is your last chance."

They stared back mutely. Reality had set in.

"Sixty minutes from now, that ship of your's ought to be backing down full. If you're not there when she gets under way, you become a statistic."

He turned back to his three team leaders and tapped Tommy Davis on the shoulder. "Go." After no more than thirty seconds, he did the same for Rick Ireland, then Jim Ellard.

In less then five minutes, Building 408 was empty. *Gettysburg*'s officers were on their way back to their ship.

If either the Vietnamese on board *Gettysburg* or the Russians on the pier had some familiarity with an American ship, they might have realized how unusual it was to find the crew already awake at dawn before the sun actually managed to peek over the horizon. The sounds of a ship become part of her personality and are accepted without notice by other sailors. Regardless of times or languages or evolutions, there is a rhythm that sustains a vessel at sea and brings her alive at the beginning of each day in port. Whether or not it is the same as another ship, those familiar with the daily cycle of sea life accept this rhythm as much as they would accept the daily functioning of their own body.

Gettysburg came alive with the sound of the boatswain's pipe and the familiar, "Now reveille, reveille, all hands . . ." There was a gradually increasing hum to the process. Voices—some sleepy, some angry—broke through that special silence that comes before full light. Faces appeared on deck to sniff the air. But they were all excited, anticipation evident on their faces, and there were those who didn't care to wait in line for the urinals and instead relieved themselves over the side. The first cigarette of the day for some brought on the first hacking coughs. The latent aromas of food, fresh bread, and coffee, that had been evident earlier now became pronounced as men began to move about the ship on their familiar duties. Sweepers manned their brooms. Hoses were broken out to wash down the decks. The metallic stink of brightwork polish spread as green scum was removed from copper fittings. It was entirely normal—*but it was an hour earlier than usual*.

The Soviet ships remained quiet, their quarterdeck watches the only sign of life. These Americans sailors were ambitious! Yet the guards on board *Gettysburg*, even the more professional Russians on the pier, failed to react as Chief Gannett feared they would. They were near the end of their watch and they were tired. As long as the Americans went about their business, there would be no trouble.

The officer in charge of the Vietnamese on board *Gettysburg* was becoming increasingly uneasy, however. His temporary office had been set up ashore where he'd been most of the night, alternating between playing cards with the base duty officer, making his once-an-hour visits to the ship, and napping. A half hour before, he'd received a call from the petty officer in charge aboard the ship. Two of the men from the previous watch section seemed to be missing.

He had no idea whether they had gone ashore and missed muster or if they might have found a hiding place aboard the ship to sneak a little sleep. It was better for his career if he reported their absence now, much better than noting it after the fact and being accused of dereliction of duty.

The Vietnamese officer was uneasy the moment he boarded *Gettysburg*. The gradual change of color on the horizon would eventually end his watch and he, too, would look bad if the two men were still missing. Somehow this American ship was already so alive it almost seemed ready to get under way. It was eerie. There was nothing he could see outright that would prove anything was amiss. Sailors, many of them in dungarees and tee shirts, performed simple jobs about the decks while others lounged in various locations talking or smoking. They paid little attention to their captors who now also eyed them uneasily. It all seemed normal, much too normal.

The previous day the Americans had pretty much been restricted to their quarters or designated sections of the ship requiring a work force after the morning field day. Today, though much earlier, they had reappeared throughout the ship as if the Vietnamese were not there. The situation was awkward. The Americans simply shrugged their lack of understanding when the guards tried to send them below. The tired guards had no idea what else could be done, so they avoided the Americans completely and reported their problems to the officer-in-charge. The situation was alien— it didn't balance—yet to them *Gettysburg*'s sailors were doing nothing more than appeared to be normal.

The Vietnamese officer called for *Gettysburg*'s Chief Master at Arms, whom he understood would solve all problems. When Chief Gannett sauntered up to the quarter-deck, the officer immediately began to gesticulate in concert with his barely adequate English. "See . . . your sailors all over ship . . . not wanted . . . like yesterday. . . ." He stammered on, alternating between Vietnamese and English, his frustration increasing when he decided he was not being understood.

Gannett was normally a happy individual. His round face often bore a slight grin even when he was chewing out a sailor. This morning, even with the dark bags under his eyes, a mischievous smile played at the corners of his lips. He folded his arms, and his black eyes twinkled as he listened to the Vietnamese officer. Then he removed his hat and ran his hand over his bald head as though he intended to smooth a patch of unruly hair. Finally replacing the hat at a rakish angle, he held both his hands up to still the sputtering officer facing him. "Wait. Calm down." And when the noise continued, "Shut up."

The officer did not understand what he'd been told, but he stopped. The tone, if nothing else, had delivered the message.

Gannett spoke as much with his hands. "Now, you," he said, pointing at the officer, "tell me slowly—what do you want?"

The officer looked about them and saw that many of the sailors had stopped whatever they were doing to watch the display on the quarterdeck. "Your men," he shouted, then stopped when he saw broad grins spread across a number of faces. "Your men . . ." he began again more quietly, ". . . they are not . . ." and he gestured by once again waving his arms, ". . . to be free out here . . . below decks," he indicated where they were supposed to be by pointing down at the deck.

Gannett loved it. His eyebrows rose in understanding. "Yes, yes, I understand. But, the ship is dirty. Clean . . . wash . . . polish . . ." he said, demonstrating each process to the amusement of the crew. "Clean ship . . . soon," he added with a satisfied smile.

"No . . . no clean," the officer said. "Sailors go below."

Gannett folded his arms stubbornly and shook his head. "Dirty ship!" he growled. "No good." He looked like an

Indian chief when he added, "Clean first," which received good-natured laughter from the sailors now gathered around him. This pidgeon English was, Gannett realized, right out of a western movie. He was enjoying every moment of his charade.

The laughter took the Vietnamese officer by surprise. He glared back at the sailors who remained totally without concern and placed his hand on the Tokarev on his hip. "Order them away."

Gannett's brow furrowed. "No need in pushing things, gents. Give us some breathing space." He waved them off the quarterdeck with his hand. "OK," he said to the officer, "what else?"

"Two men . . . my men . . . lost . . . I want . . ." He was puffing out his chest with authority when Gannett interrupted him.

"Two men?" He held up two fingers. He raised his eyebrows in understanding. "I saw two men go out on the pier." He pointed first at himself, "I saw them go off the ship." Then he pointed to the pier.

"No . . . no one left ship . . . order . . ."

Gannett nodded. "Yes, two men." And he again gestured toward the pier as if he had solved the officer's problem. "Go pee . . ." and he showed exactly what he felt they were doing before folding his arms with a satisfied grin.

"NO!" the officer shouted in frustration. "We search ship . . . now." His right hand now unsnapped the cover on the leather holster at his waist. "You help . . . or jail . . ."

His sentence was never finished. A brilliant light, illuminating all of them like a giant flashbulb, flared from within the base outlining *Gettysburg* against the sky. It was followed by a powerful explosion that echoed back and forth across Cam Ranh Bay in a series of thunderclaps.

The Vietnamese officer stared back at Gannett with widening eyes as if he might have suspected that reaching for his holster had caused the blast. His mouth opened slowly, forming an almost perfect "O." Was he about to comment on the explosion? Then, a second, more powerful one again rolled over them. This time, towering flames instantly lit up the night sky.

A series of smaller blasts followed. The ever-present gulls wheeled into the air as one, screeching their anger at this violent interruption to the start of their day. They were the first to react as the men on both the ship and the pier initially seemed transfixed by the glow of flames reflecting off billowing clouds of smoke. A third smaller blast, this time to the north in the direction of the airfield, finally jarred the Vietnamese officer from his stupor. Without a word to any of his men, he raced from the quarterdeck pushing Soviet marines aside as he headed toward the duty office at the head of the pier.

Gannett was swept along in the rush of men to the bow of the ship. There sailors and Vietnamese sentries stood shoulder to shoulder seemingly hypnotized, staring out as towering flames licked into the sky. Intense heat sent the smoke boiling high into the air to reflect the flames back to those on the ground. A series of sharp, secondary explosions continued to rumble back and forth across the bay. There was another smaller fire in the direction of the airfield that seemed to be dying down, along with the lights that were now flickering ashore. Gannett assumed that would be the reserve power station. The SEAL had explained how Dinh's Vietnamese workers would sabotage the main station.

On the pier, it was obvious the Soviets had shaken off the stupor that came with the end of a long night. An officer shouted orders above the din of the horns that whooped down the pier from the front of the duty office. The eerie howl of fire engines expanded the early morning to a scene of organized chaos. As Gannett watched, sergeants formed approximately half of the marine sentries in a loose order to sprint toward the head of the pier. *They're headed toward the source of the problem*, Gannett said to himself, *just like those crazy SEALs figured.* He was absolutely sure that not a Russian on the base had any idea that any American unit had actually infiltrated Cam Ranh Bay.

It was now time for him to initiate the next step, the responsibility Jimmy Gates had given him, if *Gettysburg* was to be ready when Captain Gold returned aboard his ship. Unnoticed by the Vietnamese sentries, who remained fascinated by the conflagration ashore, Gannett moved quietly about the decks passing the word to each of the leading petty officers.

This stage had to function in a timely manner, Gannett had explained earlier, or the Russians remaining on the pier would eventually become suspicious. The Vietnamese noticed that quite suddenly they were alone. It was an unusual experience being by themselves on this foreign ship and they were instantly uneasy. Their officer had disappeared. Flames still climbed into the sky. Smaller explosions continued to reverberate across the water. Yet the Americans, who were the first to the bow, were now paying no attention at all. What were they doing? Were their actions somehow part of this whole wild introduction to the day? Nothing had seemed right since the American sailors appeared on deck before the sun had risen. The bow was certainly no place to find out.

The first unfortunate emerged from an interior passageway and wandered slowly down the port side amidships. His rifle was now unslung, cradled nervously in his right arm. He peered over the edge at an object in the water exactly as he'd been expected to do. He never saw or heard the man who grabbed him. One moment he was walking on the deck, the next an arm had reached from a passageway and encircled his neck. A hand was clapped over his mouth at the same time he was jerked back inside. He could feel the rifle ripped away at the same time a foul-smelling cloth was clasped over his nose. The sour, chemical smell, sharp at first, rapidly disappeared with the unconsciousness that followed so quickly. He never felt his clothes removed from his body, nor did he notice the heavy line used to secure him tightly. In less than a minute, he was being lowered into Chief Ferro's engineering spaces.

A sailor in *Gettysburg*'s crew, one of a group chosen either for their oriental features or their small size, slipped into the guard's uniform, shouldered his rifle, and waited for orders to move out onto the deck.

Jimmy Gates had explained just hours before in chiefs quarters how critical the sailors' part would be to the whole effort. There were too many of the Vietnamese aboard to simply bang them over the head one by one. That was a sloppy method and it offered too much opportunity for a mistake. A single shout from a sentry who had not been knocked out would attract attention. And blood could make an awful mess of a needed uniform.

Gannett's sailors had practiced at their new talents the remainder of the night. None of the crew could have slept anyway when they were actually an integral part of liberating their own ship. Once again, Hogan, the chief corpsman, had provided the final solution. Chloroform was an old method, but the reaction was still the same a century later. It knocked people out quickly and efficiently.

The crew members who slipped into the Vietnamese uniforms stayed well out of the way as long as possible. When they did appear to display their newly acquired uniforms, they remained in groups on the bow or stern with their backs turned away from the others. None of them actually took part until there were just two of the Vietnamese guards left on duty, both on the quarterdeck. These were in full view of the Russian marines on the pier. They could prove to be the most difficult.

The first one was easier than Gannett anticipated. When a short Italian sailor, who appeared remarkably Vietnamese in his uniform, frantically waved his arms from a passageway forward of the quarterdeck, the sentry responded as they'd hoped. Sensing trouble of some kind, he followed the sailor into the passageway. He was greeted in the same manner as the others and disabled without a sound. It was a simple matter to dispose of him.

Chief Gannett had anticipated that the last problem is always the most vexing. The Russians on the pier could not be disregarded, no matter how curious they were about the fires ashore and the accompanying activity. So it was Gannett who appeared on the quarterdeck in the company of two of his own men in Vietnamese uniforms.

The last sentry had no reason to be suspicious. He was exhausted, more concerned with the activities ashore. He barely took notice of their approach. He had no interest in Gannett—none until the chief casually tapped him on the shoulder. The guard looked irritably at Gannett, who kept his back to the pier. There was no reaction until he became aware of the pistol aimed directly at his stomach. Then the other two sentries were pointed out to him, both with grinning American faces.

Gannett jerked his head back toward the midships passageway, emphasizing his silent message by pulling back the hammer on the gun. There was no opportunity for any meaningful response for the guard. He simply moved off down the deck with Gannett, his eyes magnifying the combination of respect and honest fear he had for the gun.

While a depleted group of Soviet marines remained on the pier to ensure that the ship remained secure, *Gettysburg* was once again in American hands.

To the east, the sky was now a glorious orange. Small fair-weather clouds drifted above the horizon sharply outlined by the rising sun. A new day was emerging rapidly in Cam Ranh Bay. A bright silver disk peaked over the South China Sea.

Georgi Brusilov was a survivor in a brutal, demanding system. Those who were capable of achieving flag rank did so in an era of suspicion, character assassination, and occasionally even the disappearance of competition. General Brusilov thrived in such an environment. As a result, he had grown into a thoughtful and very careful individual, introspective when the situation dictated and merciless when an opportunity to advance was presented.

He'd cut his teeth as a covert advisor in Vietnam, earning the respect that was critical in a combat situation. Afghanistan had been a place to avoid. Careers were destroyed there. So he adroitly maneuvered himself into a staff position in Moscow that catapulted him to a general officer's promotion. And when Cam Ranh Bay became the Soviets' first warm-water port and most critical military base in the Pacific, he convinced the right people in the Kremlin that the entire area should become an army command under someone who had already served in Vietnam and understood the people. The army was still the most powerful service in the Soviet military and it seemed logical that Brusilov fit the requirements he had indeed outlined himself.

Yet the past two days had been unlike anything he might ever have anticipated. His secondary mission, according to his seniors in the army, had been to convert Cam Ranh Bay into the most powerful combined military base in the Pacific, more vital even than the Navy's Pacific headquarters at Vladivostok. It would assure him future promotion and should be a guarantee of ending his career in one of those cushy billets in Moscow. But misfortune, combined with a badly flawed intelligence coup and the simple arrogance of a Vietnamese Navy captain, threatened all of that.

There had been little chance to sleep in the past forty-eight hours. His eyes were heavy, the muscles in his back and shoulders were tightening, and he found his thinking growing fuzzy as he forced himself to concentrate on the disconcerting events of the past few hours. At times like this he found that studying his problems in black and white often improved his perspective. So he jotted down the specific points that bothered him most on a blank sheet of paper.

Then, looking carefully at his notes, he waited calmly for

meaning and purpose to strike him between the eyes. Nothing seemed to fall into place. He found himself doodling with his pencil. All the figures appeared geometric, the straight, black lines neatly attached at acute angles, yet not even these seemed to make sense. They were purely an invention of his own mind. Then both the notes and the doodles grew fuzzy when he attempted to concentrate on them.

Brusilov rubbed both hands over his face, digging at tired eyes with his knuckles. The sandpaper sound of facial stubble rasped in his ears. Perhaps a shave would awaken him. But when he stepped into the adjacent bathroom, his eyes fell onto the small, dried pool of blood that the dispensary people had failed to clean up. He would insist that be done as soon as his orderly appeared. He threw a towel over the spot and stepped back into the office. He would shave in a moment. Meanwhile, out of sight, out of mind.

Perhaps a shot of chilled vodka would do. There was a small freezer in one corner of the room and he extracted a bottle and a glass, both of which instantly frosted over in the hot, sticky room. That was enough to remind him to turn up the air conditioning. Then he poured himself three ounces of the clear liquid, swirled it in the glass, sniffed at it out of habit, then took it down in one gulp. It was icy cold and dry, and at first it seemed just what he needed. Then it arrived in his stomach and began to churn what little remained of his dinner. The sensation was unpleasant. He could feel the heartburn rising and belched uncomfortably. Alcohol was definitely not the answer.

He stepped into the outer office and turned on the single burner that would heat water. When he looked for the box of tea that he liked so well, he realized that Miss Phuong must have kept it somewhere else and he was forced to get down on his hands and knees to search through the cabinet beneath until he located it. Brusilov had no idea how much she normally used so he filled the tea ball and dropped it in his glass. When the liquid looked dark enough, he would remove it.

The general was watching the tea kettle, waiting for the water to boil, irritated that it was taking so long, when the telephone rang. Who else knew he was in his office at this hour? It must have been transferred by the duty officer at his quarters.

He picked it up tentatively. What else could go wrong? "Brusilov," he snapped.

"General Brusilov, this is Major Kirov, the duty officer at the air base. We have an aircraft orbiting forty miles to the northeast at about thirty-five-thousand feet. . . ."

"Why could that possibly be reason to interrupt me at this hour?" Brusilov interrupted rudely.

"My apologies, General. This is an American aircraft . . . launched from their aircraft carrier that's been operating off the coast for the past few days. There are no others accompanying it. It is very strange, sir, very unusual considering current circumstances. I recommend we send some of our own to—"

"You'll do nothing of the kind." So, perhaps that was to be the solution. Maybe the Americans were threatening to employ a nuclear weapon . . . that's what the intelligence people in Moscow had included in their estimates. "No, that's not what I mean," he corrected. "I don't want to excite the Americans yet but I want equipment on the runway ready to intercept on my orders." He wondered why they would employ something so obvious. Why not a nuclear-tipped Tomahawk from one of the submarines? Maybe the obvious was . . . *to make their President's point obvious.*

The teapot began to whistle at him.

"Immediately, sir. Will you be in your office, sir, if I need you again?"

"I haven't the slightest idea," Brusilov growled. The whistling was increasing in strength. There was no need to be any ruder than he already was. "Use your head." He slammed the phone down.

He poured the water over the teaball, splashing himself and the cabinet and swearing under his breath. The heart-burn continued to bubble up with determination as he carried the glass of tea in its elaborate metal holder back to his own desk.

The notes that he'd made offered nothing more brilliant than before. Nothing seemed to fall into an orderly progression that would answer his questions. Even the doodles in the margins seemed the work of an illogical mind. The hook on the teaball had fallen into the glass and he fumbled with a pencil to retrieve it. Tea splashed out onto the pad of paper, blurring his notes. He sipped the hot liquid, burning his lips. The sugar—he'd forgotten the sugar. The vodka seemed to well up from his gut in a hot blast as the black, bitter tea passed it on the way to his stomach.

Brusilov was pushing back in his chair to go after the sugar when the first explosion rattled the building. It was much different to someone hearing it inside, conveying a deeper, more hollow sound. The second followed as he rose to his feet. It seemed louder, sharper, more distinct— perhaps a larger charge.

He rushed to the window in the rear of his office but he could see only the glow of fire against the buildings and trees. The source was to the north and he would have to go to the end of the building to determine the cause. In the outer hallway, he could make out dancing shadows caused by the flames. When he reached the window at the end of the hall, he had no doubt about what had taken place. It was clear that both armories had been targeted, though he could not imagine who might have done something like that. The local population was incapable . . .

Of course! Brusilov turned and darted for his office. He had encountered them before—*American SEALs!* Why hadn't he considered that earlier. They were the logical solution. As he turned into the outer office, the lights began to flicker. At first, it was pronounced—light, dark, light, dark—then they graduated to an amber glow, raising slightly once more before they were completely gone.

For a moment, he was in total darkness. Then the vague background hum of the emergency lighting came to his ears as the filament in the lantern in the upper corner of the room increased in brightness until everything was once again visible. It was nothing like normal but it was workable. The center of the spotlight fell on his desk, magnifying the stains on the blurred, wrinkled paper where the tea had splashed on his notes. No need for those. He had the answer. *He'd remembered*. He'd tangled with them before.

But now there was an emergency and there were orders to be issued. No one else understood what was happening. He must call out before he did anything else. He must contact the duty officer at the airbase. He wanted those aircraft off the ground.

But first he must alert Moscow. The Americans had more than one plan in mind for protecting their Aegis system. They would get that ship one way or another.

But when Brusilov lifted the receiver to his ear and began punching out the code numbers, he realized that the phone was dead. It was not surprising. They were very good at things like this. Very slowly, he placed the receiver back in its cradle. He had no doubt that the radios would also be dead, at least until emergency power was piped into the backup communications system. Whoever was leading this was good, very good! He remembered years ago . . . what was that name? Song Be! That was it. That was when the SEALs had done something like this when it was considered impossible by everyone else. He'd been humiliated then—but he'd also had his revenge. *Forget that for now*.

They would need him down by the pier. He removed the gun belt from his desk and strapped it around his waist, checking that the gun was loaded before slipping it into the holster. He dropped extra magazines in his pocket.

General Brusilov's eye settled on the glowing eye of the emergency lamp as he stalked from the room. He tried to remember the names of those SEALs from Song Be that intelligence had provided to him. Brusilov had created such a furor among his intelligence people that they finally dug up the names of the men on that operation. They'd meant nothing at the time, three Americans and three Vietnamese. However, the huge VC—Po had been his name—recognized one of them and Brusilov remembered his fit of anger that had been the ultimate reasons for razing that village. *He had been so humiliated by that raid.* Now the names had disappeared. He might recognize them if they were listed for him again. They had been superb at what they did. Was it possible? *The bastards were so good at what they did . . . so damn good.* Was it really . . . ?

Another explosion shook the building.

CHAPTER 18

"Coffee?" Jules Auger's voice, normally hoarse, had grown squeaky as the hours passed. The word sounded more like fingernails running down a blackboard.

"Couldn't taste it," Admiral Lyford answered. His throat was raw from a combination of cigarettes and coffee, and he was convinced his tongue would never again fit in his mouth. "I'm going to give up coffee—maybe take up gin instead."

The two of them had slipped back into Lyford's office to escape the confusion that been generated by setting wartime conditions— *conflict imminent* is the way the book defined it. Issuing orders and monitoring compliance at times like this were the reason that admirals had staffs. As Commander, Naval Special Warfare, Lyford had acknowledged the order and turned the details over to his number two. He'd proved most efficient in exercises and he would be now.

The junior officers were excited and, strangely, a little uneasy at the same time. Many of them had never come this close before, at least not on the global level. But they were SEALs and almost all of them had been involved in some type of combat or covert mission. This was different because those came under the heading of special operations

which involved small-unit missions. This time everything
was so different. Washington had no interest in spec ops for
the time being, with the exception of four SEALs at Cam
Ranh Bay, and strategy was oriented around the threat of
nuclear confrontation. That centered on a world of computers and button-pushers and that convinced Rollie Lyford to
make a little speech to his men. They reminded him of
retired athletes forced to sit in the stands and watch the
game. He explained that of course they all had better be
damned scared of a situation like this and pray with all their
might that once again the SEALs would come through.
What he had finished with was, "Pray for Chance if you
think you might have some contacts that will hear you."
Then he'd left the room with Auger.

"If only he'd waited until the time had passed, maybe
even given an extra half hour." Lyford was referring to the
President and the A-7 from *Theodore Roosevelt* that was
already orbiting off Cam Ranh Bay. "It's just going to incite
them. Sunspots have the same effect on their communications as they do on ours. What the hell would you do if you
were in their place?"

"Intercept."

"Of course you would. You ought to get shitcanned if
you didn't. So I don't think he sees that as his ultimate
weapon. He's just making good on his threats. If they shoot
it down, that shows they still think they need the ship to
compromise Aegis. If so, then he'll use a sub-launched
missile." He licked his cracked lips. His mouth was
foul-tasting. "Maybe I will have some coffee after all."

"How about the gin?" Auger croaked. "It might change
your attitude, which the President wouldn't like if he could
hear you now."

"If I had a couple of shots, I might just get him on the
pipe and tell him that I think . . . although in a couple of
hours it might not mean a shit anyway."

"Cream and sugar, I presume." The intelligence officer
was already pouring thick, black coffee into the stained

mugs. The cream was actually the powdered variety and it turned the coffee a muddy brown rather than lightening it. "This may pack more of a wallop than a couple of shots." He stirred and carried the cups over to a corner of Lyford's desk. "Do you think this might force them to pick up the phone in the Kremlin and tell the President they'll do whatever he wants if he just lays off that A-7?"

"Not a chance," Lyford answered. "They don't respond that way." He sipped at the coffee and made a face. "I'd hate to think coffee was the last drink I was ever going to have. I hope to hell Chance has got things swinging his way right now." He winked at Auger. "Got any fresh contacts we can pray to?"

David Chance reserved a second, a very short one, to congratulate himself for incomparable brilliance. When some shore-based captain he'd never met decided that York and Merry weren't that vital to the mission, and two others could just as easily replace them, Chance called Rollie Lyford. That had been all that was necessary. It took an extra couple of hours to deliver them but it had been worth the trouble.

The first two blasts were no more than fifteen seconds apart—perfect timing, even better than perfect considering how little planning time there was. What in the world did that four-stripe clown expect when he suggested two others would be just as effective? It had only taken that one call to Rollie, and York and Merry were on their way. The other two who had been suggested might . . . might have pulled it off like that, but there was no room for "mights" in this operation. In that all too brief second of self-congratulations, Chance could even imagine the expression on their faces. If York and Merry were together, they'd be into a couple of high fives like two kids. They were like that. It was a matter of pride. If you're going to blow something up, make damn sure it's done right.

It was a momentary reverie. Then Chance forced himself

to return to the real world. There were fresh, new sentries outside Brusilov's quarters, Soviet marines. It was just as Dinh had explained on his return to their little shack. And there were more by that front entry, and at the other doors also. The place was blazing with lights. A mouse wouldn't stand a chance in there! But why the hell would they put so many outside the front entrance? No one sneaks in the front door, not even in the movies.

Then he heard the thud of one more distant explosion. Perfect. *Now,* he said to himself, *if only Dinh and his people were able to hold up their end* . . .

The answer came as the street lights flickered, came back up close to original power, then faded, until only their filaments glowed. Darkness, absolute and enveloping, followed. The flames from the armories had cast an odd glow moments before even though the base had still been well-lit. Now, they were the only source of light, creating strange, dancing shadows as they reflected off billowing clouds of smoke. A weird quiet followed. It was more a product of the shock that comes with the loss of light, the disappearance of security. It was a strange effect and lasted only a few seconds but it also emphasized the secondary blasts emanating from the direction of the armories.

Surprise and darkness, after the sudden loss of the comfort of light, tend to magnify ensuing noises. The shouting back and forth between the marines around Brusilov's quarters was compounded by a general clamor that rose throughout the base. The automatic response of heightened voices was intended to instill comfort. Shouting indicated that control would soon be restored. The sirens and horns that followed, alarms, warning devices, fire engines, all contributed to a renewed sense that all would soon be well.

The din also provided a superb cover for Chance to check out the other two entrances. He scurried unobserved from one shadow to the next, until he was opposite the north door to Brusilov's headquarters. He arrived in time to see the door being secured, no doubt a reaction to the blackout. The beam of a flashlight on the inside was enough to convince him that a deadbolt had just been thrown. There would be too much noise if he tried to force it now, an exercise in futility.

Then he eased through the shadows to a position near the rear entrance where he squatted down to watch how those sentries would react. There were two of them, one with a flashlight. He was nervous, very much so if his handling of the light indicated anything. The beam scanned the surrounding area, stopped at each shadow, climbed each tree, even returned a few times to shadows that may have moved. The sweep was much too fast to locate anyone who didn't care to be found. That was good. Chance preferred them on edge. They could be distracted more easily.

The rear entrance was obviously his best shot, but one more circuit of the building was necessary. Never take the best shot for granted. They could be moving someone that had been on the north side to the back, or perhaps they even realized how foolish it was to overload that front entrance. He checked the street side once more and saw that nothing had really changed. The emergency lighting from inside the building cast a glow on the same number of marines as before, this time disciplined and at parade rest. It was no different on the inside, the same number of men at the same locations. Nothing had changed.

Why must the Russians remain so unimaginative even at a time like this? he wondered. *They were so rigid. They anticipated only the logical, and nothing that night had made sense.* Chance would have shot the officer in charge of security. This was a terrific visual display of establishing a guard, and it probably would have seemed more than adequate under usual circumstances—but this situation had called for the unusual from the minute *Gettysburg* entered Cam Ranh Bay.

Chance slipped back to the rear of the building. There were no other options. *Wasn't it simply a matter of figuring*

how to take out both of the guards at one time? He glanced
at his watch. Forty-five minutes max, no more than that.
Everyone understood. *Gettysburg* would start backing away
regardless. Whoever was on board had a life. Those
remaining ashore most likely would have no need to be
concerned—they'd be dead anyway. That ship would leave
on time because they were all professionals, and if David
Chance and Barney Gold weren't there then it was just
tough shit!

There weren't a hell of a lot of options, Chance admitted.
If one of them was to wander into the bushes for a leak in
the next five minutes, that would be just terrific. But life
didn't work that way. He couldn't take them both at the
same time. Oh, he probably could but that would most
likely involve a little too much noise.

It had to be one at a time. It had to be silent. It had to be
quick. And it had to be done right. There was no such thing
as a slight error. Even a moan as the first one died would
blow the whole thing.

Chance's greatest advantage was their nerves. Jumpy
men reacted. They didn't think. His idea could backfire just
as well, but it was his only opportunity. He scooped up a
handful of gravel and tossed it into the bushes where it
rattled off the large, waxy tropical leaves.

"What was that?"

"Probably some animal, monkey maybe . . ."

"There aren't any monkeys around here."

"Well, I don't know then. Go look if you're so curious."

"Well . . ."

"Scared?" The tone was taunting.

"I'll find out." Truculent.

Chance had dropped back into the bushes. Neither the
reddish glow from the fires nor the faintly tinged eastern sky
had yet penetrated the area. He could see the guard
approaching cautiously, his rifle unslung, poking at the
undergrowth with the barrel. The flashlight in his other
hand swept rapidly from one side to the other, then up and

down. It was almost impossible to spot someone like Chance when the beam was in constant motion. Chance didn't move a muscle. Occasionally the man would hook the barrel under a branch and sweep it back suddenly hoping whatever had made the noise might be spooked.

He stopped next to where Chance huddled and jabbed the rifle into the undergrowth directly opposite him. Nothing. Without warning, he reversed direction, whipping the tip of the barrel within an inch of Chance's face. The beam of the light swept up as the undergrowth weighted the tip of the rifle down. It took every ounce of Chance's willpower to remain stock still as the barrel came back in the opposite direction just as quickly. This time, it passed directly over his head, ruffling his hair as it swept by.

The guard looked over his shoulder, jerked the light to either side once again, then extended his arm straight out and bent forward to peer down the beam of light as if his sight were perfectly adjusted to the darkness. He hesitated, then took a step backwards, as if he was satisfied.

No . . . no . . . keep going, Chance said to himself. *If you stop now, it may be you who lives and me who'll die.*

"Find anything yet?" came the call from the other.

"Nothing."

"Check everywhere in there?"

"Almost."

"Too dark?" The brave one remained back by the door, enjoying his opportunity to tease the other. "Want me to finish the job?"

"I'll do it," the guard called back from the bushes, irritably. "After this, you can chase after things."

The man took a step past Chance, his shoulders hunched slightly forward, gun barrel swinging from side to side alternating with the flashlight. Then he took a second step . . . a third . . . one more . . .

Chance had risen to his full height on the sentry's first step, still completely masked by the shadows. On the second step he had positioned himself directly behind the man. No cat had ever stalked as perfectly or as silently. There was no sound as Chance's right arm came around the guard's neck like a whip, his forearm lifting in a swift, clean motion that slammed the man's mouth shut with tremendous force. The weight of Chance's body drove the man forward as his neck snapped back. The heel of Chance's left hand slammed forward in the same motion with a terrific force that broke his neck instantly.

Neither of them made a sound. Chance had sucked in a deep breath before moving. Now, as the flashlight clattered to the ground, he exhaled gradually. Holding the body and the rifle together, he lowered both of them down as softly as a pillow.

The other guard heard the light fall. "You all right?" he called out.

Chance picked up the flashlight and moved it back a few feet so that the body was beyond the range of the beam. Then he slipped back into the undergrowth again, moving softly toward the building.

The other guard was really the one who had been scared. There was no possibility he'd come back in as far, especially after he saw the flashlight on the ground. This time it didn't matter if there was a bit of noise.

The sound of rifle fire a few blocks away shattered the silence. It was a welcome break for Chance. That, combined with the havoc around the armories, would mask whatever was about to take place in the rear of the building.

"Alexei?" the guard called. There was a tremor in his voice that appealed to Chance. He hoped the man would be more afraid of his superior officer's reaction than the dark, and would come over to find out about Alexei.

"Did you find something?" A pause, then, "I don't think you're funny playing games like this."

He was inching slowly in Chance's direction. It was a slow process because he didn't have a light. Chance could imagine what was going on in his head, the combination of fear balanced by the desire to show that he was brave. In all probability, he was likely hoping Alexei was playing a trick on him and it was doubly important to show that he wasn't afraid.

Whatever bravery meant to the young soldier, it was short-lived. He never heard Chance, but he caught sight of him out of the corner of his eye at the last instant. He was partially able to throw up his arms to defend himself, but his reaction was much too late. Chance's knife was slightly deflected and the point was driven into his neck beneath the ear rather than slicing his throat neatly. He attempted to shout but his voice was turned into a gurgle as Chance covered his mouth with the other hand and brought the blade back across his throat. He lowered the body gently to the ground and hauled it into the undergrowth, thankful that the youngster had chosen bravery over reason.

Chance slipped through the back entrance of Brusilov's quarters. Dinh said he'd seen Barney Gold standing in exactly the same window as before. Chance was sure there would be someone either with him or staked outside the door.

Nguyen van Dinh recruited his volunteers carefully after the move to Cam Ranh Bay. Although the government in Ho Chi Minh City had undertaken a massive reeducation program for the defeated southerners, a generation of silent dissenters remained. They were men and women who had begun families even though a civil war raged, confident that the freedom they enjoyed would be passed on to their children in a better country. Even in defeat they knew they would continue to fight a personal war. They were an unseen partisan army waiting for an opportunity. Dinh had even coined a term for them that translated closely to Chance's word—*irregulars*. They liked that title.

Most, like Dinh, had lost part or all of their families. They had seen their brothers, sisters, parents, wives, even children slaughtered in a war in which few participants knew or cared whether the victims were military or civilian.

But the survivors knew—and they remembered. They carried vengeance in their hearts and they survived on patience, waiting for that proper moment to vent their rage.

There were both men and women in Dinh's private army, each able to recount stories of horrors that future generations would find difficult to comprehend. Many of them had remained alone since the war. They were a ravaged middle-aged society uninterested in starting family life over again in a country without freedom. Dinh had united those in Cam Ranh Bay under this common goal and their knowledge of each other offered as much promise as they had dared hope for in twenty years.

The individual talents within this small group were the result of careful planning. Luck had no part in it. Dinh had cut his teeth on covert operations with Chance when they worked in the Phoenix Program together. He had learned the essence of undercover machinations from the best. And during Chance's last mission in Vietnam, Dinh had convinced his American friend to spend an extra couple of days refining their training. For many of them, the opportunity to strike back, even if it was just once, was worth their lives.

It had been agreed the night before in Suoi Hoa that the SEALs would not be able to control the central power station in Cam Ranh Bay. It was too large and complex, and would require a large part of their limited explosives. Since a sustained power loss was as critical as limiting access to heavy weapons in the armories, it was a natural for Dinh's irregulars.

In addition to Dinh, three of his sergeants had remained on the base that night. Their initial responsibility would be to neutralize the alarm system along the base's perimeter to allow their comrades to cross over. They also were the ones who would appropriate the small military trucks—large ones would be too obvious at that time of night—to transport their mini-army and the weapons that had been secreted about the base.

It worked exactly as Dinh promised it would. He had

been taught that guns were dangerous and noisy and there-
fore useful only in a hazardous situation. Silence was
golden in a covert operation. There were no guards with
which to be concerned outside the power station. Inside,
their weapons easily convinced the duty officer that resistance would be a foolish choice. The Vietnamese workers
on duty inside had no desire to argue, and they were
replaced one at a time until the station was completely under
Dinh's control. Even if General Brusilov had happened by,
there would have been no apparent reason for him to be
concerned—all positions were properly manned. The first
step had been successful and there was more than enough
time to set up their defensive perimeter.

Dinh had already initiated his own countdown before the
armories blew. If York and Merry failed, Chance had
reasoned that the lack of power might still allow them an
opportunity. The few explosives they possessed had been
strategically set. Dinh couldn't have been more pleased at
the precision. There was no way they could destroy the
giant turbines, and they lacked the experience and finesse of
the SEALs, but their explosives did cause sufficient damage
to vital control panels to black out Cam Ranh Bay for more
than enough time.

Every light on the base winked out. Only makeshift
emergency systems in certain buildings activated to provide
minimal lighting. Computers, machinery, communications
equipment, alarm systems, even power to the ships at the
piers disappeared. The small backup station at the north end
of the base would have functioned automatically until main
power came back on line, but the SEALs had made sure that
was also out of commission. It would be more than an hour
before portable emergency generators could be set up in
critical areas.

Cam Ranh Bay was immobilized.

Theodore Roosevelt's commanding officer was dozing in
his chair in the pilot house when an excited voice from radio

central called on the squawk box beside him. "Captain, we've got a strange transmission down here. The pilot of some American transport plane had come up on one of our primary circuits and says there's some excitement around Cam Ranh Bay that you ought to know about. He says his call sign's *Loner* and his orders were to talk with you direct."

That was his A-7 pilot. His orders had been to use his radio only in an emergency. "Thank you. I'm aware of *Loner*. Patch that circuit up to me here." The captain knew the A-7 pilot would never compromise his position without something vital to report. It had to be a change on the ground that might affect the mission.

When the speaker above crackled into life, the captain called the A-7 pilot immediately. "*Loner*, this is *Number One*. Do you have a message for me? Over."

"Roger, *Number One*. I have a status change that could affect my cargo. I have a fireworks display taking place on the ground that looks like it could really amount to something. Someone's been setting off some heavy stuff. I have fires in sight and out of control. Also, a major power failure base wide. Over."

"This is *Number One*. You may have to deliver your cargo at another destination. Maintain your position and guard this circuit until I have further word for you. Out."

The captain's next call was to his air boss. "Be ready to scramble those Tomcats in twenty minutes." Then he headed for his cabin. He hoped he would be able to prepare the message for the President in a one-time code double-fast. Maybe—just maybe—the White House would let him send in his Tomcats as an escort. The A-7 could hold in orbit for the time being in case his mission required completion. Better yet, it sounded like those SEALs might be accomplishing something. Whatever, he had no intention of sacrificing his A-7 pilot. He suspected the aircraft was bait to test Soviet determination.

Tom Davis huddled in the shadow of a warehouse with

his team, each of whom was positive their white uniforms glowed like neon lights. That SEAL had scared the hell out of them. Naval officers had never been trained to scurry about from shadow to shadow with rifles, like marines, and they were nervous. Fifteen minutes before, Merry had promised that Cam Ranh Bay would be turned inside out. It was just a matter of waiting until the lights went out and then the rest would be easy if they used their heads. They would have preferred the lights go out before they ever left Building 408.

Davis peered at his watch and shook his head. It seemed that whenever you waited for something it took that much longer. He'd already noted that familiar glow to the east with longing. It would be a while yet but the sun would be taking away whatever advantage they might have with darkly shadowed streets after the lights went out. Davis looked over his shoulder. He couldn't make out what was behind him but he saw the figure in white shrug. That was it. All they could do was wait and hope no one was curious about five Americans in white uniforms huddled outside an old warehouse.

He had barely turned back when the first blast shattered the night air. It rattled off the metal sides of the nearby warehouses and out over the bay, which was no more than half a dozen blocks away. It was immediately followed by two others. Seconds later the street lights blinked a few times before plunging the area into total darkness. There was no doubt that the SEALs had done their share. Now it was a matter of getting back to *Gettysburg*.

Davis led his group through the cluttered alleys between the warehouses, racing from building to building as the sounds of a frantic base were magnified by the mystery of darkness. Once, they were held up crossing a major street as trucks raced frantically north toward the blazing armories.

When they drew near the main thoroughfare a block from the head of the piers, the vague forms of sentries were outlined by the reflected light of the flames on one side and a brightening sky on the other. They were mostly Soviet marines now and all of them appeared totally alert. Were they perhaps awaiting the appearance of a bunch of American naval officers in white uniforms? There was no chance to get closer to their ship without attracting attention. Davis drew them back behind the closer building. It appeared more and more likely their weapons might have to be used. But they would wait until they heard the others.

It was no different with Glen Marston's group. It took that much longer to get into position because there was more activity near the central part of the base. They took cover one street above *Gettysburg* where they could observe the remaining sentries on the pier. There were less than had been reported earlier, but that made no difference. They were more heavily armed. Marston knew they'd need help from the ship. There were no choices—just remain invisible until it was time. He hoped the junior officers a few blocks north of him would do the same.

Rick Ireland had kept his team under control much the same as those south of him, hiding his people under a loading dock less than a block from the piers. It had seemed to work almost too perfectly considering how quickly the plans had been devised.

The first problem developed when an emergency repair crew was sent to the main power station. As they came within sight of the building, they encountered protective fire from Dinh's people who had established a perimeter defense around the plant. Jim Ellard's team was caught near the edge of the firefight. They remembered Merry's warning that there were a number of Vietnamese on their side. When they saw Vietnamese civilians involved in a firefight with Russian troops, they opened fire themselves. It was the first significant mistake that morning.

CHAPTER 19

The Chief Master at Arms aboard a ship like *Gettysburg* not only is an expert at handling men, he is the liaison between the captain and the crew. He is akin to a concert master, seeking the balance between command structure and those who make the ship function. Ben Gannett was all of this, and he also knew when to listen to someone else.

When it came to handling small arms effectively, he delegated the responsibilities to the chief gunner's mate. The gunner was one of the few Vietnam veterans still on active duty. He'd sailed as a youngster in that brown-water navy serving as a gunner on the old PBRs and Swift boats. Sailors in those days handled small-caliber weapons as often as the marines. They learned how to set up ambushes, calculate fields of fire, and they could work a firefight from a high speed boat careening down a canal while the enemy remained unseen in the dense undergrowth. The gunner had done it all before he'd gone to school to learn about missiles. When Gannett turned over the responsibility of setting up a small arms defense for *Gettysburg* to him, it was like a dream come true for the gunner.

Gettysburg was to open fire on the pier on her starboard side as soon as their first team of officers was seen in an effort to create a safe passage to the ship. The gunner also set up twin automatic weapon positions to cover the shore in either direction. Gates had said that Chance wanted the Soviet marines under fire from two directions.

The ship's lighter caliber weapons had been distributed gradually from the small arms locker. It was a time-consuming process that had begun the night before but eventually the weapons were in the exact positions assigned by the chief gunner. As the light increased to the east, the sailors moved furtively about the ship one at a time to avoid attracting attention from the shore. The men wearing the Vietnamese sailors' uniforms gave the appearance of an effective guard.

By the time firing opened up near the power station, Chief Gannett knew that *Gettysburg* was as ready as she could be. The bow, the signal bridge behind the pilot house, and aft on top of the hangar became central battle stations with a chief petty officer in charge of each one. They were all coordinated over the ship's sound-powered phone system by the chief gunner, who had taken position with Gannett on top of the pilot house. The gunner felt as if he were once again back in his brown-water navy.

Below decks, all machinery had been tested and Chief Ferro had the engineering department manned and ready. The sea detail team would be ready to man the pilot house the moment Barney Gold set foot on the pier. The combat information center was prepared to light off *Gettysburg*'s Aegis system for air defense on the assumption Soviet aircraft would be scrambled from the adjacent field. And men were ready with fire axes to cut through the shore lines when the ship was ready to back down.

As the sound of firing increased ashore, Ben Gannett was sure that everything had been done to prepare *Gettysburg*'s escape.

Georgi Brusilov's car halted a reasonable distance from the burning armory. While the loss of the structure and its contents angered him, the sight that most impressed the general was not the flames themselves. It was the expression in the eyes of his driver. Sitting in the back seat and studying the reflection in the rearview mirror, Brusilov could see the man's face illuminated by the brilliance of the fire. Multicolored flames danced in those eyes magnifying the terror that tightened his face. The man's fear amazed Brusilov. There was no shooting, no threat to their lives. They were a safe distance from a fire that the base firefighters were quickly neutralizing. Yet there was fear. The general was disgusted.

"Is something bothering you?" Brusilov leaned forward in his seat as he addressed the driver.

The man jumped as if he'd received an electric shot. "Bothering . . . no . . . not at all, General." But his eyes contradicted his words.

"Then I'd like you to join me. I'll need someone to take some notes perhaps." The sound of small explosives detonating in the fire punctuated his words.

The driver's eyes grew larger as Brusilov spoke. There was no way he could refuse.

"I'm sure there's no danger now. They'll have the fire under control shortly. It's not likely there's much left to explode in that heat," he added as he opened his own door and stepped out. It hadn't been necessary to add that last sentence but he found himself thoroughly enjoying the young man's fear. It was a natural reaction, Brusilov decided, caused by his own frustration at not having an enemy to retaliate against. The driver was just one more of those two-year conscripts who was sure he'd lucked-out with a soft job during his tour of duty. Other than the marines and some of the senior officers and noncoms, there were very few in Cam Ranh Bay who had ever experienced any danger during their military time.

The man was a simple foil, Brusilov willingly admitted once again, who served the purpose of releasing some of his own tensions. "Stick close to me, and perhaps we will survive the day," he snarled caustically as he waved the driver over to his side. "We'll talk with the captain first." He gestured toward the man who was shouting orders to the firefighters over a bullhorn.

Secondary explosions continued to frustrate the battle against the flames but Brusilov moved as close as humanly possible, slowly circling the building. The fire captain's answers to his question did not satisfy him. He needed to see for himself exactly where the fire had started. Armories simply didn't explode of their own accord—not two within fifteen seconds of each other.

They had eased around one side of the building toward the rear where one of the walls seemed to have collapsed. Just the shape of the hole convinced the general it was most likely from some type of explosive. "Look, what's that?" Brusilov called out. He wasn't absolutely sure himself, but he would have wagered that he was pointing at the body of one of the missing guards.

"It looks like a body," the fire captain ventured, but he had no intention of moving any closer to find out. "I don't know what it would be doing back here. . . ."

"Send two of your men to bring it out," Brusilov interrupted.

"General, it's awfully hot that close. There won't be much to—"

Brusilov never let him finish. "There's no time for silly excuses. They have protective equipment." He moved closer to the man until their faces were no more than an inch apart. His voice was a howl against the crackle of flames. "I have no time left. If your people aren't capable of a simple effort like that, my driver and I will have to do the job ourselves, and then you and I will settle this later."

"We'll do it, sir," the captain conceded. "I'll get two of my men right away." He trotted off without another word.

Brusilov turned to his driver with a triumphant smile but that vanished as he searched that other face. There were tears forming in the man's eyes, either from fear or purely the fact that he felt he had just been saved from a frightening assignment.

In a moment, two men in protective suits rushed in close to the building under a curtain of water that raised steam from them and the object they were ordered to retrieve. What they layed at Brusilov's feet was a man, but the heat of the fire had burned off the clothes and charred the corpse to the point that he would be difficult to recognize.

"Have you ever seen this individual before?" the general asked his driver. His voice was high pitched and cruel. "Bend down, look closely to be sure." Brusilov was amazed how much he was enjoying this moment, especially since he knew he had little time for such frivilous games.

The driver's eyes had been closed. Now his entire body shook as he slowly opened them and bent down. The smell that invaded his nostrils brought the first heaves, which he managed to choke back. He looked up at Brusilov and shook his head.

"Roll him over."

The young man again closed his eyes briefly before he reached out with a shaking hand and grasped a blackened arm. Two more internal heaves, then a third racked his body as he touched the corpse for the first time.

"Not that way, you idiot. You'll just tear the skin off. This is what you do." Brusilov placed his boot on a hip and gave the body a vicious shove. It rolled over on its back. "Hah, just as I thought. Look at that." He pointed to the red, gaping wound that had been the guard's throat. "See, we are playing with some tough ones." *SEALs—it has to be SEALs!*

The driver desperately tried to hold back one final massive heave before he vomited on the ground beside the corpse. Then, very slowly, he straightened up with the tears streaming down his cheeks.

The general had no sympathy. "Now that you've gotten that out of your system, you should be able to act like a man," he snarled. "Don't ever forget what you have just seen," he continued, pointing at the body. "What that means is that we have some unwelcome guests on our base, some American special forces, I expect." He grabbed the driver by the arm. "Come on. If you stick close to me, you may just survive the day."

As soon as they were in the car, Brusilov explained that he intended to go to the piers but first there would be a single stop at Building 408. Then he called over the radio for the officer in charge of his marines to meet him at the pier. If the general was correct, his enemy would remain unseen until the last possible moment. There would be no targets. The presence of every available Soviet marine would be critical.

Building 408 was exactly as Brusilov expected—empty. The guards' corpses in the outer room were further proof that the Americans who had somehow infiltrated the base were experts at quick, covert movement. For a moment, he considered heading for his quarters to be sure that their Captain Gold was still a prisoner. Then he decided that *Gettysburg* was indeed the reason for all of this and expanding the security around the ship was more important until he had more information. After all, his quarters had been turned into a fortress.

The officer in charge of the marine detachment was already on the pier when Brusilov arrived. He was anxious to support his men. "Nothing's changed with the ship, General. No one has gone aboard or departed during the current watch."

Brusilov glanced up at the Vietnamese uniforms on the main deck. The Vietnamese, whom he currently detested, carried rifles slung from their shoulders. They paid no attention to the Russians on the pier, appearing totally unconcerned that the base commander had just arrived. Both they and a surprising number of American sailors were obviously more interested in the activity ashore.

"I thought it was understood that the American sailors were to remain below decks."

"They began to wander up as soon as reveille sounded, sir. I suppose there's only so much that can be done to keep them down unless we chase the Viets away. I'm told the Americans have just been going through the normal routines—sweeping down the decks, polishing bright work, that sort of thing."

Brusilov glanced at his watch. "Reveille?" He looked toward the east where the brilliant colors were disappearing into a normal golden sky as the sun rose. "An hour before sunrise?" Everything aboard *Gettysburg* appeared so normal that he knew something had to be very wrong. "I think it's definitely time to . . ."

That was when heavy gunfire—automatic weapons— erupted in the direction of the power station. The activity increased much too quickly to be an isolated incident. Brusilov's feet were moving with the marine officer's before he ever finished the sentence.

If ever there was a calculated risk, this was it. The captain of *Theodore Roosevelt* had always been considered a rational man. That was one of the reasons he had vaulted over so many of his peers to take command of the giant carrier. But a decision like this was reserved for presidents. A captain never ordered a launch just for the hell of it. There was a purpose in everything. In this case, after personally handing the encoded message to the communications officer who waited patiently beside his desk, the captain called the air boss. "I want to launch just as soon as we can. How long?"

"They're not all on deck yet, Captain." The air boss prided himself in the performance of *Roosevelt*'s air group but fueling, arming and lifting them to the deck took time. "Another ten minutes . . ."

"I'll join you in pri-fly in five. I want some birds in the air super fast. Their CO can round them up however he wants once they rendezvous. But I want to send a message out to shore-based radar stations as soon as the first one's in the air."

"Say again, sir. I'm not sure I understand . . ."

The captain disconnected and called his OOD on the bridge next. "Prepare to launch in five minutes. I'll be in pri-fly."

Roosevelt was bathed in a golden early morning sun as the first Tomcat roared off the catapult. The aircraft dipped slightly at the end of the flight deck even as the pilot gave her full power. Then it clawed into the air, climbing like a falcon as it banked off to starboard. The captain was surprised at his own feelings as he watched each of the fighters arch skyward. A feeling of exhilaration coursed through his body.

There was as yet no response from the President to his message, nor had he expected one so quickly. But he was confident in his decision. He was one of the chosen few to be given command of an attack carrier for situations exactly like this one. There were fires ashore—that SEAL may just be pulling it off! That *Gettysburg* would somehow be getting under way shortly in Cam Ranh Bay was pure speculation. But he preferred that if she did, there would be an escort to bring her safely out into the South China Sea. If his decision was later found to be provocative, so be it. Better that he do it this way than have to forward an order to that single A-7 orbiting off the Vietnamese coast. That one deserved to be protected, too, until it was on the ground in Thailand, depositing that strange cargo in a hangar on some distant airbase.

David Chance stopped before he had climbed halfway up the back stairs of Brusilov's quarters. He was panting like a puppy dog out of breath, and he was making sounds more like a rusty old steam engine than the cat he was supposed to be.

Covert meant *secret* which meant *unseen*—and how was he to remain unseen if he sounded like this? Obviously, he realized, it was the end result of the action in the back garden. It was habit. In the past, when it had been critical to remain silent, Chance would hold his breath. It wasn't at all difficult. He'd learned early on, during the first days of SEAL training, that he had a tremendous capacity for holding his breath. If a man couldn't, and he had a problem with breathing apparatus underwater, he would most likely be a dead man. In school, you became an automatic flunk-out because none of the others needed a partner who might give away their position. David Chance was the champion in his class. In Vietnam, it was more instinct the first time it happened. He had no idea he was actually holding his breath until a VC sentry lay dead at his feet, and his chest began to hurt from the effort. But the discomfort was nothing because the VC never heard him and Chance was very much alive. He was convinced it was a habit that kept him alive a number of other times.

But this was twenty years later, and lungs that had been in business for upwards of forty years simply didn't react the way they used to. He still remained unaware at times when he held his breath—it really was a habit—but he was no longer going for the record. The pain in the chest came sooner, as did the first sensations of dizziness. When breathing resumed, he found himself gasping more than in the past and he was sure he was making too much noise.

No, it wasn't logical to hit the top of the stairs sounding like a steam engine. Instead, he crouched low in the shadows and modulated his breathing as quickly as possible. He went over the security system in his mind. Most of it would be useless until they had some emergency generators on line. Somewhere down the above hallway there was an emergency lantern which cast a somber shadow just at the break of the stairs.

He listened for any hint that someone else was above. But there was nothing, not a footstep, not a sigh, not even the scrape of someone shifting their position.

Satisfied that he had complete control of himself once

again, Chance crept to the top of the stairs. Remaining in the shadow of the emergency light, he peeked over the lip of the last stair. Nothing. He saw the lantern bolted to the ceiling at the far end of the corridor casting its dim glow toward both the stairway and another hallway that ran off at a right angle. Halfway down that one, there was one more set of stairs that led up to the top floor where Barney Gold was kept. Rooms were on either side of the hallway but all the doors were shut. He had no intention of checking any of them.

Chance moved silently down the corridor to the break. He halted there, held his breath, and listened. This time he was even more surprised. Considering the abnormality of everything that had happened the past two days, even more in the last hour, Chance would have circulated guards throughout the building. It still made no sense to him to put all that firepower in the front, the least logical place to gain entry, if you thought someone might attempt to release your prisoner. Yet that was exactly how it seemed to be going. Maybe there was even more advantage to turning out the lights than he'd thought!

One hand rested on the gun under his shirt as he crouched and peered around the corner—nothing—before proceeding up the hall to the next stairway. This last stage would be just a little more hairy. There were also stairs leading down to the main room on the first floor. Voices flowed up the stairwell and he caught snatches of conversation concerning the explosions at the armories and the power plant. But there was nothing that indicated great concern about the man held prisoner in the room on the top floor. Chance was amazed. They were more concerned about what had already occurred rather than what could happen next.

He snaked across the open space on his stomach, almost invisible in the weak light, unless someone came up towards him. Rising to his knees on the far side of the stairs, he once again concentrated on the sounds from below until he was certain there was no one coming in his direction.

Then he moved up the darkened stairs toward the glow that came from another emergency light—probably near the door to Barney Gold's room.

Crouching just below the top step, gun now in his right hand, Chance gradually raised his head until he could peer down the corridor. *Bingo!* Gold had to be in there again because there was a Soviet officer outside the door, perched on a chair that was balanced on two legs with the back leaning against the wall. He was reading a magazine, holding it close to his face in the dim light. Outwardly, it didn't look difficult, with one exception—a gun lay casually on his lap and Chance was sure anything unusual would bring that gun into his hand in an instant. The only approach to the room was from exactly where Chance crouched. The distance between the stairs and the sentry was no more than thirty feet. A shot would bring a horde of people from below.

Okay, sit back and think about this, Chance. If you've come this far, you can afford an extra thirty seconds. There was no way he was going to use a gun here. The minute he showed himself that sentry was going to pull the trigger— *one dead Chance!* If he shot that guard, it would be quite simple to break Gold out of there. But there would be one major problem after that—the hail of bullets as they tried to escape. *One dead Chance, one dead Gold.* There was no way, none at all, that he was going to get any closer to the sentry either.

His knife was the only answer. *How long has it been since you've thrown the damn thing?* That brought back memories of SEAL training and of instructors who weren't all that damned sharp themselves trying to teach novices how to throw one. He remembered one of them who was so good. The man had saved his own neck more than once before by killing men that way and he promised that some of Chance's class would do so during their tours. There were not many military types who could throw a knife well, the man had explained. The ones who were the best had

been African hunters, New Guinea mountain dwellers,
American Indians—those who had first learned to function
without gunpowder. If they could do it, SEALs better damn
well learn also.

Chance had learned. And he had also used the knife on
his first tour. That first time he'd taken out a sentry guarding
a VC ammo cache. They had no idea if there were mines or
booby traps surrounding the area and the lieutenant in
charge was willing to consider any ideas. Gunfire would
bring all the guard's buddies who were swimming in the
river. Chance had said nothing. He took out his knife, and
before the guard could respond he was clawing at the hilt of
the knife embedded in his throat. Then they were able to
blow the cache and take out the swimmers, all within
minutes.

From the moment that patrol returned to base, every
SEAL was required to take lessons from Chance until they
were considered qualified. Most of them never had the
opportunity to use their new talent but those who did always
made sure to set up as many beers as Chance could drink
when they returned.

Now, as he crouched in the shadow of the stairs, he
slipped the knife from the sheath and balanced it in his
palm, feeling its weight, remembering exactly how this one
should be held. His man was sitting, a motionless target.
There was no need to lead him. On the other hand, he was
holding a magazine in front of his face. The throat, always
a good spot, wasn't exposed. The arms covered either side
of the upper chest. If he happened to mistakenly hit an arm,
he pictured what would happen in the next second, and how
the stairs below would fill with every goddamn marine in
the building.

Chance closed his eyes and snapped his wrist a few times
to get the feel once again. He dug back in his memory to
remember the care he had taken each time. The only
mistakes had come when he was practicing, never when it
might have been life or death.

Then he reared up on his toes, uncoiling in one fluid motion, his right arm back, then arching forward, wrist snapping at the precise moment, his entire weight coordinating with the flow of his body. He did not see the knife fly. His entire being was concentrated on the sentry. The magazine had not yet dropped from the man's grasp although the hands had opened. His mouth had dropped, more from surprise, because there was no time to actually identify what was taking place.

The knife buried itself just below the guard's sternum and the impact that knocked the wind out of him also slammed him back against the wall. There'd been no chance to cry out. The gun in his lap clattered to the floor as Chance vaulted down the corridor. Before any other sound could be made, the heel of Chance's hand jammed up under the sentry's chin, snapping his head back against the wall. Then, yanking him forward by the hair, Chance snapped his neck. Only seconds had passed. It would have been impossible for anyone downstairs to have heard what had just taken place if their conversation was still going on.

Chance scooped up the guard's gun and pushed open the door. Barney Gold had just turned from the window at the sound and his mouth hung open in surprise as he stared back. "I was beginning to think that girl was crazy until that first blast went off." Then he smiled casually as if this were a common, everyday situation. "Then I knew there had to be such a thing as SEALs."

"Here." Chance handed him the guard's gun. "You and I are out of time. Your ship is going to be leaving here real soon." He turned, beckoning with his hand. "Just stick close. Don't use that thing unless you absolutely have to because there's a hell of a lot more of them than there are of us."

"Love a SEAL," Gold murmured to himself as he followed David Chance out the door.

Phuong had served her purpose—at least that was the

way she interpreted it when she learned her part in the operation was considered over. Chance supported Dinh when he presented it as a final decision, no argument allowed. It was for her own good. The next few hours would be much too dangerous. She'd anticipated it would happen that way but that didn't make the prospect any more palatable.

Her father had held her tight and whispered that she shouldn't worry because whatever happened would make him happier regardless. Then he was off. She knew he would be involved in defending the power station with his people—his *irregulars* as he called them. She had no doubt he would have little regard for his own life in his effort to destroy Brusilov. What concerned her even more was the fallout from the rebellion of Dinh's small band. It would all be over in the next hour. Where did they think they could all go once the Americans and their ship were gone? The Russians would root them out—*one by one.*

Chance was the last of the SEALs to leave that little shack. Somehow she'd understood that her father knew how she felt because it was his wish that Chance should be the last to leave her. David had held her tightly for longer than she had hoped for, less than she wished. He kissed her, wiped away her tears, said everything that she had wanted to hear, then had slipped away into the night.

Phuong had no idea whether she would ever see any of them again.

They simply didn't want her involved. Her father had insisted she'd already taken too many chances in Brusilov's office. This wasn't her battle, Dinh said. Those involved were in it because they had earned the right years before— and they had scores to settle. After it was all over, she would still be safe.

Phuong had decided ahead of time that silence was her only option. She gave them no argument. Let them believe what they wanted. But, just as soon as she heard the firing near the power station, she slipped away from the little shack that had been their meeting place and followed the alleys down toward the piers. When she approached the firefight at the power station, she was very careful to keep herself hidden but she desperately needed to see what was taking place. She wanted—needed—to help!

Somehow she'd known she must remain involved. Her subconscious seemed to dictate it. There was no memory of the massacre at Can Fat, nor did she possess a concrete picture of her mother in her mind. Yet there was something that seemed to be driving her. The survivors of Can Fat, she and her father, owed a debt to those who had died—Dinh was in the process of meeting that obligation and Phuong accepted the same responsibility even though she had no actual memory of the event.

But now that she was here . . . what? She remained secure in her little sanctuary as the firing increased, surprised at how calm she remained. Why wasn't she terrified? The noise was deafening. The sound of automatic weapons, the whine of bullets ricocheting, the shouts of men on both sides—all of it seemed part of another world, one that shouldn't have existed. Men were being hit, perhaps dying right then. Their screams of pain were magnified by the realization of what had happened to them.

Was this the way it had been at Can Fat? Had her relatives experienced this same horror? If so, had they also wondered why they had been singled out to suffer in that fashion? The people involved here were military—even Dinh and his *irregulars* considered themselves soldiers for their cause. Was it easier to accept because of that? Was that why she had come here to be part of this? To pay the debt that was part of surviving Can Fat?

She couldn't see her father, but she could tell approximately where he and his men were located because the Russians seemed to be concentrating their fire in one direction. And as they did, some of the Soviet marines were apparently ordered to spread out because she saw men run off to either side. Then one of the Russians who seemed to be heading directly toward the place she was hiding went down. He had been trying to make it to the alley and had fallen just before he reached safety.

Phuong stared as he struggled to rise to his feet. Bullets spattered around him. As she stared with a sick fascination, he looked up and his eyes locked on hers. She saw the enemy suffering—yet she could not imagine that this man was guilty of any crimes as his eyes pleaded with her for help. They were the eyes of a lost human being, terrified that he would die in this street so far from home. *Why was it this way?* She experienced an unanticipated sorrow for the young soldier. As much as she searched, there was no hatred for him in her heart. All she could see in those eyes that were pleading with her was fear.

She scurried from the safety of her shelter and, with stray bullets still hitting nearby, she helped the wounded man as he struggled to make it to the alley with her assistance. This was no longer a Russian marine who might have fired the bullet that killed her father. It was a young man no older than she who was in pain and was frightened. Her actions were entirely instinctive as she helped him to drag himself to safety.

The Russian was more dead than alive. No word ever passed between them. Her only reward was a personal one and that had come from the look in his eyes as he sank to the ground safe from the gunfire in the street. He reached out and she took his hand, holding it in both of her own. Then he fell mercifully into shock. Had this been the way it had happened in Can Fat? Did her mother . . . the other members of her family, too . . . did they suffer as much? Did they experience that moment of fear, or did death come swiftly and mercifully? Was that what had drawn her here?

Phuong very carefully placed her hand inside his shirt. There was only a faint heartbeat, almost no breathing. Then she removed his ammunition belt, which she hung around her neck. She had seen photographs of people doing that during the war years. His rifle had landed at the edge of the alley when he fell and she picked that up, cradling it in her arms as her father had shown her years before. Dinh had taught her how to shoot.

Leaving the unconscious Russian in the alley, she headed back in the direction she'd come from. She circled around a couple of blocks to the south before heading back toward the piers. She had no feeling for the other Russians—she'd learned in an instant to hate one—Brusilov! Phuong knew what had drawn her there. She intended to exact her own revenge.

CHAPTER 20

"What do you make of it?" Rollie Lyford slid the message across his desk to Jules Auger. It had been addressed from *Roosevelt* to the White House with Naval Special Warfare, Admiral Lyford, for information, and it had arrived in slightly garbled form.

"I don't make anything out of this 'protective shield' thing. I don't remember the President calling for anything like that." There was a look of genuine concern in his eyes that had not been there until now. Was this for *Gettysburg* if she got under way or to prepare for retaliation by the Russians?

"My gut feeling is that somehow it looks like Chance may have something going."

Auger moistened his dry lips as he studied the sheet of paper. His eyes were more tired than he could ever remember. He read the message three times in an effort to fill in the blanks, then remarked, "That would be my first reaction, too. But there's something we must have missed, a recent message." His red-rimmed eyes stared in Lyford's direction without really seeing him. "I wouldn't be surprised if *Roosevelt*'s CO sent something along to Washington without letting the rest of us in on it, or else it's swimming around in a sunspot out there."

"So we're missing something. . . ." That was the trouble with the system. It could have been an errant operator aboard the carrier, or even one under his own command, but most likely it was Mother Nature—playing games at a time like this! Perhaps the carrier's CO decided it was something too critical to take a chance on with anyone else. But with it all so close . . . "I'm going to dial that number . . ."

"Before you call up the President like he was an old drinking buddy, let's cover all the angles. He could be worried about security, or contravening orders, or he may even be taking something into his own hands. After all, he's on scene. The rest of us have to rely on him," Auger mused. Then he winked at Lyford. "There's only fourteen guys in the whole navy allowed to command those things and we tell them they have to use their heads. Remember, the President has a gift for the Russians orbiting off Cam Ranh Bay. The man in the White House is giving every indication that he seems set on delivering that right on schedule. If he does, I got everything in my pocket saying that *Roosevelt* is the first Soviet target if they react the way I think they're going to. So maybe the CO of *Roosevelt*'s thinking the way we are."

Lyford glanced at his watch again. "Less than half an hour and the man says Cam Ranh Bay is going to disappear. Maybe you've got something there." He reached in his pocket for some change. "I couldn't handle another coffee. How about a Coke? You could sure as hell use something if you plan to keep talking." His five o'clock shadow was no longer a shadow, and it itched.

Auger reached in his own pocket for some change. "Sure, I'll flip you to see who gets it." He tossed a coin in the air. "Call it." Auger was fascinated with their reaction. It was surprising how casual they both seemed when there was a distinct possibility that the President appeared set on sending in a nuclear weapon in less than thirty minutes. Once faced with the reality, any alternatives became pale in comparison. There would never be another time like this for either of them again.

"Heads."

"Heads it is. You win. I got the duty." Auger looked at the coins in his palm. "Just one problem. I don't have enough change. I need another quarter."

Lyford snorted and tossed a quarter across the desk. "Why did I bother?" Then his voice changed and he folded his arms and stared down at his desk. "I hope David Chance is doing better with his odds than I am today." And, just as quickly, his expression changed and he laughed softly. "Did you ever imagine it would be like this—I mean, we'd be talking like this when there's a chance the whole world could go up?"

Auger smiled. "Funny. I was thinking the same thing." As he left the room, he added over his shoulder, "I've got some ideas but let's drink on it before you call again. I've been wondering how we can get the White House to extend their deadline and still look as mean and tough as hell to the other guy. After all, we were the ones that told him that if Chance didn't have *Gettysburg* out of there by this time then it was going to be bad. He was acting on our recommendation. Right?"

"But he didn't tell us what options he was considering." Lyford waved him away. "Go on. I'm thirsty. We'll bang it around when our throats start working again."

When Auger returned half a minute later, Lyford saw that a radioman was holding the door for him. "Look what I just ran into barreling down the passageway," he said to Lyford, placing a cold can on his desk. "Maybe we've got a message here that will settle everything. He says it's from the top man."

Lyford reached across his desk for the message board. He scanned it quickly before extending it toward Auger. "Something's wrong." He nodded at the board. "I don't think he got the first one from the carrier yet. He wants to send in that bomb." If there was such a possibility as fear appearing on Lyford's face, only someone like Auger would have noticed it. If that A-7 ever went in for the wrong reasons . . .

"Don't go away," Auger muttered to the radioman. He moved to Lyford's side. He tapped the message which lay flat on the desk as he said, "It's too late to be sending messages back and forth. You've been playing with that special telephone number. How do you feel about calling the White House and really getting yourself in hot water?"

"What difference can it make at this point?" The admiral's face was drawn and he yawned involuntarily. "How do you think we should approach him if we get through, I mean with everyone else trying to give him advice at the same time?"

"First, we find out if he got that message that *Roosevelt* apparently sent direct to him. If not, then we beg—and I mean beg—for some extra time since there's apparently something going on at that base that none of us know about. If he did get it, then we tell him that it's just possible Chance is pulling this thing off, or getting damn close to it. That's when we really start begging."

Lyford picked up his phone and pressed a button. He gave his aide on the other end the phone number. "Tell the party who answers that Admiral Lyford has an urgent—repeat urgent—message for the President." He replaced the receiver and sat down, taking a long pull on his Coke. "You know, Jules, if you're wrong about some missing message, and the boys in Moscow are about to one up the President, we're going to look very, very bad." He raised his eyebrows and shrugged, watching the sweat from the can run onto his desk blotter. "But it may not make a hell of a lot of difference an hour from now anyway."

Auger raised his can in a mock toast. "It's a shot in the dark. If we're right, Chance may just pull off the impossible. If not, well . . ." He shrugged and drank deeply from his Coke. "We ought to have champagne if we're toasting something that special."

• • •

Jim Ellard had been placed in charge of a four-man team of *Gettysburg*'s junior officers after being cautioned repeatedly by Glen Marston. Yet he came close to leading them into the middle of the firefight that was starting near the power plant. Fran York had emphasized again when they were picking up their weapons that their only purpose was self-defense. The most important contribution they could have made would be to avoid contact with the Russians. But they were all young, anxious, and they moved too fast. Any one of them might have been just as foolhardy. They arrived at the intersection of the main street passing by the power plant at about the same time as the first Soviet forces were moving into position and into the sights of Dinh's men.

Dinh knew beforehand that his tiny group of *irregulars* was outmanned. On the other hand, he decided their age and their memories of a past war was a benefit. They had careful planning on their side, they were disciplined, and their motivation was extreme. Chance and Dinh had studied the layout around the plant before the SEALs ever set foot on the base. They selected what appeared to be the best locations on the chart to defend, then Chance confirmed that the following day visually.

After that, it was Dinh and his men who had formulated their own strategy. Each of them had fought through much of the war. They were survivors. They knew their weapons and understood each other's capabilities, so it became a matter of placing the proper weapon in each location and manning it with the individual who was most familiar with it.

When the first Soviet marines appeared, approaching very cautiously in the faint early morning light, Dinh was wise enough to hold his fire. The Russians were split, working their way down either side of the wide street, moving from shadow to shadow, unsure of what they might encounter. The closest ones were no more than twenty to thirty yards away when Dinh gave the signal. His riflemen aimed at the closest marines, hitting three of them.

Then the men who had fired disappeared from their positions. The Russians opened up with small arms unaware their enemy was no longer there. It was a tactic Dinh had acquired in another era, an old Indian trick, Chance said, that had worked for generations of guerrilla warriors. When the Soviets brought their heavier weapons up, two teams of Dinh's men who had remained hidden opened up with old-fashioned rocket launchers. They, too, shifted their positions as soon as they fired.

It was after the small arms fire, as the Russians were frantically calling for some of their heavier equipment, that Jim Ellard's team barely avoided rushing directly into a crossfire. Ellard assumed the firefight was near the piers and raced on without scouting ahead. At about the same moment the five young officers eased out into the main street, Dinh's rocket launchers opened up.

The first rounds seemed to neutralize their targets. At that point, untrained troops would have retreated. The Russians took cover, laying down a heavy fire with their automatic weapons until they could regroup. The next round of fire from Dinh's launchers was directed toward the Soviets' assumed location. That was when one of the shells exploded against a wall where the Americans had taken shelter, killing one and wounding another.

Ellard had no idea where the round had come from, much less which side was the enemy. The street was wide and it seemed there was firing from every direction—*his ship was on the other side*! Retreating in the direction they'd just come from, they were confronted by two Soviet marines in the process of flanking the power plant. Neither could possibly have anticipated encountering the other. The Russians were heading gingerly for an objective that the Americans were leaving. A navy officer opened fire wildly. The marines took cover.

One of the Russians, a sergeant, quite sensibly realized there was no purpose in flanking someone if the path was blocked. Both agreed that withdrawal was the only logical

solution. They were able to retreat into the street to their
rear where they ran directly into Rick Ireland's group.
Neither of the Soviet marines had a chance; Ireland lost one
man.

They had gone off separately, two groups of Americans
whose youth seemed to guarantee immortality. They had
taken casualties and inflicted them, and their world was
quite suddenly changed. Their attitude was now moderated
by the necessity of returning to their ship safely. The final
decision was a simple one—their best option was to circle
around behind the power plant, which they knew had to be
under Dinh's control.

Each of Dinh's men knew exactly what was required of
them. They no longer depended on his presence. Since it
would take the Russians more than an hour after gaining
access to the plant to get even emergency power on line,
less than ten more minutes were planned for its defense.
Then they would be on their own, each one responsible for
his own escape. They understood Dinh—that he had his
own battle to wage—and they respected his wishes. The
massacre at Can Fat demanded vengeance. They had
wished each other well before starting out for the plant.
Now their silent messages of success seemed to be transmitted through the air as Dinh slipped away from them.

He circled away from the action in the street and moved
in a southerly direction to a position alongside a warehouse
that looked out on the piers. He studied *Gettysburg* in the
early morning light, pleased that her outward appearance
was no different than the previous day. To the casual
observer, Vietnamese sailors still seemed to be standing
guard on the ship. Yet Dinh smiled to himself. She was in
good hands once again.

He saw that the Soviet marines remaining on the pier
were restless. They were attempting to set up a defense,
yet there was little on the pier to use. That pleased him
even more. Dinh knew why they were like that. He

remembered his own feelings in those days when he was young and combat was so near, about to envelop one with the possibility of death at any moment. That kind of fear magnified itself the longer one waited . . . help-lessly . . . thinking of what was to come.

Dinh also recognized there was no real leadership. A young lieutenant appeared to be in charge. If Dinh was correct, the youngster had never been involved in a fire-fight, never seen anything beyond infantry training, or he would have known enough to take advantage of the minimal protection of pier facilities to establish fields of fire. *Gettysburg* was the objective of this action! Instead, these troops were simply waiting for whatever might occur, attempting to find individual protection. What in the world could that lieutenant be thinking of? Wasn't he aware that the reason for the nearby action was directly related to the ship beside him? Of course, Dinh acknowledged, even the best defense would be useless with *Gettysburg*'s small arms at their backs.

Dinh waited patiently. He knew Brusilov would have to appear. The general would know by now exactly what was happening. But what the general didn't realize—what he couldn't possibly imagine after all these years—was that there was one final element of the Phoenix Program yet to be completed.

Chance found his men exactly where they said they would be—three blocks north of the piers, behind a well-tended tropical garden of palm trees and thick bushes. Gates, Merry, and York had performed their assignments perfectly. They had also brought automatic weapons for Chance and Barney Gold.

The intensity of fighting between Dinh's irregulars and the Soviets was increasing. That, too, was just as they'd anticipated. The defense of the power plant was more a ruse, a calculated risk. The ship would be under way before the power would ever be back on the line—or they would be dead. But the longer the Soviet marines were kept occupied there, the better the opportunity to release *Gettysburg.* Chance knew they had been both efficient and lucky, but their luck couldn't last forever. Eventually, the fighting would spill over onto the piers. Every Soviet on the base would be involved if they didn't get aboard the ship very, very soon. It was even possible the sailors on the Soviet ships might have to be reckoned with.

Barney Gold was impressed, even just a bit in awe of how the SEALs had planned their operation. "You said my officers divided into groups. Who managed that?" he asked curiously.

"Your XO handled it." Fran York was checking the Soviet AK-74s he'd reserved for them once more. "He sure was beat to hell but there's a lot of spirit in that man. He should be waiting close to the piers right now with your department heads. Mr. Davis should be just south of the pier with some of the senior ones. And the XO sent off two groups of the junior officers who should be somewhere up here near us."

"You decided to separate out the younger ones?"

York grinned, holding the Russian weapon to his shoulder and sighting it at a sea gull. "I always did like these 74s—hell of a weapon." Then he glanced back at Gold. "We figured it was the best idea to try to get the most critical ones there first, and your XO was afraid some of those younger officers would do something that might draw fire . . . sort of like triage, I suppose. I'm afraid I insisted. Hated to do it, but hell, from what he said I guess I wouldn't want to be too close to them either. They sure mean well but they've got no idea about the real world . . . still think they're impossible to kill I guess." There was an increase in automatic weapon fire a few blocks away. "That might be what I mean. They sounded like they were looking for bear and maybe they just found some." He finished softly, "Good boys, but a little danger-ous." Each one of them had survived that way—if they were ever going to buy it, it would be their own fault, not someone else's.

Gold nodded without responding.

Chance placed a hand on Jimmy Gates's arm as he peered down the street where he could see *Gettysburg*'s mast rearing up against the morning sky. "No way we could get the captain to his ship across the water?"

"I considered it," Gates answered. "It might have worked at night, but not now. No way the sailors on those Soviet ships are going to stay in the rack with all this racket going on around them. The captain would make too nice a target out there about now. Fran says to move right down toward the ship and no one's going to notice us for a while. Between here and the piers, the gardeners have done a terrific job, plenty of greenery to play in if we have to."

Chance turned and his eyes settled on Barney Gold. "There's no guarantees from here on."

"I'm ready," Gold said.

"Let's go."

With Chance taking point, they moved cautiously toward *Gettysburg*, taking advantage of the dense gardens.

Once again, Barney Gold repeated the phrase to himself he'd coined when he first saw Chance—"*Love a SEAL!*"

Tom Davis saw something out of the corner of his eye, a movement of some kind. He was sure of that even though he had no idea what he'd seen. He wheeled about, his pistol held tightly in both hands at arm's length. Directly in front of him was a narrow alley between two buildings. The sun hadn't risen high enough above the horizon to melt the shadows.

What the hell . . . ? He sensed, rather than saw, movement once again. His index finger tightened on the trigger. They were so close to *Gettysburg*, no more than a hundred yards ahead, and they had made it without attracting attention—and now . . .

"No, please . . . no!" The voice was urgent—and feminine.

Davis would have been the last man to claim any sort of bravado at a moment like this. He was just plain scared, no matter who was in that alley. But that voice, an equally frightened cry from the shadows, was enough to hold his fire. It also allowed him to come face to face with a Vietnamese girl—a very pretty, though slightly disheveled, one who happened to be toting an automatic rifle still pointing at his midsection. There was fear rather than anger evident on her face. He would wonder many times afterwards what made him do it, but he let his own gun fall to his side, then gestured toward her with his free hand, pointing at the Soviet-made weapon.

She looked down and saw that the rifle was shaking like a leaf, a reflection of her own terror, yet her finger remained on the trigger. She shifted it in her arms, cradling it close to her chest. "I didn't want to . . ." she began in English. "I just didn't know . . ."

Tom Davis let out a sigh of relief. "Who are you?" He had no idea what else to say, nor did it really matter. He remembered the SEAL indicated that there were some women involved.

"My name is Phuong . . . Nguyen thi Phuong," she replied gravely. When she saw this meant nothing to the man who addressed her or the other Americans behind him, she added, "My father is Nguyen van Dinh . . ."

"The one with the SEALs," one of them said.

"Yes, yes, that is correct," she agreed hastily. "But I don't know where my father is. He was involved with the power station. He . . ." she shook her head from side to side in confusion. Everything had seemed so normal two days before.

Her voice was drowned out by the sound of renewed small arms fire coupled with tremendous explosions. She could tell by the sounds—the irregulars had nothing like that, only the rocket launchers—that the Soviets would soon regain the power station.

"We ought to get our butts aboard that ship while we got a chance, Tommy. It'll never get any easier." Each of the Americans was scared. Only one objective had any meaning out here—get back aboard that ship.

Davis had no idea what to say to the girl. "Your father . . ." he guessed, ". . . all of them, are supposed to show up at the ship." He was already moving toward *Gettysburg*. No one had said anything about this girl and he had no reason to include her now. But she had said her father's name was Dinh, and the SEAL, York, had said that was the Vietnamese who would get them out of Cam Ranh Bay. It seemed logical that she could be just as important to them.

There was a long, low building running alongside the waterfront almost to the head of the pier. The Americans used it for cover to avoid being seen by the marines on the pier, stopping only when they got to the end. Davis peered around the corner. The Soviet troops hadn't been able to do a great deal for their own protection. Their attention remained concentrated toward the smoke rising from just beyond the warehouse directly opposite the pier. They had established weak defensive positions that might hold off anyone attempting to challenge the pier, at least for a time. And that's when he understood why that SEAL said the men on the ship were so critical. Those marines wouldn't have a chance—not when the ship opened fire! The Russians must have felt more comfortable facing the head of the pier, assuming they were protected from the rear by *Gettysburg*.

Davis had no idea what to do other than what York had told him—*wait*. It made sense. Those marines could cut them down instantly. *Wait* until the shooting started here. When he looked over his shoulder toward the others, he saw that the girl remained with them, the fear still evident in her eyes, her rifle tightly clutched to her chest.

• • •

Glen Marston crept forward slowly, keeping as close to the ground as possible. Somehow he felt that the rising sun, gradually changing from its hazy, early morning red-orange glow to a brilliant tropical white, would search him out and indicate to the world exactly where he was. Never in his life had he ever imagined being in such a position.

The executive officer and his group had arrived ten minutes before behind a building across from *Gettysburg* and had done exactly as York had insisted—*wait*. They'd hidden behind a pile of junk beside that building as the firefight just a block away from them increased until they were sure it would break on top of them at any moment. Every two minutes, Marston crawled around the corner of the building, inched down a filthy alley between the warehouses, and peered out onto the pier beside *Gettysburg*.

As he did so now, he watched as Tom Davis and his men crept alongside the low building just to the left of the pier. Marston was tempted to get their attention, to call or wave or whatever was necessary, anything that might reinforce their confidence. But he also was absolutely sure that no matter how unaware the Soviet troops on the pier seemed to be, someone would see him. Instead, he squirmed about on his stomach and worked his way back to the others.

When he reappeared back by the pile of junk again, he and the officers who ran each department of the ship huddled once again in the filth that had accumulated between the buildings and waited.

CHAPTER 21

Georgi Brusilov's driver, whose eyes had grown large as saucers as they neared the fighting at the power plant, had stopped the car at a safe distance. This allowed the general to move to a position on foot where he could analyze the action without becoming involved.

It became immediately obvious that this was a delaying effort rather than any sort of stout defense. It was just a matter of time until his marines overpowered the small force that defended the damaged power plant. There was no purpose in remaining there. The defenders' fire was already decreasing and it would be impossible to capture survivors. He'd seen that tactic before—the SEALs had taught the PRU well. His order to the senior officer was simple: As soon as resistance weakened enough, detach as many men as possible and send them to the American ship. If there was to be heavier fighting, it would be on the piers, and that would be no delaying effort.

The ride back to *Gettysburg* was more difficult than Brusilov had anticipated. Two of the streets leading directly to the road at the head of the pier were blocked by civilian trucks that had been parked across the entrances. There was more here, the general realized, than met the eye, more than SEALs. This was also an indigenous operation, one that must have involved Vietnamese working on this base. He shuddered, remembering the Parrot's Beak twenty years before and how hard it was to tell friend from foe.

This was so much more than a few covert terrorists could have perpetrated. He was forced to continue a few blocks north before he could turn toward the water. His anger increased even more with the actions of his driver, who seemed to have forgotten the finer points of shifting gears as fear overcame reason. The engine raced out of gear, the transmission ground incessantly, and the tires squealed when corners were cut too sharply.

Jimmy Gates had survived by his senses. His ears were attuned to odd or unnatural sounds. Grinding gears, even a few blocks away, piercing the still morning air during a momentary lull in firing were an alien sound to him, intruding on a brief moment of peace.

They were slipping through another garden lush with bougainvillaea and towering shrubs when Gates shouted his warning. Just before the car squealed around the corner into the main road, they leaped for the protection of the tropical plants, remaining on their bellies until it had roared by.

Fran York peered over the broad, waxy leaves. "Our friend, Brusilov, no doubt." He turned to Barney Gold, whose white uniform was now covered with rich, black dirt. "I hope your officers are where I sent them because they no longer have to wait for anything. Time just ran out."

Chance rose to his feet. "Okay. No more playing with the flowers. Jimmy, you're going to make sure Captain Gold gets aboard . . . and I don't care how. Do it however you want. Fran and I will worry about the others . . . if they've made it."

What none of them could be aware of was the urgent call General Brusilov was taking as his car careened down the street—the duty officer at the air-base was reporting multiple aircraft on his radar screens apparently launched from *Roosevelt*. The single aircraft, the one the general was convinced carried a nuclear device, remained in its previous position and the additional ones seemed to be headed for it.

Brusilov's orders were specific. Launch interceptors the moment there was any indication of radar emission from the American aircraft, whether it was search or fire control. But don't go up to meet them yet—not if they don't pose an immediate threat. He wasn't ready to initiate combat with them.

Admiral Lyford, his head crooked to the side to balance the telephone receiver on his shoulder, had lost any patience he might have retained. "I can hear all sorts of noise in the background. There seems to be an assortment of bureau crats wondering what the hell I could want at a time like this." He winked at Jules Auger. "No one's supposed to bother him at a time like this . . . you know," he gestured with a wave of his hand, "when he's making weighty decisions to end the world . . ."

Auger looked up as the admiral's voice broke off in mid-sentence. The expression on Lyford's face had quickly changed from irritation to absolute seriousness.

"Yes, sir, I think there could be a change . . ." He scowled at the interruption. "No, sir, I have nothing absolute other than that last message from the captain of *Roosevelt*. Fires within the base at Cam Ranh Bay and a power blackout should indicate that Chance is accomplishing his mission, and it . . ." Another interruption. "I agree there's no telling if he's going to be successful, but my considered advice is that we should allow more time before—I mean, after all it would border on insan—" This time it was Lyford's pause. "It would create a problem of tremendous impact if we were to go ahead and destroy their base, if there's a possibility that we may be able to release the ship under different circumstances. Otherwise, there are substantial indications of retaliation . . ."

Auger noticed from Lyford's look of disgust that the admiral did not appear able to continue the conversation. "Is he considering what you've said?"

Lyford shrugged. "Beats me. He just interrupted to tell me to wait. I suppose that means he's going to talk with someone who thinks they know more about this than either one of us."

Auger cradled his chin in his hand. "If it's one of his yes-men, we're in trouble. Then again, it could be someone who understands the Soviet mentality. We might have a shot there." He closed his eyes tightly and rubbed them. There were visions of expanding mushroom clouds on his eyelids, but they disappeared when he opened them and stared back at Lyford. The admiral appeared to be listening again.

"How about fifteen minutes extra, sir? I know voice communications are very tenuous because of the sunspots, but I'd recommend attempting to establish direct communications with the commanding officer of *Roosevelt*. He's apparently having no problem talking with that A-7 pilot orbiting off the coast, and that one pilot seems to be the eyes for all of us." He paused and winked again at Auger. "And it's more than likely that Moscow might be eavesdropping. Overhearing you would allow them to understand that we're making an attempt. I don't think there's any secrets at this point . . ."

Auger watched as the admiral listened for a few seconds, then replaced the phone in the cradle. He was smiling. "Fifteen minutes. But I don't think we'll get another reprieve."

Before a hot, steaming sun rose completely above the horizon to erase the comforting shadows, Ben Gannett had settled on the top of *Gettysburg*'s pilot house with the gunner. They were stretched out flat on their bellies watching the tactical situation develop. It seemed that in less time than it took to accustom themselves to their surroundings, the sun's rays were already baking the metal beneath them.

Each man had powerful binoculars and wore a set of sound-powered phones which connected them to each of their action stations. The gunner was thoroughly enjoying his new position but he'd insisted they back each other up. He'd seen too many situations where a firefight took out the leader, and there was no time for *Gettysburg* to acquire another at this stage.

Their location provided a superb view of all the piers, the main street that ran parallel to the waterfront, and most of the side roads leading inland. It was a perfect position to scan the entire base, from the point to the south where Cam Ranh Bay abruptly turned inland at a right angle all the way north to the airfield on the northern boundary.

Activity appeared to be increasing aboard the ships at the other piers, but it seemed to Gannett to be more of an inquisitive nature at first. One by one, they were going to general quarters but there was little they could do in this situation. These ships were designed for a different kind of combat. Sleepy crews peered curiously at the commotion near the American ship while signalmen flashed frantic messages back and forth. He saw civilian workers lined up at distant gates, which had been closed to them, and he noted the activity at the airfield as the Soviet jet fighters taxied to the end of the runway to await their orders. He also noted the rapid progress of the Soviet marines around the power station as Dinh's irregulars disappeared. The action ended abruptly when the marines stormed empty barricades. At about the same time, General Brusilov's car screeched to a halt on the pier below, and he strode rapidly over to the officer in charge.

Gannett had watched the progress of Tom Davis's group from the moment they'd appeared beyond one of the warehouses and he followed their approach from the south until they halted at the corner of a nearby building near the head of the pier. He also caught sight of Glen Marston as the executive officer peered cautiously out from the shadows across the way. Barney Gold swam into sight in his binoculars from the moment he and the SEALs came out of the gardens a few blocks to the north. He even noticed Dinh climb into the back of a battered old truck parked on the waterfront.

What was occurring made sense. Considering how little time had passed since *Gettysburg* arrived in Cam Ranh Bay, things seemed to be following a pattern. It was similar to piecing a puzzle together although he was not allowed to select or fit the various pieces. They appeared on their own and proceeded much as they desired, generally unaware of the approach of the other parts. In that respect, the SEALs' method of operation was a total surprise regardless of their numbers. The final pieces appeared quite suddenly off to Gannett's right. He saw flashes of white racing between two buildings, then more than half a dozen officers, with Ensign Ireland in the lead, raced out into the middle of the main street along the waterfront. They were all armed and they instantly drew the attention of the Soviet marines.

That was how the action began on the waterfront.

For perhaps the first time in his life, General Brusilov experienced feelings of his own mortality. He understood how precarious the situation had become even before stepping out of his car. He was disturbed by how rapidly it had developed, more so than even he would have anticipated. His only comfort, if it could be called that, was that he had predicted something like this to Moscow.

The Vietnamese on *Gettysburg*'s deck suddenly looked too large—they were taller, more broad-shouldered than he remembered. Had they been like that before? The sentries on duty on the pier appeared more agitated by whatever was still happening with their friends at the power station. If anything was to happen to them, that was the direction it would come from. The ship seemed to be the last of their concerns—why not, wasn't it secure? Why had he allowed that lieutenant to remain in charge? Rather than calling the officer to him, Brusilov strode rapidly up to the man and grasped him by the shoulders, shaking him as he barked a series of orders. These men looked more like a gaggle of geese than a platoon of Soviet marines. He wanted them in position, ready to take advantage of specific fields of fire that still could be established. There was time!

As Brusilov turned to head back up the pier, one of those marines pointed in the direction of a band of American officers in filthy white uniforms who had just appeared in the street less than a hundred yards away. His excited shouts were picked up by others. Without waiting for orders, many of them began firing toward the men in white. The general turned on them in a rage and raced back to the officer in charge. There was almost no chance of hitting anyone at that range—or in that manner!

Brusilov appropriated the young lieutenant's communicator. These men were barely in control. They knew they were at the main objective and that they were the targets, yet they had no idea what was happening or how they should counter it. There was too little time to reclaim discipline. Envisioning the chaos that would follow if more Americans appeared in the next few minutes without a return to order, the general called for immediate reinforcements from the captain in charge at the power station.

The young American officers were not returning fire. Their effort was as indiscriminate as the Soviets'. It was a stalemate!

Glen Marston understood what was happening, intuitively knew what Brusilov was calling for when he took the lieutenant's communicator, and could also picture disaster if more marines appeared. His observation period was over as fast as it began. He raced back for his own group.

Tom Davis had seen how devastating even small arms fire could be, so he remained rational. There was nothing to be gained from attracting attention when real bullets were being used. He kept his own people flat on the ground, waiting for the ship to open fire.

Chance was approximately a hundred yards from the head of the pier when the Soviets opened fire. He'd taken no more than another ten steps when one of the American officers fell, then a Russian. It was all fear and reaction, no organization, no command. But there were too many marines to make any losses a fair exchange. "You said he's in the pilot house?" he asked Jimmy Gates.

"Should be on the top if he could make it." Gates squinted against a golden sun behind the ship's superstructure. "There's someone up there, two of them."

The Soviet marines were inching toward their white-uniformed targets hesitantly, urged on by a confused officer and a bellowing General Brusilov.

"I can't imagine a better time to open fire," Chance muttered, squeezing his eyes shut as if he could will *Gettysburg* to commence firing.

"I told him to use his own judgement—not to give himself away too soon."

A second American fell. They'd been taken by surprise when the marines opened fire. There was no nearby cover. Their instinctive reaction was to fire back—to hold their ground. But two of them were down and the Soviets were moving toward them. Following Davis's example, they flattened themselves, wondering if they would all die before the promised help came.

The SEALs had worked about fifty yards closer without being seen when Glen Marston reappeared with his team and opened fire. Five more automatic weapons—American firepower had just doubled! The front rank of Russian marines fell back. They had no more cover than the Americans. Three more marines fell before they could find cover.

"Jimmy, there's no better time than now." Chance placed a hand on Barney Gold's shoulder. "You take our friend here and get him aboard somehow. We're going to lay down a covering fire. You know you can't get through the way things are now—but get as close as you can. Your buddy on the pilot house had better come to life when he sees us or Brusilov's going to feed us to his dogs." He gave Gates a solid slap on the rump. "Go! Take care!"

Chance, Merry, and York sprinted down the street in the open. They would attract attention—enough so that Gates and Gold could get close.

Ben Gannett saw the flash of white to his left and recognized Barney Gold moving toward the pier with a man dressed completely in black. There was little enough cover to use as they seemed to dance from one spot to the next. "Son of a bitch, they're going to get as close to the head of the pier as possible without being seen because of those other three." Gannett recognized the suppressing fire from the other SEALs as he pointed them out to the gunner. "Captain's coming," he shouted into the mouthpiece of his sound powered phone.

The gunner had been patient. He wanted to open fire when the first officer went down but he knew it was too soon. Now the time was right. "Helo deck cover the section of the pier aft of the quarterdeck. Don't leave a soul alive. Signal bridge take out the marines forward and let the ones retreating this way see where it's coming from," he shouted into the mouthpiece. "Bow has covering fire at the head of the pier. Hold the heavy stuff until I give the order. We're sure they've called for reinforcements. Repeat—hold the heavy stuff. We don't want to give that away. Anyone who sees any activity on the ships near us, sweep their decks."

Heavy, automatic fire erupted from three separate sections of *Gettysburg*, tearing into Soviets who had no cover, scattering them like dolls across the pier. Brusilov literally dove over the hood of his car to escape the hail of bullets that swept through his marines. He saw the lieutenant whirl to fire his weapon for the first time and watched the man's body fly backwards before he ever pulled the trigger. Those few marines remaining alive after the first ten seconds were the lucky ones who'd found some kind of shelter, but hardly one of them was able to return fire. The general had seen ambushes before, had set up some so perfectly that there was no return fire—but he'd never witnessed such a brutal one. Nothing could withstand that volume of fire!

As Brusilov peered out from his position, he was positive there were more white uniforms on the waterfront than marines. How had the Americans made it this far? He glanced at his watch—no more than a minute had passed. He bellowed angrily into his radio for reinforcements.

"We see you," was the immediate response. "We've got to spot their heavy stuff first. I can't just send these men into that crossfire without assigning targets. We wouldn't have anyone left."

"How many men do you have?" Brusilov snapped.

"One company—the one from the power station."

"Where are the rest?"

"I don't know. There's no radio contact. It's almost as if they were intercepted." There was a pause, then, "I can only see the fire from the bow. What else can you see?"

Brusilov sensed a moment of *déjà vu* as he peered over the hood of his car. This is what he had done as a young man when the general officers remained behind the lines, and now—"I have targets on the bow, and the signal bridge . . . and somewhere toward the stern. I can't see the last from here." He saw Barney Gold and a man in black racing down the far side of the pier. No one was shooting at them!

Brusilov reached instinctively for his own Makarov. But, as he rose slightly to take aim at Gold, a flurry of bullets slammed into the car. Hot metal spattered the concrete all around, showering him with chips. Instinctively, he fell to the ground and was aware of the pressure of the container of film against his stomach. There was no possible way he could get off a shot and live long enough to see if Gold fell. *The bastard was going to make it aboard that ship and* Gettysburg *was going to . . .* NO!

The general switched channels on his radio to raise the duty officer at the airfield. "Launch aircraft," he bellowed. "If the American ship gets under way, I want your pilots to hole her at the waterline. Don't let her get out of this harbor."

Brusilov switched back to the channel with his marines. "In less than a minute," he snarled, "all those American officers wearing those lovely white uniforms are going to be back aboard their ship." He could feel an animal rage growing in his chest. What had taken place in the past few minutes should have been impossible. "And if they do, the investigation that will follow . . ."

Squads of Soviet marines appeared behind the American officers to the south and directly behind Marston who was also heading up the pier. For an instant, the Americans were in a crossfire. Two more white uniforms fell. Just as suddenly, the balance was shifting to the Soviet side—but only for an instant.

The gunner gave the signal for the heavier weapons to open up at the same moment the first of those new marines pulled the trigger. The air was shattered by heavy caliber machine guns and grenade launchers. Such an overwhelming concentration of firepower stopped the Russians in their tracks. Survivors ducked for the cover that had seemed unnecessary only seconds before.

Then an even louder roar rose above the din as—first one, then a second, then a third American fighter plane roared down Cam Ranh Bay almost at water level. Gannett found himself actually looking down into the cockpits as the Tomcats passed no more than thirty yards off *Gettysburg*'s stern.

Brusilov saw them bank ever so slightly to starboard and he knew instantly what they intended to do. He had seen none of his own aircraft yet. If they were still on the ground, the Americans would buzz them, confuse ground control, hold them down just long enough . . .

The general had been a survivor for so many years that he was able to make a decision that normally would have revolted him—he was definitely in the wrong place. If he remained, he would die and he would not be remembered as a hero of the Soviet Union. None of this had been his idea; he was a victim of circumstances now beyond any single man's control. The Kremlin would be looking for some heads after this incident was over and a dead general would be an attractive target. It was time to leave.

Reaching cautiously above his head, he pulled open the door of his car. There, still perched behind the wheel, was his driver, blood streaming over his body, eyes fixed straight ahead and very, very dead. Brusilov reached in and grabbed the man's arm. The body teetered for a moment, seemed to right itself, then pitched sideways onto the shattered glass covering the seat. The general grasped the man's collar and pulled, bracing himself against the side of the car until the body hung halfway out the door. Then he eased onto his knees and yanked until the driver's corpse tumbled onto the pier. Brusilov slithered through the glass into the front seat, keeping below the line of sight. He turned the key. The engine stuttered for . . . was it ever going to . . . ? He was overjoyed when the engine roared into life.

Chance was at the head of the pier with York and Merry, helping the surviving officers with their wounded, when he first caught sight of Dinh. The Vietnamese had leaped from the back of a truck and was running down the pier, an old AK-74 held out in front of him like a vaulter's pole.

"Dinh!"

No response.

Chance ran toward him. "Dinh . . . wait!" Then he recognized what Dinh had seen.

Brusilov's head peered above the dashboard of the car. No mistaking that face.

For a moment, everything seemed frozen in slow motion, even the movement of the car. Was it actually moving after the pounding it had received?

Dinh's face was contorted into an unrecognizable mask of hatred. He heard nothing. He'd seen Chance out of the corner of his eye and somewhere in his brain a voice had told him that was a friend. Another voice, a much louder one that seemed to drown out every other sound, was urging him on. He had seen Brusilov climb behind the wheel of the car. *The butcher was attempting to escape.*

Pictures of Can Fat swam before Dinh's eyes. It seemed that each of the souls who had been massacred were clambering to be recognized one more time as he'd leaped from the back of the truck. They followed each of his steps down the pier. The last image, the one that remained in front of him those final steps, was his wife, Mai. She was no longer being torn by bullets as she had been in all the other visions over those years—instead, she was smiling at him because she knew she was finally being avenged.

The rear tires on the car spun. Little puffs of white dust formed behind as the car shot forward.

"Dinh . . . Dinh, look out!" Chance stopped running. He knew the ending so clearly before it took place.

The car roared down the pier with bullets spattering around it. Dinh never lost stride. On the run, he leveled the AK-47 from under his arm and fired short bursts toward the man peering from behind the wheel. He saw Brusilov's lips drawn back in a howl of rage and fear and Dinh was sure that he could hear that sound above the noise around him.

Then Dinh stopped in his tracks. The car was still moving, the face was still alive, and they were almost upon him. This was no way to gain revenge. *The butcher of Can Fat would escape!* He calmly lifted the gun to his shoulder, dropped his cheek down to bring the sights into line, and took quick aim. He squeezed off two more quick bursts, bringing the sights carefully back to position after the first. It was but an instant between each but he knew one was on target because he saw Brusilov's head jerk back—just before the car slammed into him.

Chance saw Dinh's body fly into the air, arching above the vehicle in a tragic, slow-motion ballet before it fell in a heap on the pier. Chance found himself frozen, fascinated with the horror of Dinh's mad charge. That form crumpled on the pier—his friend, Dinh—would never smile back at him with that flashing gold tooth again, never glance up at him with that serious expression before explaining why he thought one of his own ideas was better. It was much too late as he lifted his own weapon and fired. The vehicle was past. The bullets were peppering the car's body, but not the driver. *Brusilov was escaping them!*

That was when Phuong, who had not followed Tom Davis and his men down the pier, brought her own weapon to her shoulder. Very carefully, as Brusilov's car careened down the pier toward her, she opened fire, one bullet at a time just as Dinh had taught her when she was younger.

Phuong watched Brusilov, blood already splashed across his face, swing the wheel first one way and then the other. After the third shot, she knew which direction the car would turn next. As it did, she was looking directly into Brusilov's eyes and she was sure he recognized her as her next bullet slammed into his throat.

She saw one hand go to his neck as the car veered away. Then both hands were back on the wheel, struggling to control the vehicle when the next bullet tore into his forehead. Phuong desperately wanted to see the expression on Brusilov's face as he realized he was a dead man, but the car swung wildly in the other direction. She watched expressionlessly as it crashed directly into a truck that had been parked near the head of the pier. There was a tiny popping sound as the gas tank in Brusilov's car exploded, then both vehicles were enveloped in flames.

When she finally looked away, the first person she caught sight of through the tears that were now blurring her vision was Chance. *He was running . . . to her!* Then she was in his arms and he was racing with her back down toward the ship. Phuong could see nothing but she could hear the sputter of machine guns and the explosion of shells around her as her world went blank.

Ben Gannett had seen the trucks coming when they were still more than a mile away. He could count the troops in the back when they were six blocks away. He'd already given the order to cut the lines to the pier when he saw Chance race up the narrow gangway to *Gettysburg*'s quarterdeck.

Gannett lay on his stomach and peered over the edge of the roof into the pilot house. "All aboard, Captain!"

Barney Gold gave the order: "All back full!" There was no time for finesse.

Gettysburg hesitated for only a second before plunging backward. Her hull scraped down the pilings. The sound of tearing metal broke through the howl of the firefight that was all around them. Bullets shattered the pilot house windows. Rockets from shore tore into *Gettysburg*'s hull.

Three more Tomcats screamed across Cam Ranh Bay, climbing slightly before they dove on the marines now flooding the pier. The ear shattering scream of jet planes rolled over them as their winking guns covered the pier. Rockets tore into the trucks. After the second pass, there were no longer any heavy weapons firing at the ship.

Once their bow was three hundred yards off the pier, Barney Gold ordered, "All stop." Then, "All ahead flank." *Gettysburg* shuddered as the propellors reversed direction and dug into Cam Ranh Bay. Her stern dipped visibly. Muddy water swirled in the froth that rose behind. "Right full rudder."

Gettysburg's bow swung toward open water as three more Tomcats roared down her starboard side. There were no Soviet aircraft in sight.

"Mr. Marston," Gold shouted across the pilot house, "try to raise *Roosevelt*." He knew the pilots would already have reported what was taking place. "Tell them we intend to rendezvous with her as soon as possible to transfer our wounded."

EPILOGUE

A fact of life at the end of the twentieth century is deeply planted moles! They are insidious creatures who for some unknown reason turn against their own country. While they are the antithesis of all that we feel is decent, their value is often inestimable.

In the case of *USS Gettysburg*, gaining the release of the ship was critical to avoiding a superpower confrontation, one that might have led to a nuclear exchange. It was that close—*minutes*! But her release was only the initial phase of an even greater concern. The United States had invested billions of dollars over the years to send Aegis to sea with the fleet and it was the key to the defense of the carrier battle group. The American strategy of power projection was constructed around the aircraft carrier and the defense of that group was the cornerstone of naval strategy.

Two days after *Gettysburg*'s release, the President met at the White House with the Chairman of the Joint Chiefs of Staff, the Chief of Naval Operations, the Secretary of Defense, and the Director of the Central Intelligence Agency. Their purpose was singular—to consider the compromise of Aegis. They were joined by four other individuals—Admiral Lyford, Captain Auger, David Chance, and Nguyen thi Phuong. After two hours of detailed analysis, no resolution was reached. The film of the Aegis system had never been discovered, nor was there any indication that it had ever left Cam Ranh Bay.

The Director of the CIA was then forced to activate that deepest of all moles in the Kremlin. If indeed Aegis was now in Soviet hands, the intelligence would eventually filter down. And, if it was learned that Moscow possessed the secret to Aegis, then American sea power would be severely crippled for years to come.

That deepest mole plumbed every available source in the Soviet Union over the ninety-day period designated by the President. He reported a frantic search of every square inch of Cam Ranh Bay, an in-depth investigation of the Kremlin power structure, and a major overhaul of the executive level of the KGB. But there was no indication that the Aegis system had been compromised.

In the end, it was determined that a lovely Vietnamese girl named Nguyen thi Phuong had likely preserved the mainstay of American sea power when she avenged the massacre at Can Fat.

The President wished to present her with the country's highest civilian award; his desire was to make her heroic stand an example to the nation. Phuong declined. She was the daughter of Nguyen van Dinh, a patient man who had never asked for more than one final reward: a vision of Mai smiling back at him.

David Chance returned with Phuong to that tiny community of Navy SEALs, men and women who understand that it is better that they remain anonymous.

95